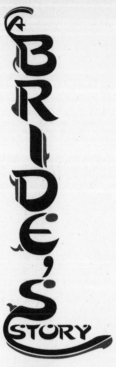

A BRIDE'S STORY

4

Kaoru
Mori

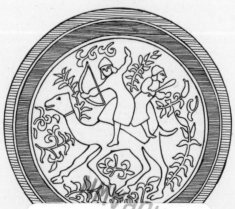

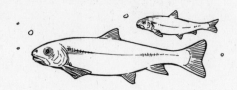

TABLE OF
CONTENTS

CHAPTER 18
VISITATION ——————————— 003

CHAPTER 19
THE TWINS OF THE ARAL SEA——— 035

CHAPTER 20
AFTER THE BIG ONE ——————— 059

CHAPTER 21
POSSIBILITIES FOR THE TWINS——— 107

CHAPTER 22
A CRASH COURSE IN BRIDEHOOD——— 155

SIDE STORY
AT THE HORSE MARKET——————— 175

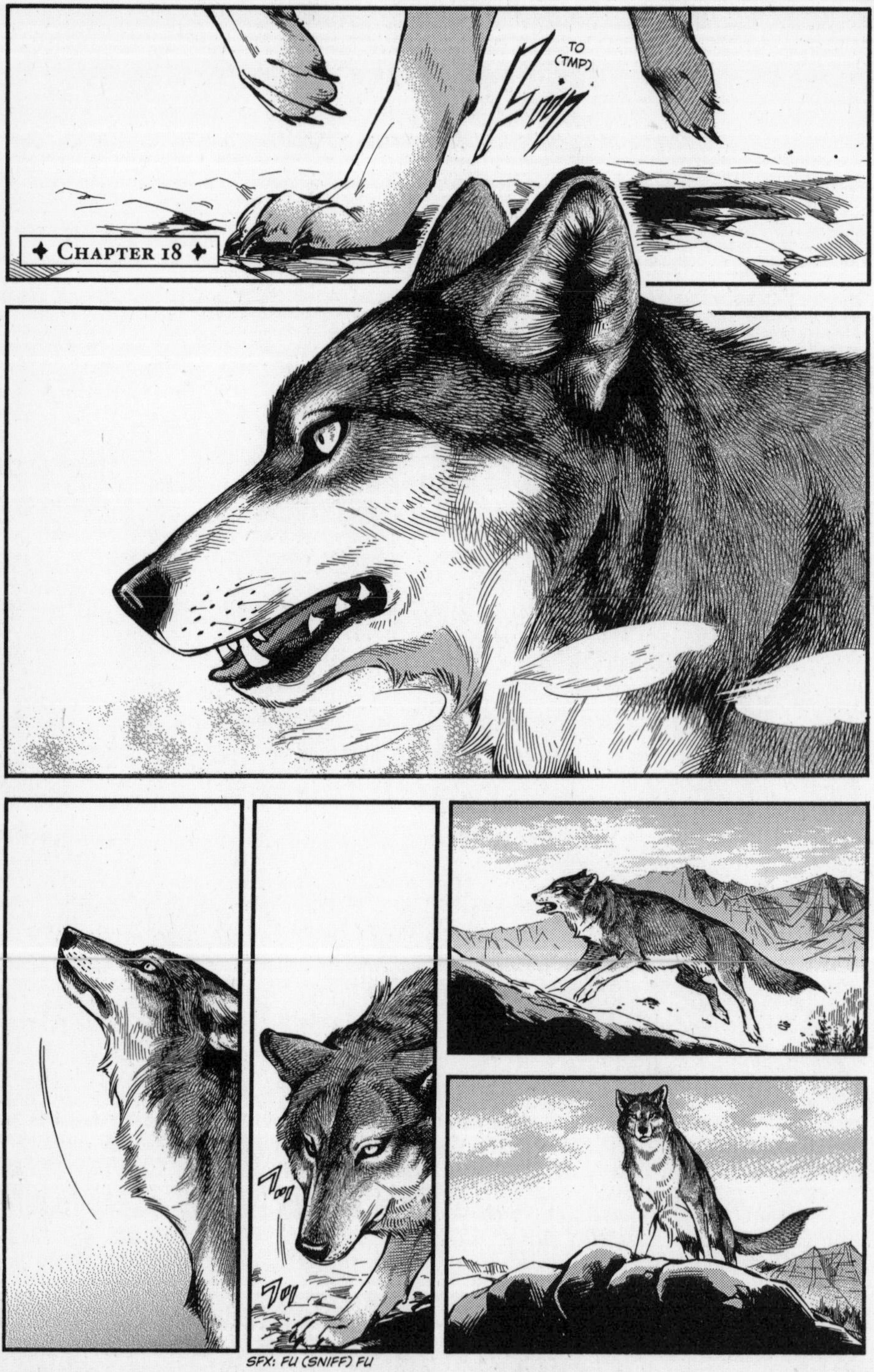
TO (TMP)
✦ Chapter 18 ✦
SFX: FU (SNIFF) FU

Chapter Eighteen
Visitation

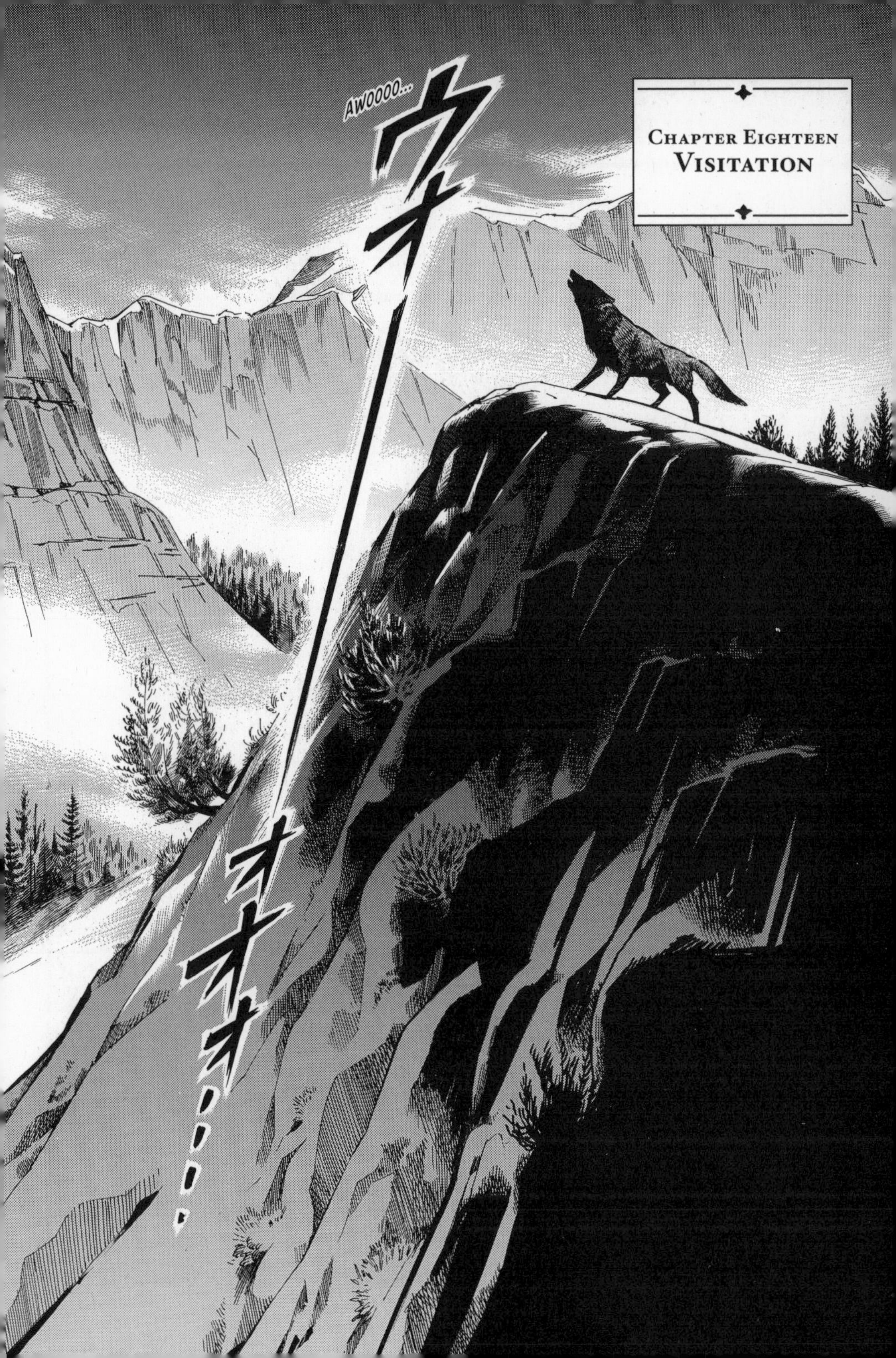
AWOOOO...
ウオーオオオ

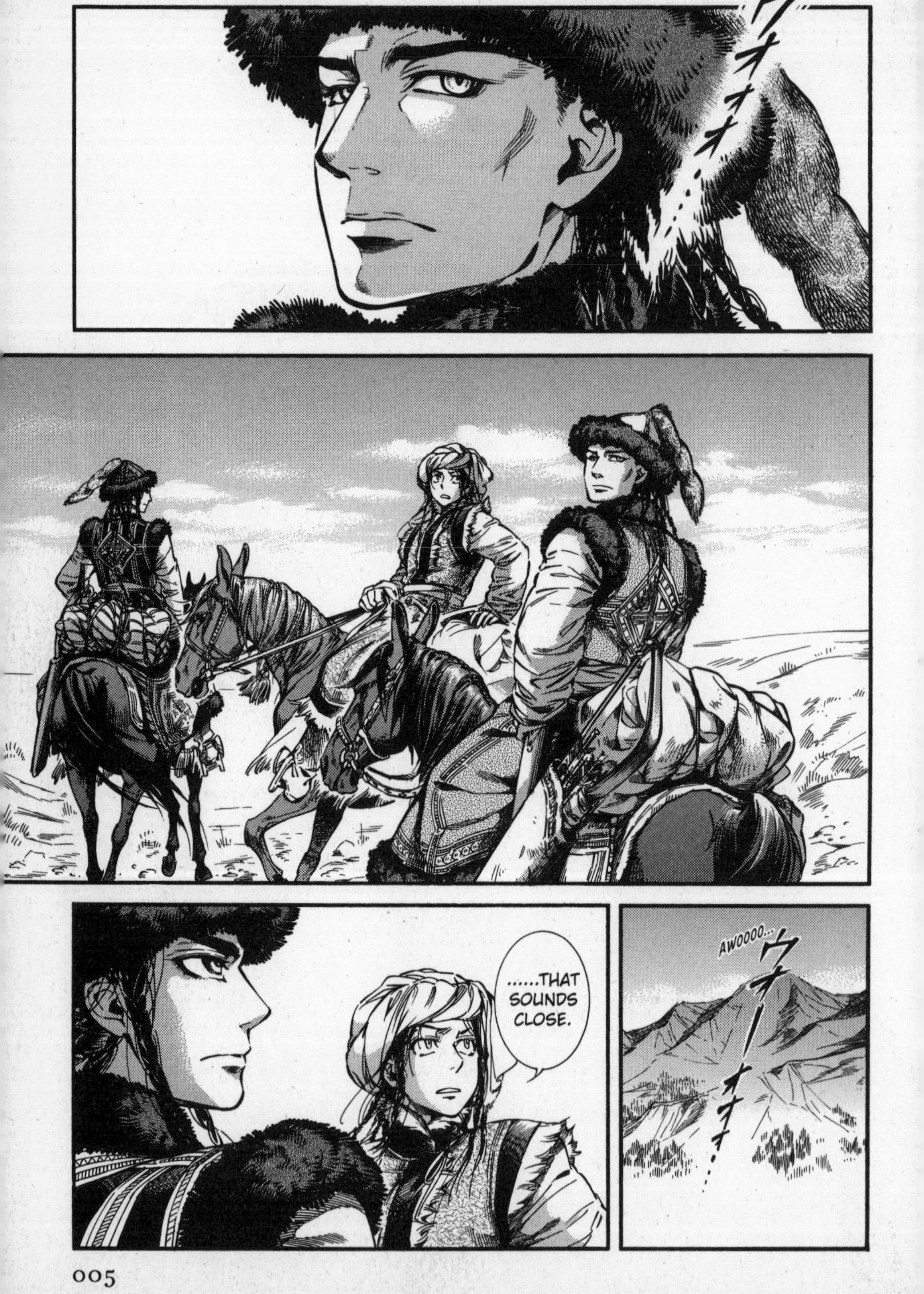
WOOOO...
AWOOOO...
......THAT SOUNDS CLOSE.

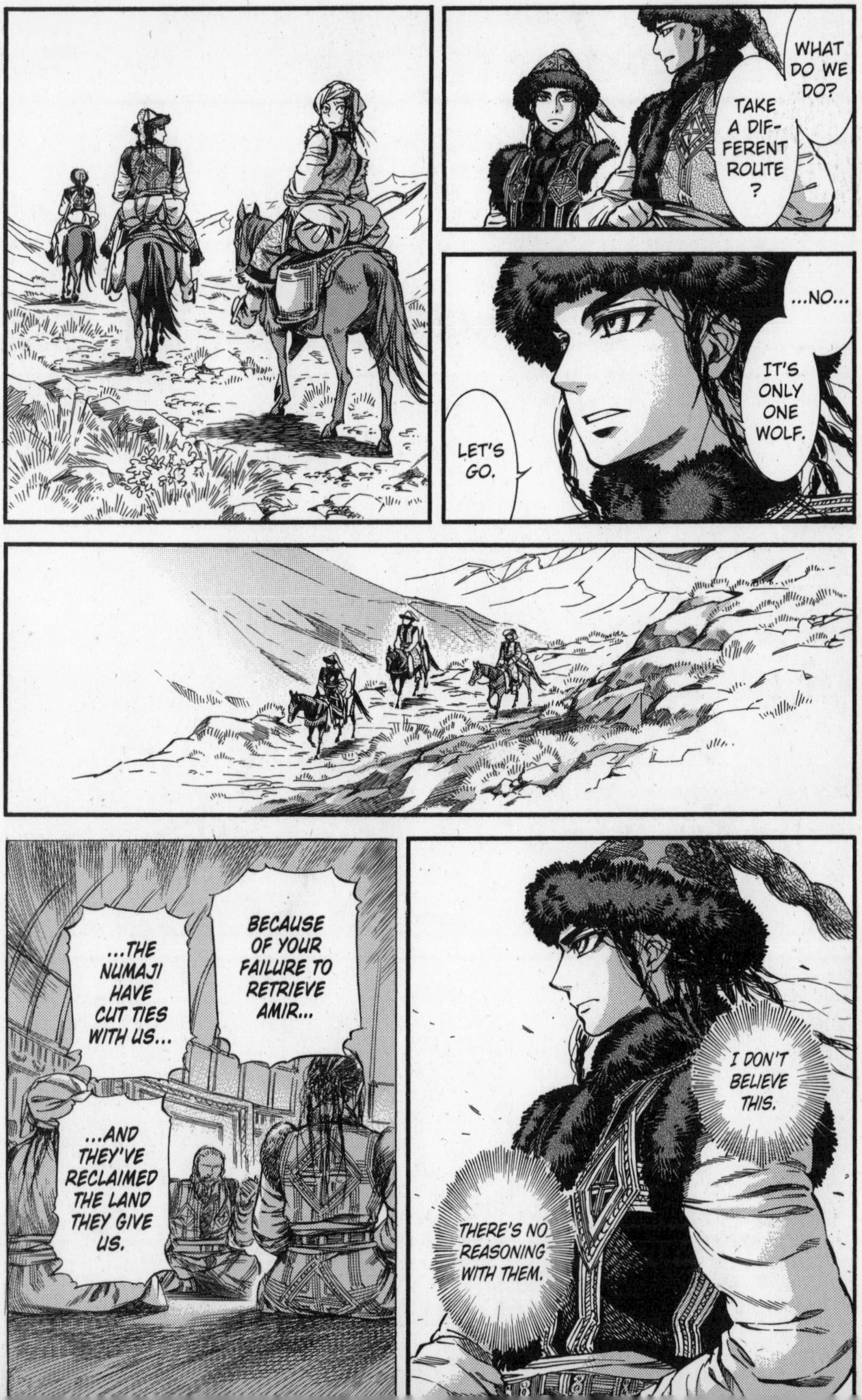
WHAT DO WE DO?
TAKE A DIF-FERENT ROUTE?
...NO...
IT'S ONLY ONE WOLF.
LET'S GO.
I DON'T BELIEVE THIS.
THERE'S NO REASONING WITH THEM.
BECAUSE OF YOUR FAILURE TO RETRIEVE AMIR...
...THE NUMAJI HAVE CUT TIES WITH US...
...AND THEY'VE RECLAIMED THE LAND THEY GIVE US.

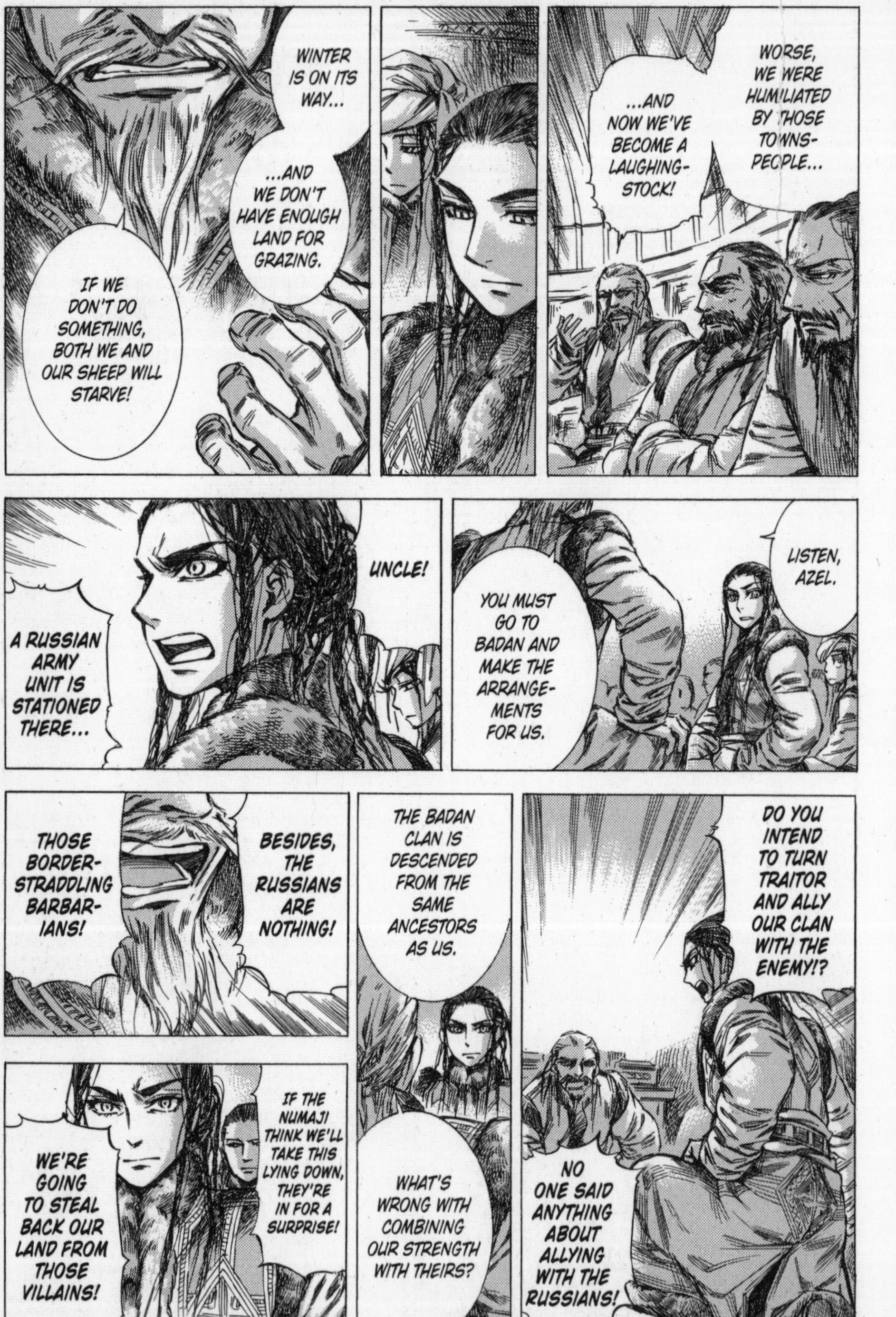
WORSE, WE WERE HUMILIATED BY THOSE TOWNS-PEOPLE...
...AND NOW WE'VE BECOME A LAUGHING-STOCK!
WINTER IS ON ITS WAY...
...AND WE DON'T HAVE ENOUGH LAND FOR GRAZING.
IF WE DON'T DO SOMETHING, BOTH WE AND OUR SHEEP WILL STARVE!
LISTEN, AZEL.
YOU MUST GO TO BADAN AND MAKE THE ARRANGE-MENTS FOR US.
UNCLE!
A RUSSIAN ARMY UNIT IS STATIONED THERE...
DO YOU INTEND TO TURN TRAITOR AND ALLY OUR CLAN WITH THE ENEMY!?
NO ONE SAID ANYTHING ABOUT ALLYING WITH THE RUSSIANS!
THE BADAN CLAN IS DESCENDED FROM THE SAME ANCESTORS AS US.
WHAT'S WRONG WITH COMBINING OUR STRENGTH WITH THEIRS?
BESIDES, THE RUSSIANS ARE NOTHING!
THOSE BORDER-STRADDLING BARBAR-IANS!
IF THE NUMAJI THINK WE'LL TAKE THIS LYING DOWN, THEY'RE IN FOR A SURPRISE!
WE'RE GOING TO STEAL BACK OUR LAND FROM THOSE VILLAINS!

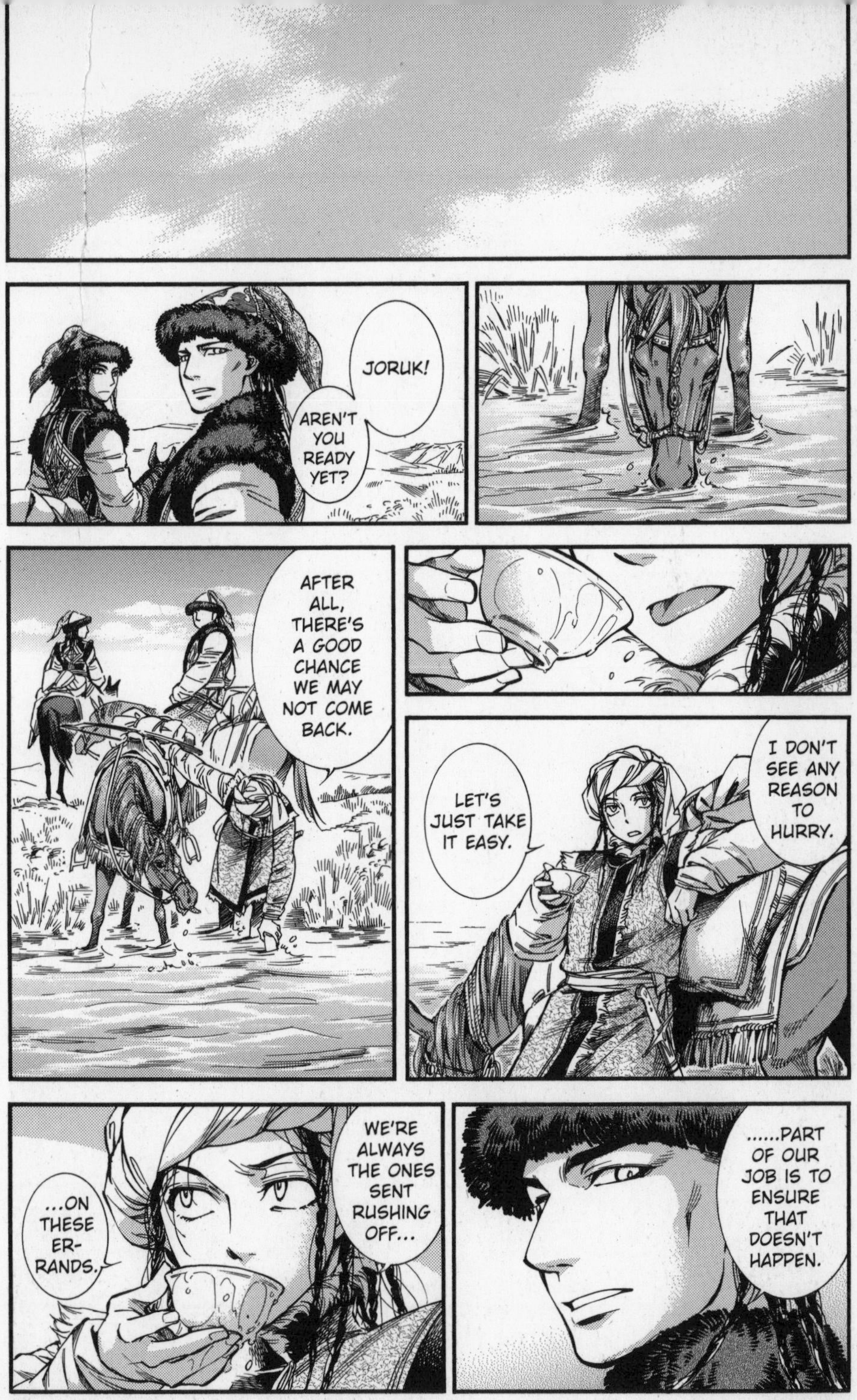
JORUK!
AREN'T YOU READY YET?
I DON'T SEE ANY REASON TO HURRY.
LET'S JUST TAKE IT EASY.
AFTER ALL, THERE'S A GOOD CHANCE WE MAY NOT COME BACK.
......PART OF OUR JOB IS TO ENSURE THAT DOESN'T HAPPEN.
WE'RE ALWAYS THE ONES SENT RUSHING OFF...
...ON THESE ER-RANDS.

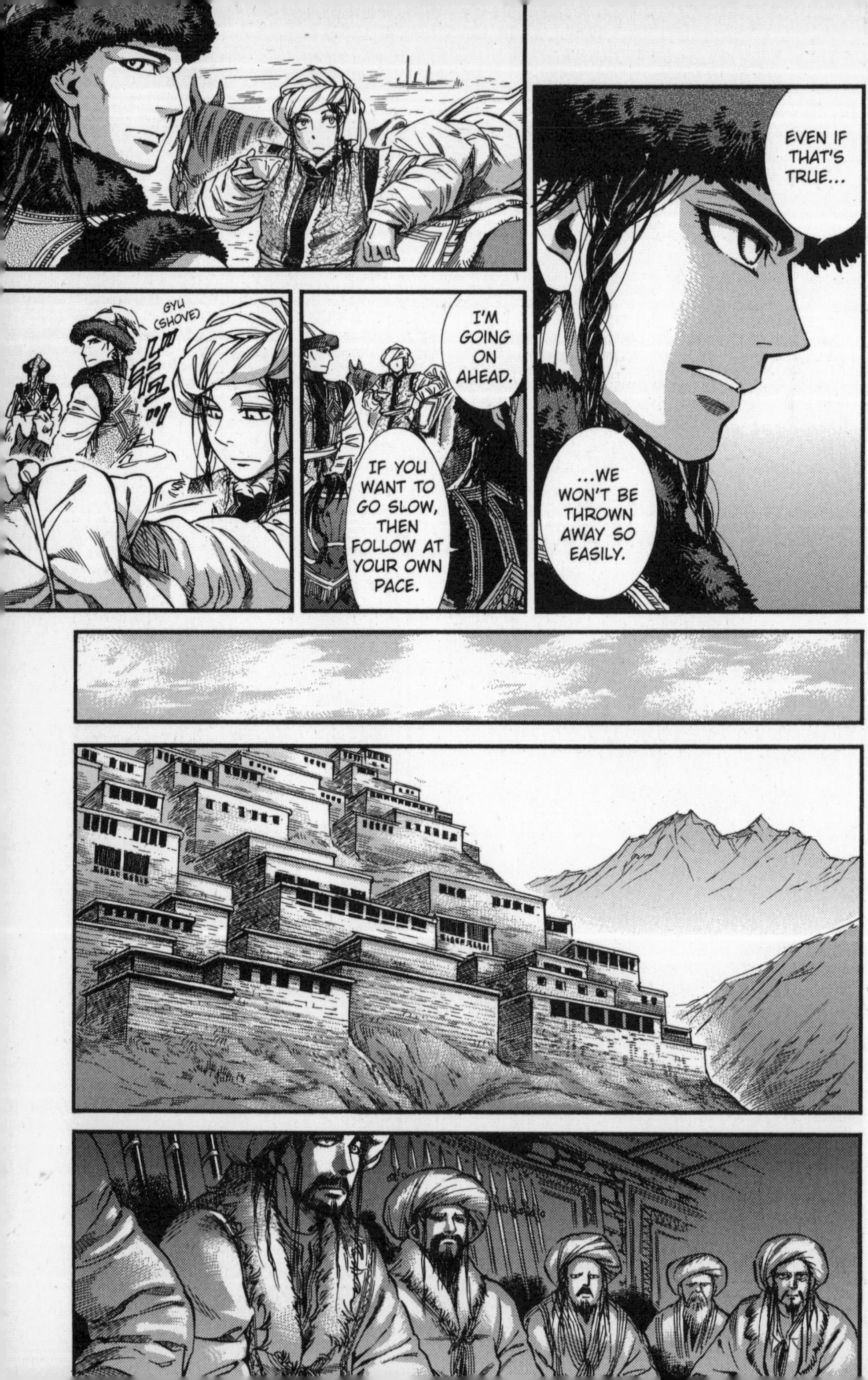
EVEN IF THAT'S TRUE...
...WE WON'T BE THROWN AWAY SO EASILY.
I'M GOING ON AHEAD.
IF YOU WANT TO GO SLOW, THEN FOLLOW AT YOUR OWN PACE.
GYU (SHOVE)

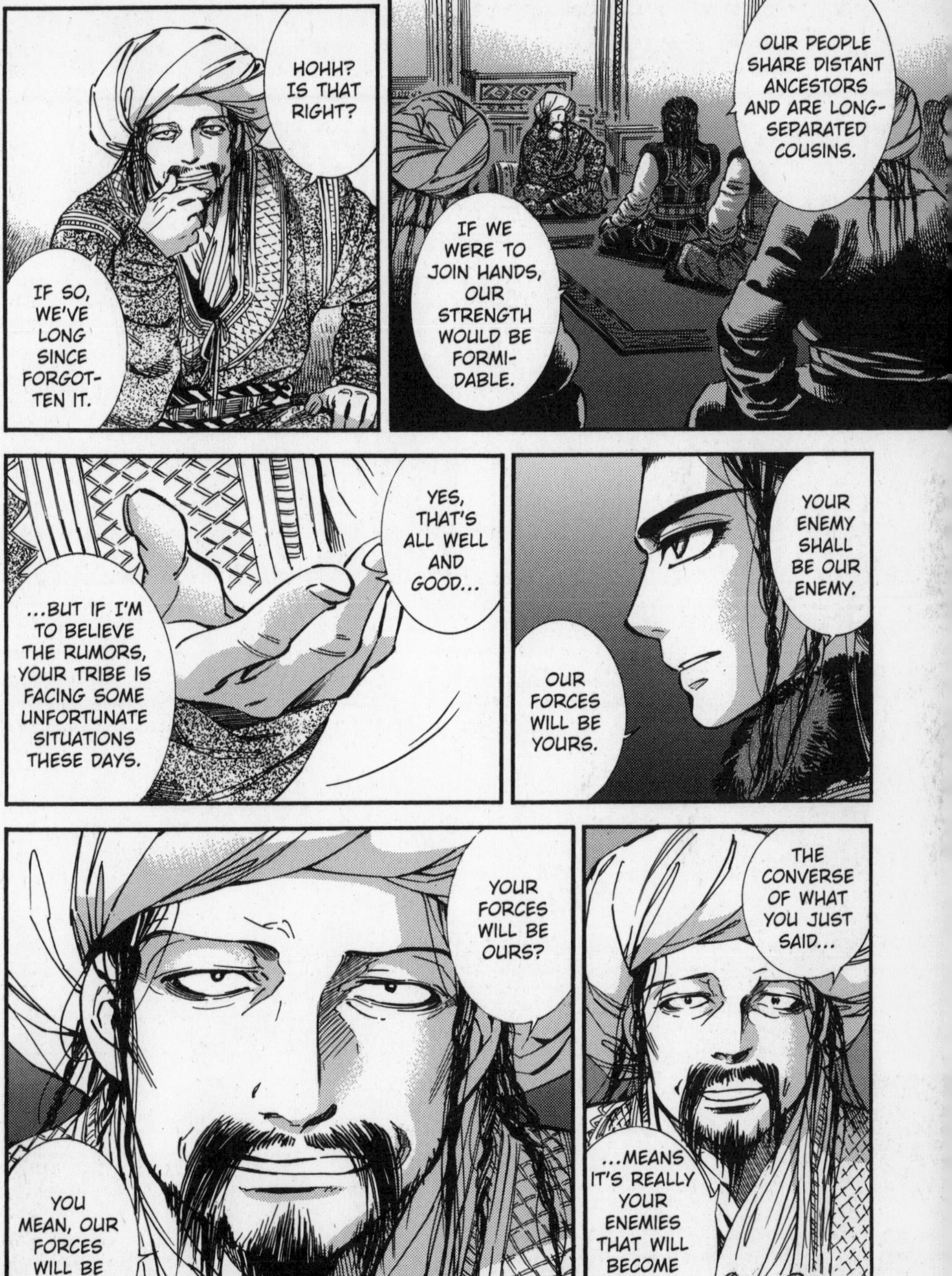
OUR PEOPLE SHARE DISTANT ANCESTORS AND ARE LONG-SEPARATED COUSINS.
IF WE WERE TO JOIN HANDS, OUR STRENGTH WOULD BE FORMIDABLE.
HOHH? IS THAT RIGHT?
IF SO, WE'VE LONG SINCE FORGOTTEN IT.
YOUR ENEMY SHALL BE OUR ENEMY.
OUR FORCES WILL BE YOURS.
YES, THAT'S ALL WELL AND GOOD...
...BUT IF I'M TO BELIEVE THE RUMORS, YOUR TRIBE IS FACING SOME UNFORTUNATE SITUATIONS THESE DAYS.
THE CONVERSE OF WHAT YOU JUST SAID...
...MEANS IT'S REALLY YOUR ENEMIES THAT WILL BECOME OUR ENEMIES, RIGHT?
YOUR FORCES WILL BE OURS?
YOU MEAN, OUR FORCES WILL BE YOURS.

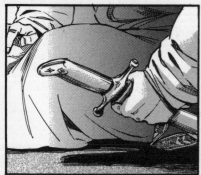

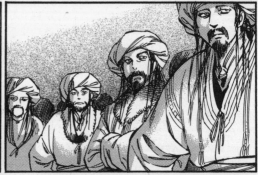

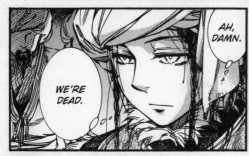

AH, DAMN.

WE'RE DEAD.

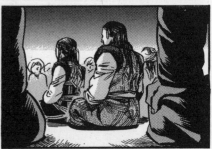

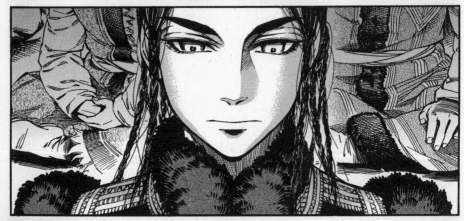

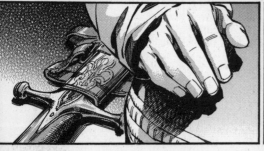

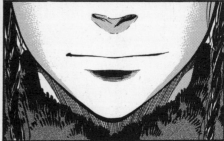

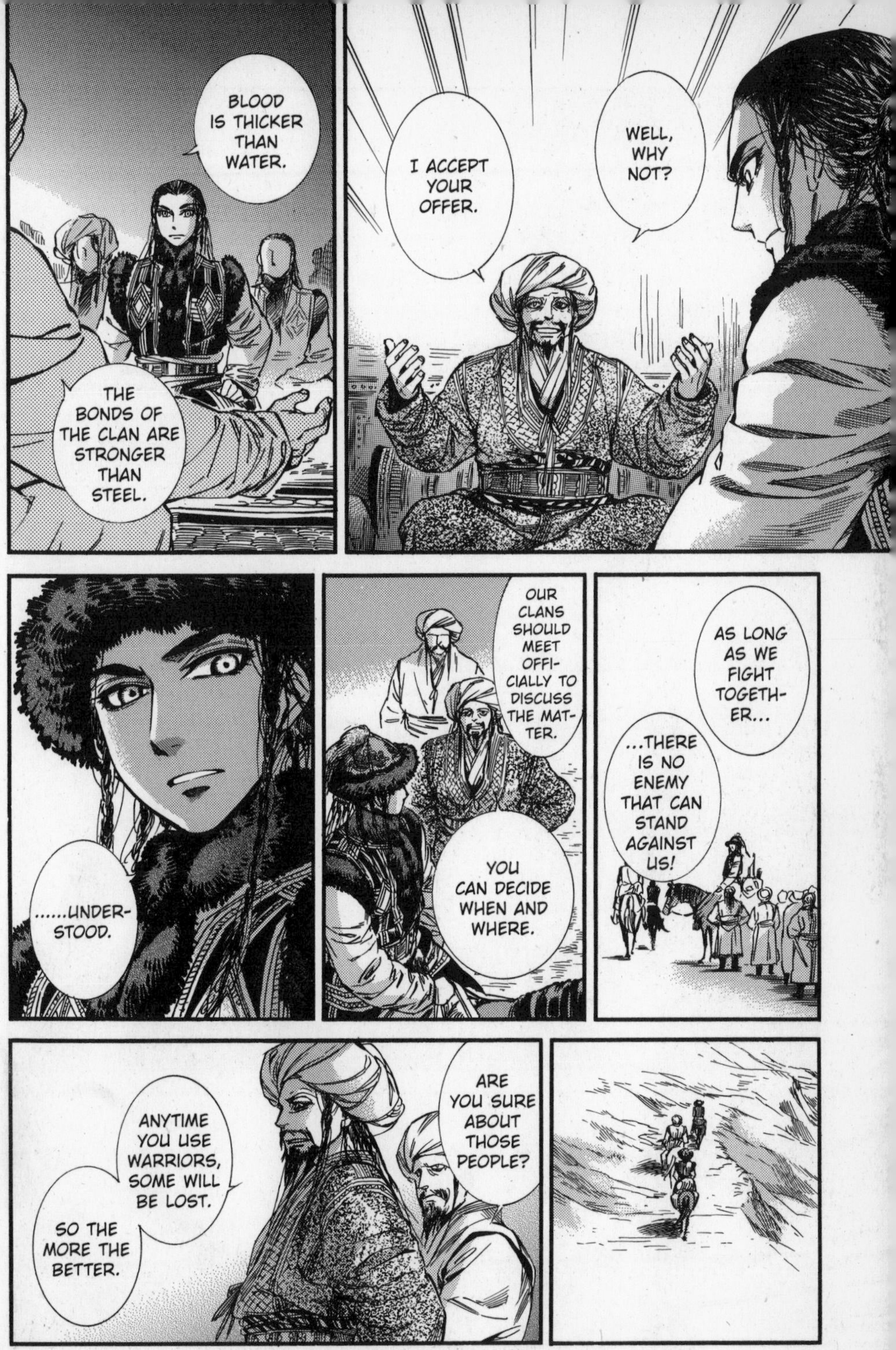
WELL, WHY NOT?
I ACCEPT YOUR OFFER.
BLOOD IS THICKER THAN WATER.
THE BONDS OF THE CLAN ARE STRONGER THAN STEEL.
AS LONG AS WE FIGHT TOGETHER...
...THERE IS NO ENEMY THAT CAN STAND AGAINST US!
OUR CLANS SHOULD MEET OFFICIALLY TO DISCUSS THE MATTER.
YOU CAN DECIDE WHEN AND WHERE.
......UNDERSTOOD.
ARE YOU SURE ABOUT THOSE PEOPLE?
ANYTIME YOU USE WARRIORS, SOME WILL BE LOST.
SO THE MORE THE BETTER.

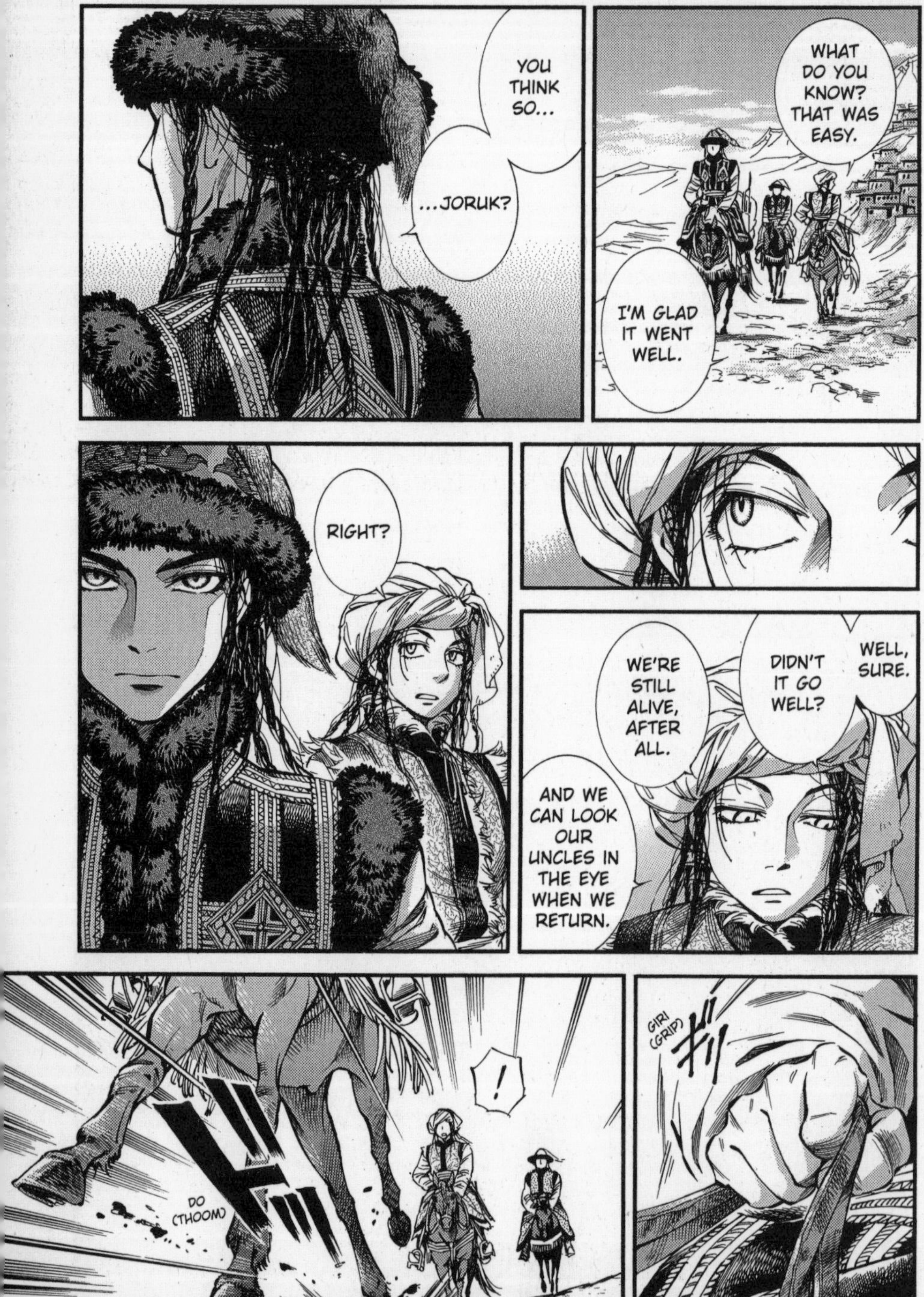
WHAT DO YOU KNOW? THAT WAS EASY.
I'M GLAD IT WENT WELL.
YOU THINK SO...
...JORUK?
WELL, SURE.
DIDN'T IT GO WELL?
WE'RE STILL ALIVE, AFTER ALL.
AND WE CAN LOOK OUR UNCLES IN THE EYE WHEN WE RETURN.
RIGHT?
GIRI (GRIP)
!
DO (THOOM)

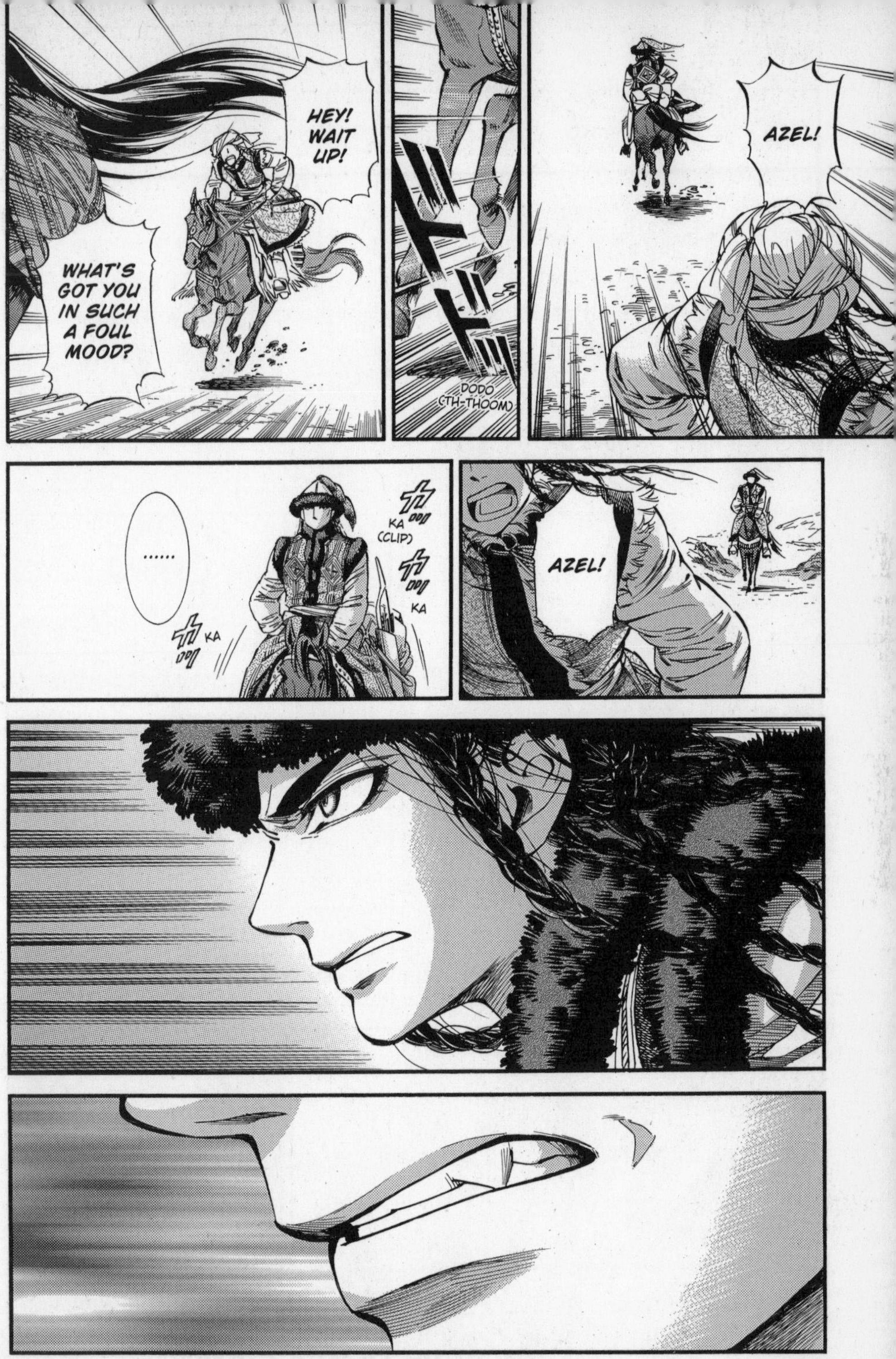
AZEL!
DODO
(TH-THOOM)
HEY! WAIT UP!
WHAT'S GOT YOU IN SUCH A FOUL MOOD?
AZEL!
......
KA
(CLIP)
KA
KA

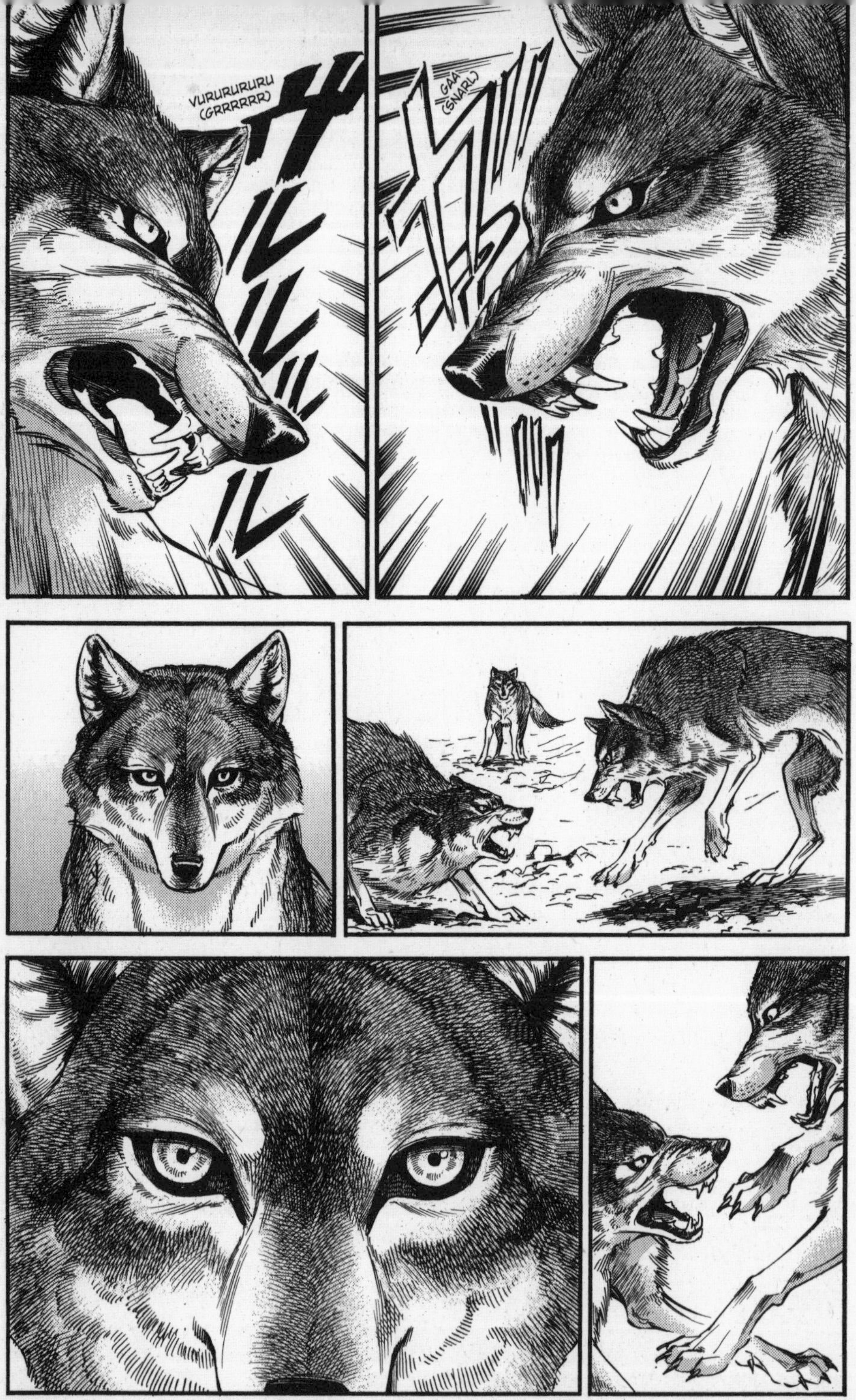
GAA
(SNARL)
VURURURURU
(GRRRRRR)

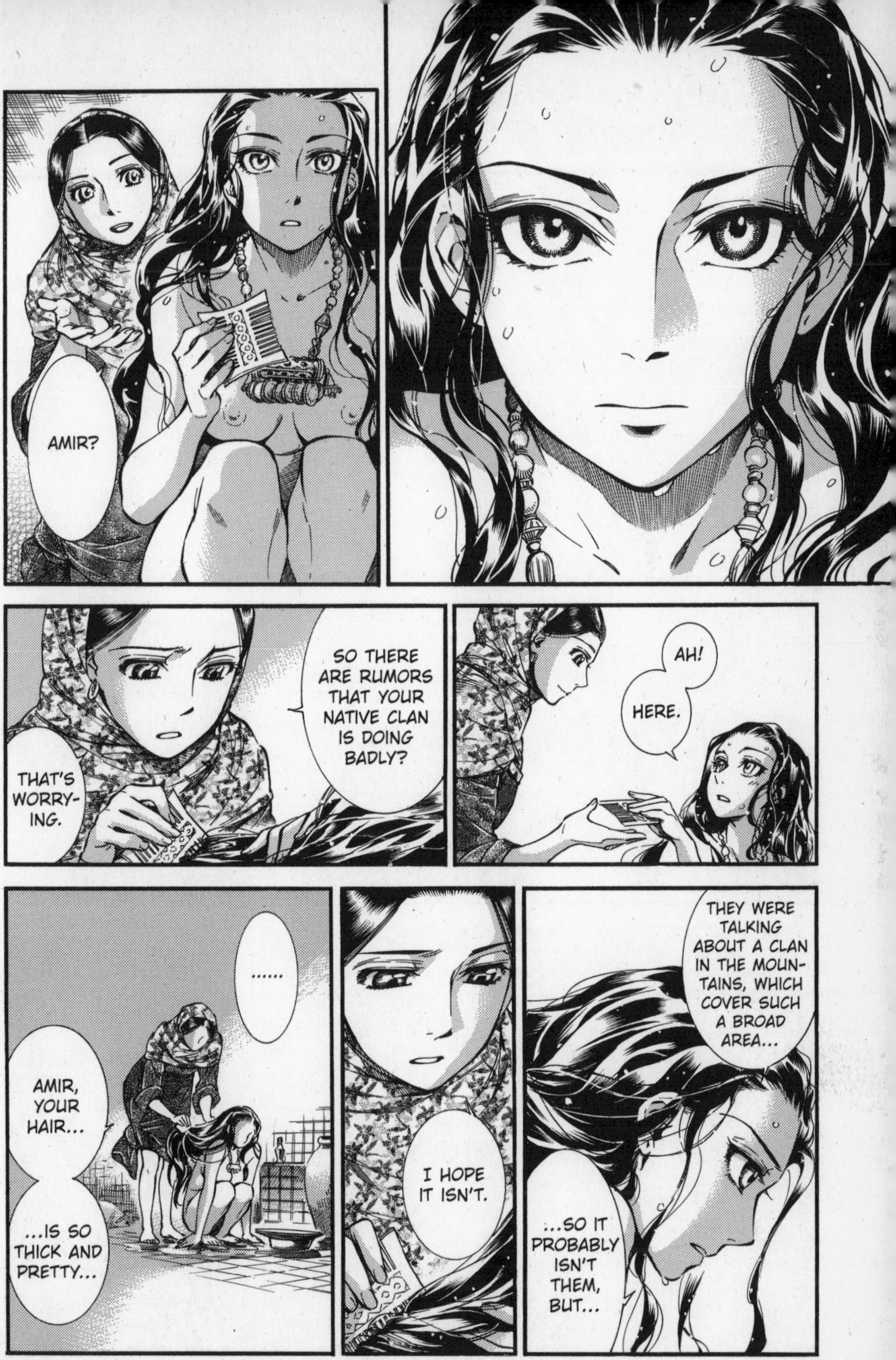
AMIR?
AH!
HERE.
SO THERE ARE RUMORS THAT YOUR NATIVE CLAN IS DOING BADLY?
THAT'S WORRYING.
THEY WERE TALKING ABOUT A CLAN IN THE MOUNTAINS, WHICH COVER SUCH A BROAD AREA...
...SO IT PROBABLY ISN'T THEM, BUT...
I HOPE IT ISN'T.
......
AMIR, YOUR HAIR...
...IS SO THICK AND PRETTY...

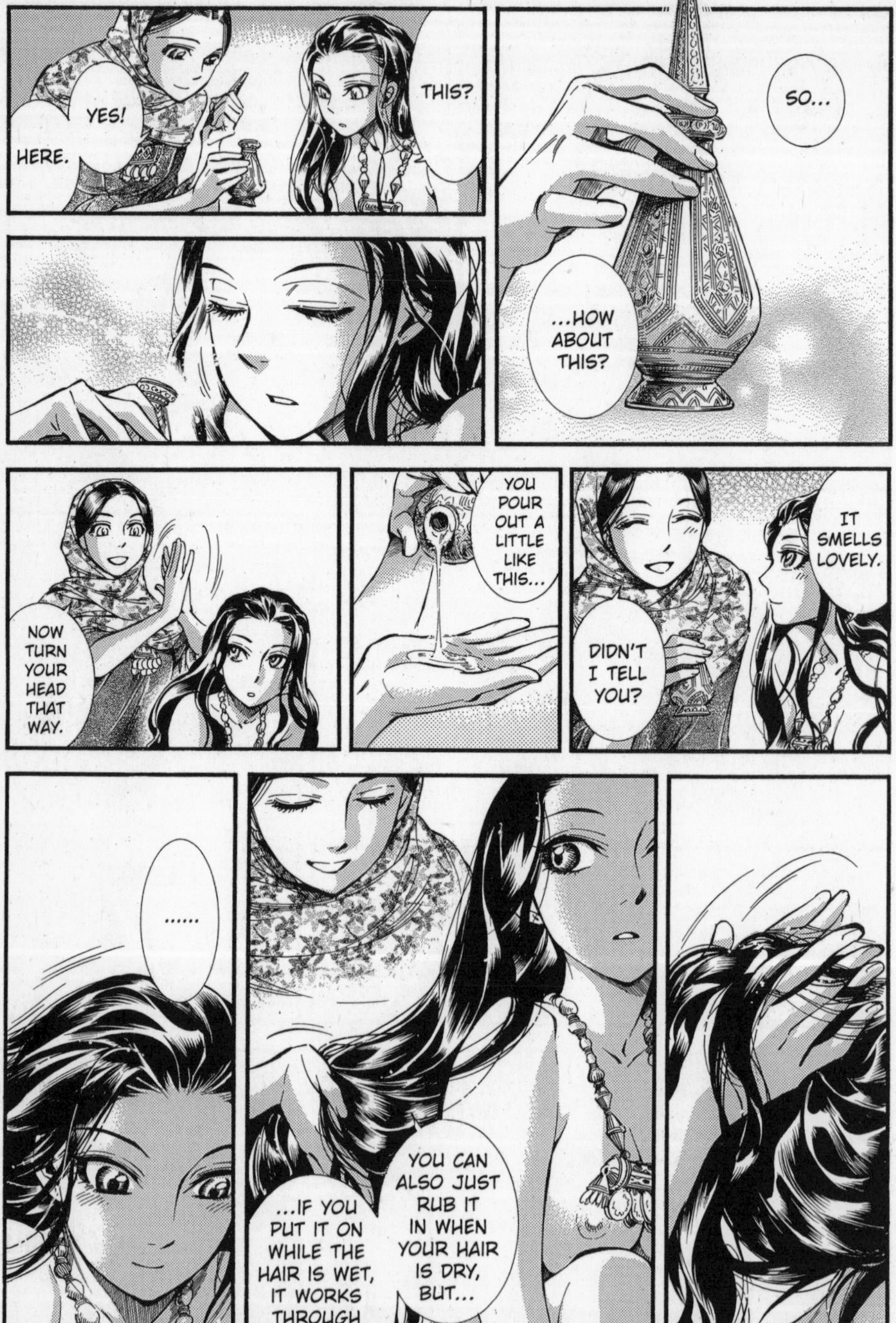
SO...
...HOW ABOUT THIS?
THIS?
YES!
HERE.
IT SMELLS LOVELY.
DIDN'T I TELL YOU?
YOU POUR OUT A LITTLE LIKE THIS...
NOW TURN YOUR HEAD THAT WAY.
YOU CAN ALSO JUST RUB IT IN WHEN YOUR HAIR IS DRY, BUT...
...IF YOU PUT IT ON WHILE THE HAIR IS WET, IT WORKS THROUGH BETTER AND SMELLS WON-DERFUL!
......

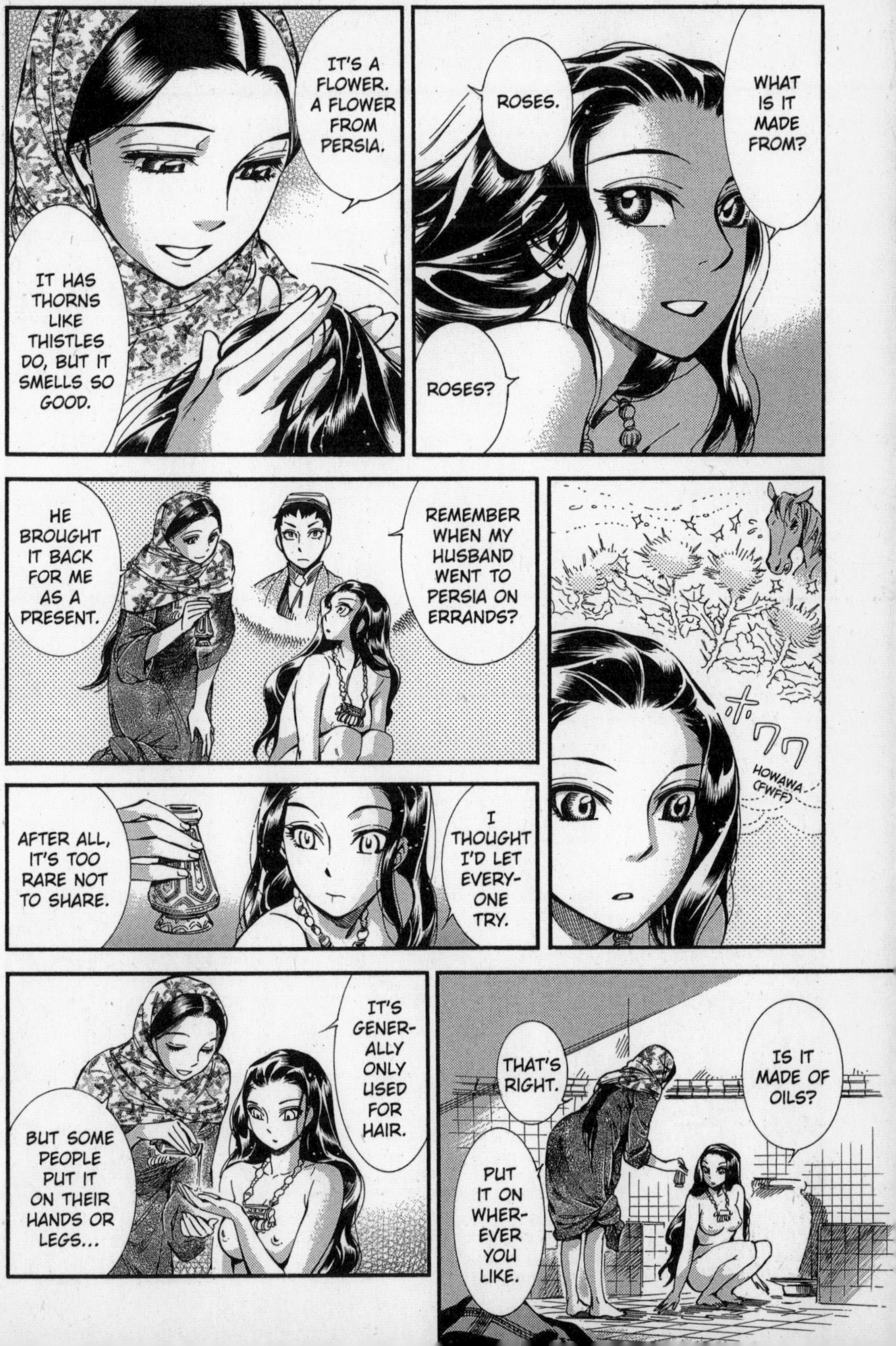
WHAT IS IT MADE FROM?
ROSES.
ROSES?
IT'S A FLOWER. A FLOWER FROM PERSIA.
IT HAS THORNS LIKE THISTLES DO, BUT IT SMELLS SO GOOD.
ホワワ
HOWAWA (FWFF)
REMEMBER WHEN MY HUSBAND WENT TO PERSIA ON ERRANDS?
HE BROUGHT IT BACK FOR ME AS A PRESENT.
I THOUGHT I'D LET EVERY-ONE TRY.
AFTER ALL, IT'S TOO RARE NOT TO SHARE.
IS IT MADE OF OILS?
THAT'S RIGHT.
PUT IT ON WHER-EVER YOU LIKE.
IT'S GENER-ALLY ONLY USED FOR HAIR.
BUT SOME PEOPLE PUT IT ON THEIR HANDS OR LEGS...

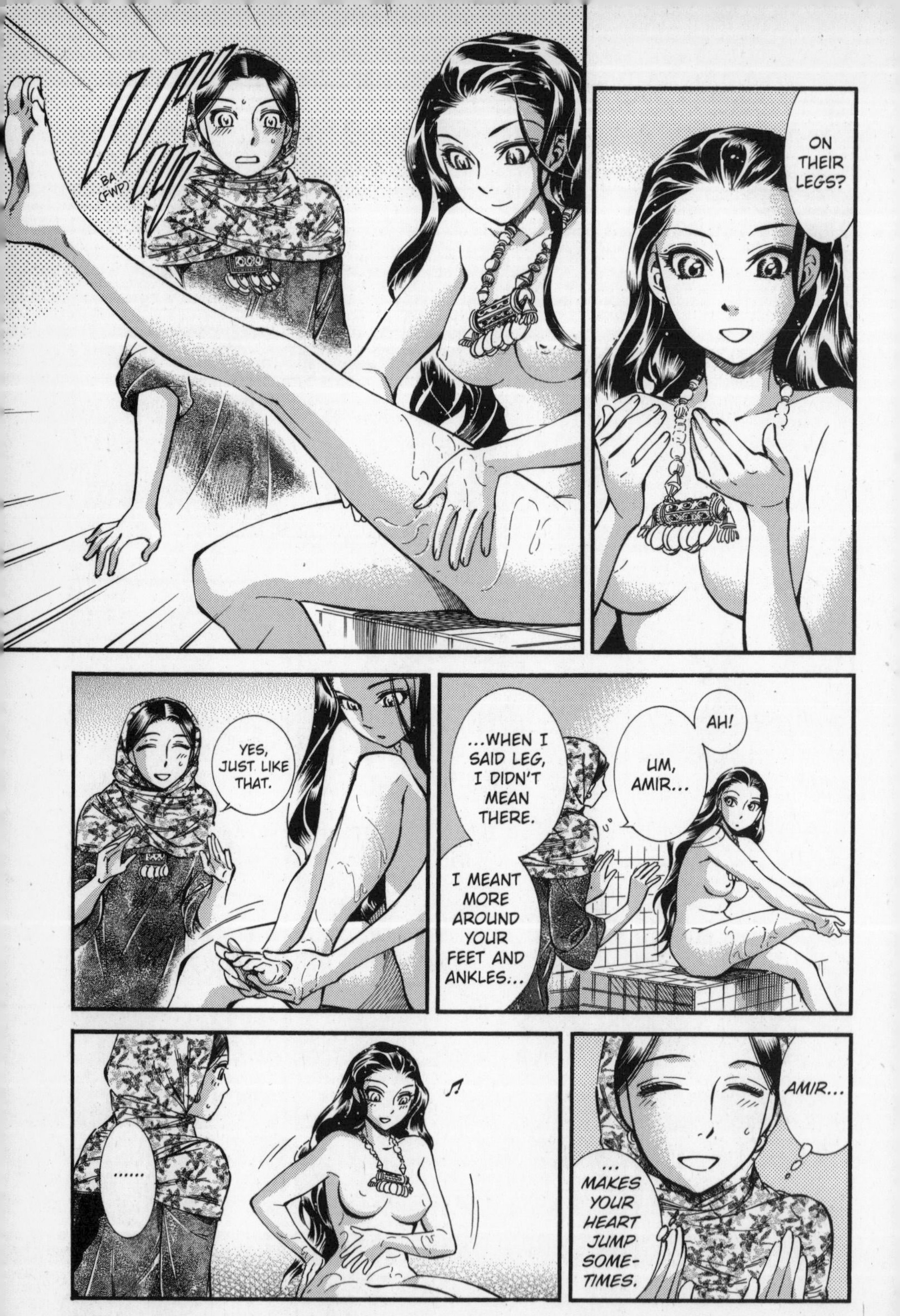
ON THEIR LEGS?
BA (FWP)
AH!
UM, AMIR...
...WHEN I SAID LEG, I DIDN'T MEAN THERE.
I MEANT MORE AROUND YOUR FEET AND ANKLES...
YES, JUST LIKE THAT.
AMIR...
...MAKES YOUR HEART JUMP SOME-TIMES.
......

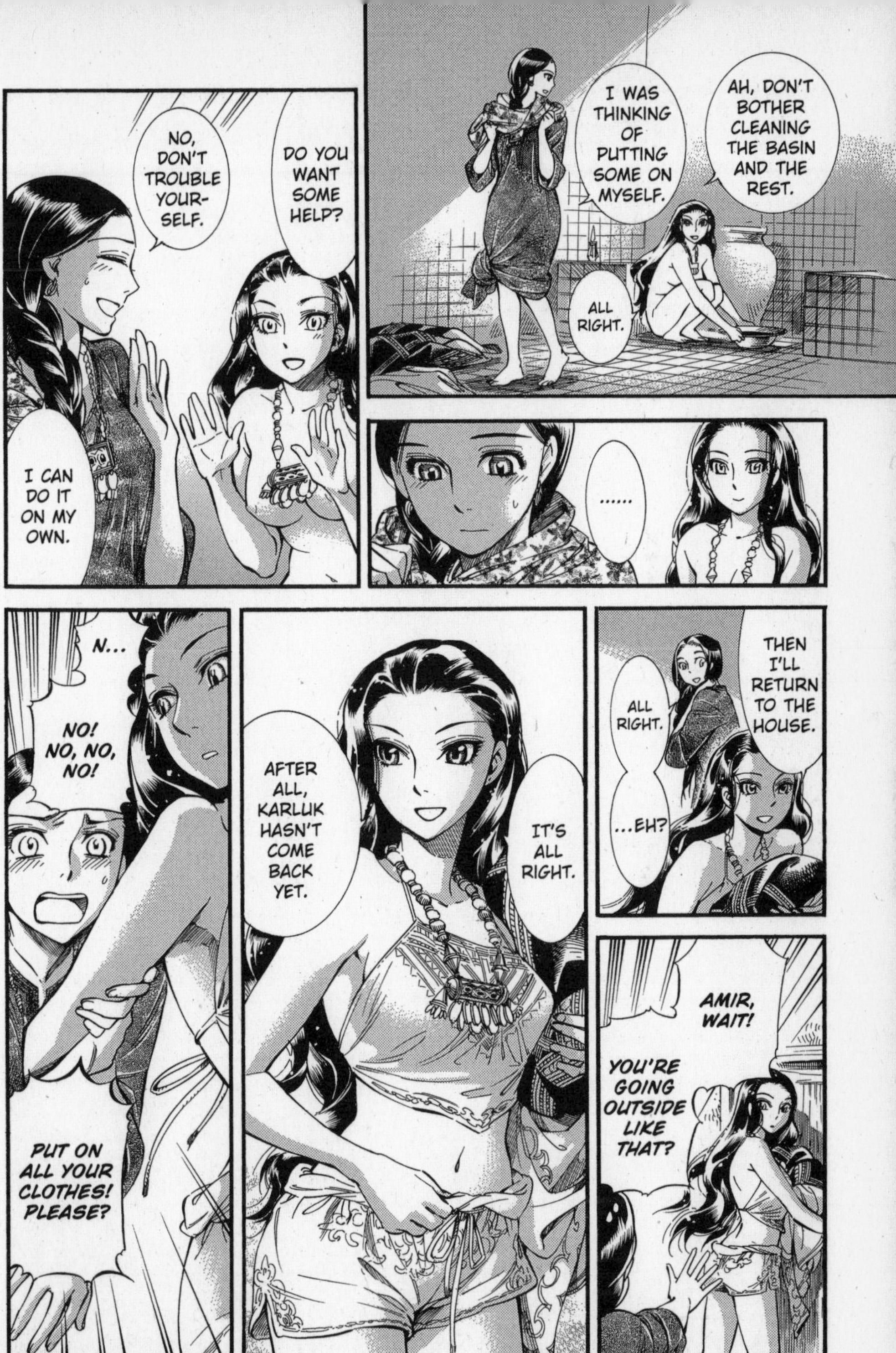
AH, DON'T BOTHER CLEANING THE BASIN AND THE REST.
I WAS THINKING OF PUTTING SOME ON MYSELF.
ALL RIGHT.
......
DO YOU WANT SOME HELP?
NO, DON'T TROUBLE YOUR-SELF.
I CAN DO IT ON MY OWN.
THEN I'LL RETURN TO THE HOUSE.
ALL RIGHT.
...EH?
AMIR, WAIT!
YOU'RE GOING OUTSIDE LIKE THAT?
IT'S ALL RIGHT.
AFTER ALL, KARLUK HASN'T COME BACK YET.
N...
NO! NO, NO, NO!
PUT ON ALL YOUR CLOTHES! PLEASE?

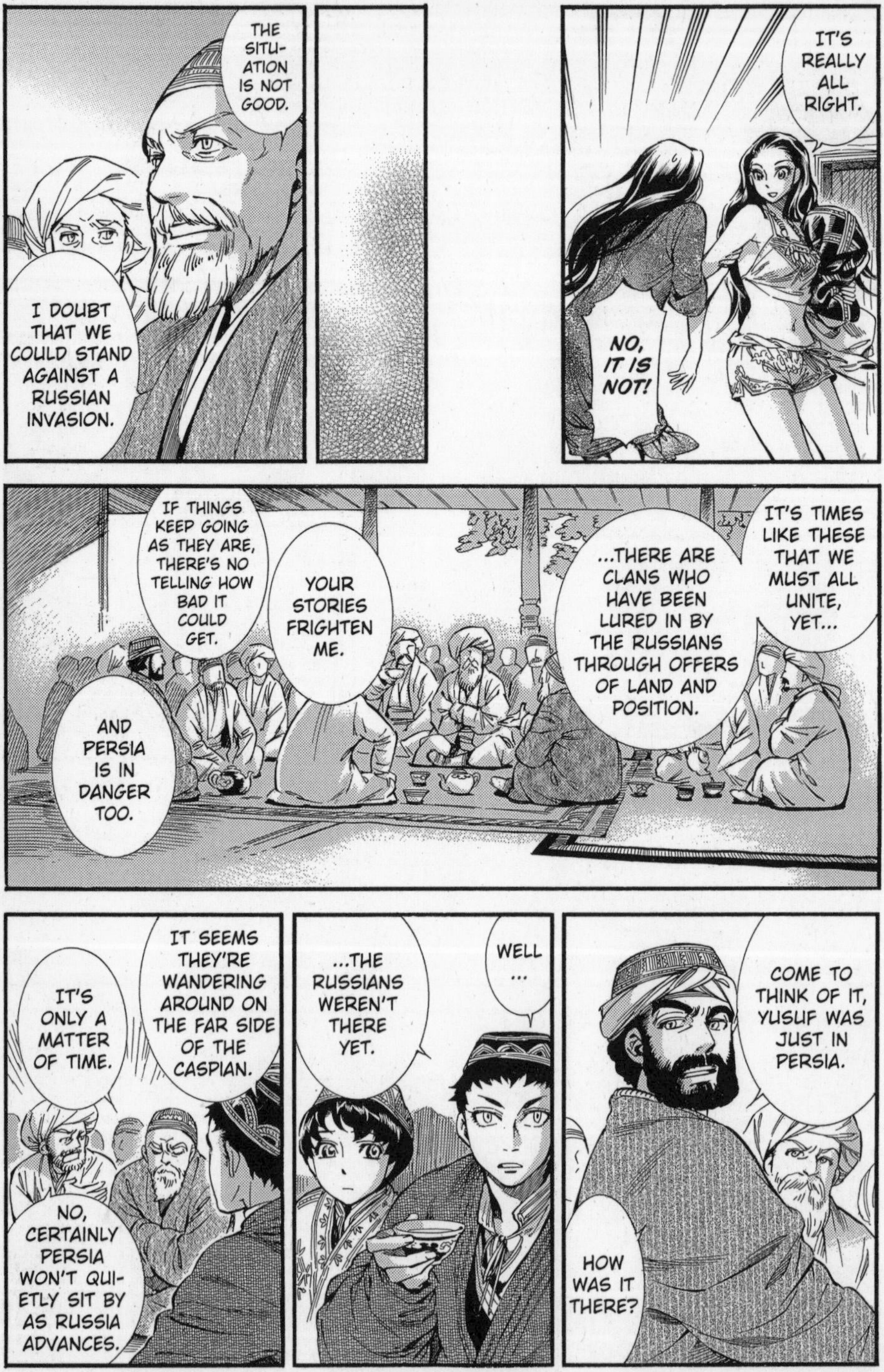

IT'S REALLY ALL RIGHT.
NO, IT IS NOT!
THE SITUATION IS NOT GOOD.
I DOUBT THAT WE COULD STAND AGAINST A RUSSIAN INVASION.
IT'S TIMES LIKE THESE THAT WE MUST ALL UNITE, YET...
...THERE ARE CLANS WHO HAVE BEEN LURED IN BY THE RUSSIANS THROUGH OFFERS OF LAND AND POSITION.
YOUR STORIES FRIGHTEN ME.
IF THINGS KEEP GOING AS THEY ARE, THERE'S NO TELLING HOW BAD IT COULD GET.
AND PERSIA IS IN DANGER TOO.
COME TO THINK OF IT, YUSUF WAS JUST IN PERSIA.
HOW WAS IT THERE?
WELL ...
...THE RUSSIANS WEREN'T THERE YET.
IT SEEMS THEY'RE WANDERING AROUND ON THE FAR SIDE OF THE CASPIAN.
IT'S ONLY A MATTER OF TIME.
NO, CERTAINLY PERSIA WON'T QUIETLY SIT BY AS RUSSIA ADVANCES.

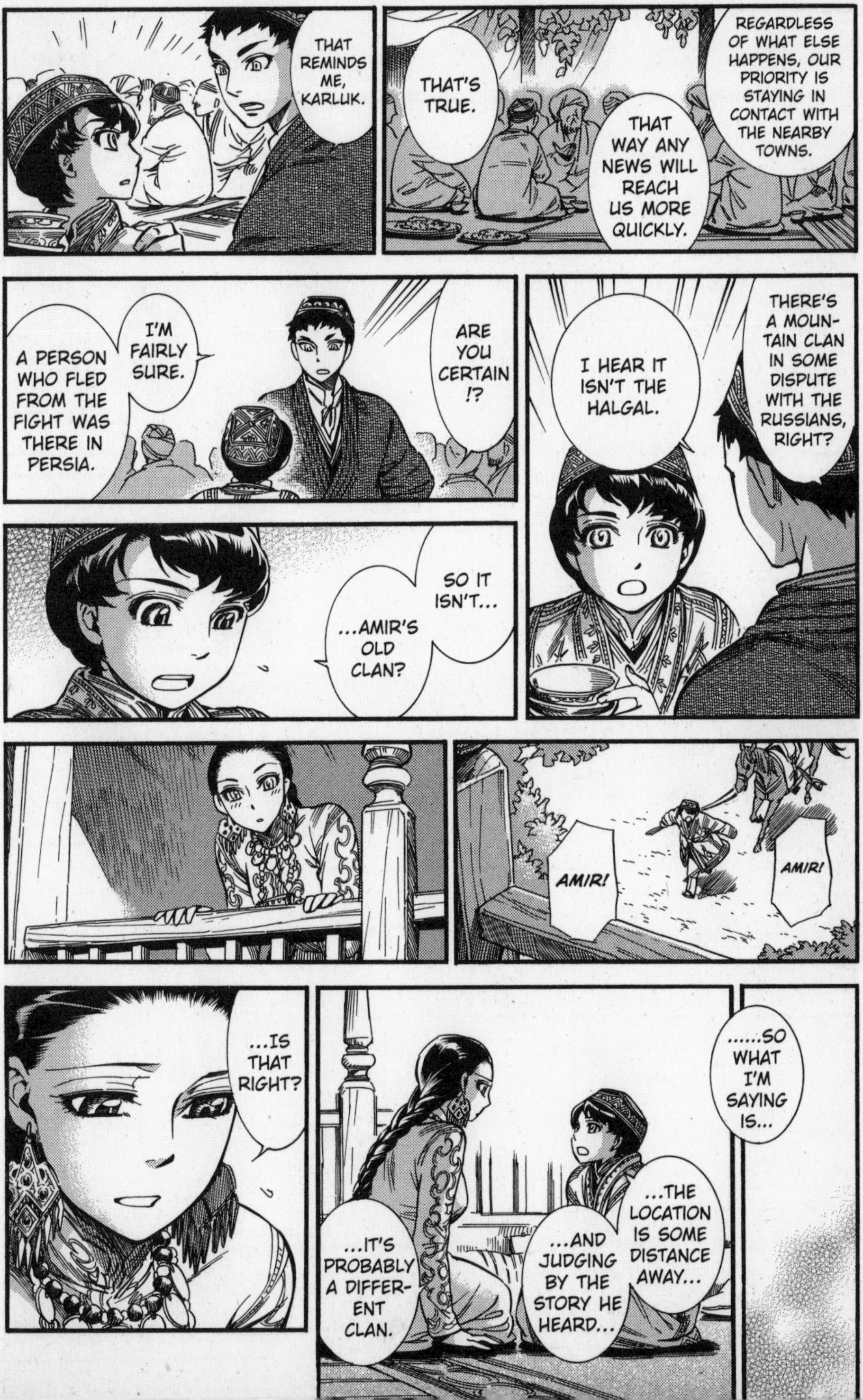
REGARDLESS OF WHAT ELSE HAPPENS, OUR PRIORITY IS STAYING IN CONTACT WITH THE NEARBY TOWNS.
THAT WAY ANY NEWS WILL REACH US MORE QUICKLY.
THAT'S TRUE.
THAT REMINDS ME, KARLUK.
THERE'S A MOUNTAIN CLAN IN SOME DISPUTE WITH THE RUSSIANS, RIGHT?
I HEAR IT ISN'T THE HALGAL.
ARE YOU CERTAIN!?
I'M FAIRLY SURE.
A PERSON WHO FLED FROM THE FIGHT WAS THERE IN PERSIA.
SO IT ISN'T...
...AMIR'S OLD CLAN?
AMIR!
AMIR!
......SO WHAT I'M SAYING IS...
...THE LOCATION IS SOME DISTANCE AWAY...
...AND JUDGING BY THE STORY HE HEARD...
...IT'S PROBABLY A DIFFER-ENT CLAN.
...IS THAT RIGHT?

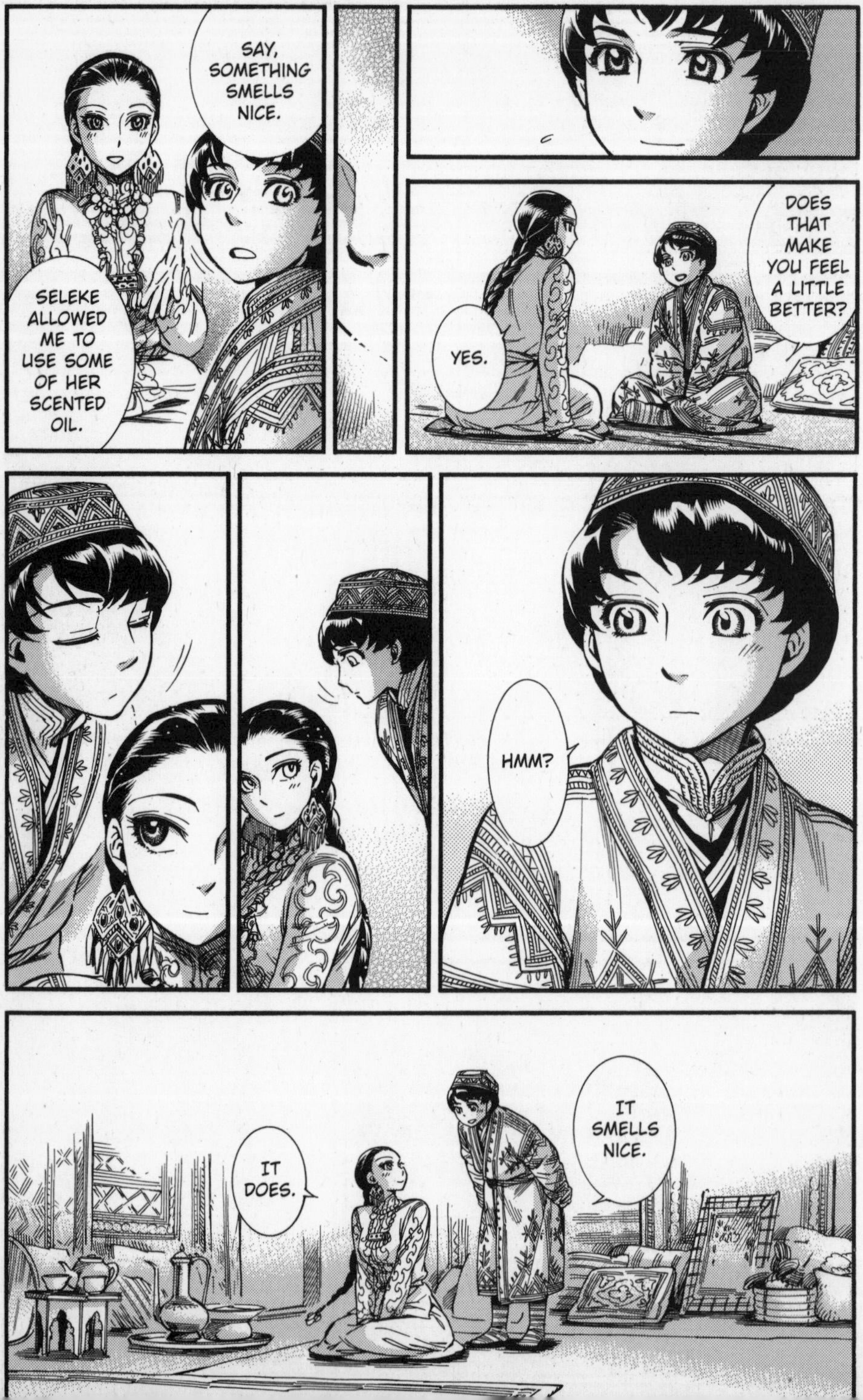
DOES THAT MAKE YOU FEEL A LITTLE BETTER?
YES.
SAY, SOMETHING SMELLS NICE.
SELEKE ALLOWED ME TO USE SOME OF HER SCENTED OIL.
HMM?
IT SMELLS NICE.
IT DOES.

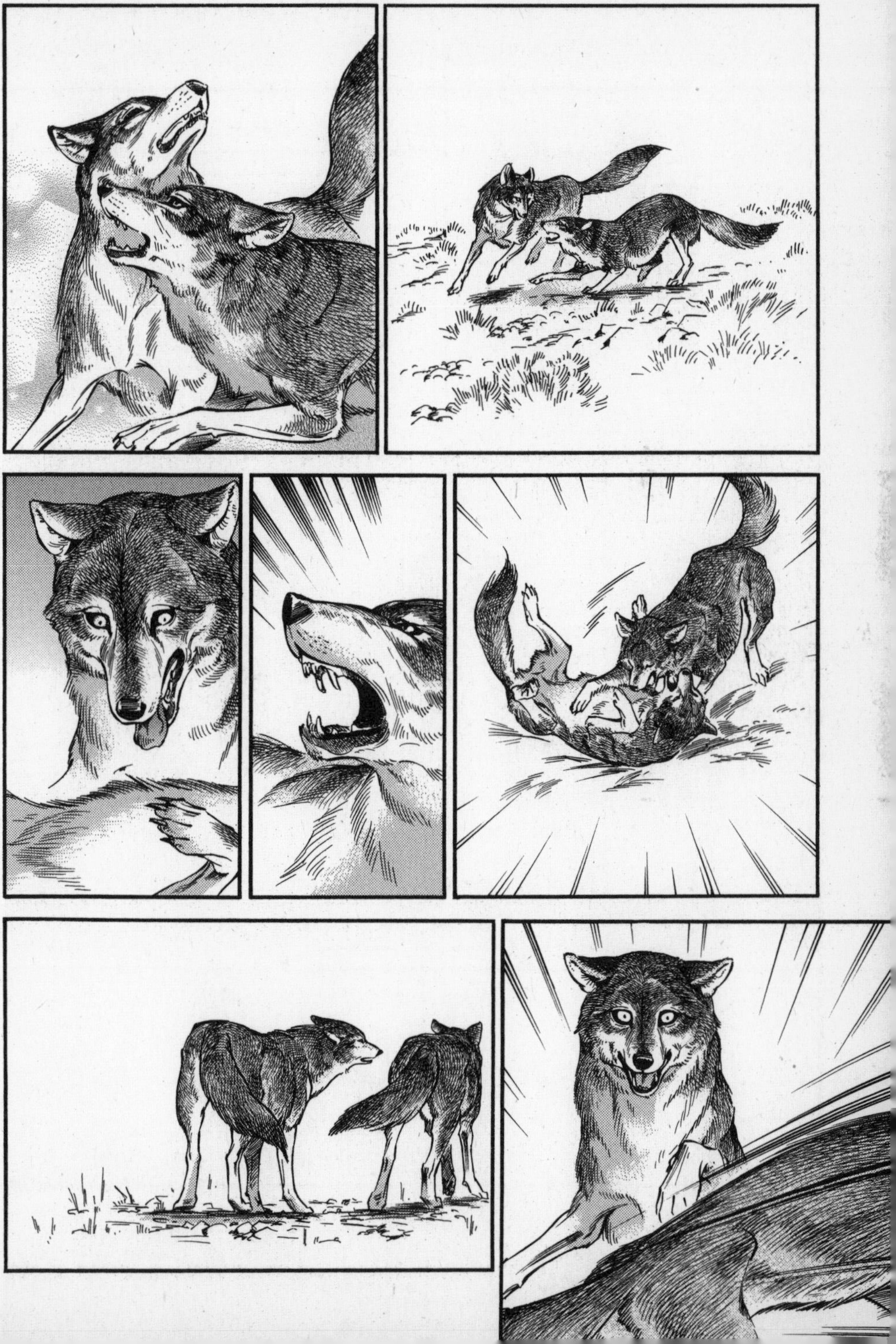

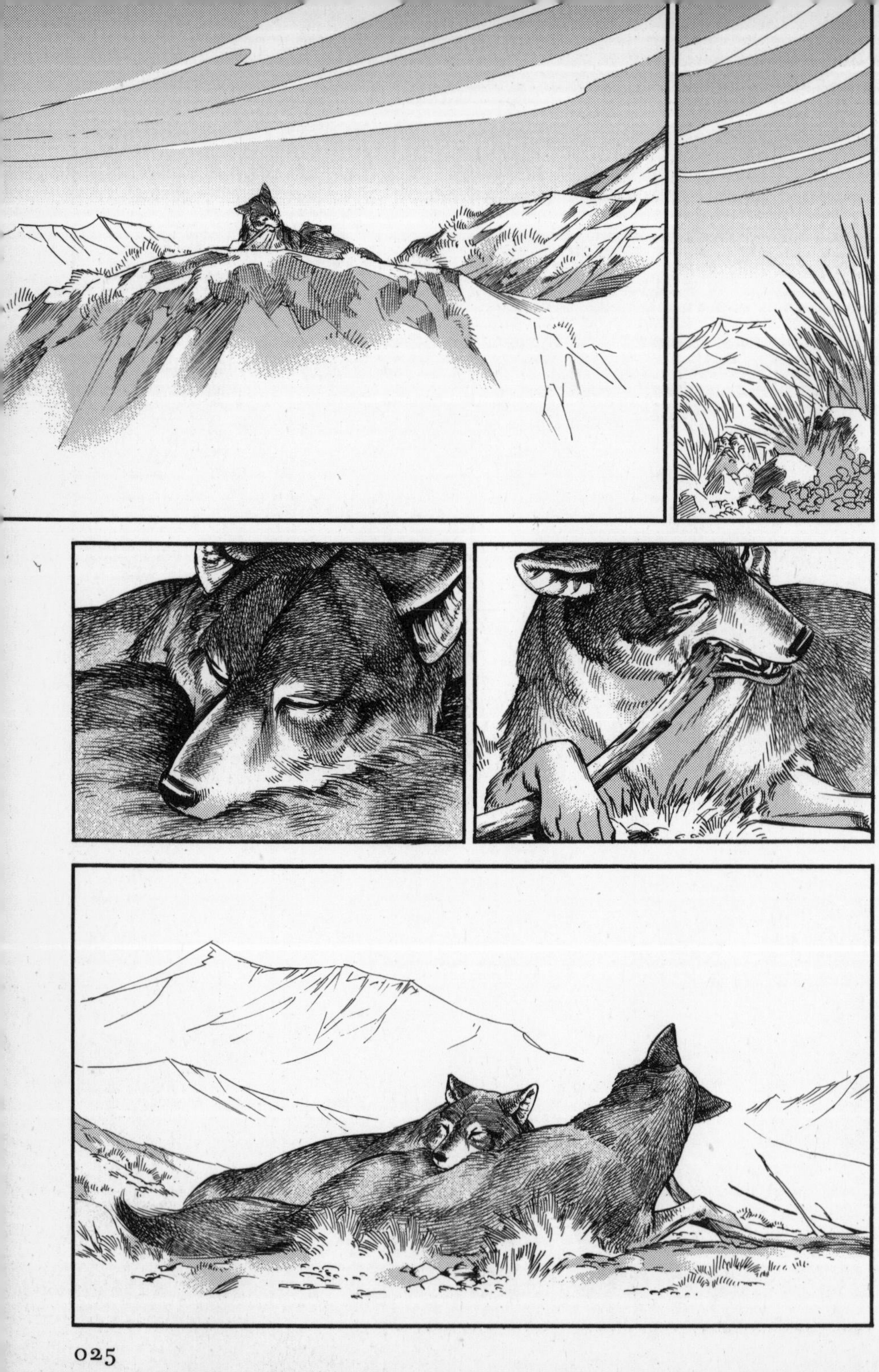

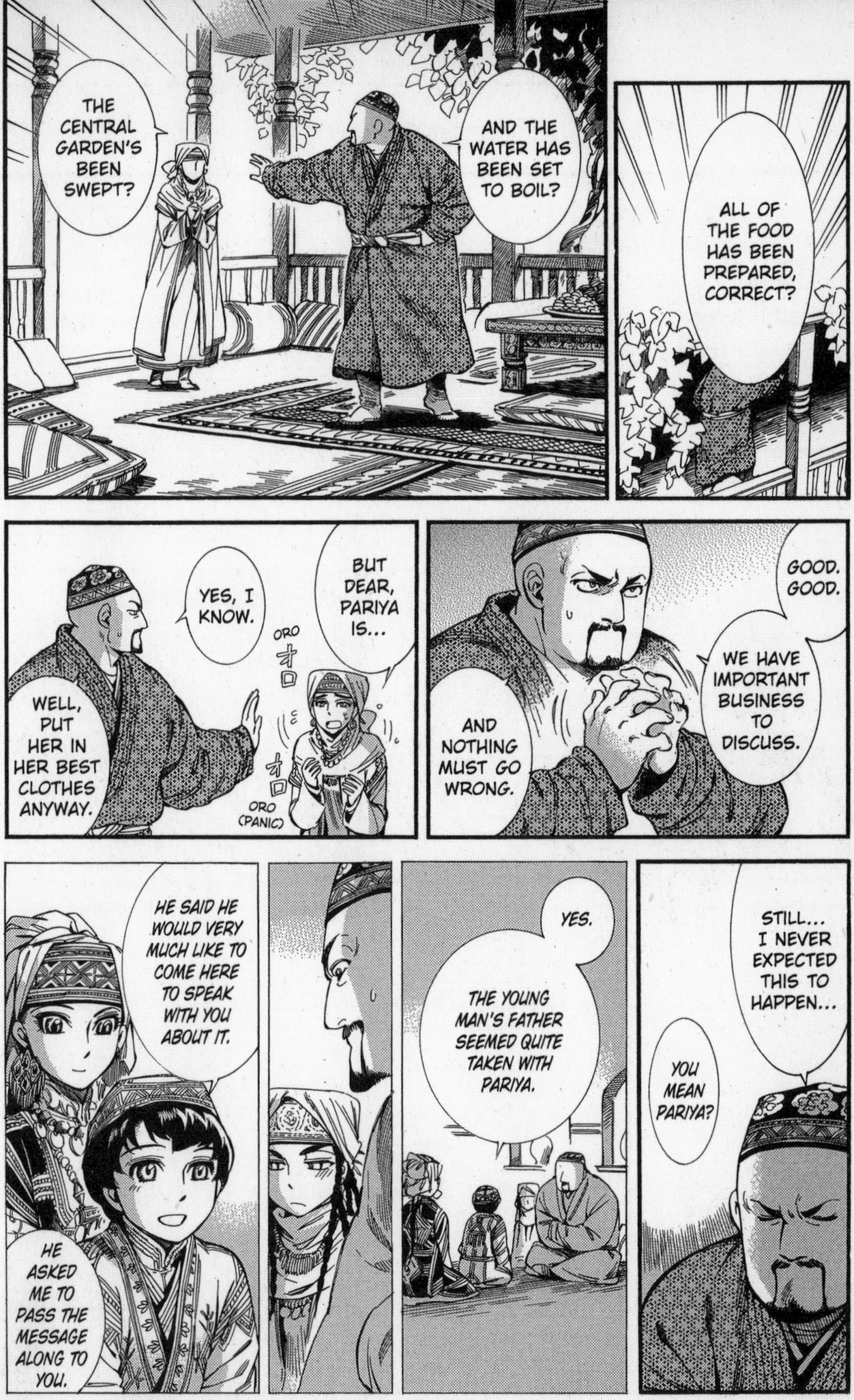
ALL OF THE FOOD HAS BEEN PREPARED, CORRECT?
AND THE WATER HAS BEEN SET TO BOIL?
THE CENTRAL GARDEN'S BEEN SWEPT?
GOOD. GOOD.
WE HAVE IMPORTANT BUSINESS TO DISCUSS.
AND NOTHING MUST GO WRONG.
BUT DEAR, PARIYA IS...
ORO オロ
YES, I KNOW.
WELL, PUT HER IN HER BEST CLOTHES ANYWAY.
オロ ORO (PANIC)
STILL... I NEVER EXPECTED THIS TO HAPPEN...
YOU MEAN PARIYA?
YES.
THE YOUNG MAN'S FATHER SEEMED QUITE TAKEN WITH PARIYA.
HE SAID HE WOULD VERY MUCH LIKE TO COME HERE TO SPEAK WITH YOU ABOUT IT.
HE ASKED ME TO PASS THE MESSAGE ALONG TO YOU.

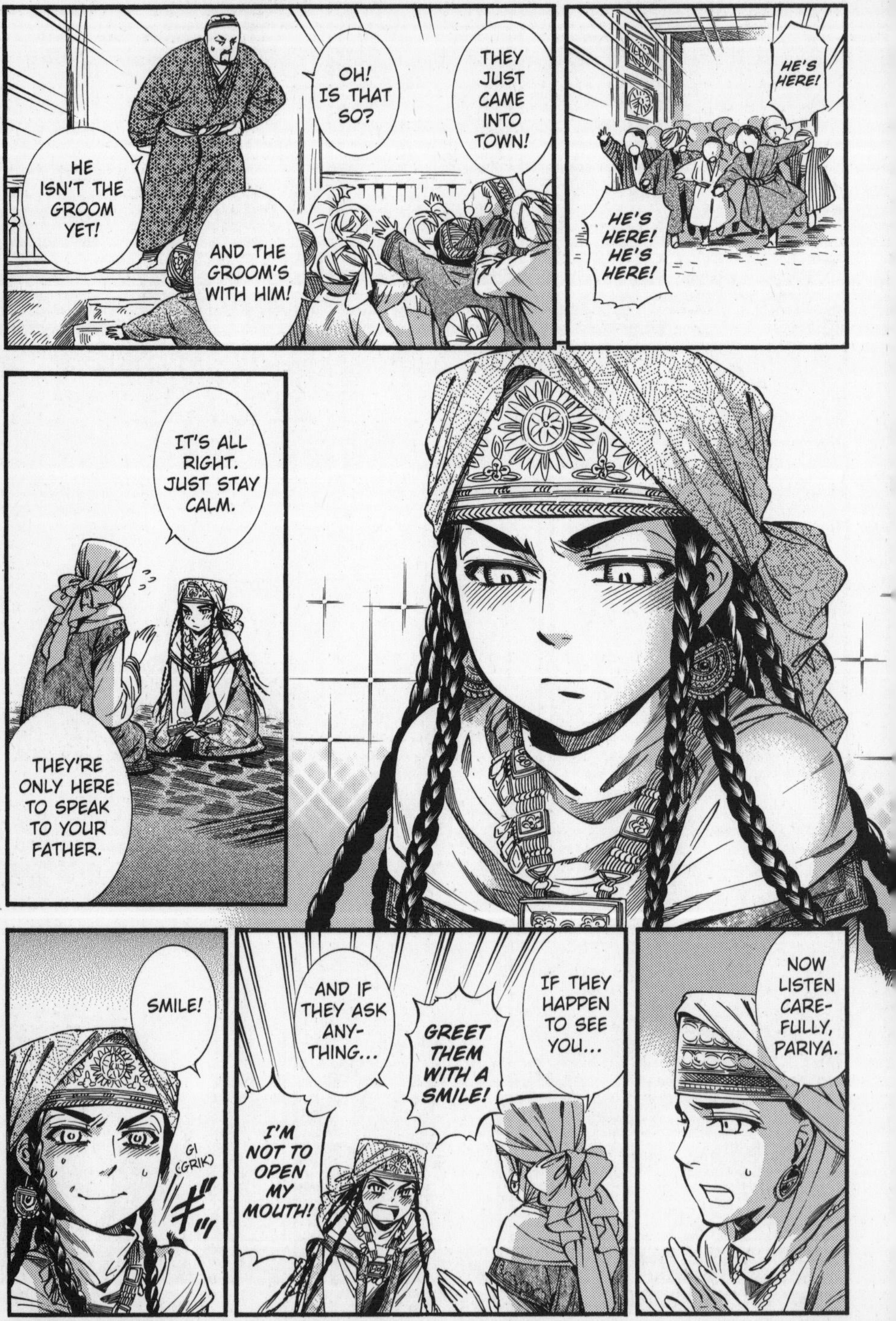
HE'S HERE!
HE'S HERE! HE'S HERE!
THEY JUST CAME INTO TOWN!
OH! IS THAT SO?
AND THE GROOM'S WITH HIM!
HE ISN'T THE GROOM YET!
IT'S ALL RIGHT. JUST STAY CALM.
THEY'RE ONLY HERE TO SPEAK TO YOUR FATHER.
NOW LISTEN CARE-FULLY, PARIYA.
IF THEY HAPPEN TO SEE YOU...
GREET THEM WITH A SMILE!
AND IF THEY ASK ANY-THING...
I'M NOT TO OPEN MY MOUTH!
SMILE!
GI (GRIK)

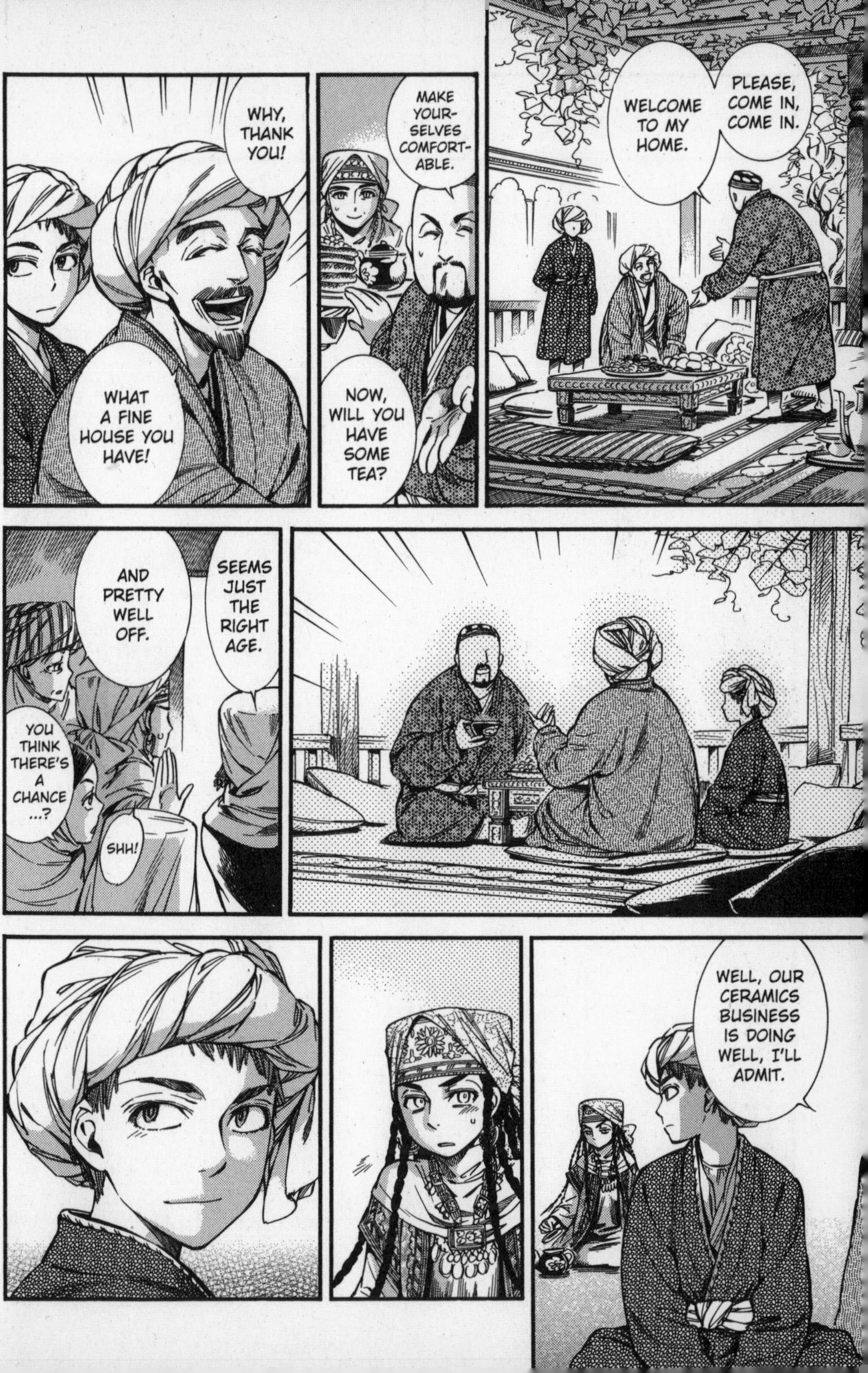
PLEASE, COME IN, COME IN.
WELCOME TO MY HOME.
MAKE YOUR-SELVES COMFORT-ABLE.
NOW, WILL YOU HAVE SOME TEA?
WHY, THANK YOU!
WHAT A FINE HOUSE YOU HAVE!
SEEMS JUST THE RIGHT AGE.
AND PRETTY WELL OFF.
YOU THINK THERE'S A CHANCE ...?
SHH!
WELL, OUR CERAMICS BUSINESS IS DOING WELL, I'LL ADMIT.

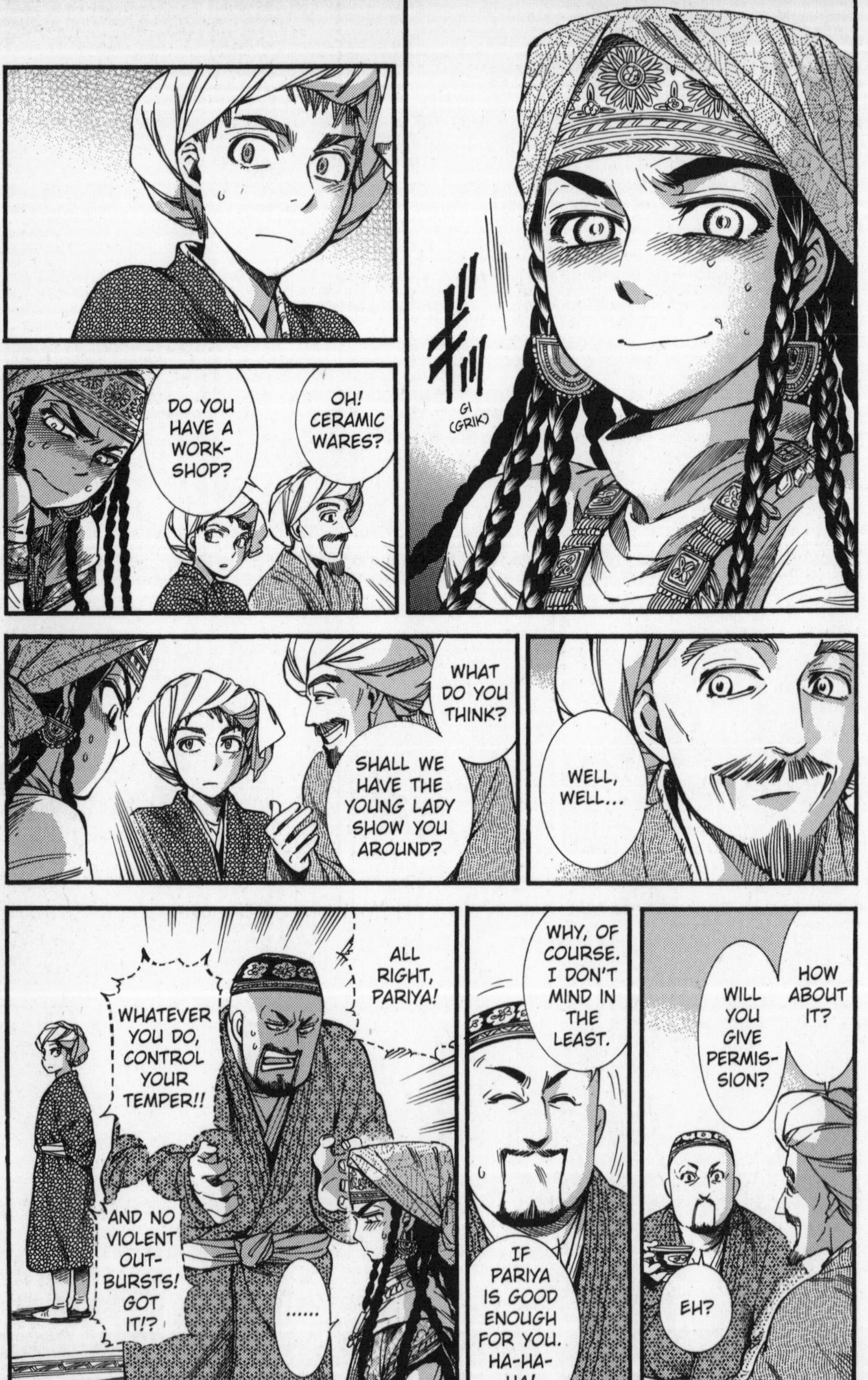
GI (GRIK)
OH! CERAMIC WARES?
DO YOU HAVE A WORK-SHOP?
WELL, WELL...
WHAT DO YOU THINK?
SHALL WE HAVE THE YOUNG LADY SHOW YOU AROUND?
HOW ABOUT IT?
WILL YOU GIVE PERMIS-SION?
EH?
WHY, OF COURSE. I DON'T MIND IN THE LEAST.
IF PARIYA IS GOOD ENOUGH FOR YOU. HA-HA-HA!
ALL RIGHT, PARIYA!
WHATEVER YOU DO, CONTROL YOUR TEMPER!!
AND NO VIOLENT OUT-BURSTS! GOT IT!?
......

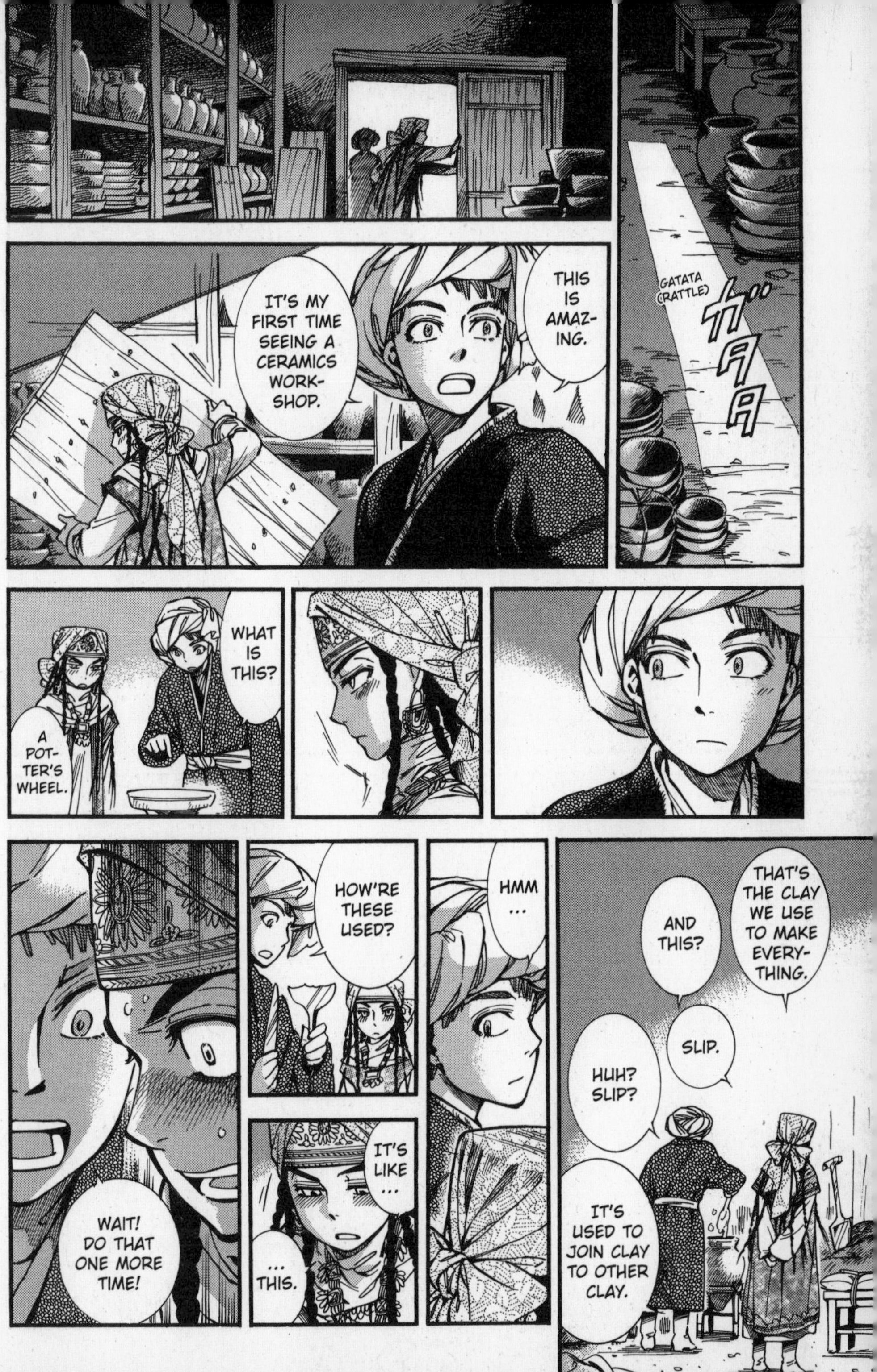
GATATA (RATTLE)
ガタタ
THIS IS AMAZ-ING.
IT'S MY FIRST TIME SEEING A CERAMICS WORK-SHOP.
WHAT IS THIS?
A POTTER'S WHEEL.
THAT'S THE CLAY WE USE TO MAKE EVERY-THING.
AND THIS?
SLIP.
HUH? SLIP?
IT'S USED TO JOIN CLAY TO OTHER CLAY.
HMM...
HOW'RE THESE USED?
IT'S LIKE...
...THIS.
WAIT! DO THAT ONE MORE TIME!

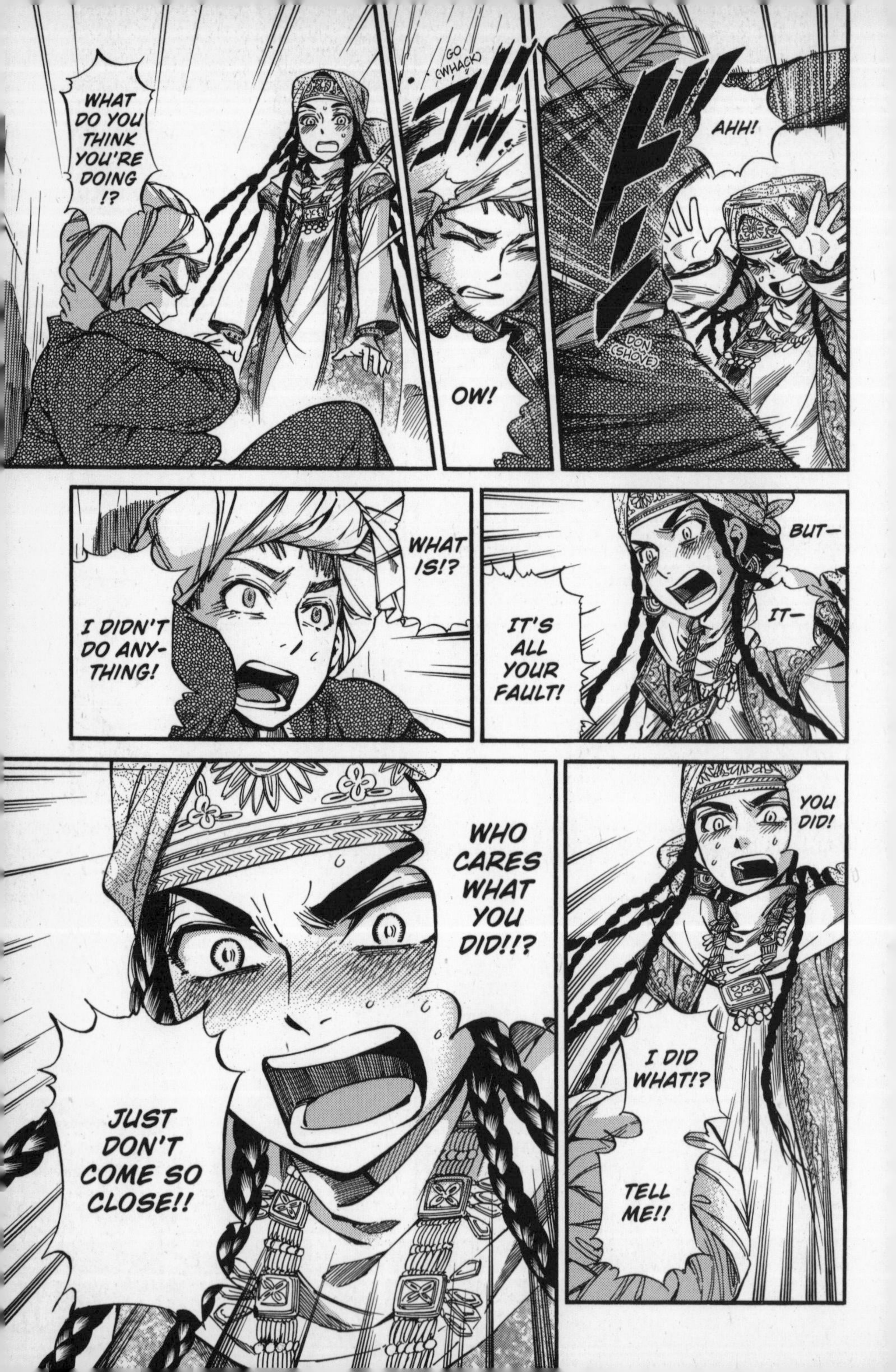
AHH!
DON (SHOVE)
GO (WHACK)
OW!
WHAT DO YOU THINK YOU'RE DOING!?
BUT—
IT—
IT'S ALL YOUR FAULT!
WHAT IS!?
I DIDN'T DO ANYTHING!
YOU DID!
I DID WHAT!?
TELL ME!!
WHO CARES WHAT YOU DID!!?
JUST DON'T COME SO CLOSE!!

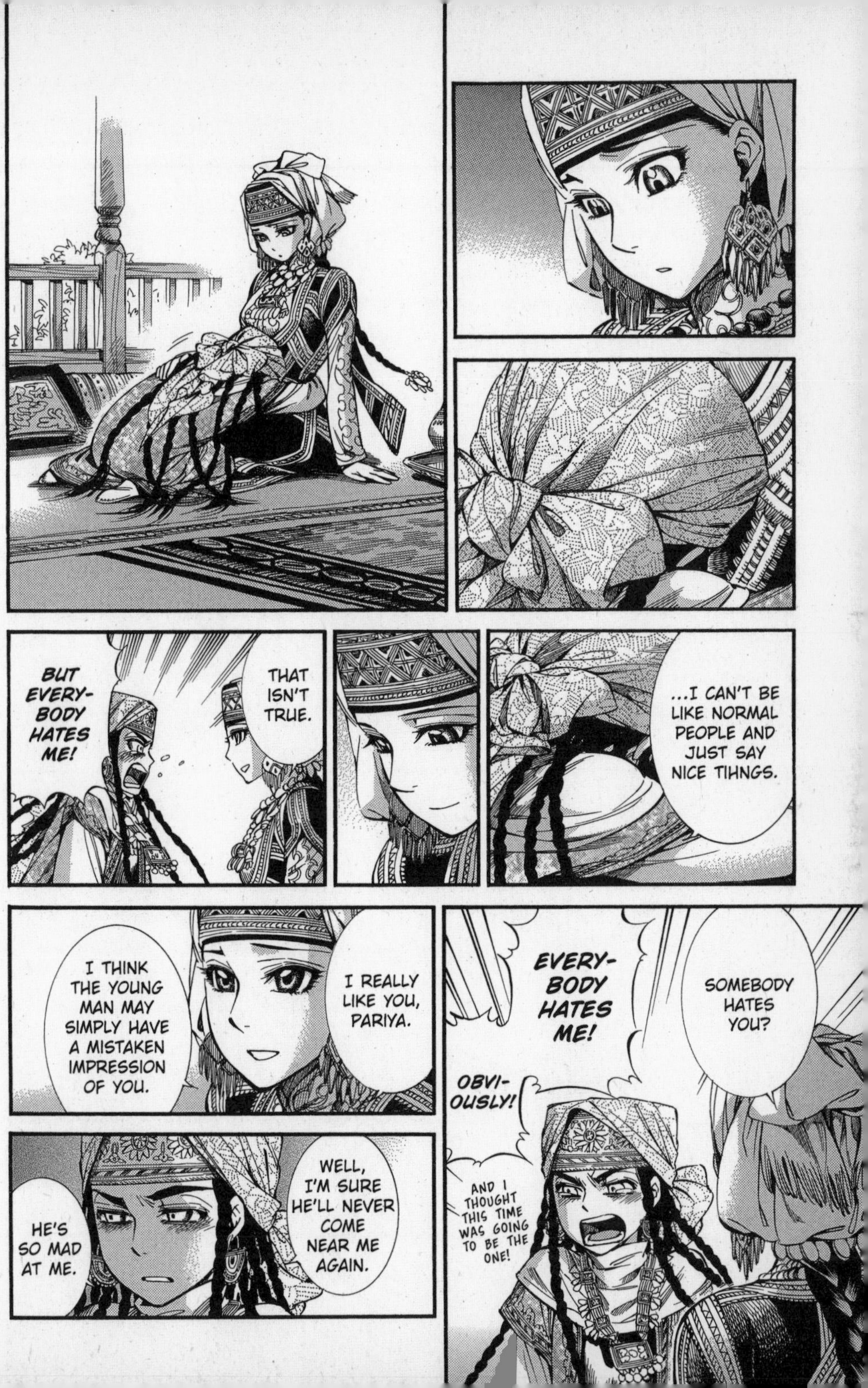
...I CAN'T BE LIKE NORMAL PEOPLE AND JUST SAY NICE TIHNGS.
THAT ISN'T TRUE.
BUT EVERY-BODY HATES ME!
SOMEBODY HATES YOU?
EVERY-BODY HATES ME!
OBVI-OUSLY!
AND I THOUGHT THIS TIME WAS GOING TO BE THE ONE!
I REALLY LIKE YOU, PARIYA.
I THINK THE YOUNG MAN MAY SIMPLY HAVE A MISTAKEN IMPRESSION OF YOU.
WELL, I'M SURE HE'LL NEVER COME NEAR ME AGAIN.
HE'S SO MAD AT ME.

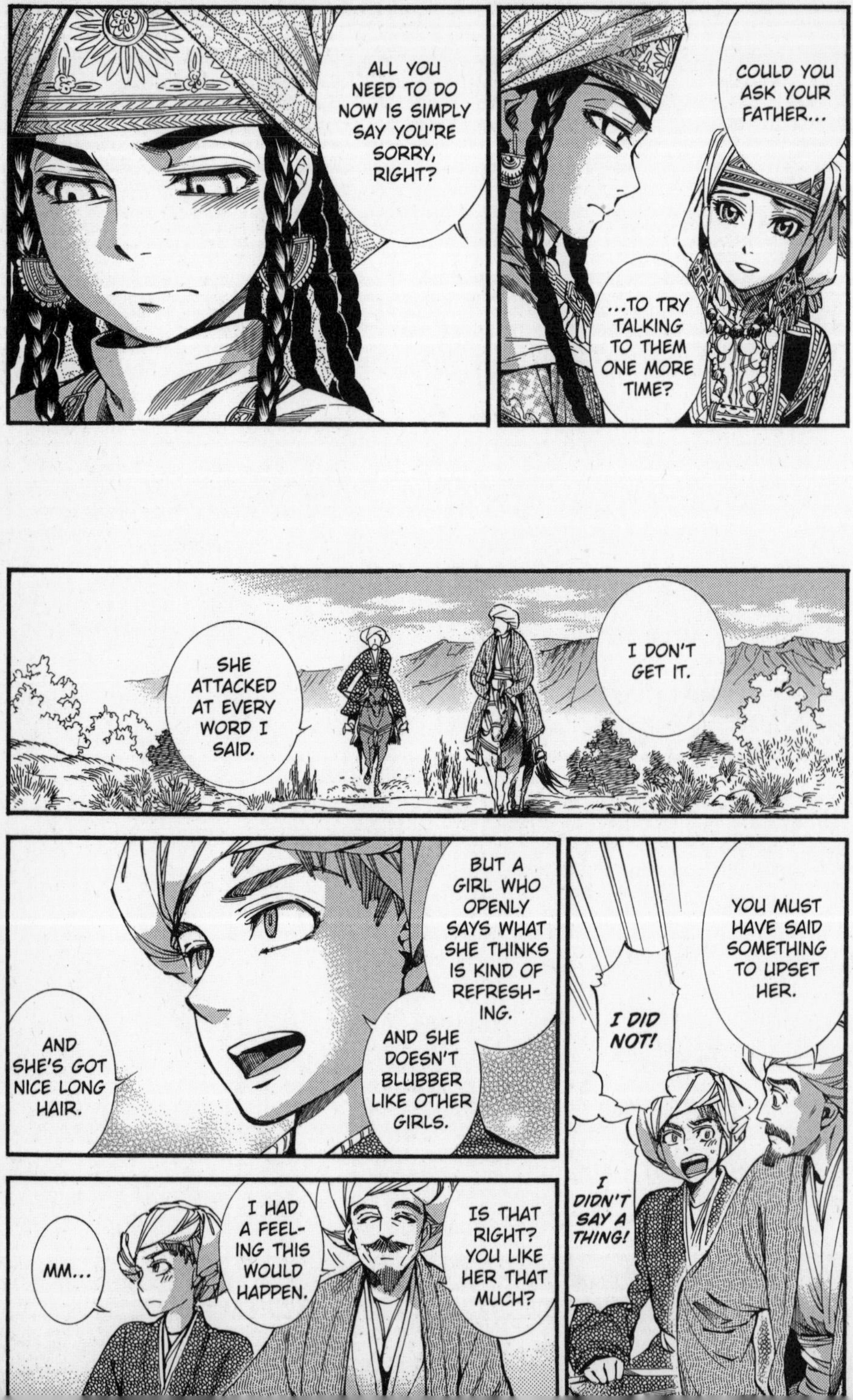
COULD YOU ASK YOUR FATHER...
...TO TRY TALKING TO THEM ONE MORE TIME?
ALL YOU NEED TO DO NOW IS SIMPLY SAY YOU'RE SORRY, RIGHT?
I DON'T GET IT.
SHE ATTACKED AT EVERY WORD I SAID.
YOU MUST HAVE SAID SOMETHING TO UPSET HER.
I DID NOT!
I DIDN'T SAY A THING!
BUT A GIRL WHO OPENLY SAYS WHAT SHE THINKS IS KIND OF REFRESHING.
AND SHE DOESN'T BLUBBER LIKE OTHER GIRLS.
AND SHE'S GOT NICE LONG HAIR.
IS THAT RIGHT? YOU LIKE HER THAT MUCH?
I HAD A FEELING THIS WOULD HAPPEN.
MM...

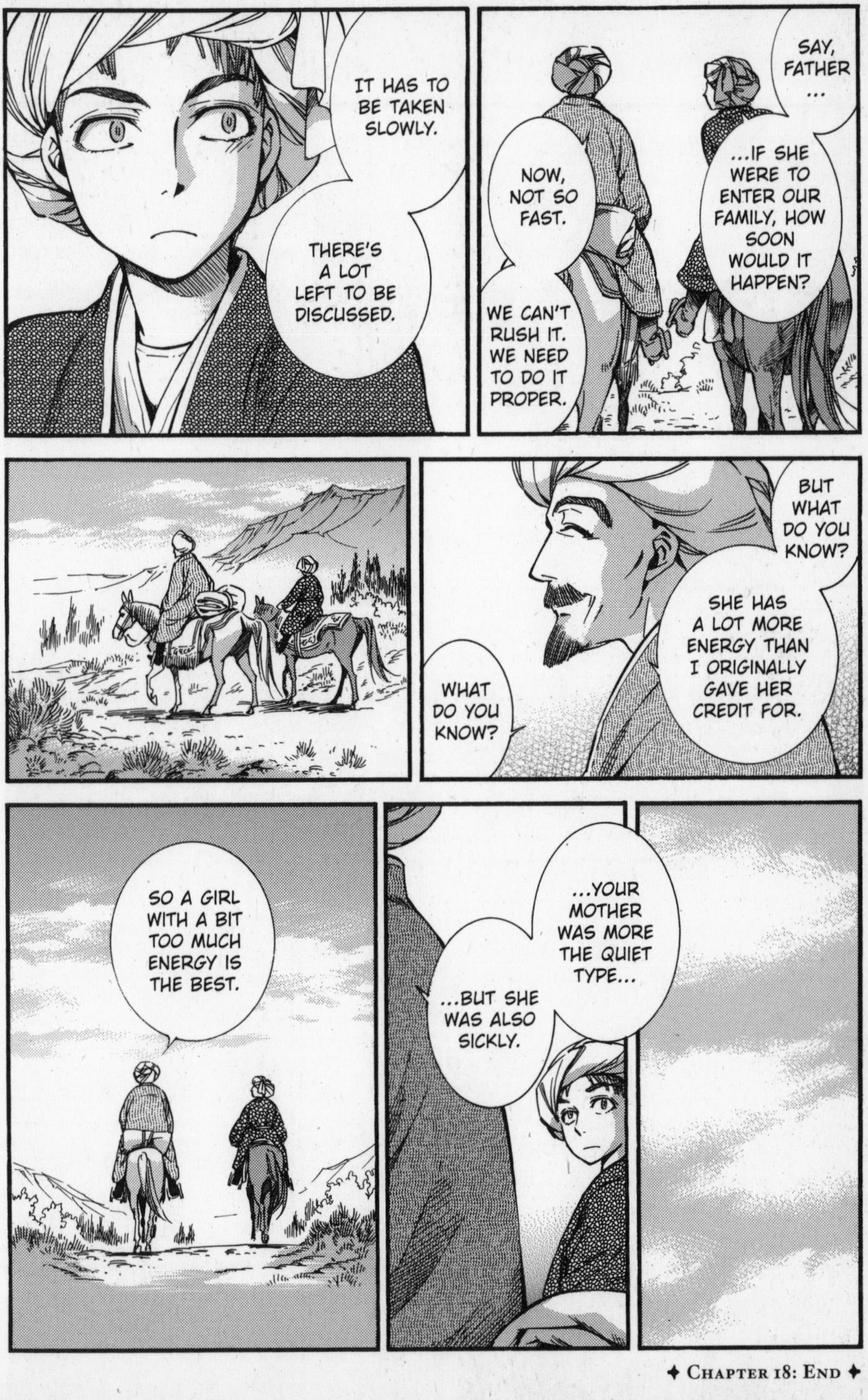
SAY, FATHER ...
...IF SHE WERE TO ENTER OUR FAMILY, HOW SOON WOULD IT HAPPEN?
NOW, NOT SO FAST.
WE CAN'T RUSH IT. WE NEED TO DO IT PROPER.
IT HAS TO BE TAKEN SLOWLY.
THERE'S A LOT LEFT TO BE DISCUSSED.
BUT WHAT DO YOU KNOW?
SHE HAS A LOT MORE ENERGY THAN I ORIGINALLY GAVE HER CREDIT FOR.
WHAT DO YOU KNOW?
...YOUR MOTHER WAS MORE THE QUIET TYPE...
...BUT SHE WAS ALSO SICKLY.
SO A GIRL WITH A BIT TOO MUCH ENERGY IS THE BEST.

✦ Chapter 18: End ✦

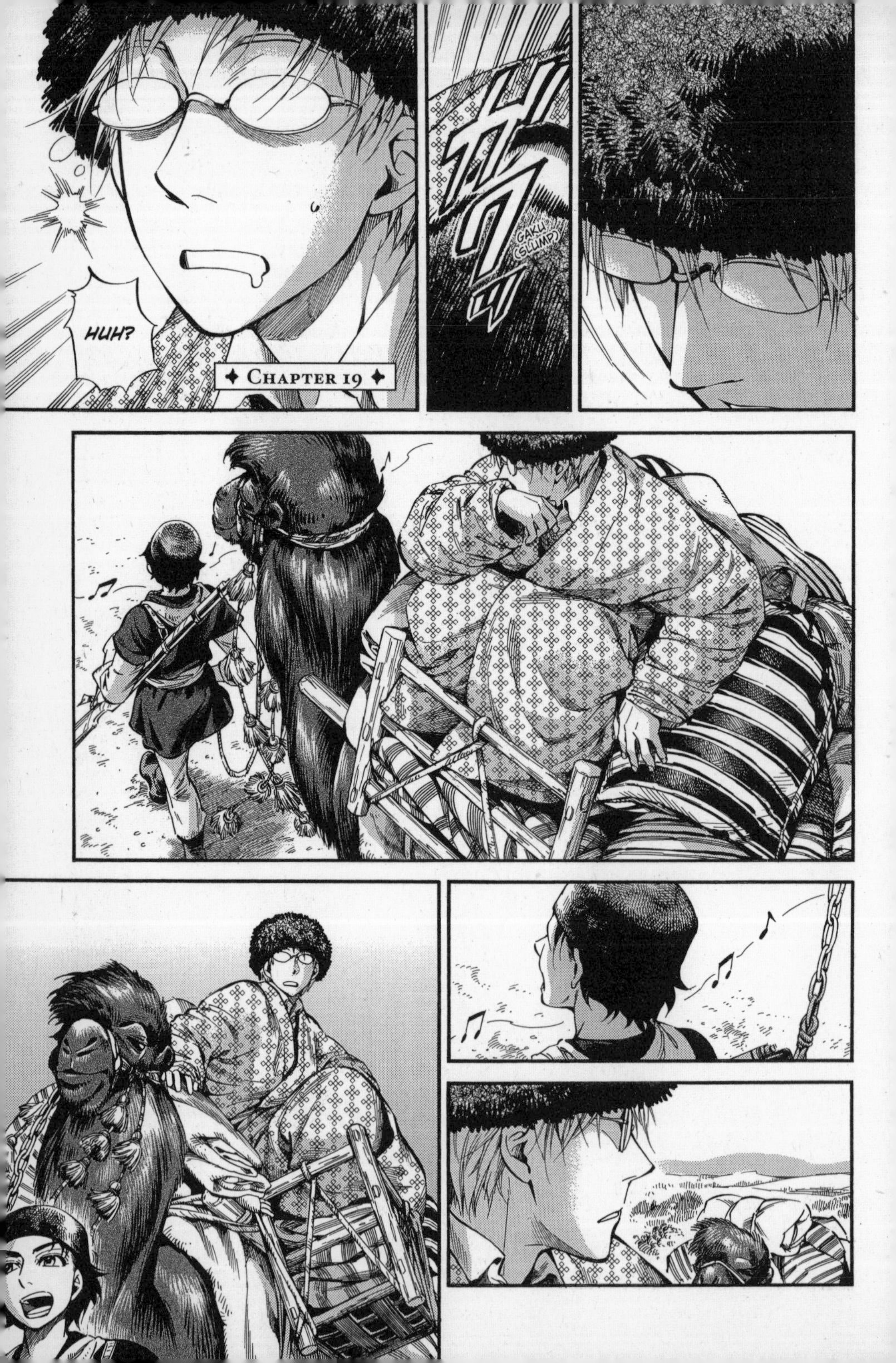
GAKU (SLUMP)
HUH?
✦ Chapter 19 ✦

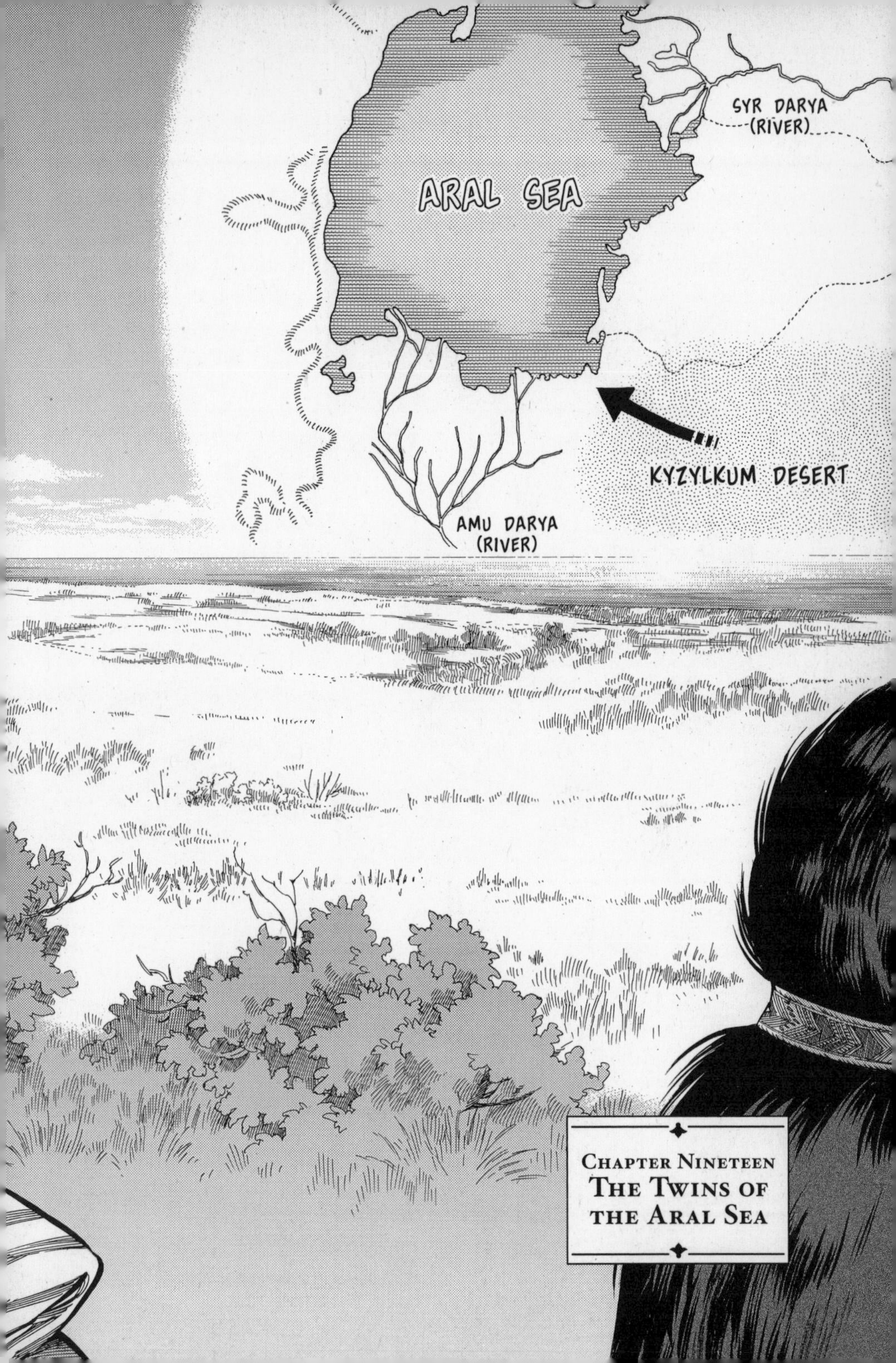
ARAL SEA
SYR DARYA (RIVER)
AMU DARYA (RIVER)
KYZYLKUM DESERT
Chapter Nineteen
The Twins of the Aral Sea

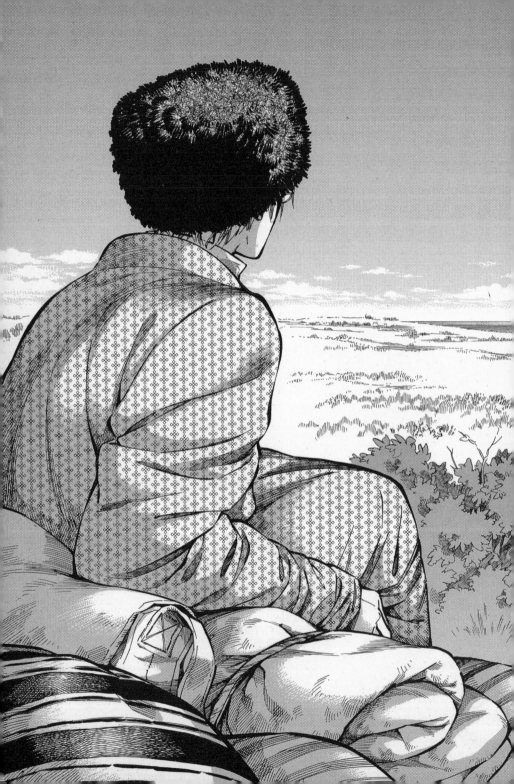

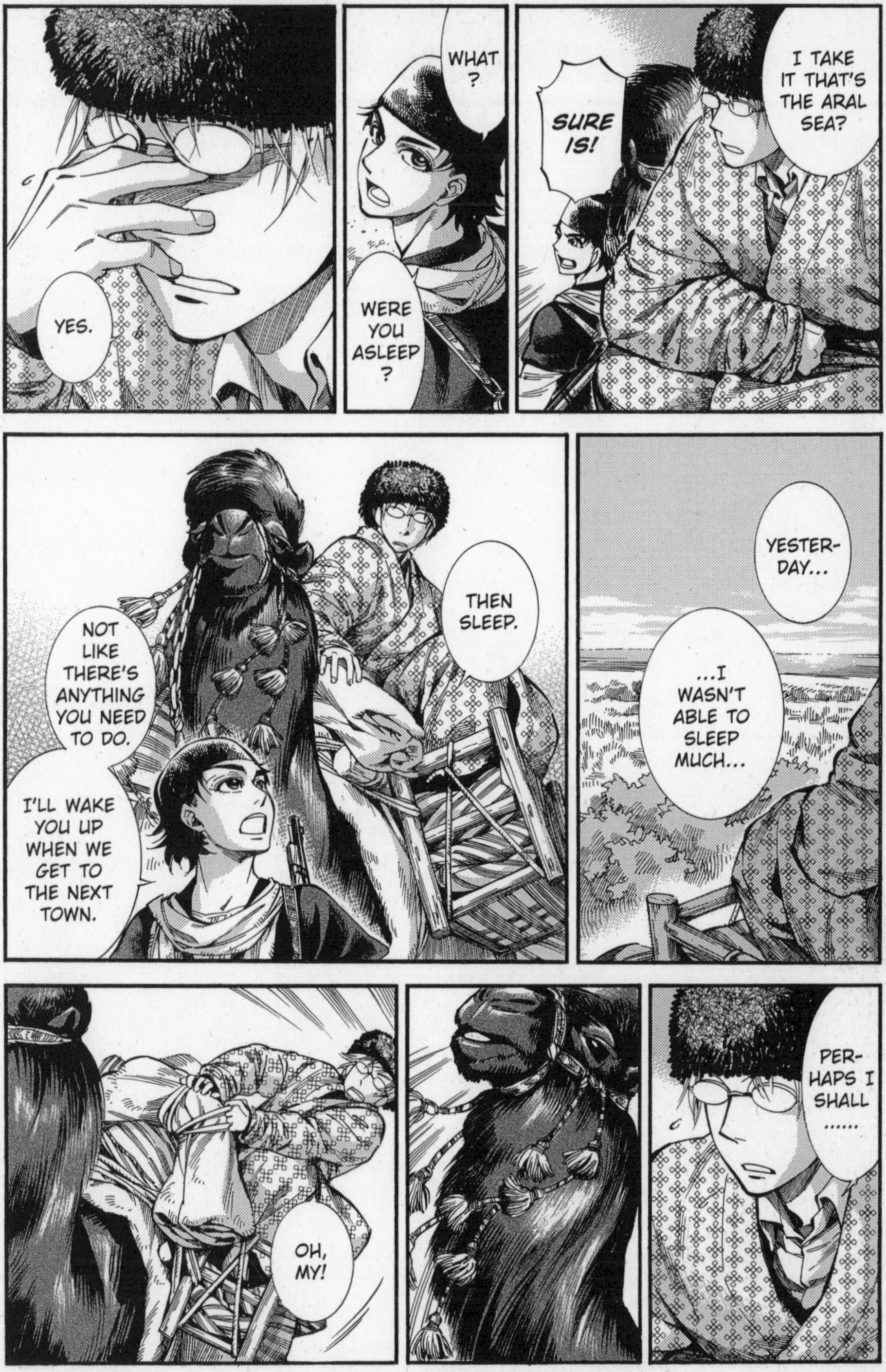
I TAKE IT THAT'S THE ARAL SEA?
SURE IS!
WHAT?
WERE YOU ASLEEP?
YES.
YESTER-DAY...
...I WASN'T ABLE TO SLEEP MUCH...
THEN SLEEP.
NOT LIKE THERE'S ANYTHING YOU NEED TO DO.
I'LL WAKE YOU UP WHEN WE GET TO THE NEXT TOWN.
PER-HAPS I SHALL ......
OH, MY!

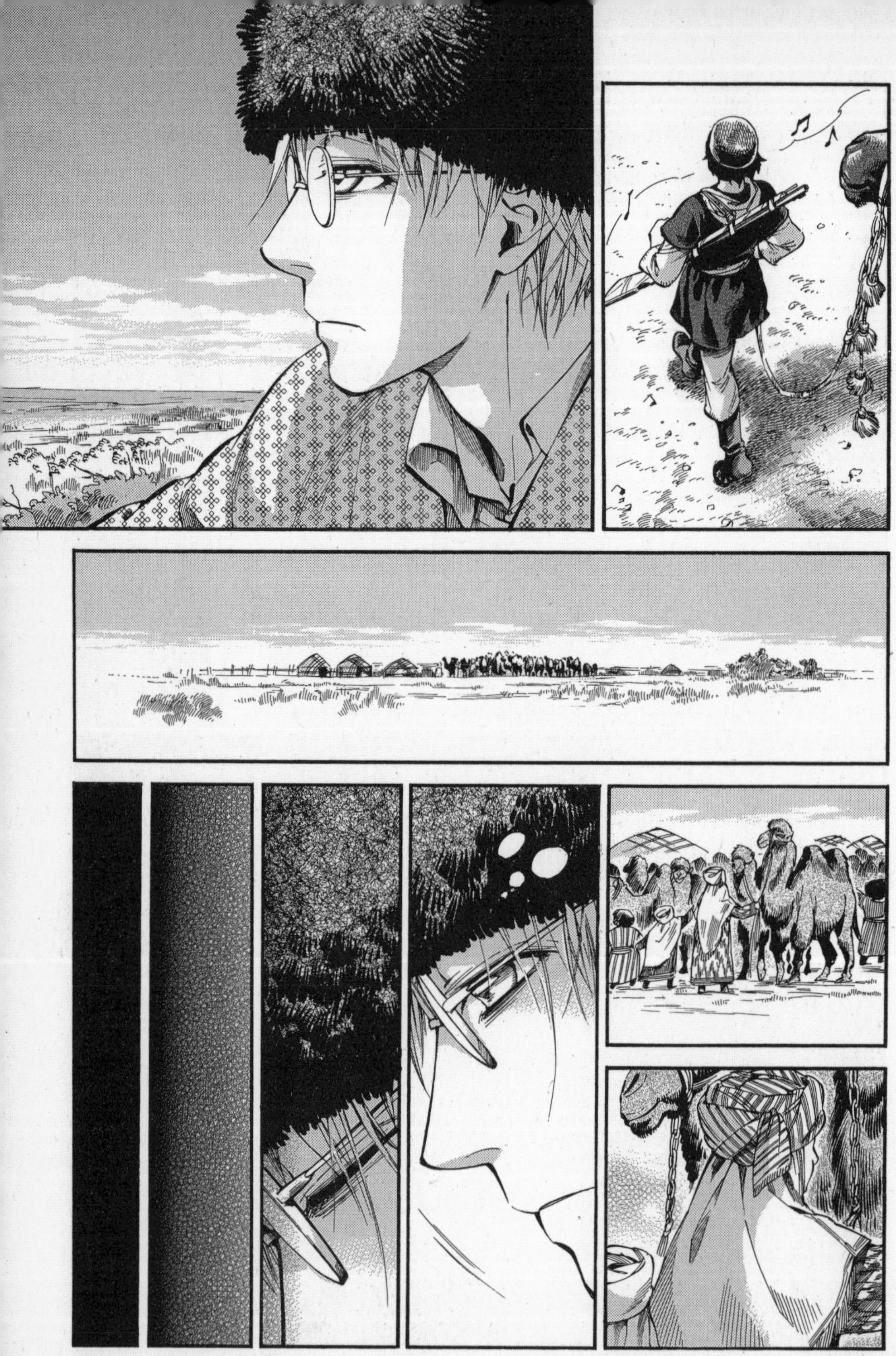

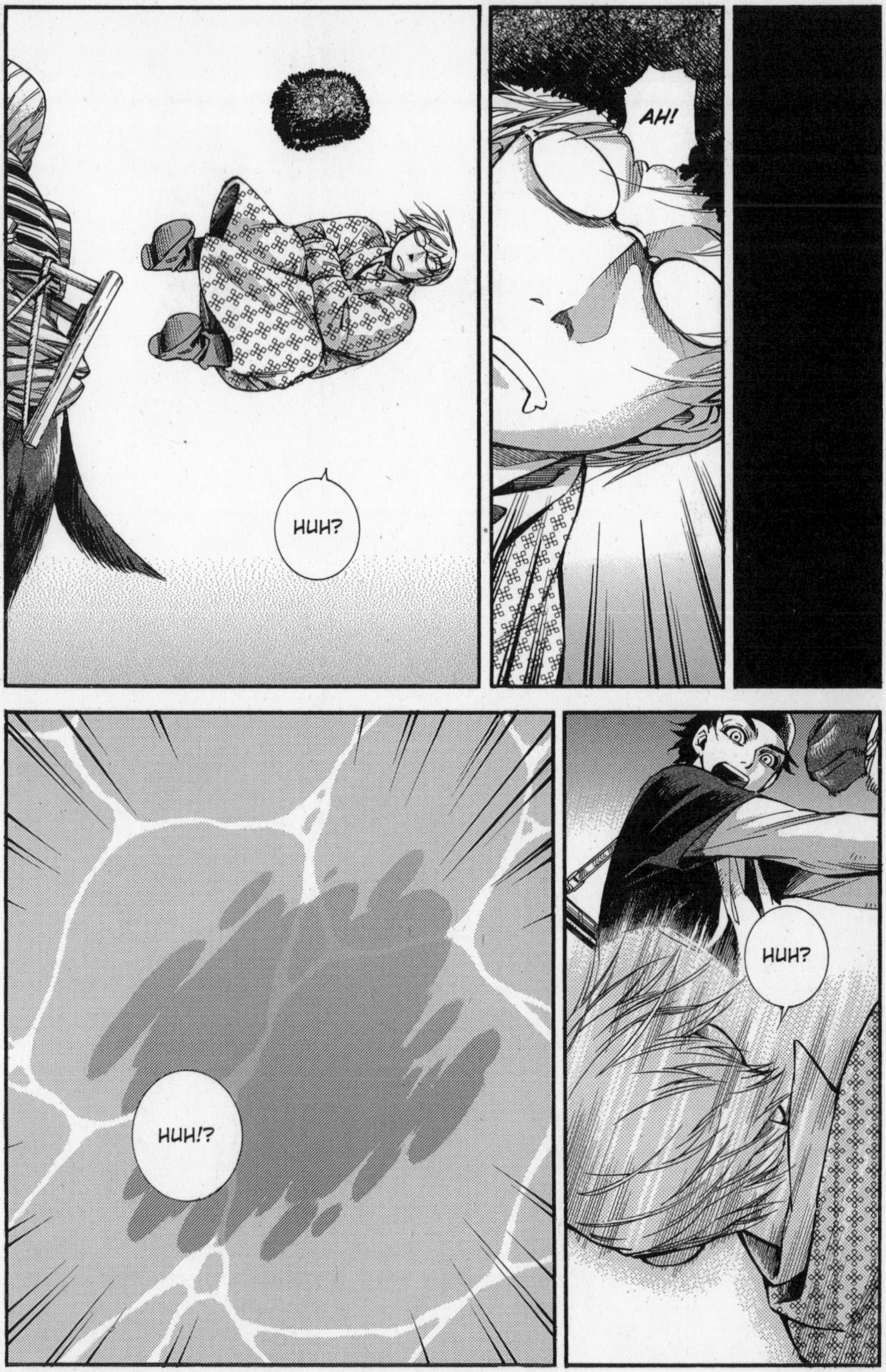
AH!
HUH?
HUH?
HUH!?

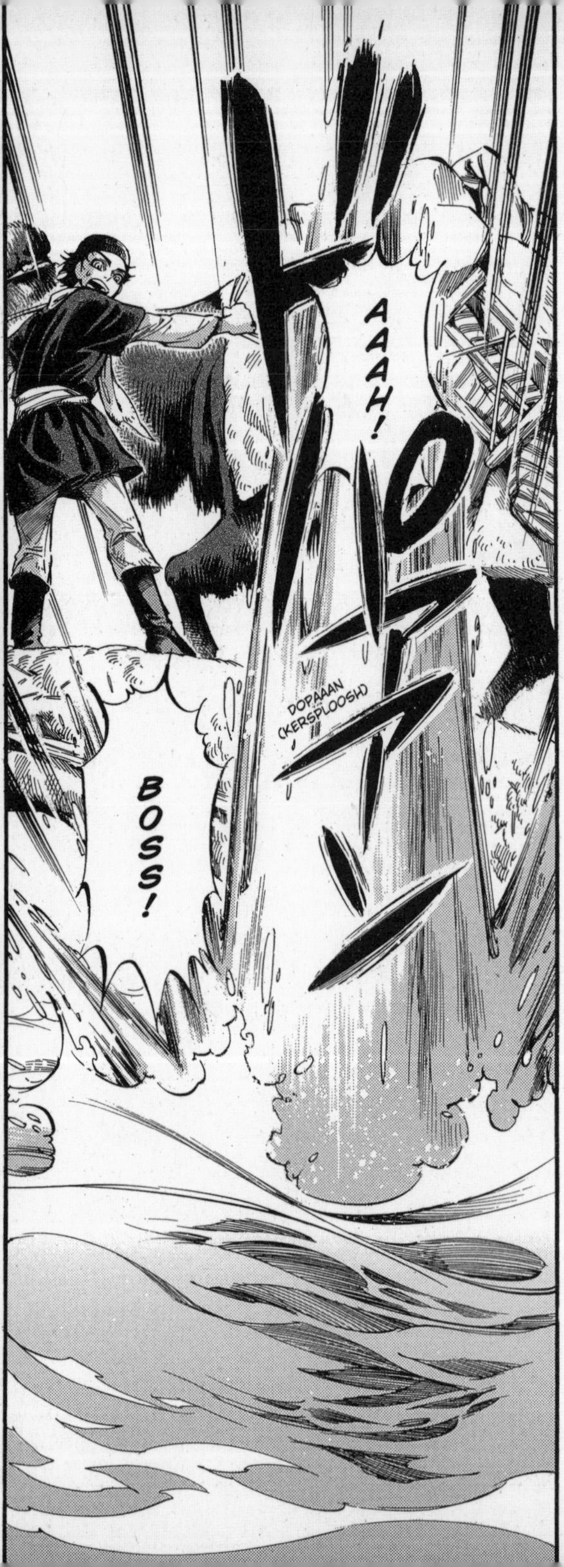
AAAH!
DOPAAAN (KERSPLOOSH)
BOSS!

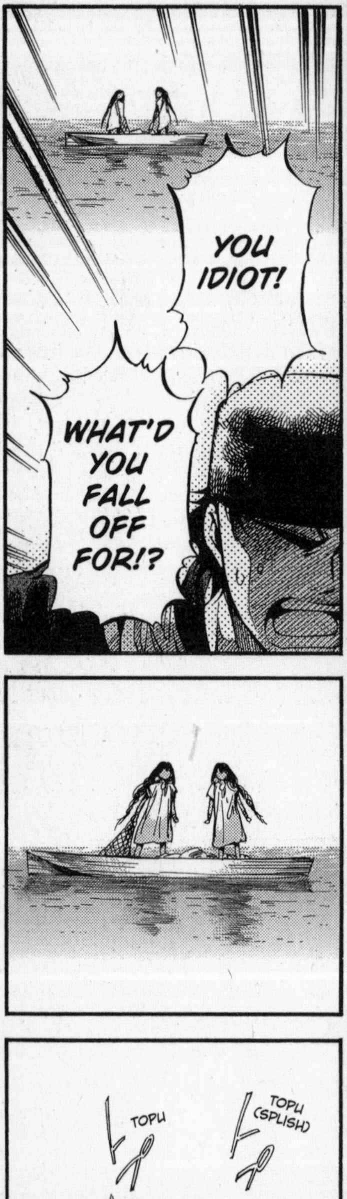
YOU IDIOT!
WHAT'D YOU FALL OFF FOR!?
TOPU (SPLISH)
TOPU

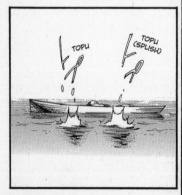

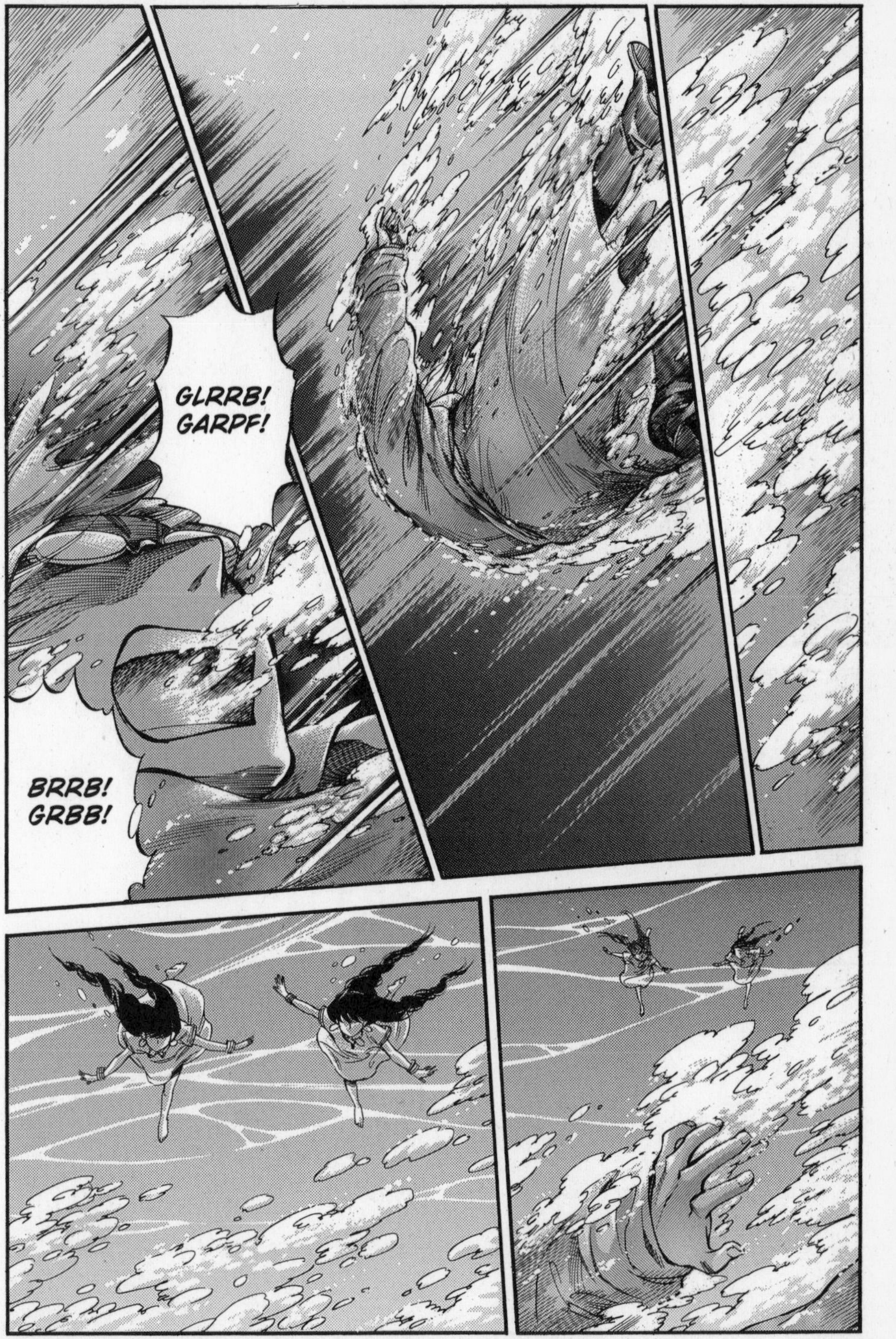
GLRRB! GARPF!
BRRB! GRBB!

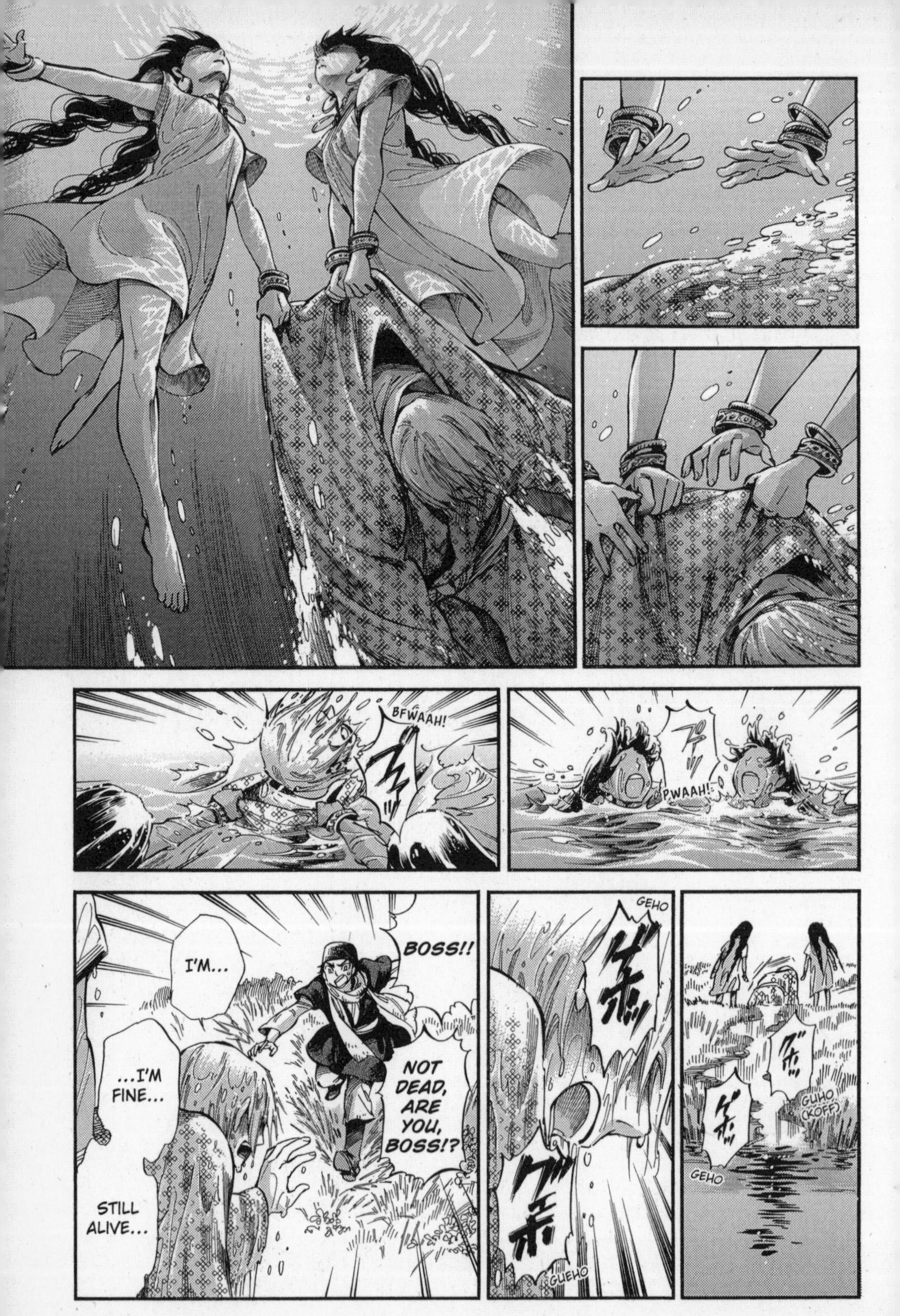
PWAAH!
BFWAAH!
GUHO (KOFF)
GEHO
GEHO
GUEHO
BOSS!!
NOT DEAD, ARE YOU, BOSS!?
I'M...
...I'M FINE...
STILL ALIVE...

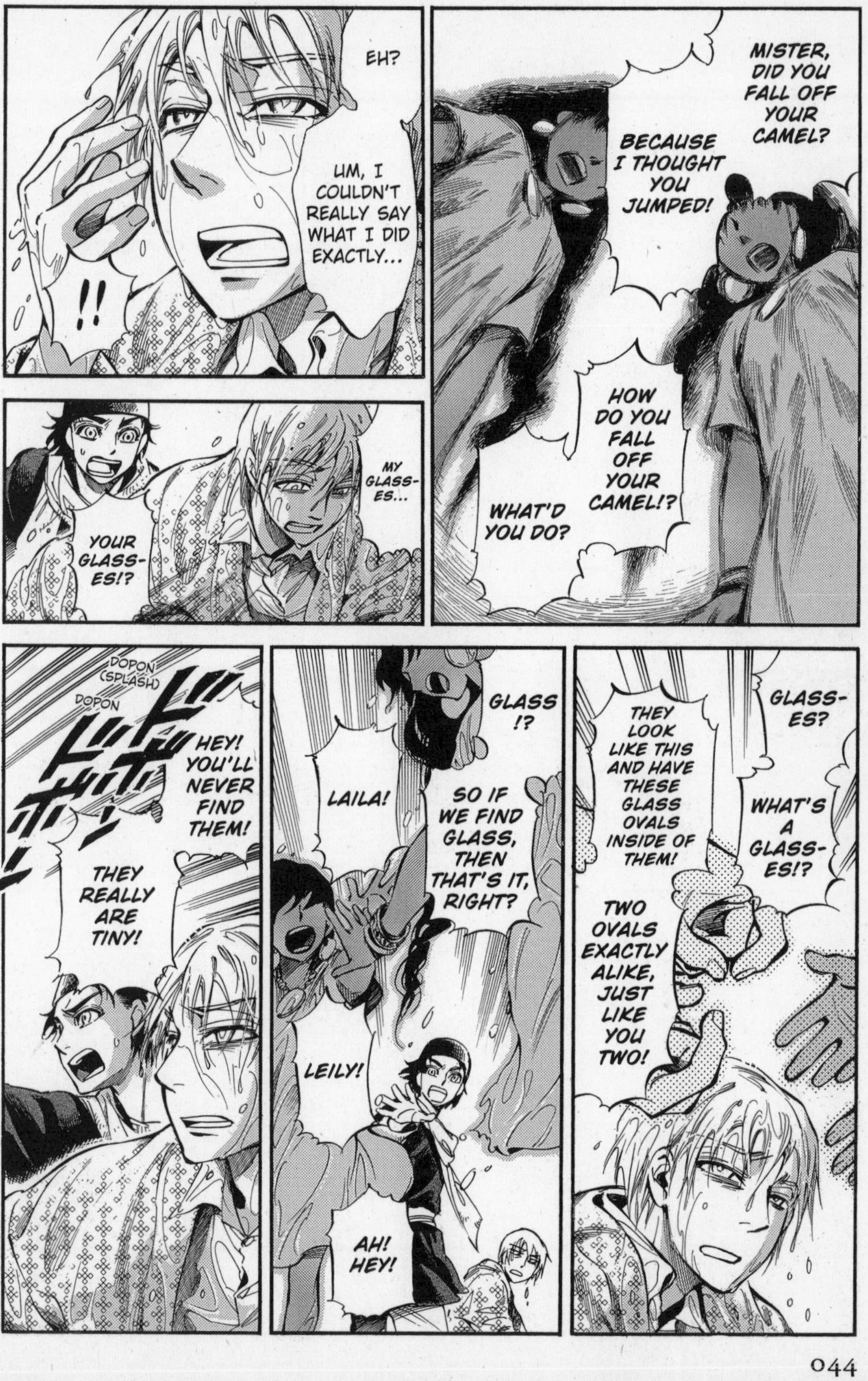
MISTER, DID YOU FALL OFF YOUR CAMEL?
BECAUSE I THOUGHT YOU JUMPED!
HOW DO YOU FALL OFF YOUR CAMEL!?
WHAT'D YOU DO?
EH?
UM, I COULDN'T REALLY SAY WHAT I DID EXACTLY...
!!
MY GLASS-ES...
YOUR GLASS-ES!?
GLASS-ES?
WHAT'S A GLASS-ES!?
THEY LOOK LIKE THIS AND HAVE THESE GLASS OVALS INSIDE OF THEM!
TWO OVALS EXACTLY ALIKE, JUST LIKE YOU TWO!
GLASS !?
SO IF WE FIND GLASS, THEN THAT'S IT, RIGHT?
LAILA!
LEILY!
AH! HEY!
DOPON (SPLASH)
DOPON
HEY! YOU'LL NEVER FIND THEM!
THEY REALLY ARE TINY!

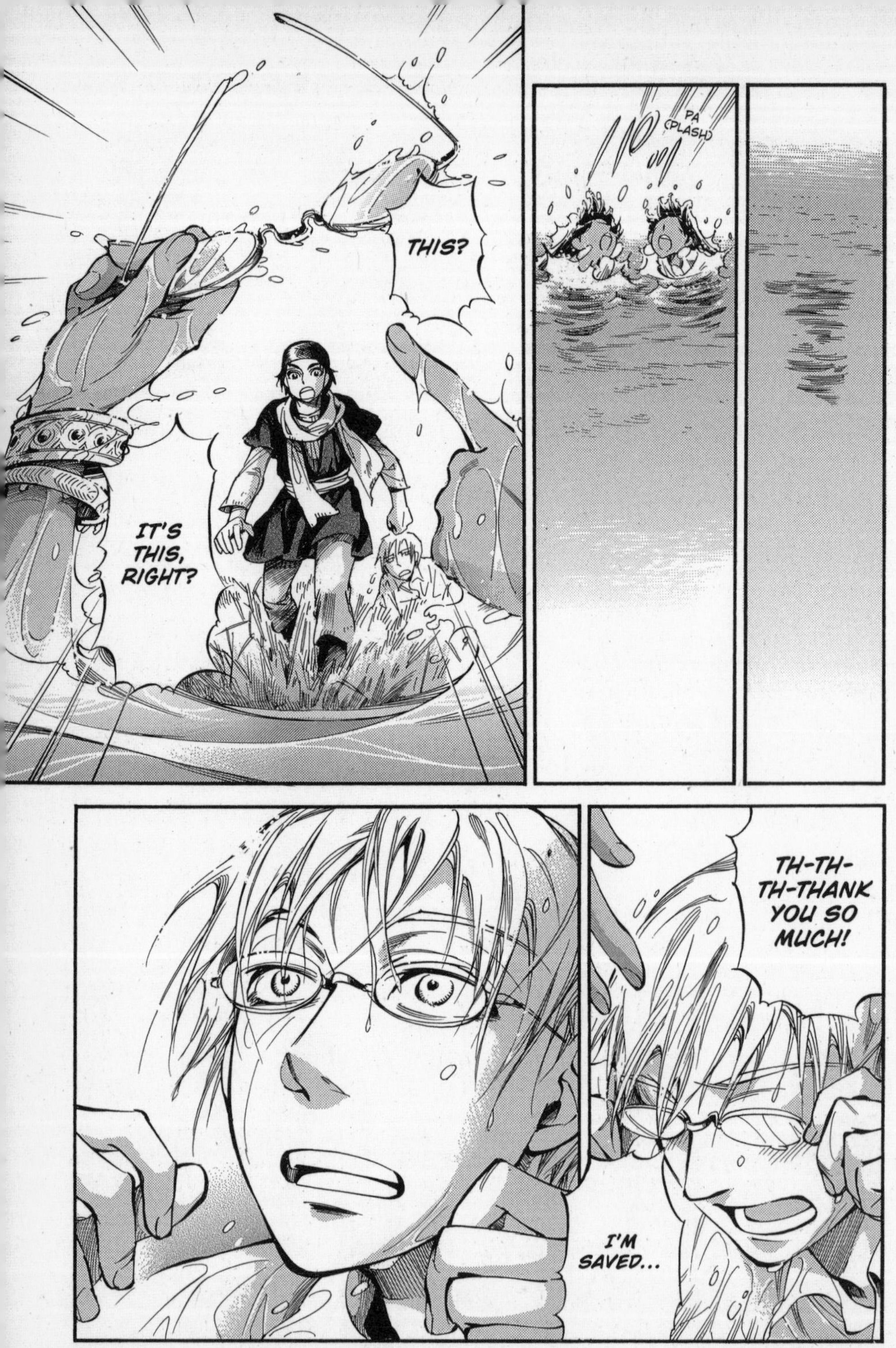
PA (PLASH)
THIS?
IT'S THIS, RIGHT?
TH-TH-TH-THANK YOU SO MUCH!
I'M SAVED...

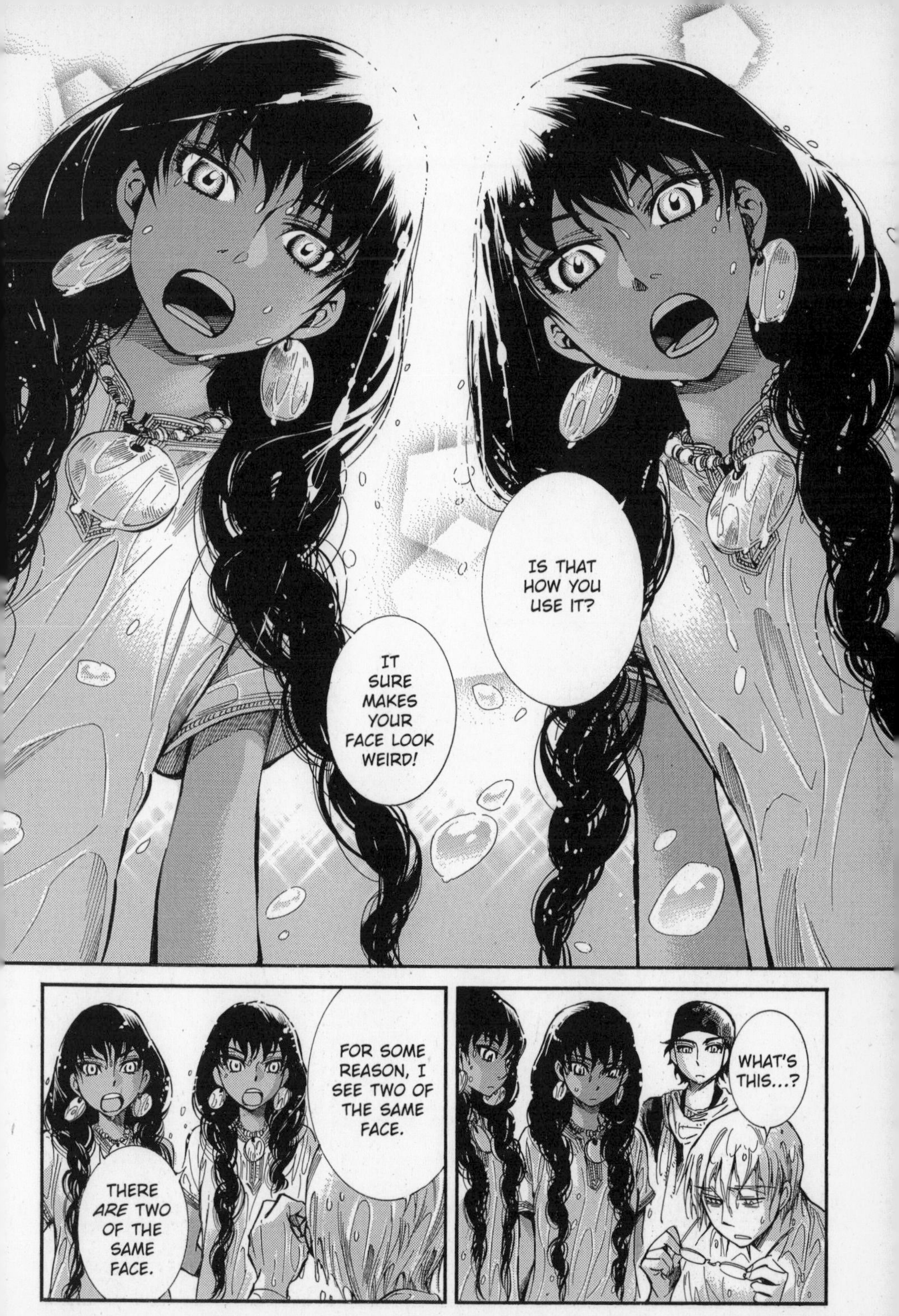
IS THAT HOW YOU USE IT?
IT SURE MAKES YOUR FACE LOOK WEIRD!
WHAT'S THIS...?
FOR SOME REASON, I SEE TWO OF THE SAME FACE.
THERE *ARE* TWO OF THE SAME FACE.

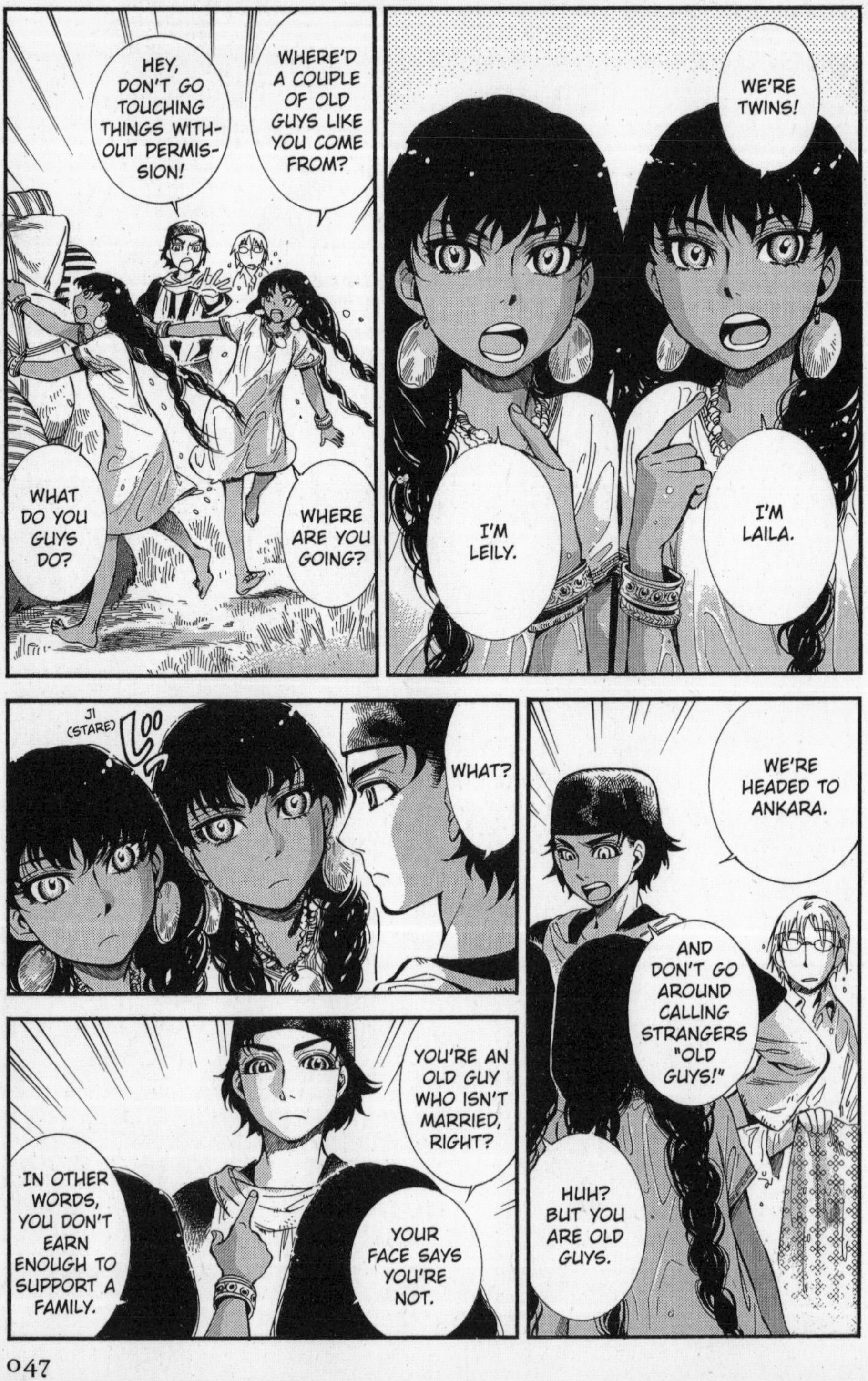
WE'RE TWINS!
I'M LAILA.
I'M LEILY.
WHERE'D A COUPLE OF OLD GUYS LIKE YOU COME FROM?
HEY, DON'T GO TOUCHING THINGS WITH-OUT PERMIS-SION!
WHERE ARE YOU GOING?
WHAT DO YOU GUYS DO?
WE'RE HEADED TO ANKARA.
AND DON'T GO AROUND CALLING STRANGERS "OLD GUYS!"
HUH? BUT YOU ARE OLD GUYS.
JI (STARE)
WHAT?
YOU'RE AN OLD GUY WHO ISN'T MARRIED, RIGHT?
YOUR FACE SAYS YOU'RE NOT.
IN OTHER WORDS, YOU DON'T EARN ENOUGH TO SUPPORT A FAMILY.

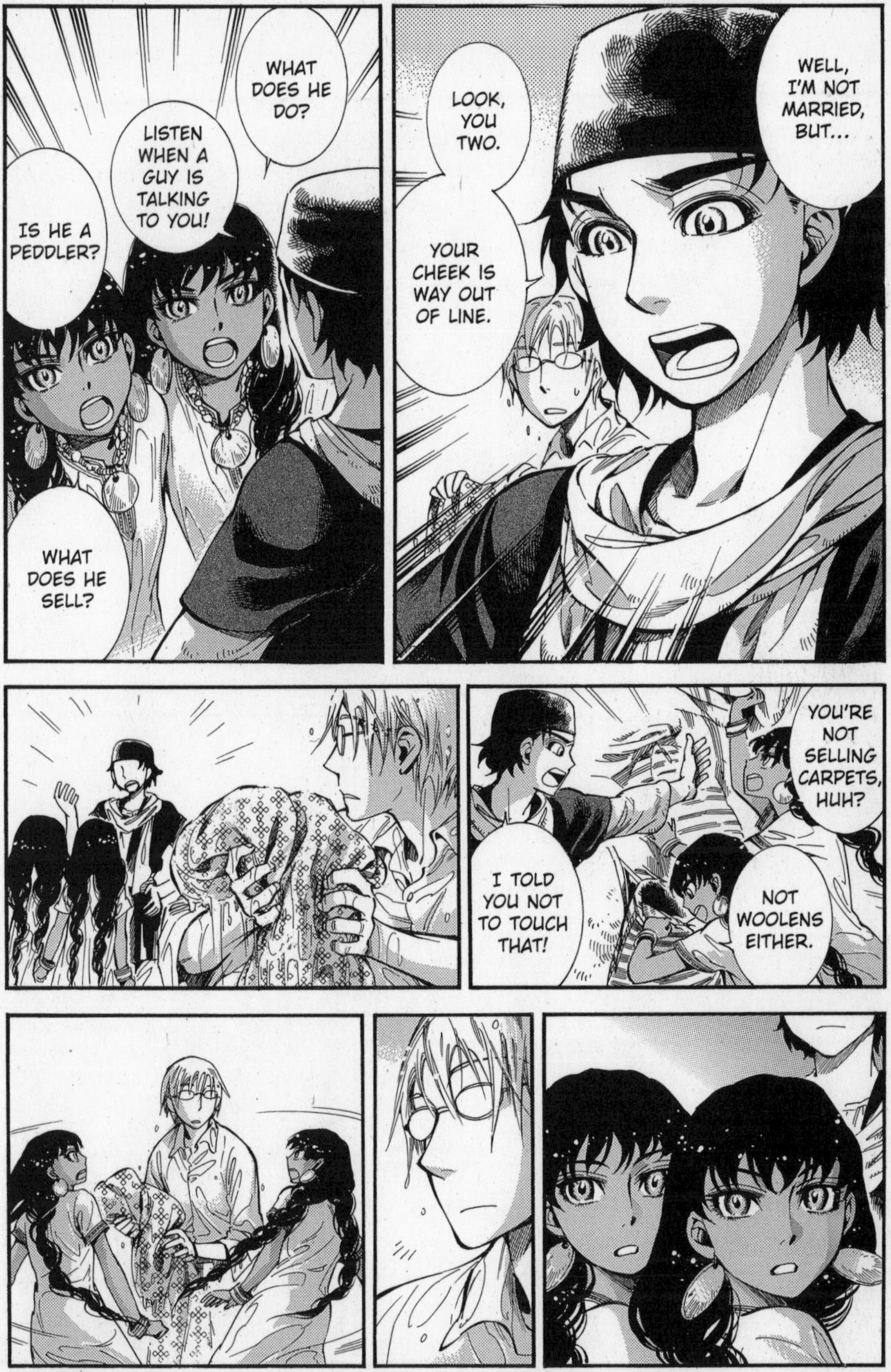
WELL, I'M NOT MARRIED, BUT...
LOOK, YOU TWO.
YOUR CHEEK IS WAY OUT OF LINE.
WHAT DOES HE DO?
LISTEN WHEN A GUY IS TALKING TO YOU!
IS HE A PEDDLER?
WHAT DOES HE SELL?
YOU'RE NOT SELLING CARPETS, HUH?
NOT WOOLENS EITHER.
I TOLD YOU NOT TO TOUCH THAT!

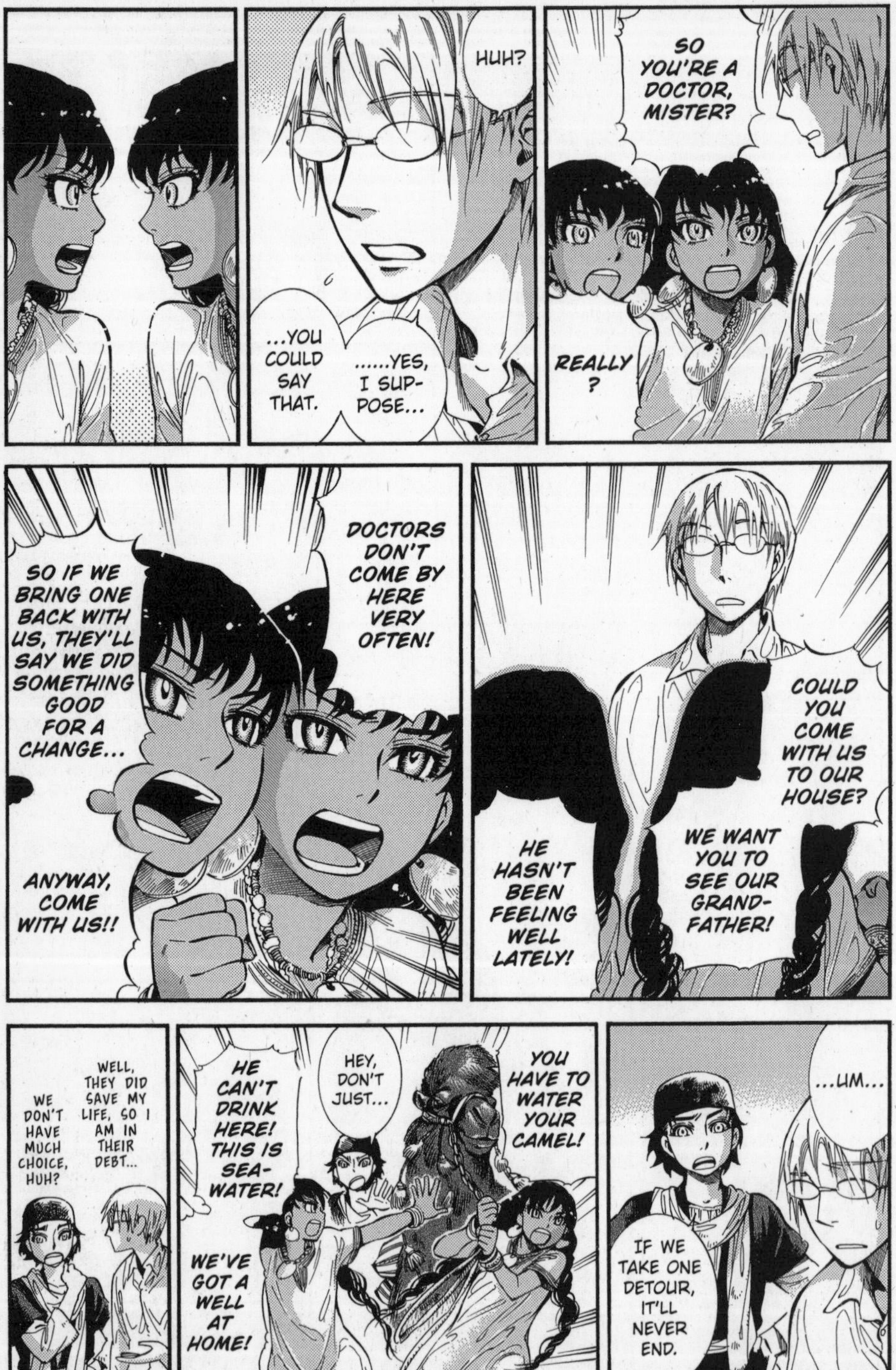
SO YOU'RE A DOCTOR, MISTER?
REALLY?
HUH?
......YES, I SUP-POSE...
...YOU COULD SAY THAT.
COULD YOU COME WITH US TO OUR HOUSE?
WE WANT YOU TO SEE OUR GRAND-FATHER!
HE HASN'T BEEN FEELING WELL LATELY!
DOCTORS DON'T COME BY HERE VERY OFTEN!
SO IF WE BRING ONE BACK WITH US, THEY'LL SAY WE DID SOMETHING GOOD FOR A CHANGE...
ANYWAY, COME WITH US!!
...UM...
IF WE TAKE ONE DETOUR, IT'LL NEVER END.
YOU HAVE TO WATER YOUR CAMEL!
HEY, DON'T JUST...
HE CAN'T DRINK HERE! THIS IS SEA-WATER!
WE'VE GOT A WELL AT HOME!
WELL, THEY DID SAVE MY LIFE, SO I AM IN THEIR DEBT...
WE DON'T HAVE MUCH CHOICE, HUH?

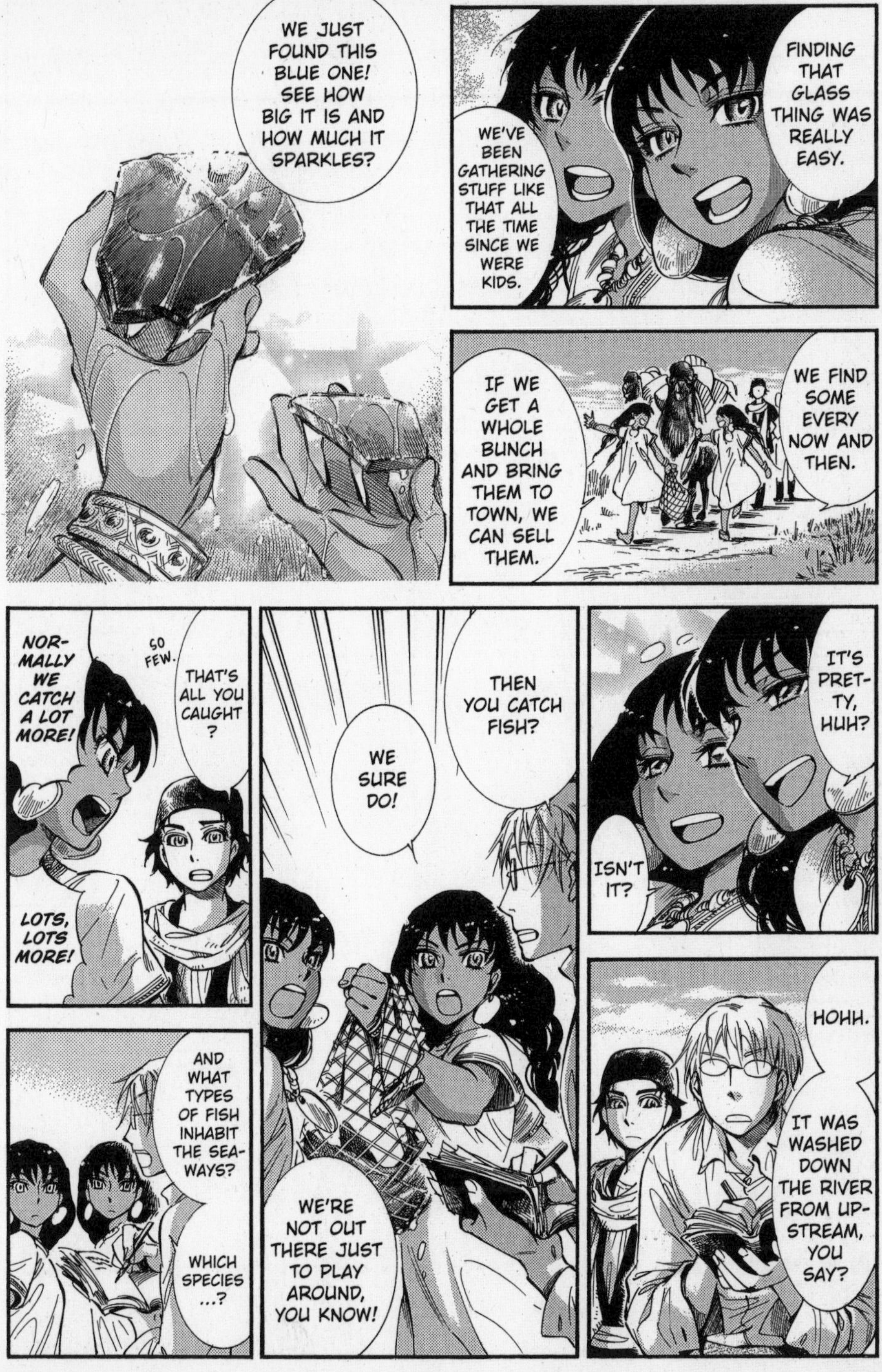
FINDING THAT GLASS THING WAS REALLY EASY.
WE'VE BEEN GATHERING STUFF LIKE THAT ALL THE TIME SINCE WE WERE KIDS.
WE FIND SOME EVERY NOW AND THEN.
IF WE GET A WHOLE BUNCH AND BRING THEM TO TOWN, WE CAN SELL THEM.
WE JUST FOUND THIS BLUE ONE! SEE HOW BIG IT IS AND HOW MUCH IT SPARKLES?
IT'S PRET-TY, HUH?
ISN'T IT?
HOHH.
IT WAS WASHED DOWN THE RIVER FROM UP-STREAM, YOU SAY?
THEN YOU CATCH FISH?
WE SURE DO!
WE'RE NOT OUT THERE JUST TO PLAY AROUND, YOU KNOW!
THAT'S ALL YOU CAUGHT?
SO FEW.
NOR-MALLY WE CATCH A LOT MORE!
LOTS, LOTS MORE!
AND WHAT TYPES OF FISH INHABIT THE SEA-WAYS?
WHICH SPECIES ...?

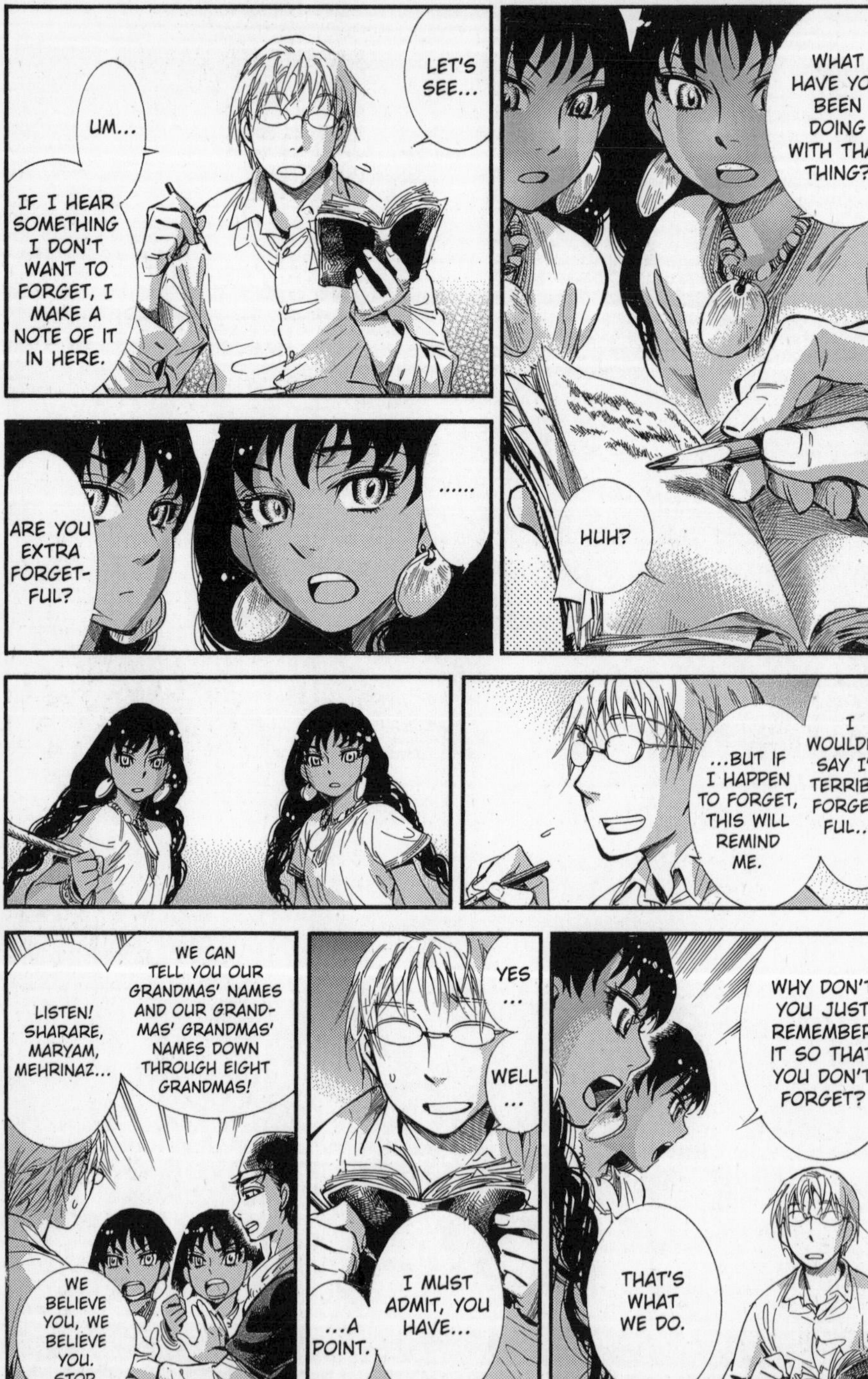
WHAT HAVE YOU BEEN DOING WITH THAT THING?
HUH?
LET'S SEE...
UM...
IF I HEAR SOMETHING I DON'T WANT TO FORGET, I MAKE A NOTE OF IT IN HERE.
......
ARE YOU EXTRA FORGET-FUL?
I WOULDN'T SAY I'M TERRIBLY FORGET-FUL...
...BUT IF I HAPPEN TO FORGET, THIS WILL REMIND ME.
WHY DON'T YOU JUST REMEMBER IT SO THAT YOU DON'T FORGET?
THAT'S WHAT WE DO.
YES ...
WELL ...
I MUST ADMIT, YOU HAVE...
...A POINT.
WE CAN TELL YOU OUR GRANDMAS' NAMES AND OUR GRAND-MAS' GRANDMAS' NAMES DOWN THROUGH EIGHT GRANDMAS!
LISTEN! SHARARE, MARYAM, MEHRINAZ...
WE BELIEVE YOU, WE BELIEVE YOU. STOP.

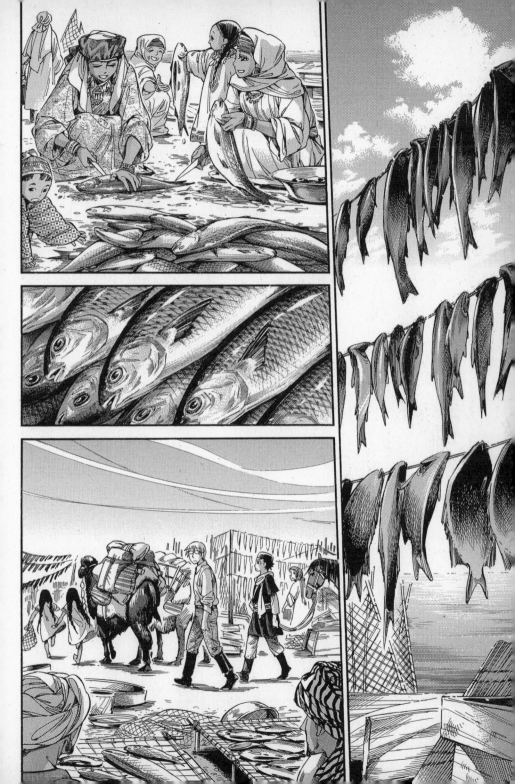

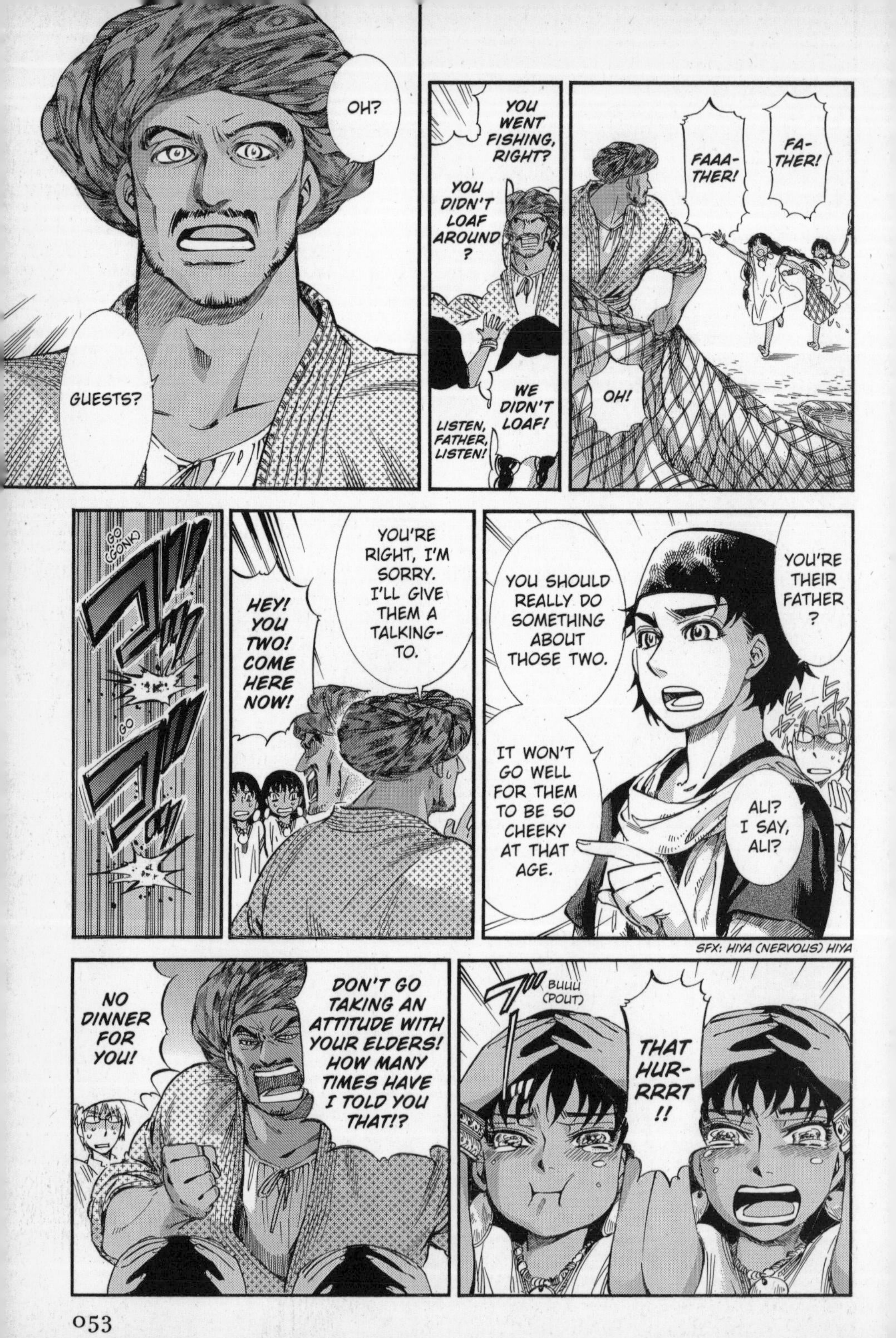
FA-THER!
FAAAA-THER!
OH!
YOU WENT FISHING, RIGHT?
YOU DIDN'T LOAF AROUND?
WE DIDN'T LOAF!
LISTEN, FATHER, LISTEN!
OH?
GUESTS?
YOU'RE THEIR FATHER?
YOU SHOULD REALLY DO SOMETHING ABOUT THOSE TWO.
IT WON'T GO WELL FOR THEM TO BE SO CHEEKY AT THAT AGE.
ALI? I SAY, ALI?
SFX: HIYA (NERVOUS) HIYA
YOU'RE RIGHT, I'M SORRY. I'LL GIVE THEM A TALKING-TO.
HEY! YOU TWO! COME HERE NOW!
GO (GONK)
GO
BUUU (POUT)
THAT HURRRRT!!
DON'T GO TAKING AN ATTITUDE WITH YOUR ELDERS! HOW MANY TIMES HAVE I TOLD YOU THAT!?
NO DINNER FOR YOU!

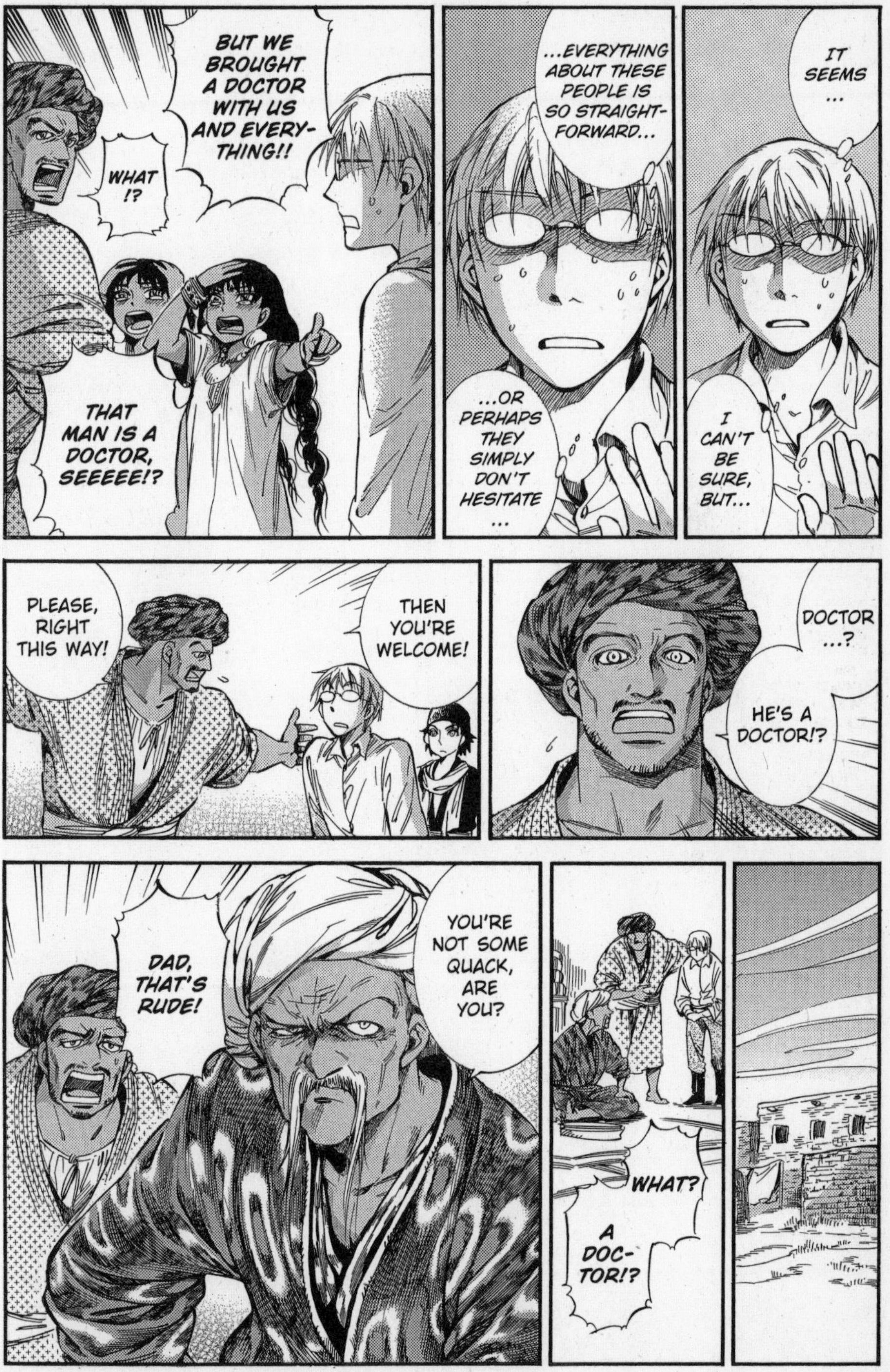
IT SEEMS ...
I CAN'T BE SURE, BUT...
...EVERYTHING ABOUT THESE PEOPLE IS SO STRAIGHT-FORWARD...
...OR PERHAPS THEY SIMPLY DON'T HESITATE ...
BUT WE BROUGHT A DOCTOR WITH US AND EVERY-THING!!
WHAT !?
THAT MAN IS A DOCTOR, SEEEEEE!?
DOCTOR ...?
HE'S A DOCTOR!?
THEN YOU'RE WELCOME!
PLEASE, RIGHT THIS WAY!
WHAT?
A DOC-TOR!?
YOU'RE NOT SOME QUACK, ARE YOU?
DAD, THAT'S RUDE!

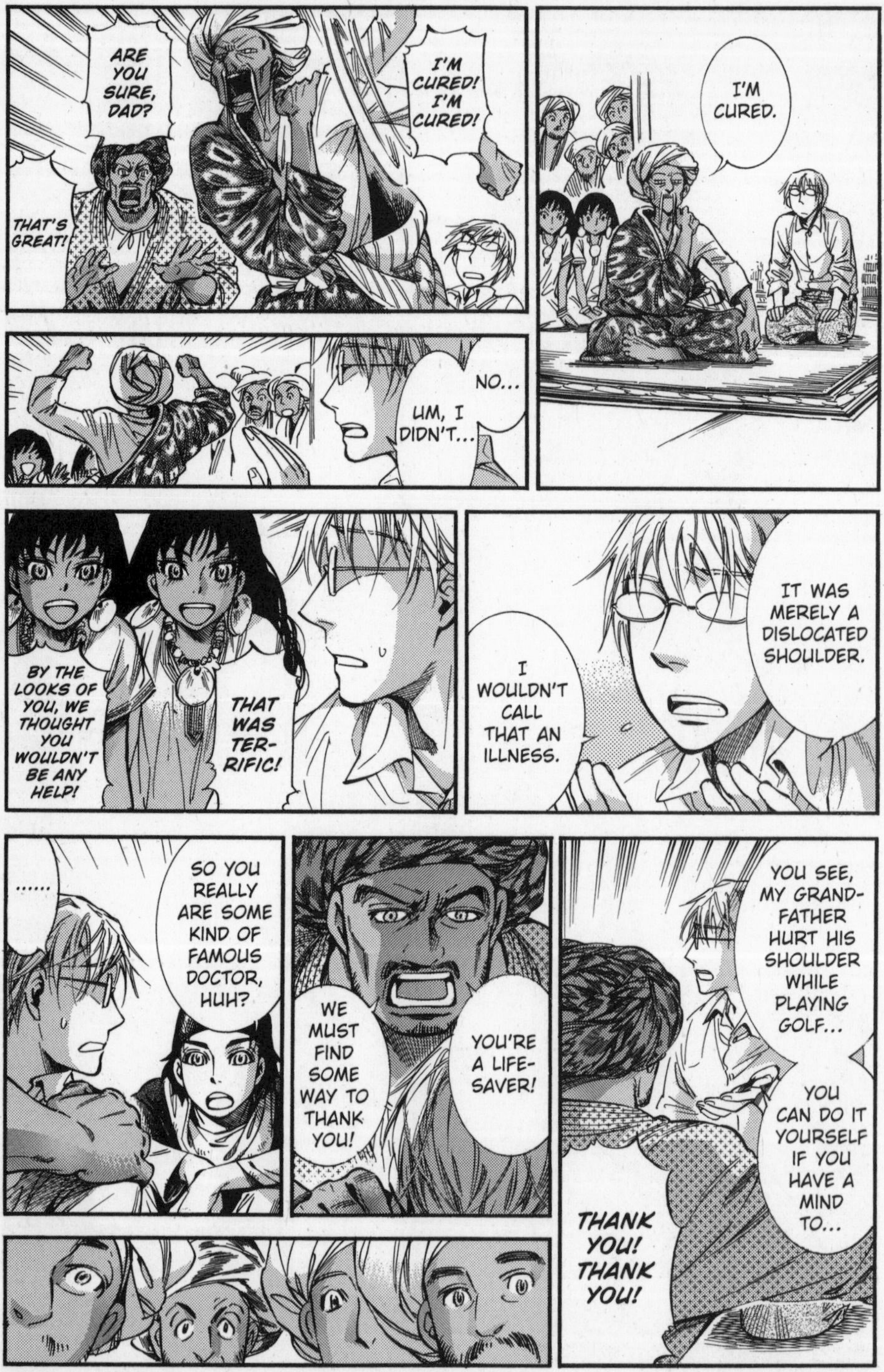
I'M CURED.
I'M CURED! I'M CURED!
ARE YOU SURE, DAD?
THAT'S GREAT!
NO... UM, I DIDN'T...
IT WAS MERELY A DISLOCATED SHOULDER.
I WOULDN'T CALL THAT AN ILLNESS.
THAT WAS TER-RIFIC!
BY THE LOOKS OF YOU, WE THOUGHT YOU WOULDN'T BE ANY HELP!
YOU SEE, MY GRAND-FATHER HURT HIS SHOULDER WHILE PLAYING GOLF...
YOU CAN DO IT YOURSELF IF YOU HAVE A MIND TO...
THANK YOU! THANK YOU!
YOU'RE A LIFE-SAVER!
WE MUST FIND SOME WAY TO THANK YOU!
SO YOU REALLY ARE SOME KIND OF FAMOUS DOCTOR, HUH?
......

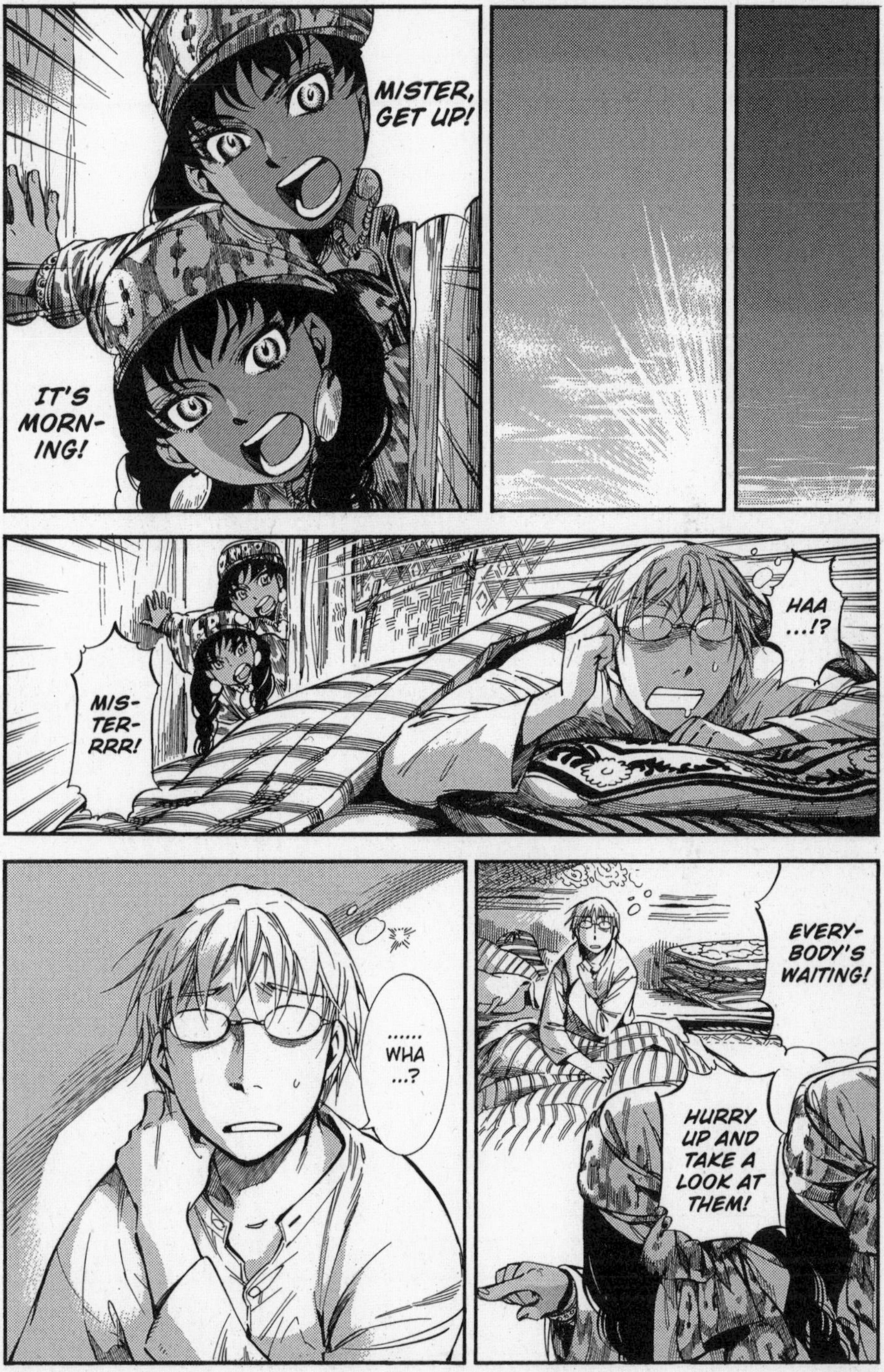
MISTER, GET UP!
IT'S MORNING!
HAA ...!?
MISTERRRR!
EVERYBODY'S WAITING!
HURRY UP AND TAKE A LOOK AT THEM!
...... WHA ...?

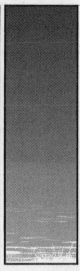

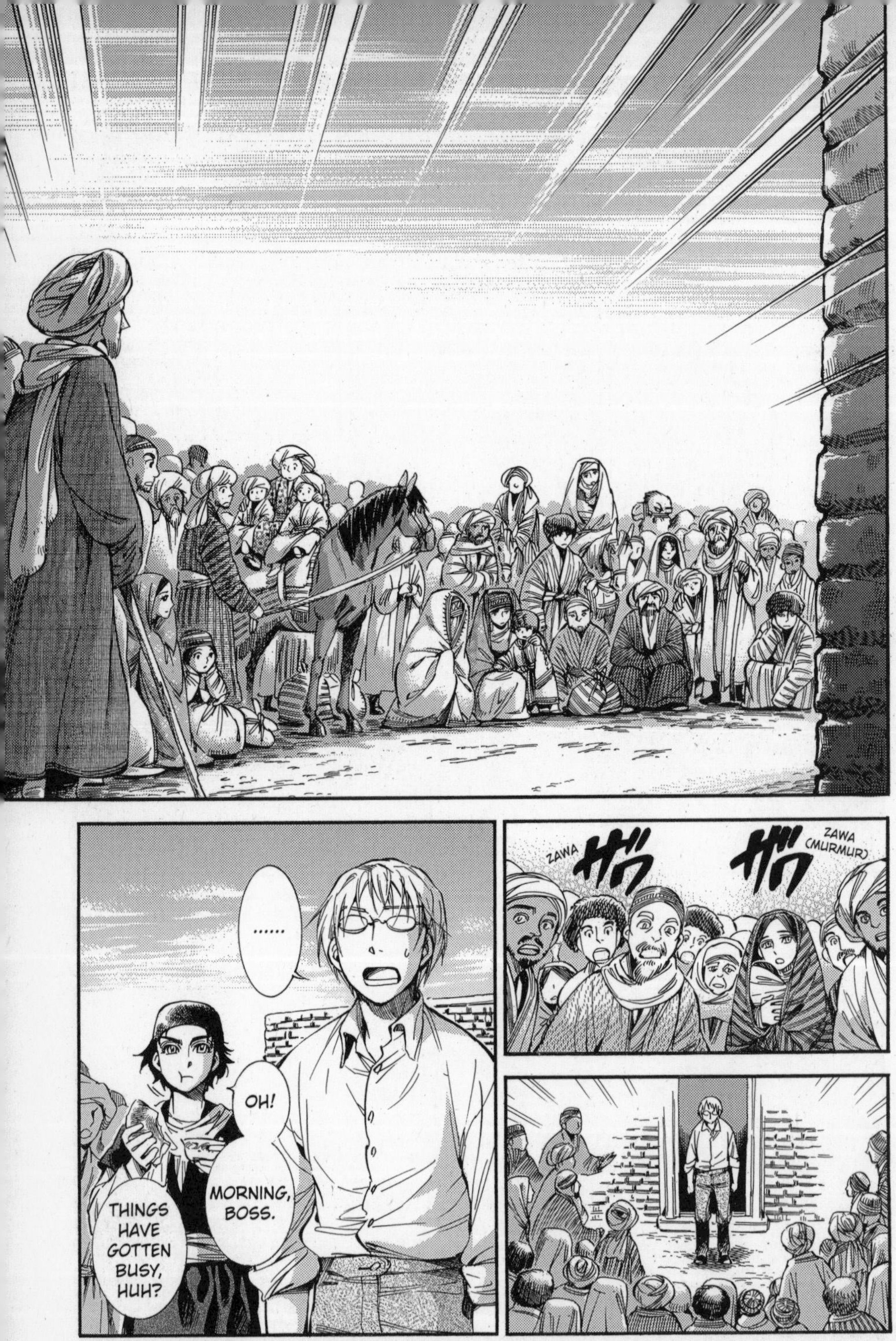
ZAWA (MURMUR)
ザワ
ザワ
ZAWA
......
OH!
MORNING, BOSS.
THINGS HAVE GOTTEN BUSY, HUH?

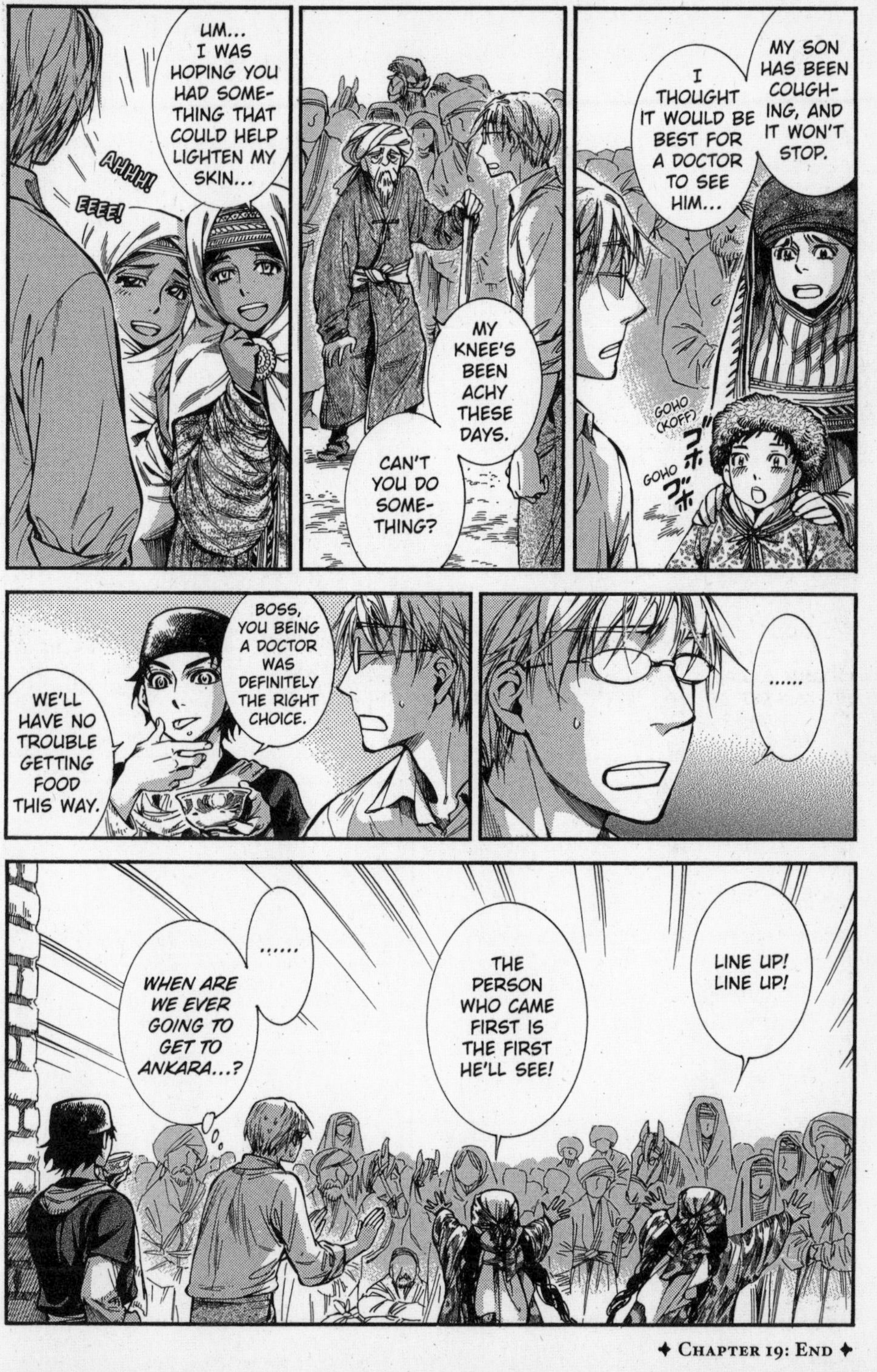

MY SON HAS BEEN COUGHING, AND IT WON'T STOP.
I THOUGHT IT WOULD BE BEST FOR A DOCTOR TO SEE HIM...
GOHO (KOFF)
ゴホ
GOHO
ゴホ
MY KNEE'S BEEN ACHY THESE DAYS.
CAN'T YOU DO SOMETHING?
UM... I WAS HOPING YOU HAD SOME-THING THAT COULD HELP LIGHTEN MY SKIN...
AHHH!
EEEE!
......
BOSS, YOU BEING A DOCTOR WAS DEFINITELY THE RIGHT CHOICE.
WE'LL HAVE NO TROUBLE GETTING FOOD THIS WAY.
LINE UP! LINE UP!
THE PERSON WHO CAME FIRST IS THE FIRST HE'LL SEE!
......
WHEN ARE WE EVER GOING TO GET TO ANKARA...?

✦ Chapter 19: End ✦

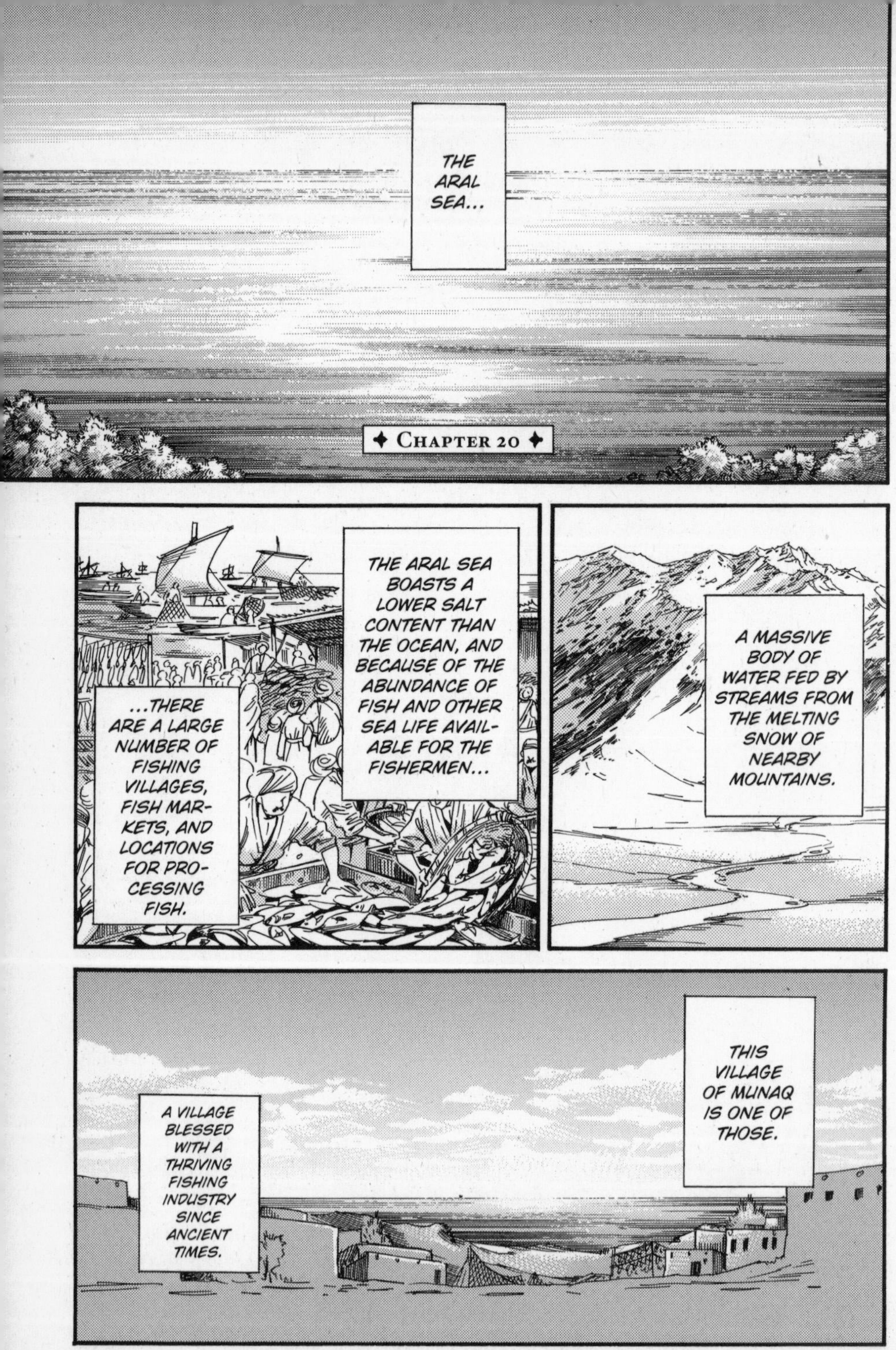
THE ARAL SEA...
✦ CHAPTER 20 ✦
A MASSIVE BODY OF WATER FED BY STREAMS FROM THE MELTING SNOW OF NEARBY MOUNTAINS.
THE ARAL SEA BOASTS A LOWER SALT CONTENT THAN THE OCEAN, AND BECAUSE OF THE ABUNDANCE OF FISH AND OTHER SEA LIFE AVAIL-ABLE FOR THE FISHERMEN...
...THERE ARE A LARGE NUMBER OF FISHING VILLAGES, FISH MAR-KETS, AND LOCATIONS FOR PRO-CESSING FISH.
THIS VILLAGE OF MUNAQ IS ONE OF THOSE.
A VILLAGE BLESSED WITH A THRIVING FISHING INDUSTRY SINCE ANCIENT TIMES.

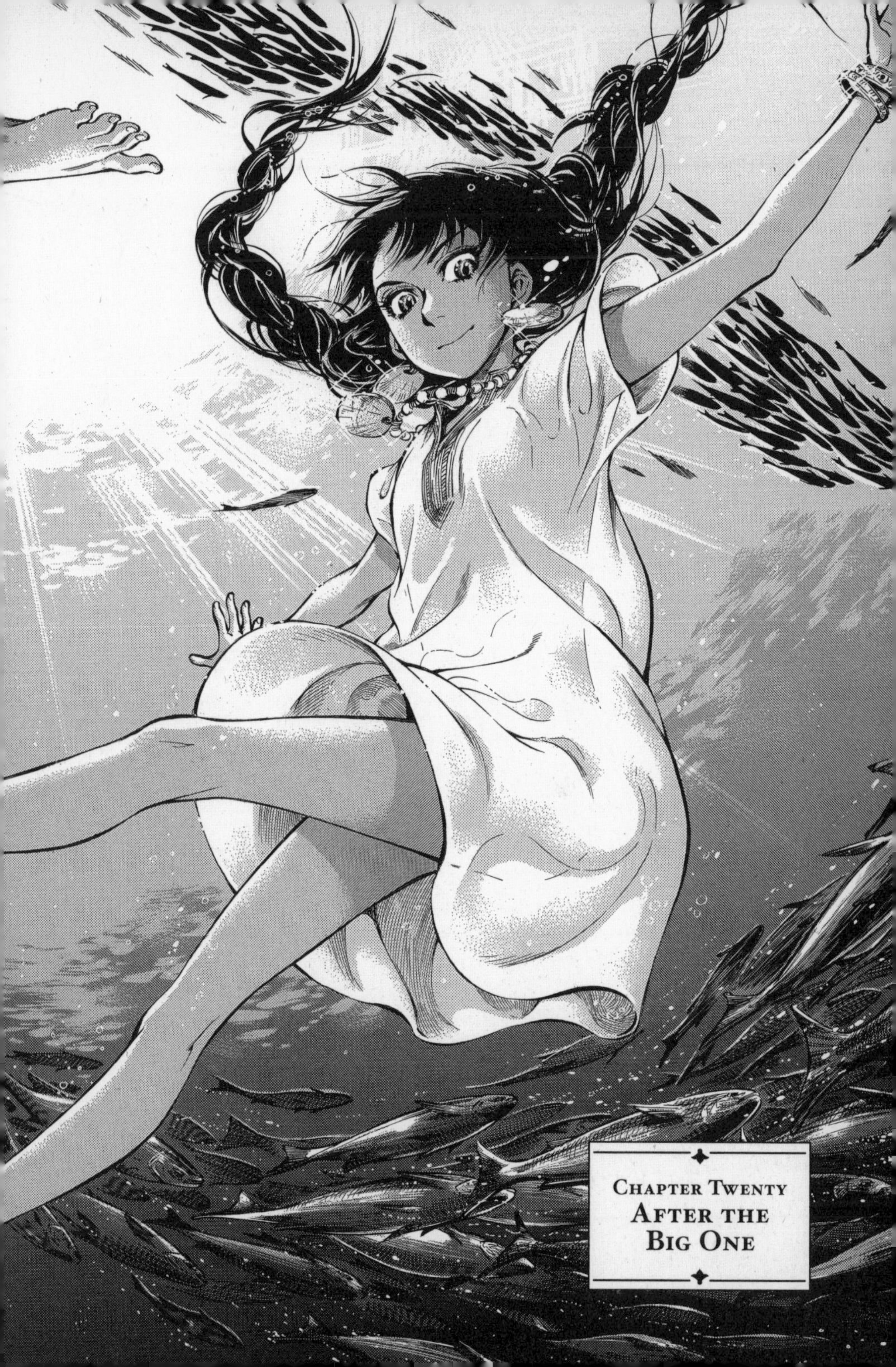
Chapter Twenty
After the
Big One

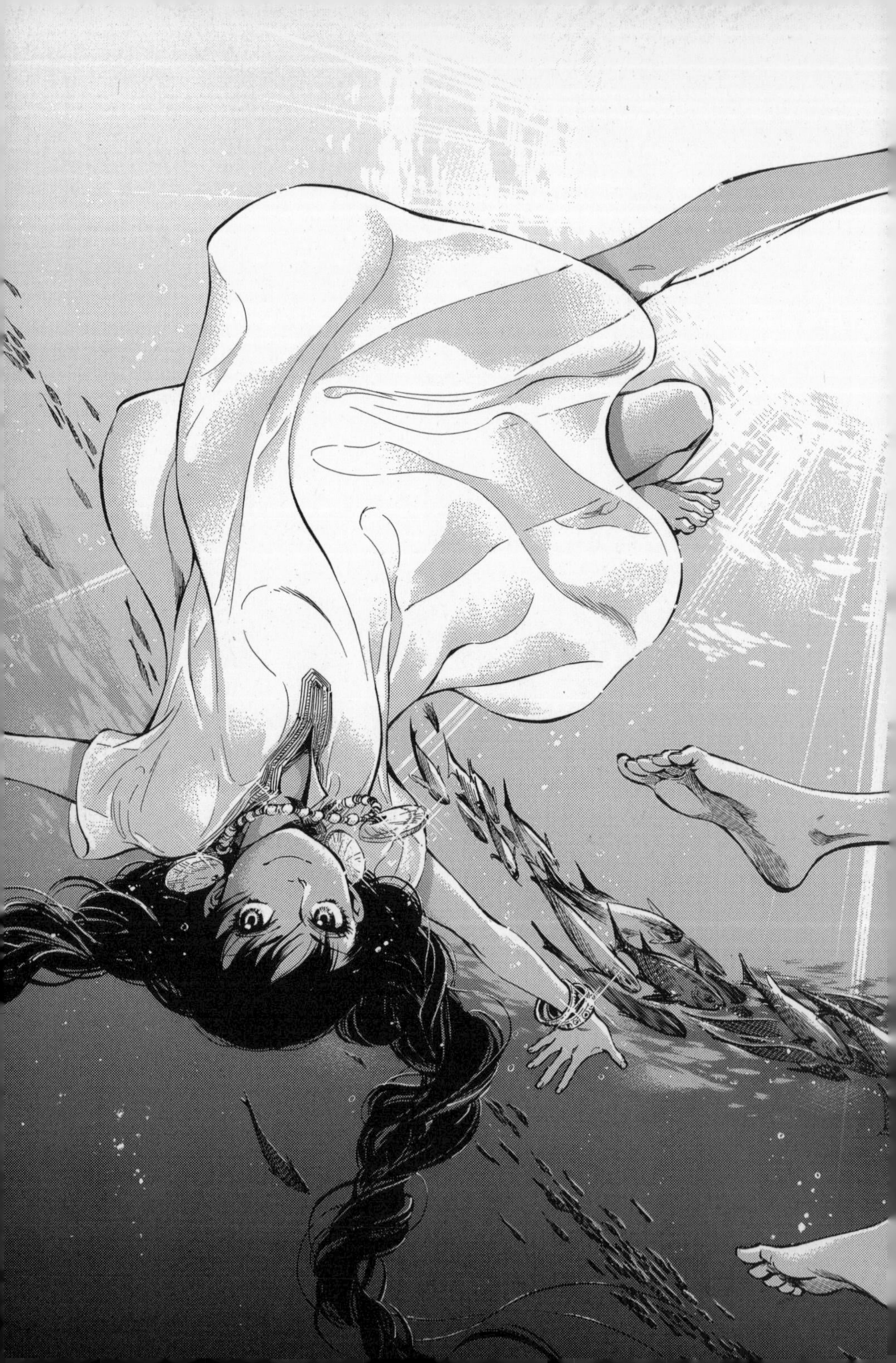

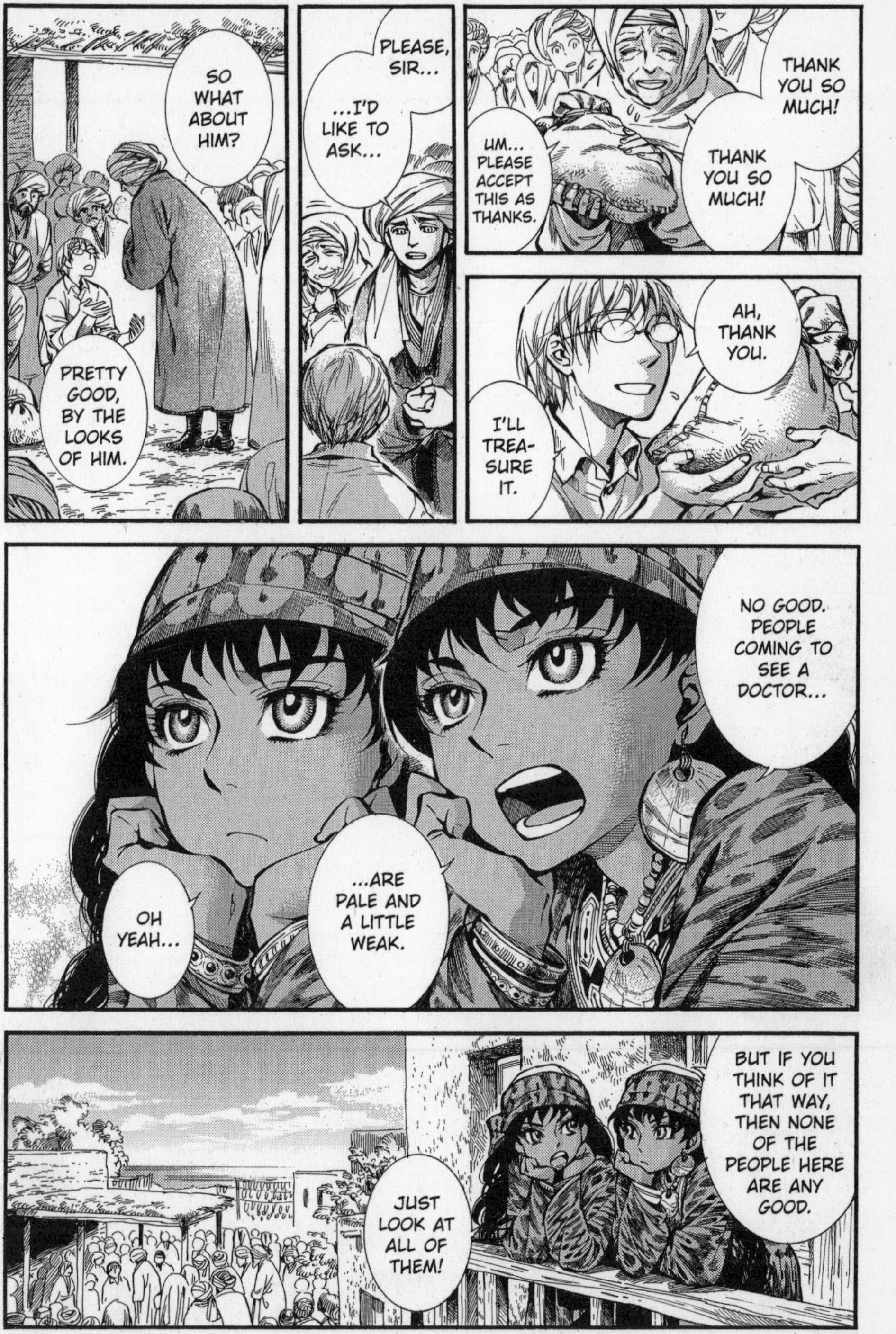
THANK YOU SO MUCH!
THANK YOU SO MUCH!
UM... PLEASE ACCEPT THIS AS THANKS.
AH, THANK YOU.
I'LL TREA-SURE IT.
PLEASE, SIR...
...I'D LIKE TO ASK...
SO WHAT ABOUT HIM?
PRETTY GOOD, BY THE LOOKS OF HIM.
NO GOOD. PEOPLE COMING TO SEE A DOCTOR...
...ARE PALE AND A LITTLE WEAK.
OH YEAH...
BUT IF YOU THINK OF IT THAT WAY, THEN NONE OF THE PEOPLE HERE ARE ANY GOOD.
JUST LOOK AT ALL OF THEM!

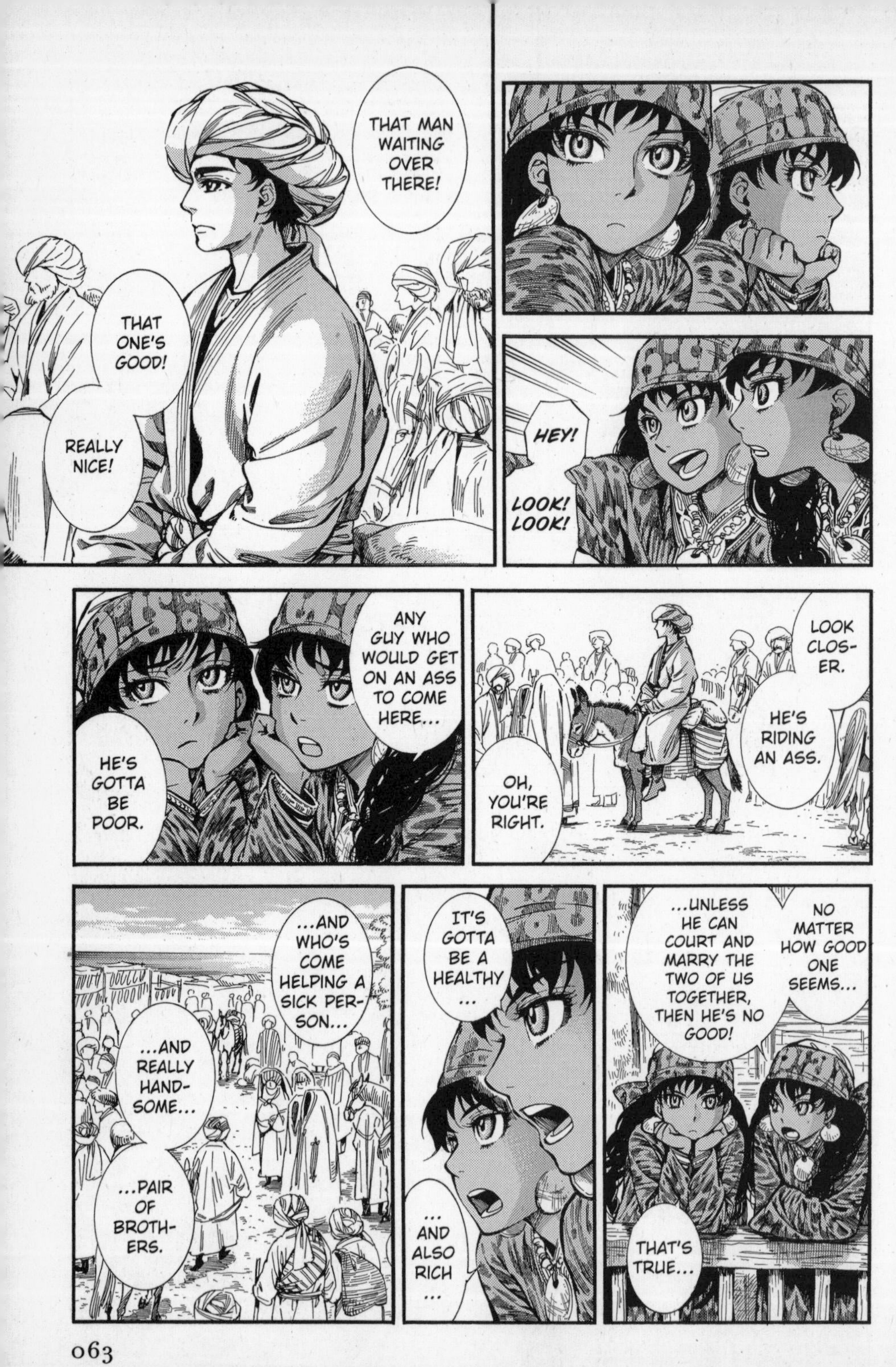
HEY!
LOOK! LOOK!
THAT MAN WAITING OVER THERE!
THAT ONE'S GOOD!
REALLY NICE!
LOOK CLOSER.
HE'S RIDING AN ASS.
OH, YOU'RE RIGHT.
ANY GUY WHO WOULD GET ON AN ASS TO COME HERE...
HE'S GOTTA BE POOR.
NO MATTER HOW GOOD ONE SEEMS...
...UNLESS HE CAN COURT AND MARRY THE TWO OF US TOGETHER, THEN HE'S NO GOOD!
THAT'S TRUE...
IT'S GOTTA BE A HEALTHY...
...AND ALSO RICH...
...AND WHO'S COME HELPING A SICK PERSON...
...AND REALLY HANDSOME...
...PAIR OF BROTHERS.

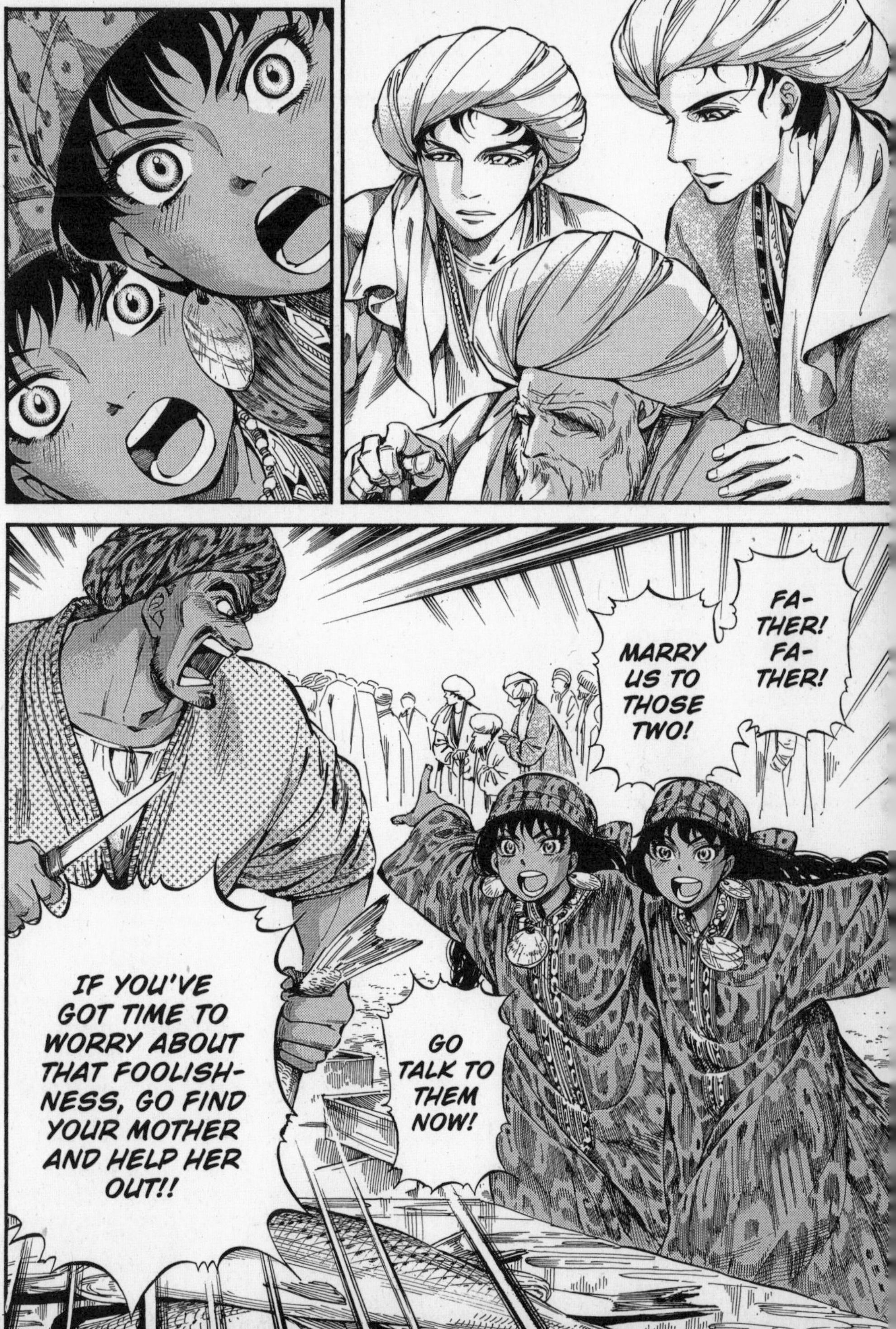
FA-THER! FA-THER!
MARRY US TO THOSE TWO!
GO TALK TO THEM NOW!
IF YOU'VE GOT TIME TO WORRY ABOUT THAT FOOLISH-NESS, GO FIND YOUR MOTHER AND HELP HER OUT!!

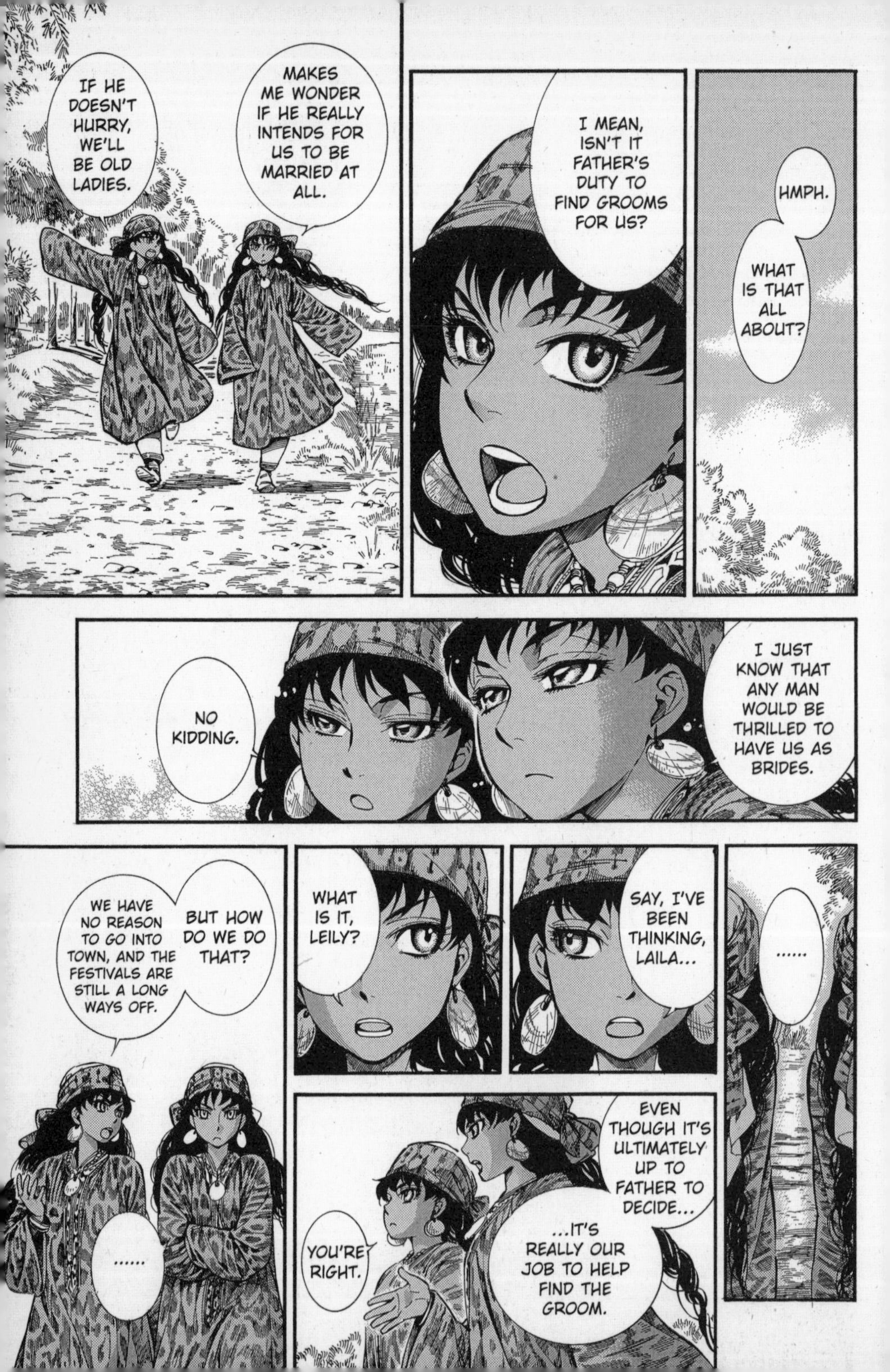
HMPH.
WHAT IS THAT ALL ABOUT?
I MEAN, ISN'T IT FATHER'S DUTY TO FIND GROOMS FOR US?
MAKES ME WONDER IF HE REALLY INTENDS FOR US TO BE MARRIED AT ALL.
IF HE DOESN'T HURRY, WE'LL BE OLD LADIES.
I JUST KNOW THAT ANY MAN WOULD BE THRILLED TO HAVE US AS BRIDES.
NO KIDDING.
......
SAY, I'VE BEEN THINKING, LAILA...
WHAT IS IT, LEILY?
EVEN THOUGH IT'S ULTIMATELY UP TO FATHER TO DECIDE...
...IT'S REALLY OUR JOB TO HELP FIND THE GROOM.
YOU'RE RIGHT.
BUT HOW DO WE DO THAT?
WE HAVE NO REASON TO GO INTO TOWN, AND THE FESTIVALS ARE STILL A LONG WAYS OFF.
......

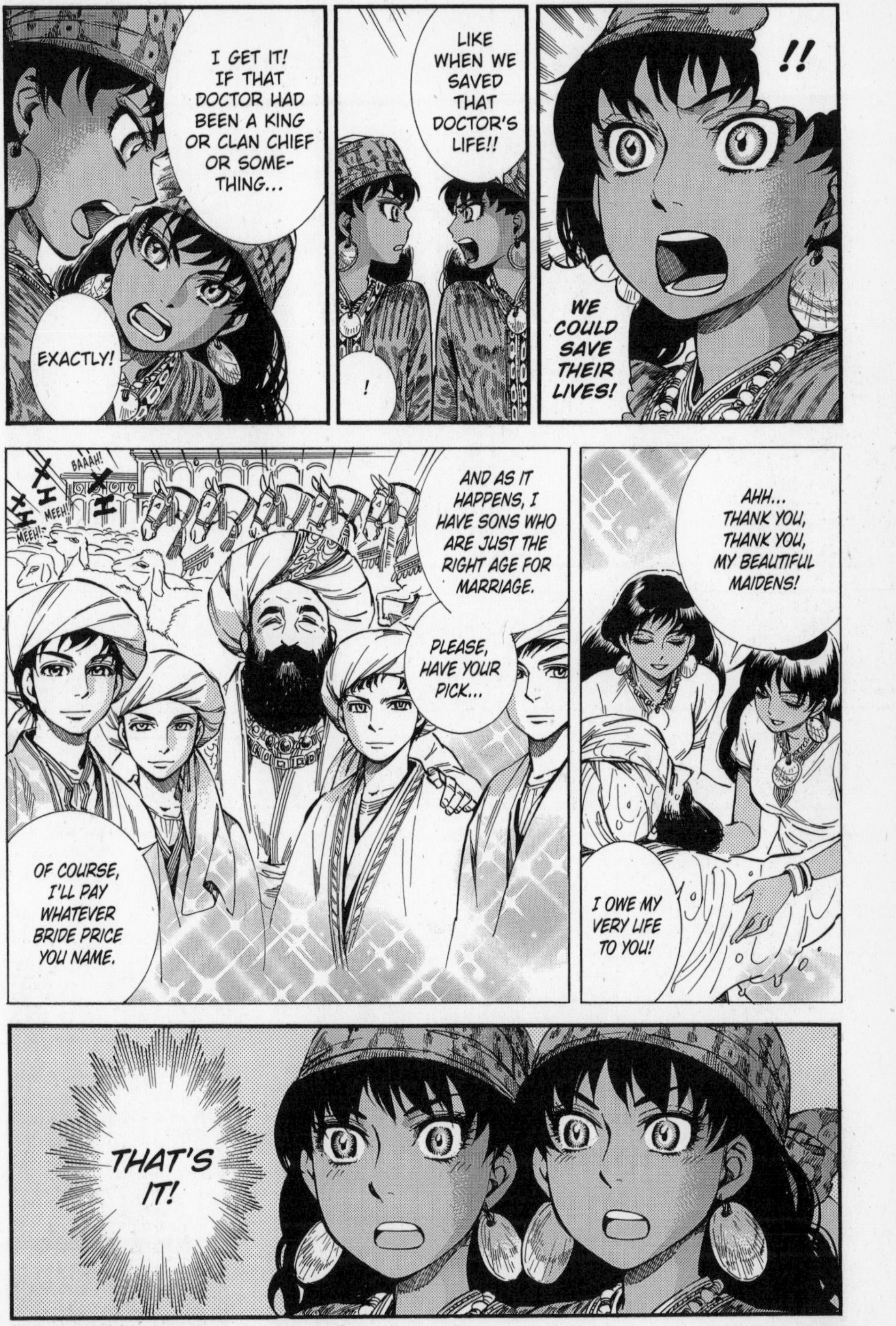
!!
WE COULD SAVE THEIR LIVES!
LIKE WHEN WE SAVED THAT DOCTOR'S LIFE!!
!
I GET IT! IF THAT DOCTOR HAD BEEN A KING OR CLAN CHIEF OR SOME-THING...
EXACTLY!
AHH... THANK YOU, THANK YOU, MY BEAUTIFUL MAIDENS!
I OWE MY VERY LIFE TO YOU!
AND AS IT HAPPENS, I HAVE SONS WHO ARE JUST THE RIGHT AGE FOR MARRIAGE.
PLEASE, HAVE YOUR PICK...
OF COURSE, I'LL PAY WHATEVER BRIDE PRICE YOU NAME.
HIH
HIH
BAAAH!
MEEH!
MEEH!
THAT'S IT!

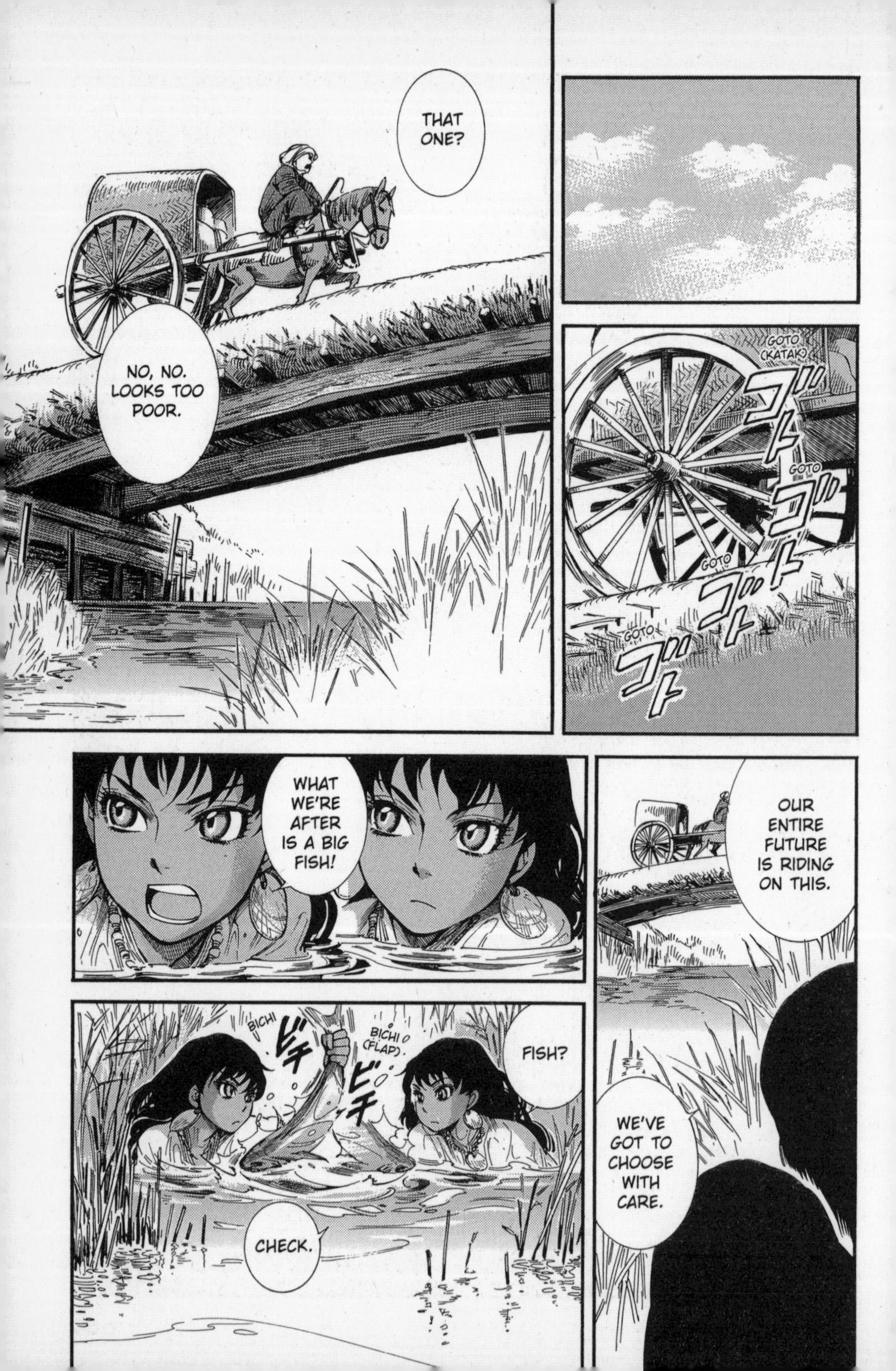
GOTO (KATAK)
ゴト
GOTO
ゴト
GOTO
ゴト
GOTO
ゴト
THAT ONE?
NO, NO. LOOKS TOO POOR.
OUR ENTIRE FUTURE IS RIDING ON THIS.
WE'VE GOT TO CHOOSE WITH CARE.
WHAT WE'RE AFTER IS A BIG FISH!
FISH?
BICHI
ビチ
BICHI (FLAP)
ビチ
CHECK.

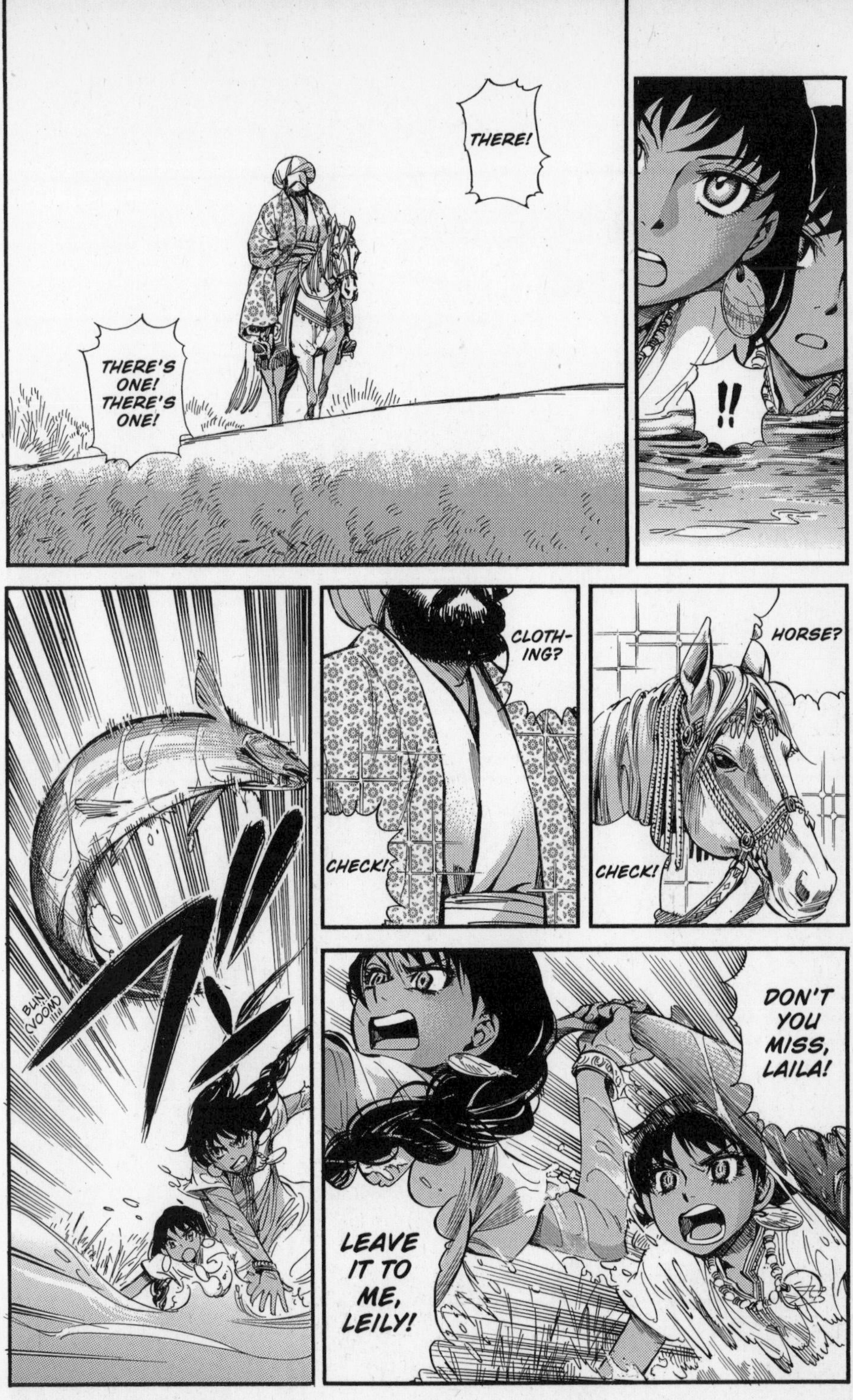
!!
THERE!
THERE'S ONE! THERE'S ONE!
HORSE?
CHECK!
CLOTHING?
CHECK!
DON'T YOU MISS, LAILA!
LEAVE IT TO ME, LEILY!
BUN (VOOM)

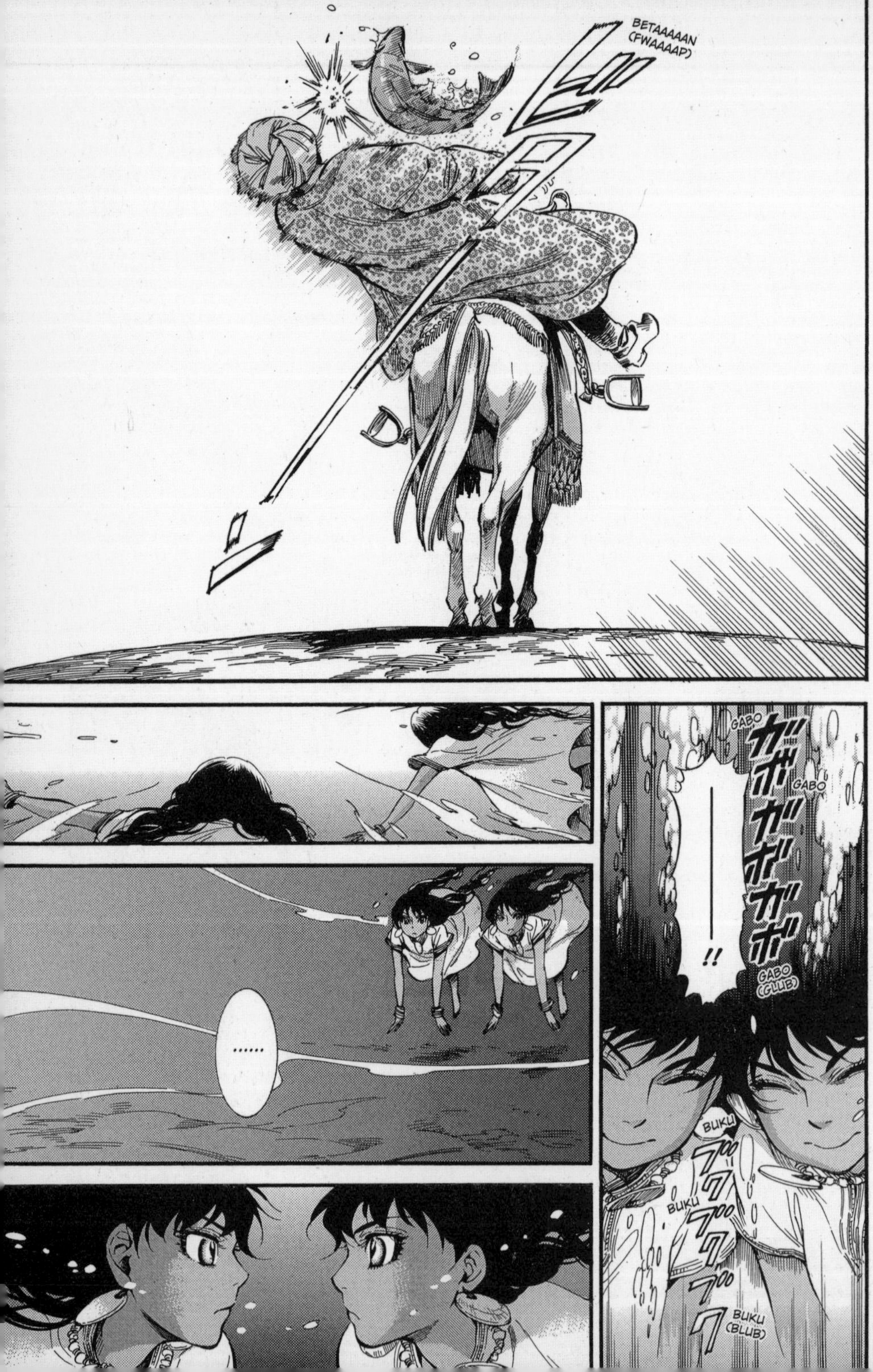
BETAAAAAN
(FWAAAAP)
GABO
GABO
——!!
GABO
(GLUB)
BUKU
BUKU
BUKU
(BLUB)
......

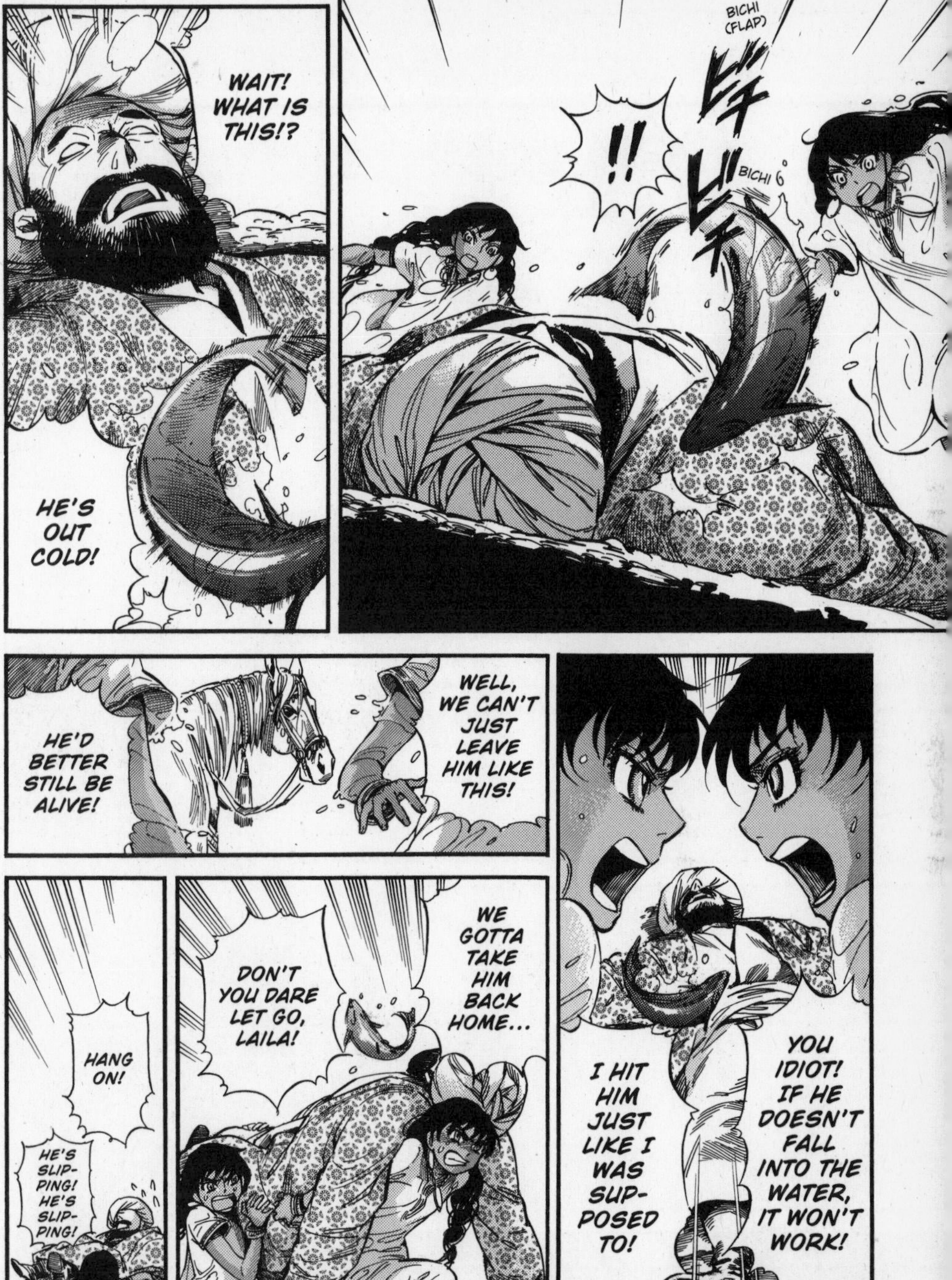

BICHI (FLAP)
ビチ
!!
BICHI
ビチ
WAIT! WHAT IS THIS!?
HE'S OUT COLD!
YOU IDIOT! IF HE DOESN'T FALL INTO THE WATER, IT WON'T WORK!
I HIT HIM JUST LIKE I WAS SUP-POSED TO!
WELL, WE CAN'T JUST LEAVE HIM LIKE THIS!
HE'D BETTER STILL BE ALIVE!
WE GOTTA TAKE HIM BACK HOME...
DON'T YOU DARE LET GO, LAILA!
HANG ON!
HE'S SLIP-PING! HE'S SLIP-PING!

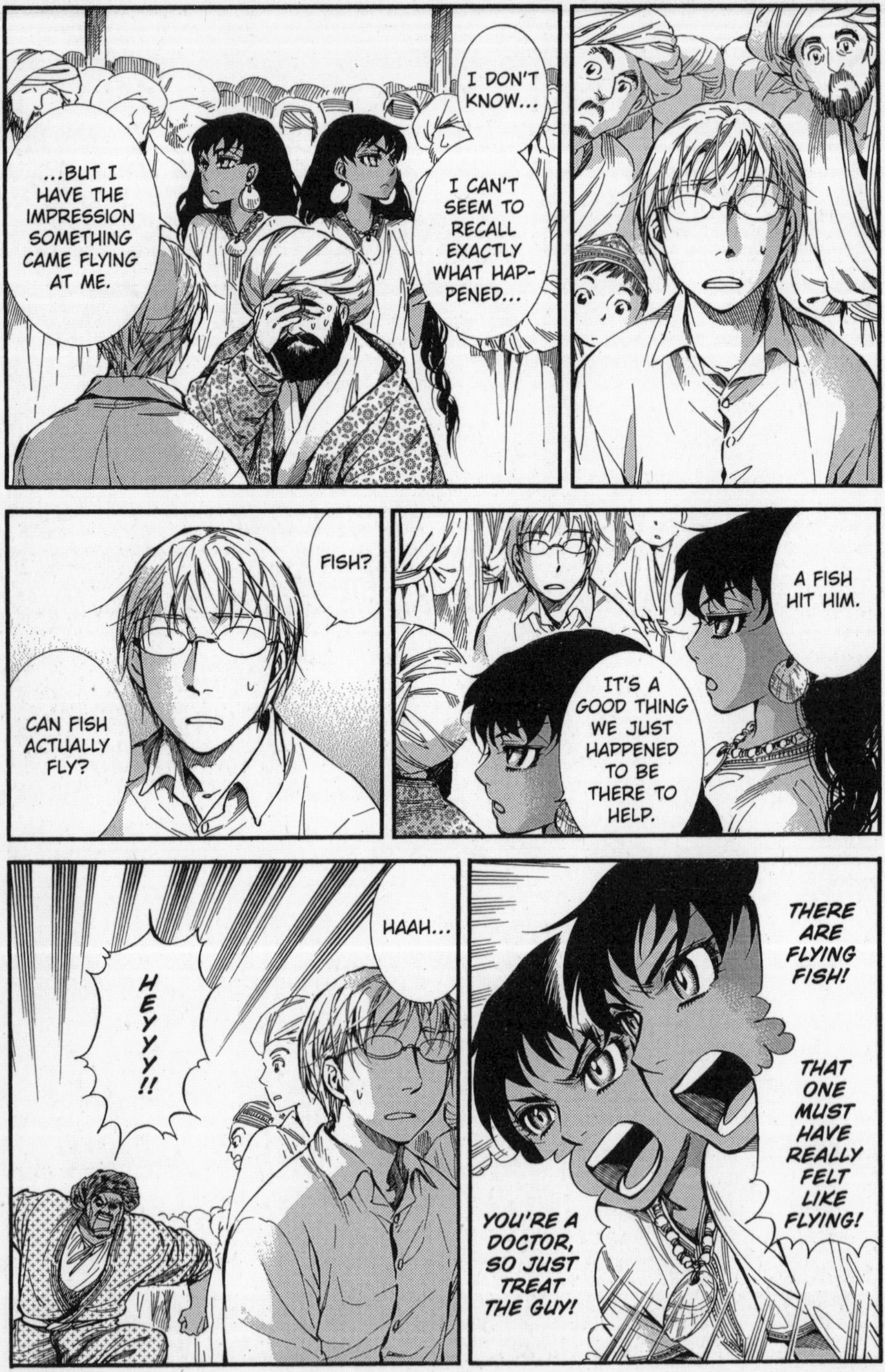
I DON'T KNOW...
I CAN'T SEEM TO RECALL EXACTLY WHAT HAPPENED...
...BUT I HAVE THE IMPRESSION SOMETHING CAME FLYING AT ME.
A FISH HIT HIM.
IT'S A GOOD THING WE JUST HAPPENED TO BE THERE TO HELP.
FISH?
CAN FISH ACTUALLY FLY?
THERE ARE FLYING FISH!
THAT ONE MUST HAVE REALLY FELT LIKE FLYING!
YOU'RE A DOCTOR, SO JUST TREAT THE GUY!
HAAH...
HEYYY!!

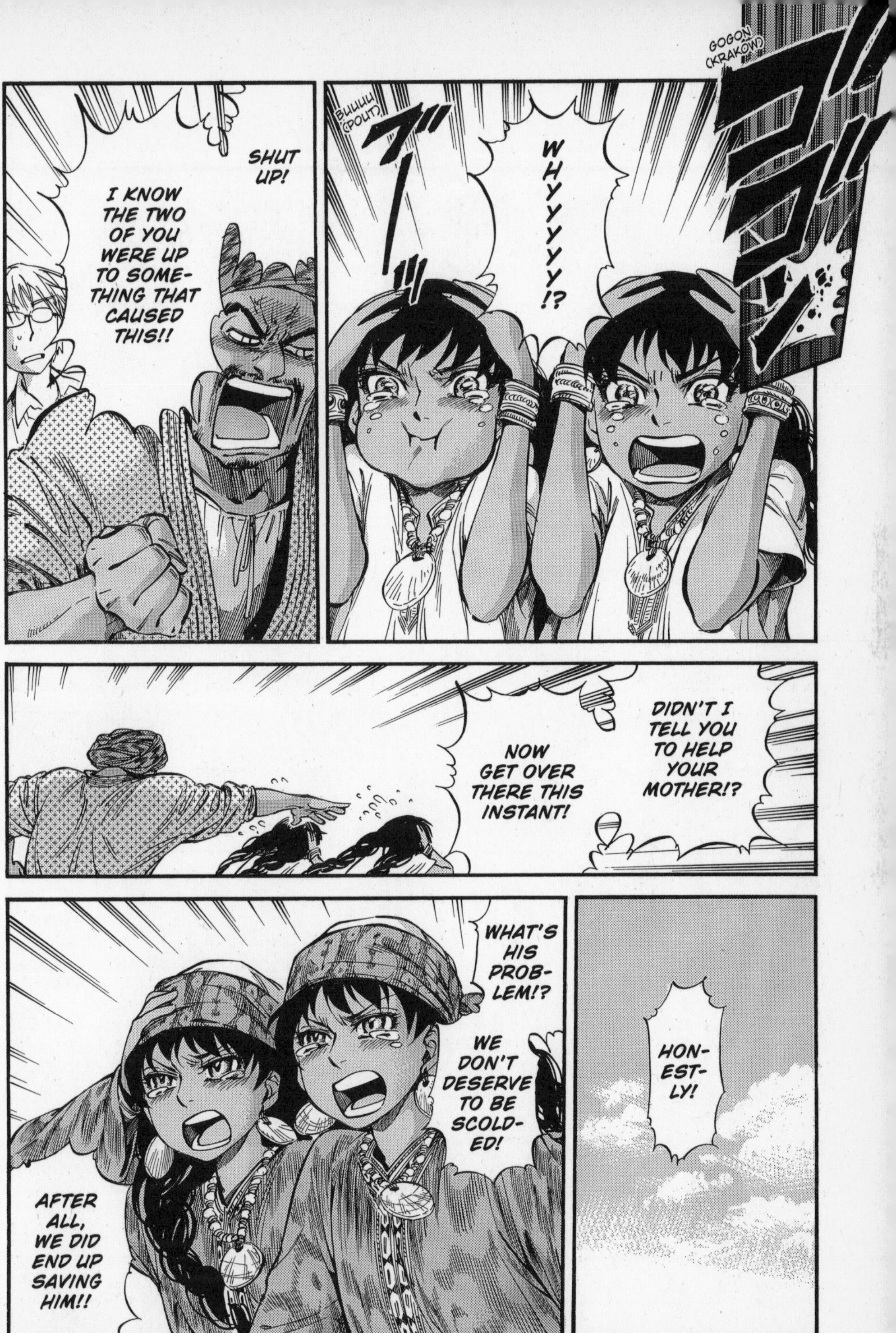
GOGON (KRAKOW)
WHYYYYYY!?
Buuuu (POUT)
SHUT UP!
I KNOW THE TWO OF YOU WERE UP TO SOME-THING THAT CAUSED THIS!!
DIDN'T I TELL YOU TO HELP YOUR MOTHER!?
NOW GET OVER THERE THIS INSTANT!
HON-EST-LY!
WHAT'S HIS PROB-LEM!?
WE DON'T DESERVE TO BE SCOLD-ED!
AFTER ALL, WE DID END UP SAVING HIM!!

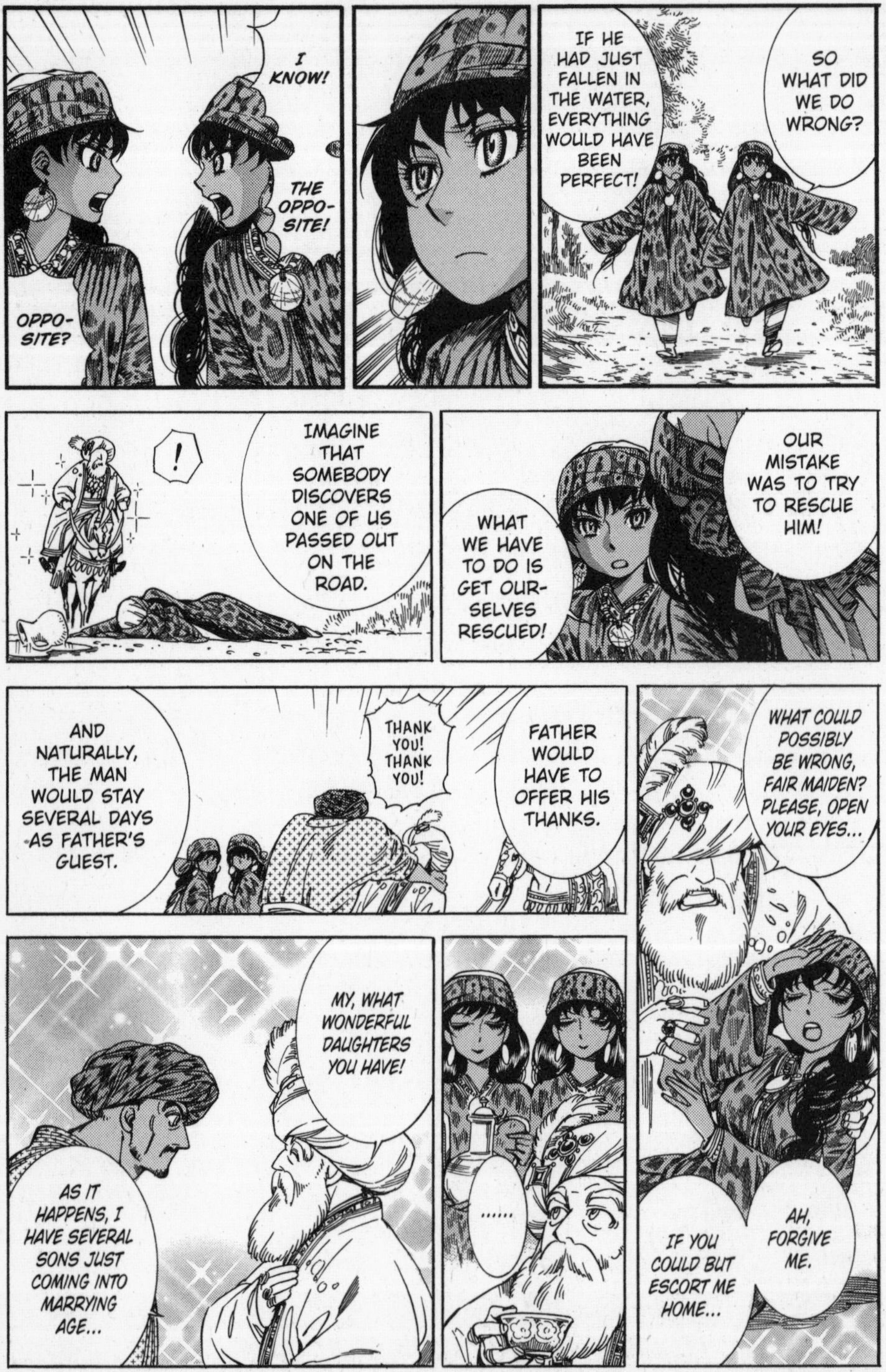
SO WHAT DID WE DO WRONG?
IF HE HAD JUST FALLEN IN THE WATER, EVERYTHING WOULD HAVE BEEN PERFECT!
I KNOW!
THE OPPO-SITE!
OPPO-SITE?
OUR MISTAKE WAS TO TRY TO RESCUE HIM!
WHAT WE HAVE TO DO IS GET OUR-SELVES RESCUED!
IMAGINE THAT SOMEBODY DISCOVERS ONE OF US PASSED OUT ON THE ROAD.
!
WHAT COULD POSSIBLY BE WRONG, FAIR MAIDEN? PLEASE, OPEN YOUR EYES...
AH, FORGIVE ME.
IF YOU COULD BUT ESCORT ME HOME...
FATHER WOULD HAVE TO OFFER HIS THANKS.
THANK YOU! THANK YOU!
AND NATURALLY, THE MAN WOULD STAY SEVERAL DAYS AS FATHER'S GUEST.
......
MY, WHAT WONDERFUL DAUGHTERS YOU HAVE!
AS IT HAPPENS, I HAVE SEVERAL SONS JUST COMING INTO MARRYING AGE...

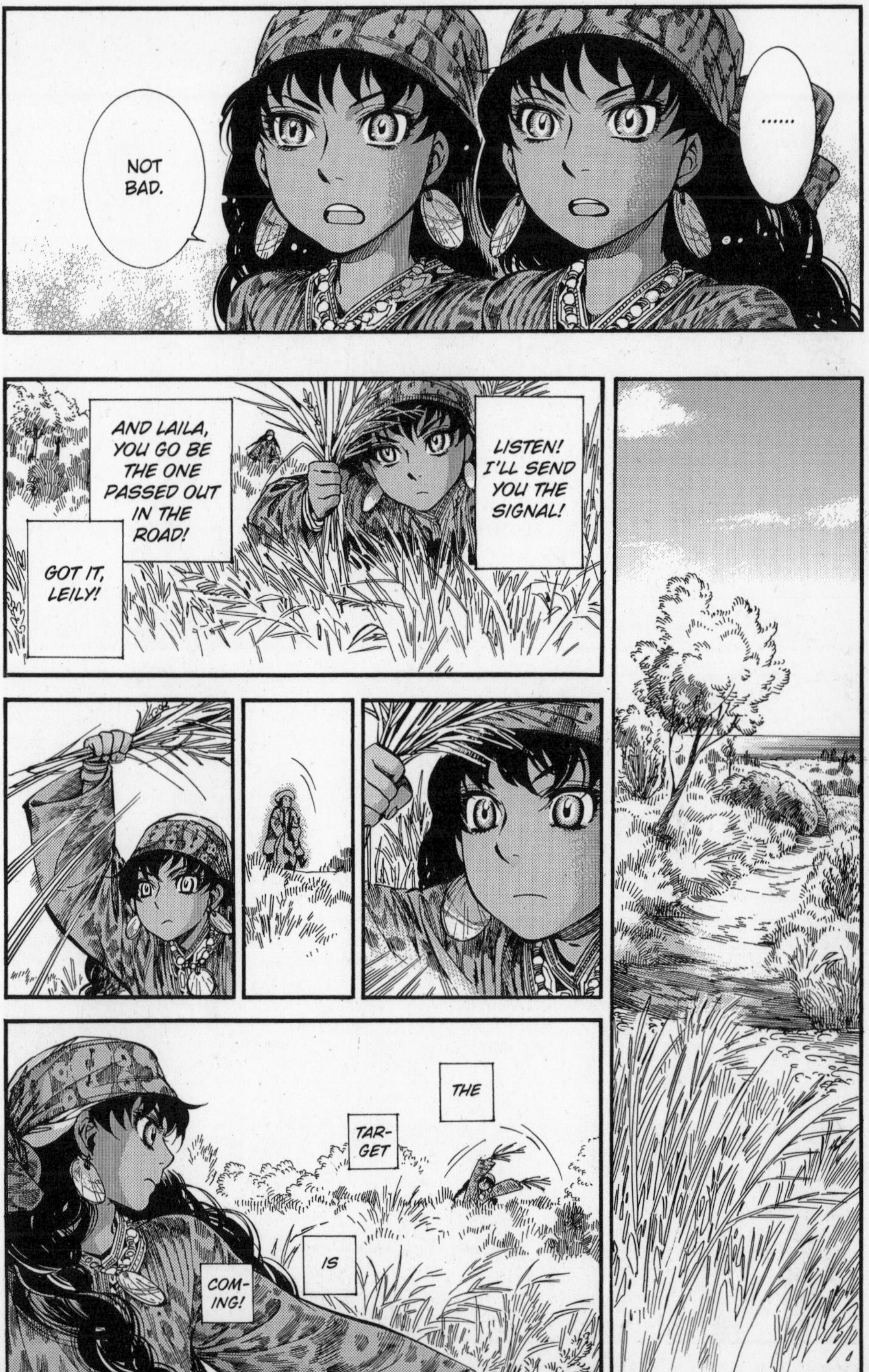
......
NOT BAD.
LISTEN! I'LL SEND YOU THE SIGNAL!
AND LAILA, YOU GO BE THE ONE PASSED OUT IN THE ROAD!
GOT IT, LEILY!
THE
TAR-GET
IS
COM-ING!

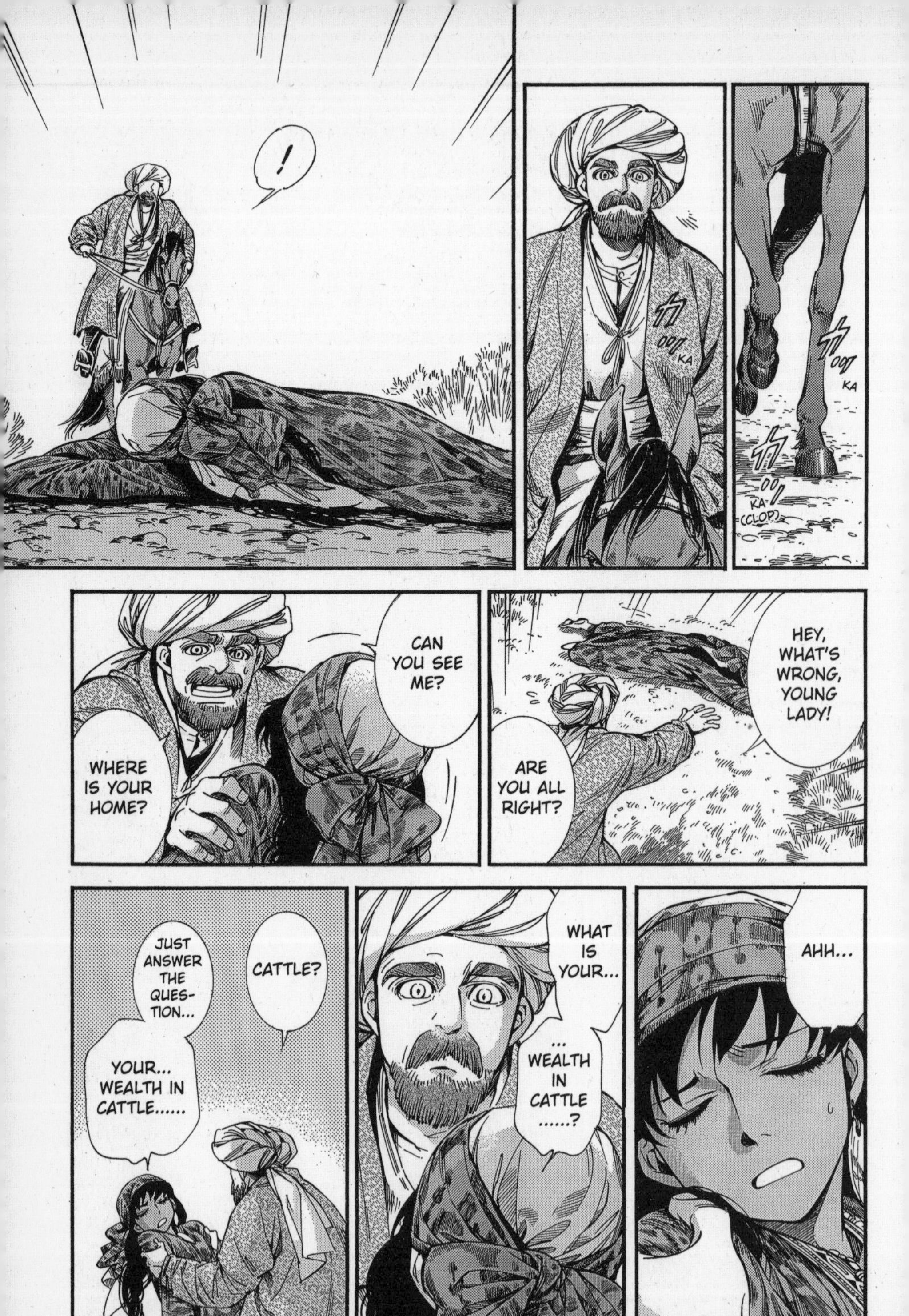
KA
KA
KA
(CLOP)
KA
!
HEY, WHAT'S WRONG, YOUNG LADY!
ARE YOU ALL RIGHT?
CAN YOU SEE ME?
WHERE IS YOUR HOME?
AHH...
WHAT IS YOUR...
... WEALTH IN CATTLE ......?
CATTLE?
JUST ANSWER THE QUES-TION...
YOUR... WEALTH IN CATTLE......

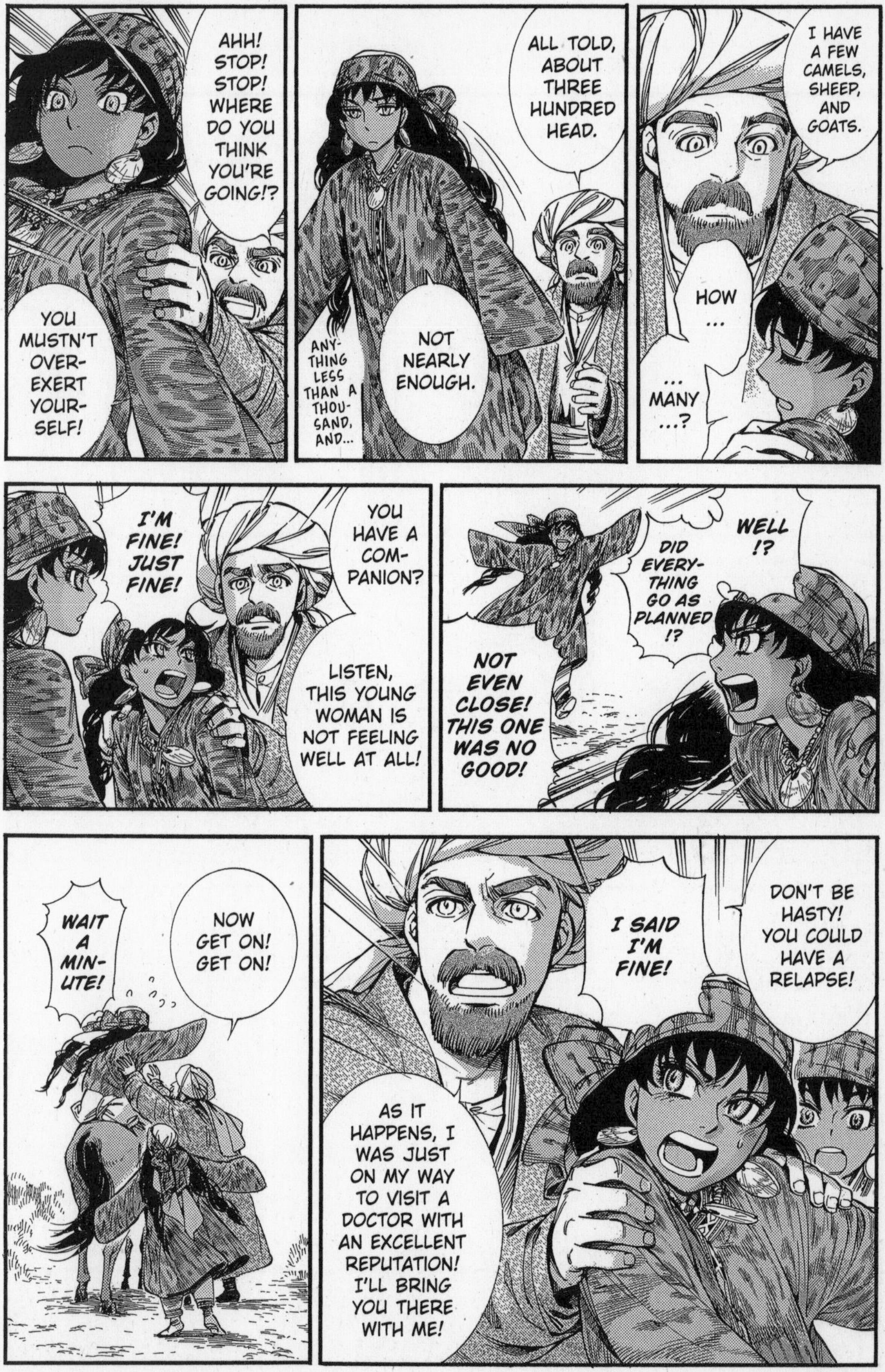
I HAVE A FEW CAMELS, SHEEP, AND GOATS.
HOW ...
... MANY ...?
ALL TOLD, ABOUT THREE HUNDRED HEAD.
NOT NEARLY ENOUGH.
ANYTHING LESS THAN A THOUSAND, AND...
AHH! STOP! STOP! WHERE DO YOU THINK YOU'RE GOING!?
YOU MUSTN'T OVEREXERT YOURSELF!
WELL !?
DID EVERYTHING GO AS PLANNED !?
NOT EVEN CLOSE! THIS ONE WAS NO GOOD!
YOU HAVE A COMPANION?
I'M FINE! JUST FINE!
LISTEN, THIS YOUNG WOMAN IS NOT FEELING WELL AT ALL!
DON'T BE HASTY! YOU COULD HAVE A RELAPSE!
I SAID I'M FINE!
AS IT HAPPENS, I WAS JUST ON MY WAY TO VISIT A DOCTOR WITH AN EXCELLENT REPUTATION! I'LL BRING YOU THERE WITH ME!
NOW GET ON! GET ON!
WAIT A MINUTE!

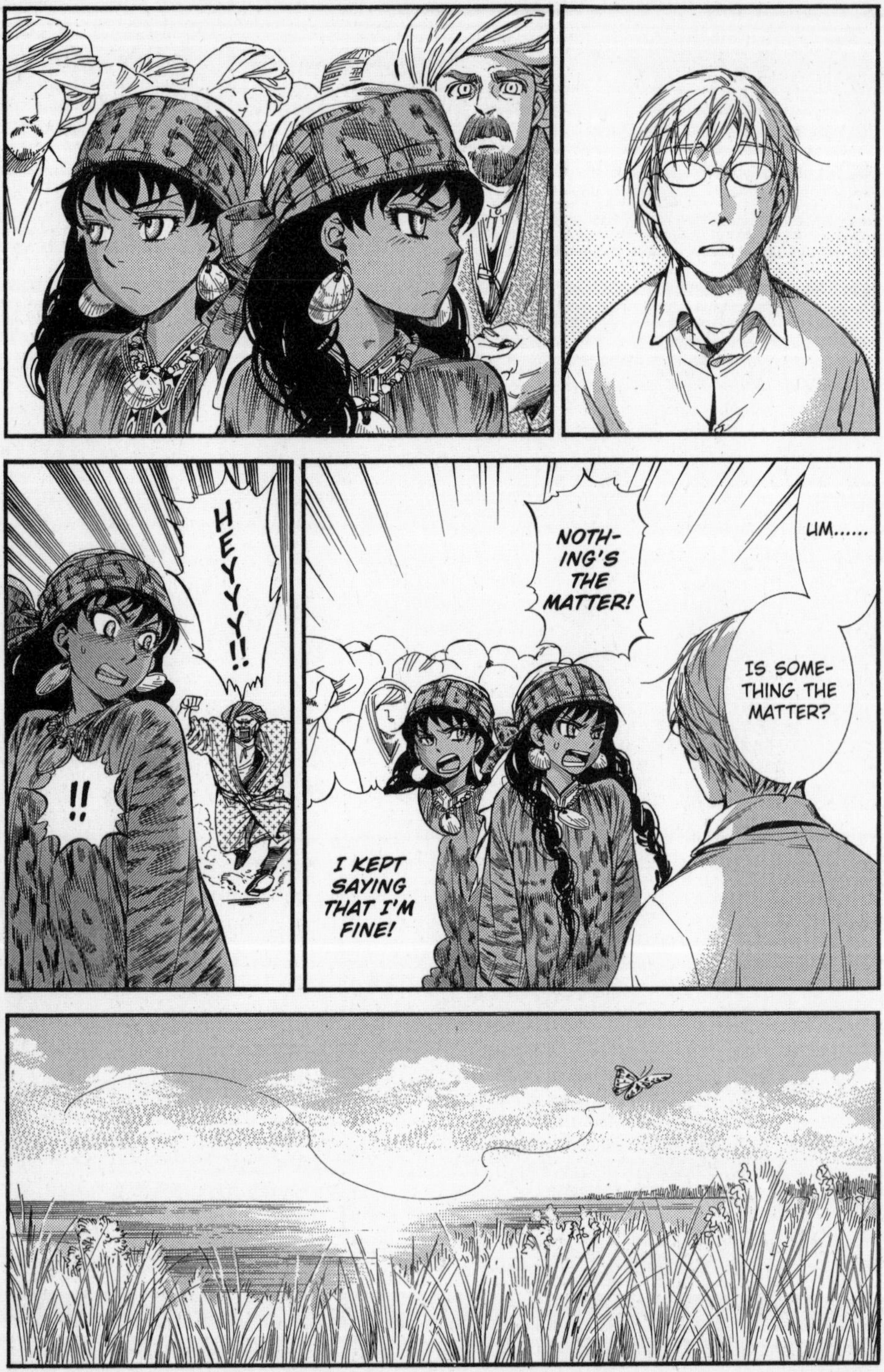
UM......
IS SOME-THING THE MATTER?
NOTH-ING'S THE MATTER!
I KEPT SAYING THAT I'M FINE!
HEYYY!!
!!

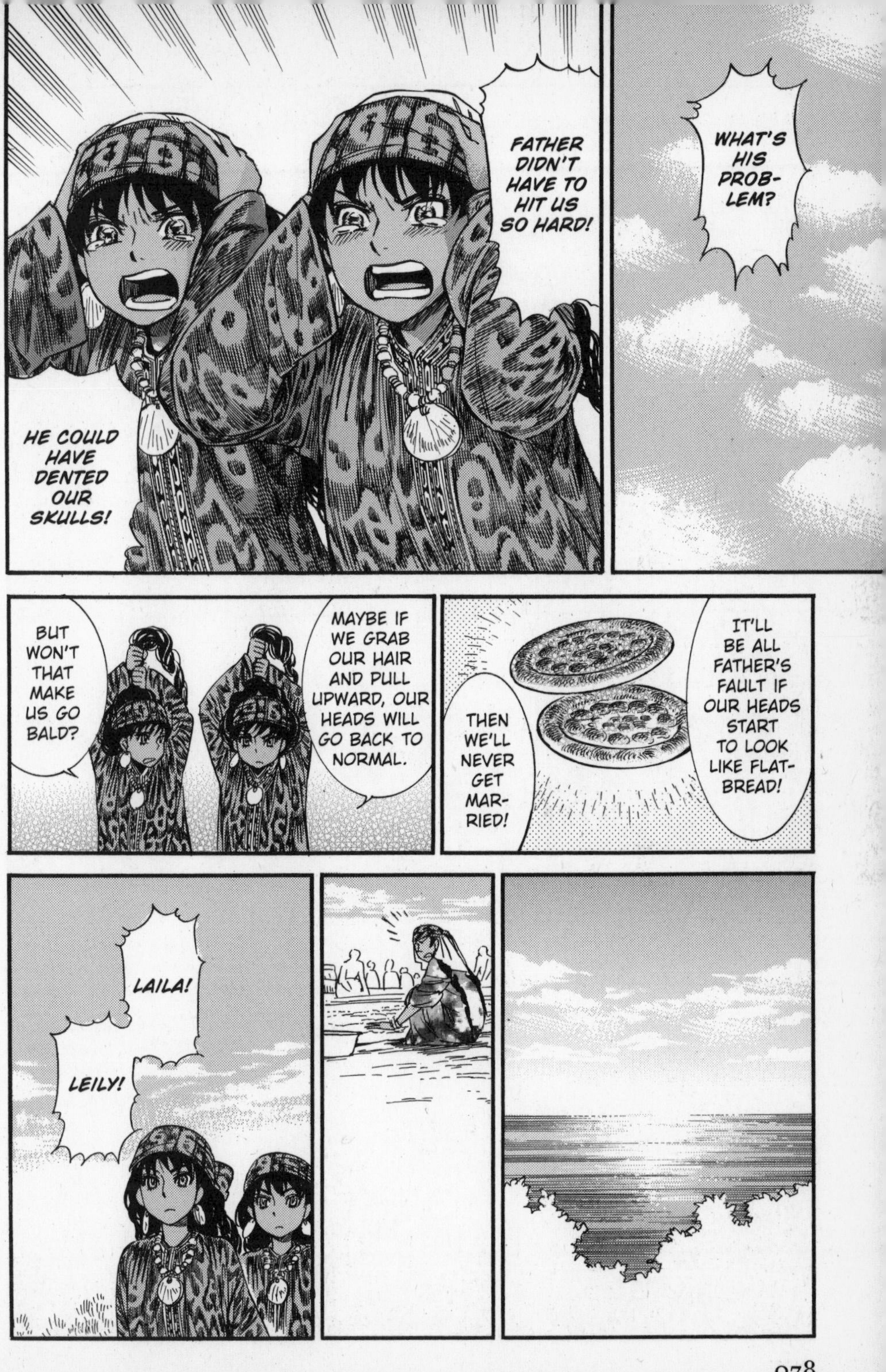
WHAT'S HIS PROBLEM?
FATHER DIDN'T HAVE TO HIT US SO HARD!
HE COULD HAVE DENTED OUR SKULLS!
IT'LL BE ALL FATHER'S FAULT IF OUR HEADS START TO LOOK LIKE FLATBREAD!
THEN WE'LL NEVER GET MARRIED!
MAYBE IF WE GRAB OUR HAIR AND PULL UPWARD, OUR HEADS WILL GO BACK TO NORMAL.
BUT WON'T THAT MAKE US GO BALD?
LAILA!
LEILY!

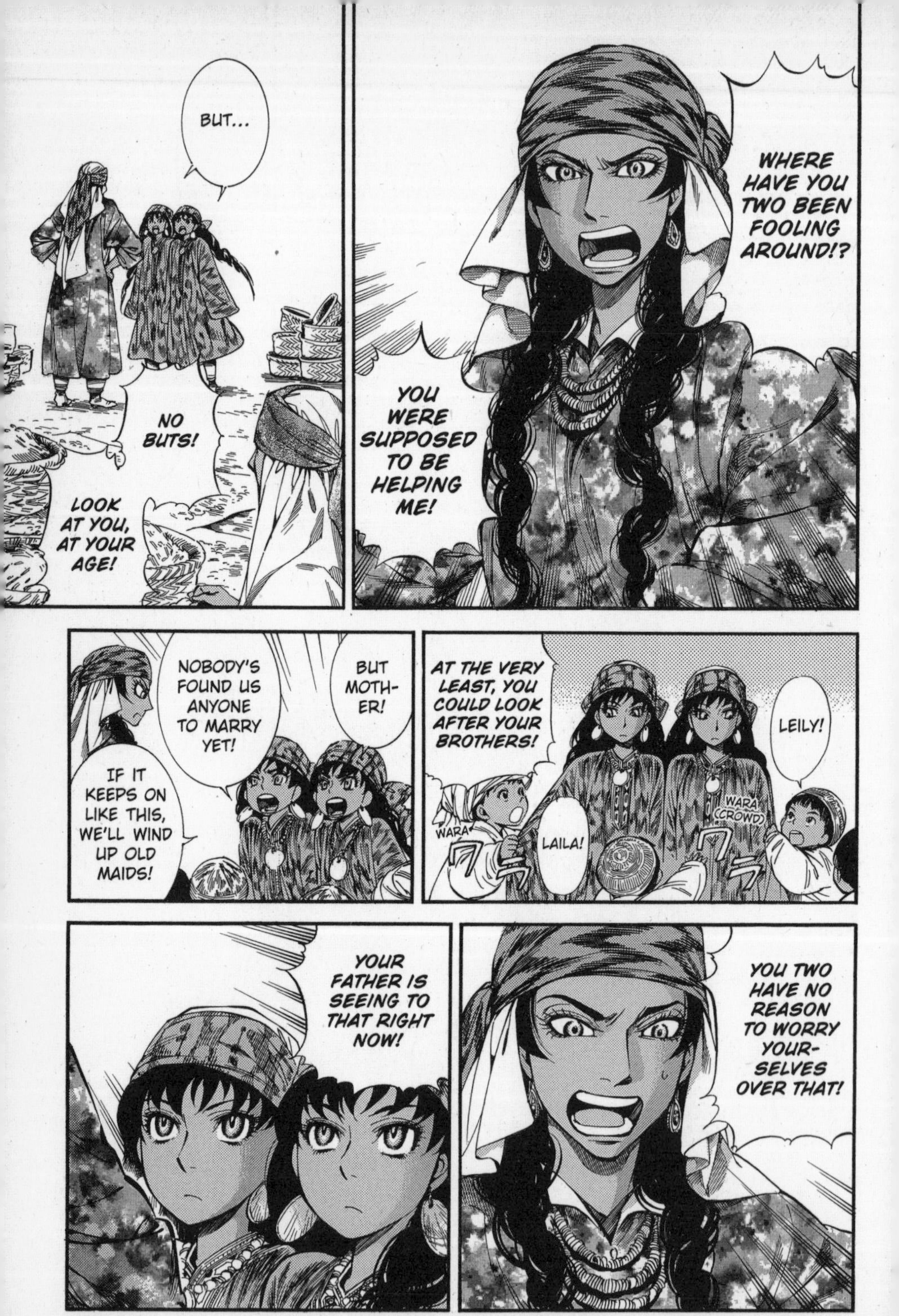
WHERE HAVE YOU TWO BEEN FOOLING AROUND!?
YOU WERE SUPPOSED TO BE HELPING ME!
BUT...
NO BUTS!
LOOK AT YOU, AT YOUR AGE!
AT THE VERY LEAST, YOU COULD LOOK AFTER YOUR BROTHERS!
LEILY!
WARA (CROWD)
LAILA!
WARA
BUT MOTH-ER!
NOBODY'S FOUND US ANYONE TO MARRY YET!
IF IT KEEPS ON LIKE THIS, WE'LL WIND UP OLD MAIDS!
YOU TWO HAVE NO REASON TO WORRY YOUR-SELVES OVER THAT!
YOUR FATHER IS SEEING TO THAT RIGHT NOW!

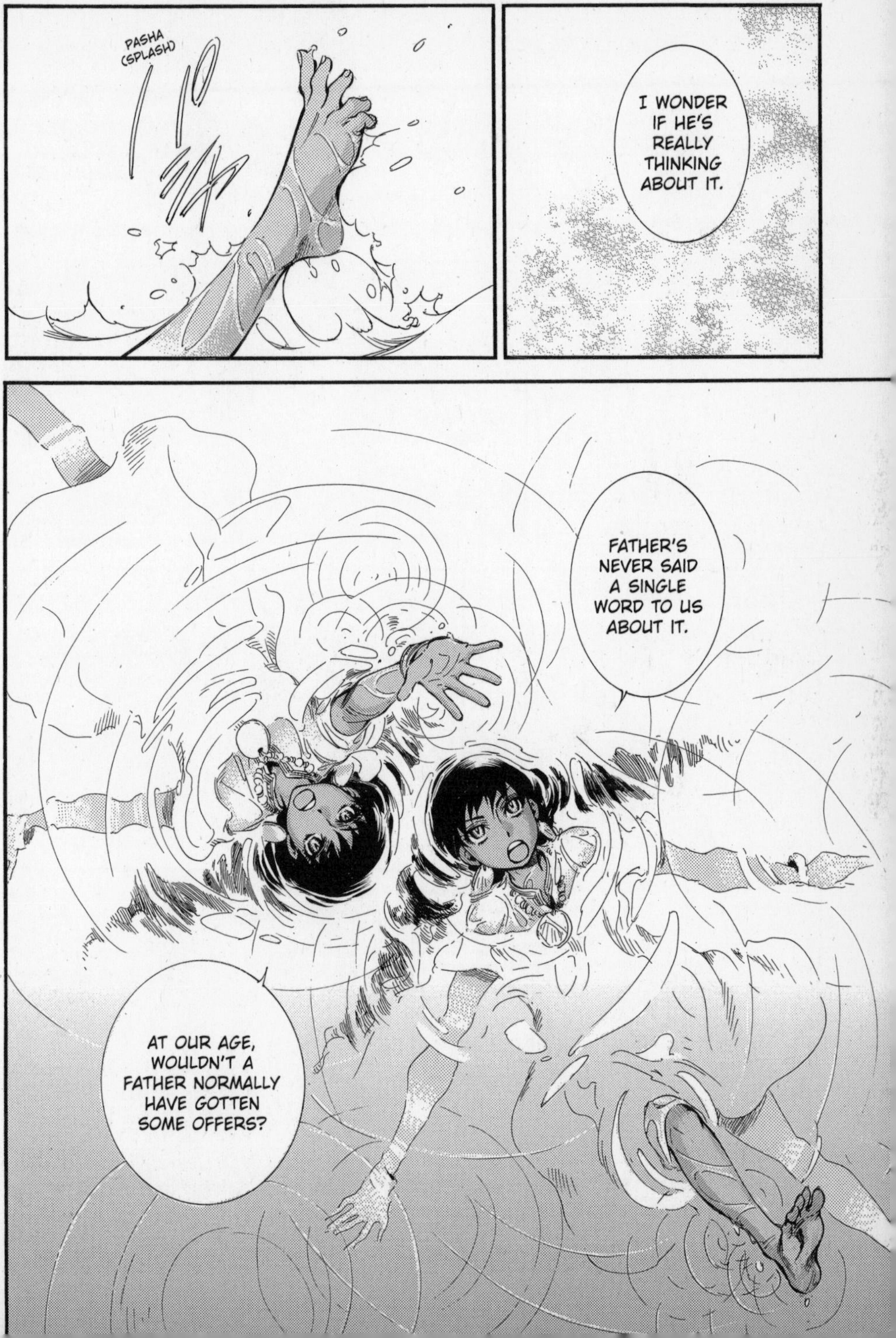
I WONDER IF HE'S REALLY THINKING ABOUT IT.
PASHA (SPLASH)
FATHER'S NEVER SAID A SINGLE WORD TO US ABOUT IT.
AT OUR AGE, WOULDN'T A FATHER NORMALLY HAVE GOTTEN SOME OFFERS?

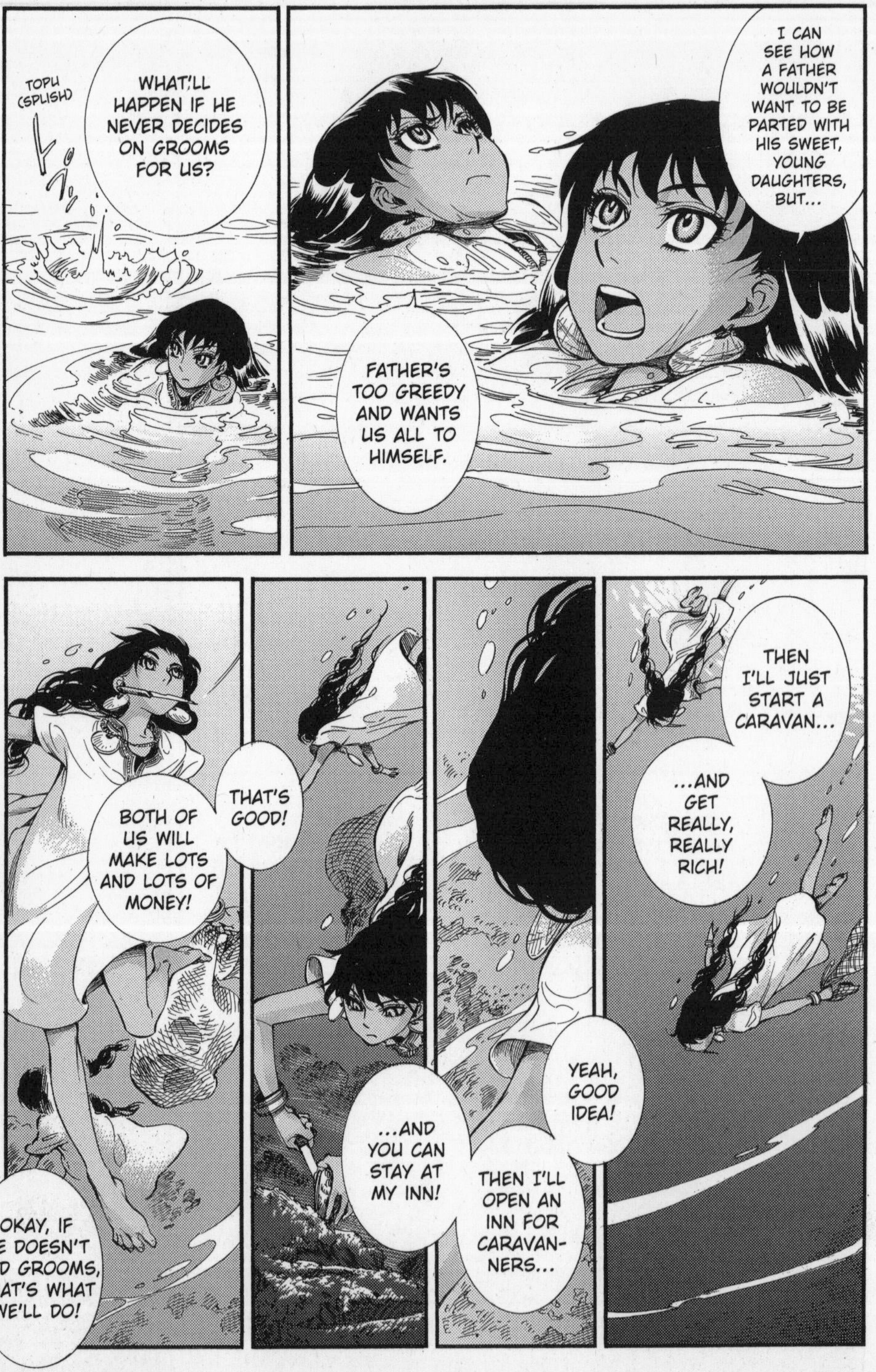
I CAN SEE HOW A FATHER WOULDN'T WANT TO BE PARTED WITH HIS SWEET, YOUNG DAUGHTERS, BUT...
FATHER'S TOO GREEDY AND WANTS US ALL TO HIMSELF.
WHAT'LL HAPPEN IF HE NEVER DECIDES ON GROOMS FOR US?
TOPU (SPLISH)
THEN I'LL JUST START A CARAVAN...
...AND GET REALLY, REALLY RICH!
YEAH, GOOD IDEA!
THEN I'LL OPEN AN INN FOR CARAVAN-NERS...
...AND YOU CAN STAY AT MY INN!
THAT'S GOOD!
BOTH OF US WILL MAKE LOTS AND LOTS OF MONEY!
OKAY, IF HE DOESN'T FIND GROOMS, THAT'S WHAT WE'LL DO!

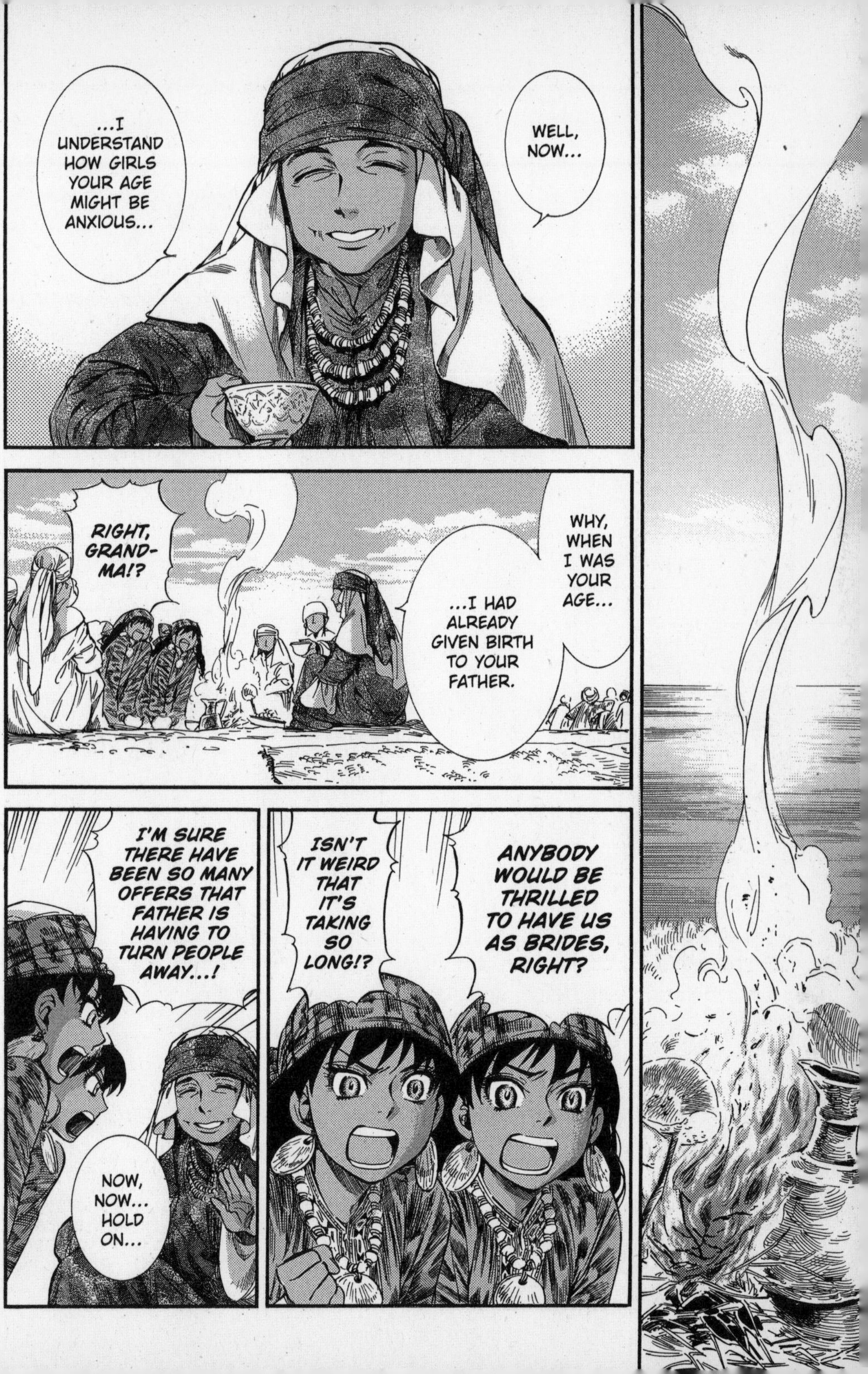
WELL, NOW...
...I UNDERSTAND HOW GIRLS YOUR AGE MIGHT BE ANXIOUS...
WHY, WHEN I WAS YOUR AGE...
...I HAD ALREADY GIVEN BIRTH TO YOUR FATHER.
RIGHT, GRANDMA!?
ANYBODY WOULD BE THRILLED TO HAVE US AS BRIDES, RIGHT?
ISN'T IT WEIRD THAT IT'S TAKING SO LONG!?
I'M SURE THERE HAVE BEEN SO MANY OFFERS THAT FATHER IS HAVING TO TURN PEOPLE AWAY...!
NOW, NOW... HOLD ON...

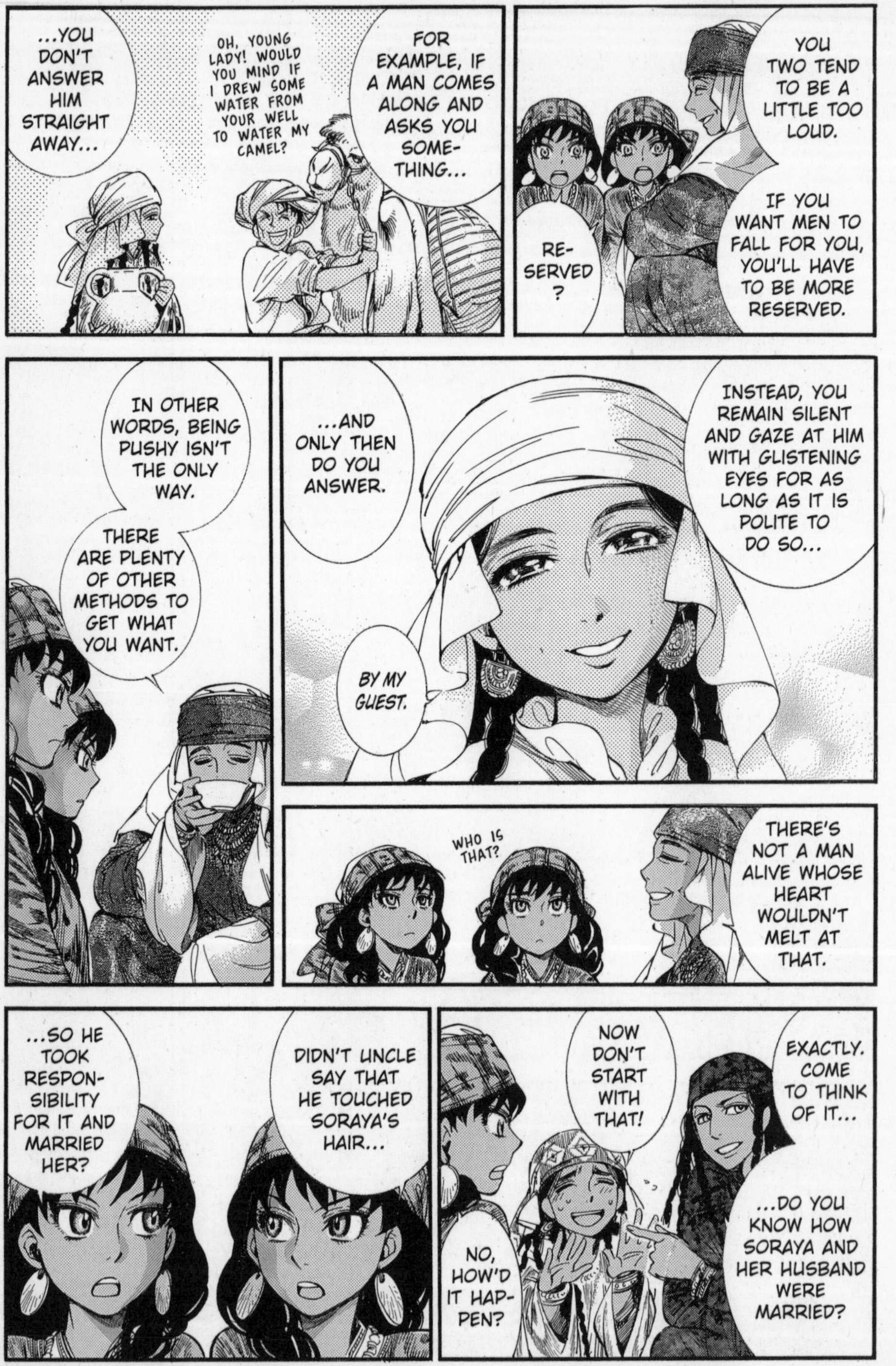
YOU TWO TEND TO BE A LITTLE TOO LOUD.
IF YOU WANT MEN TO FALL FOR YOU, YOU'LL HAVE TO BE MORE RESERVED.
RE-SERVED?
FOR EXAMPLE, IF A MAN COMES ALONG AND ASKS YOU SOME-THING...
OH, YOUNG LADY! WOULD YOU MIND IF I DREW SOME WATER FROM YOUR WELL TO WATER MY CAMEL?
...YOU DON'T ANSWER HIM STRAIGHT AWAY...
INSTEAD, YOU REMAIN SILENT AND GAZE AT HIM WITH GLISTENING EYES FOR AS LONG AS IT IS POLITE TO DO SO...
...AND ONLY THEN DO YOU ANSWER.
BY MY GUEST.
THERE'S NOT A MAN ALIVE WHOSE HEART WOULDN'T MELT AT THAT.
WHO IS THAT?
IN OTHER WORDS, BEING PUSHY ISN'T THE ONLY WAY.
THERE ARE PLENTY OF OTHER METHODS TO GET WHAT YOU WANT.
EXACTLY. COME TO THINK OF IT...
NOW DON'T START WITH THAT!
...DO YOU KNOW HOW SORAYA AND HER HUSBAND WERE MARRIED?
NO, HOW'D IT HAP-PEN?
DIDN'T UNCLE SAY THAT HE TOUCHED SORAYA'S HAIR...
...SO HE TOOK RESPON-SIBILITY FOR IT AND MARRIED HER?

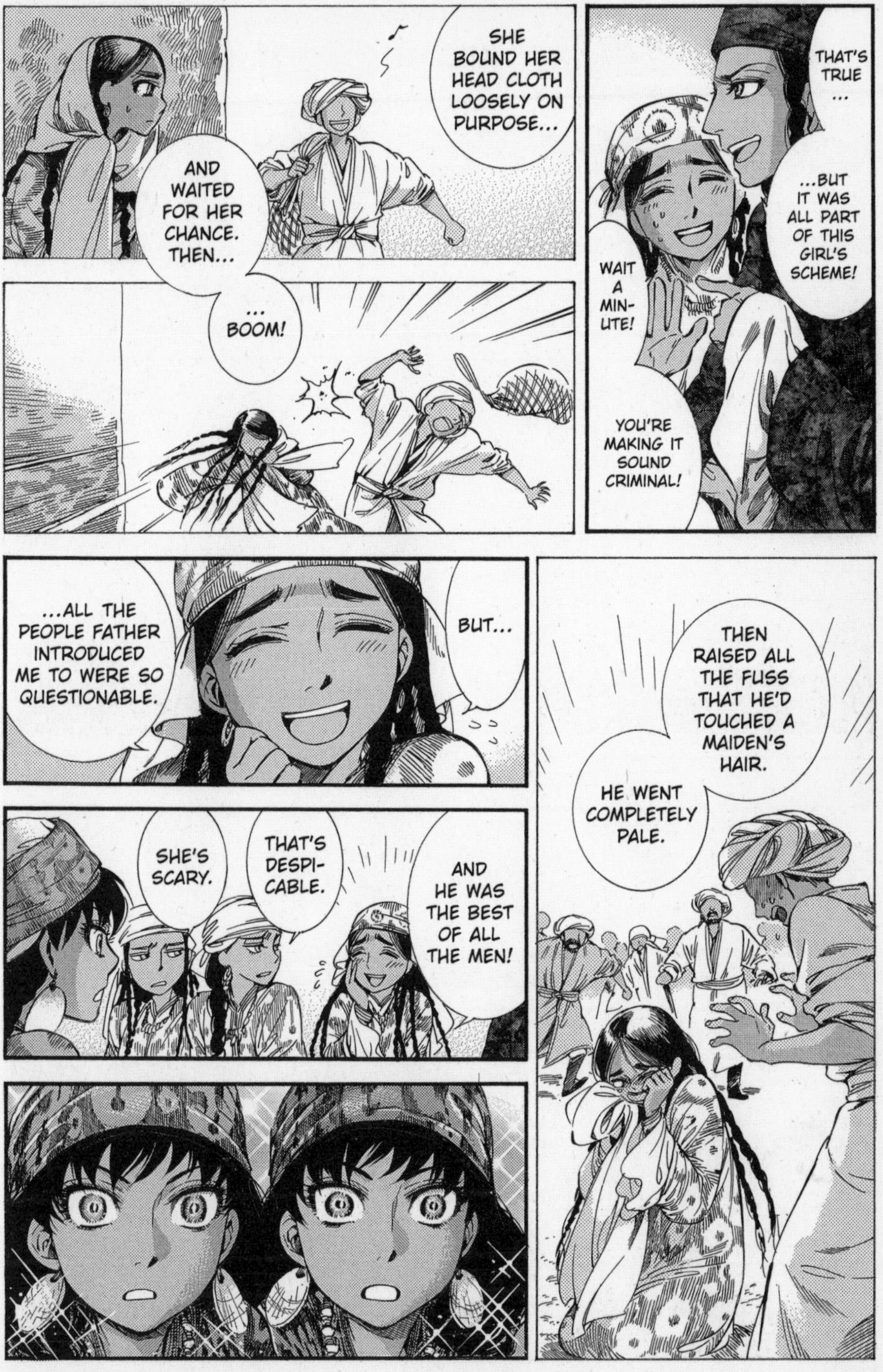
THAT'S TRUE ...
...BUT IT WAS ALL PART OF THIS GIRL'S SCHEME!
WAIT A MIN-UTE!
YOU'RE MAKING IT SOUND CRIMINAL!
SHE BOUND HER HEAD CLOTH LOOSELY ON PURPOSE...
AND WAITED FOR HER CHANCE. THEN...
... BOOM!
THEN RAISED ALL THE FUSS THAT HE'D TOUCHED A MAIDEN'S HAIR.
HE WENT COMPLETELY PALE.
BUT...
...ALL THE PEOPLE FATHER INTRODUCED ME TO WERE SO QUESTIONABLE.
AND HE WAS THE BEST OF ALL THE MEN!
THAT'S DESPI-CABLE.
SHE'S SCARY.

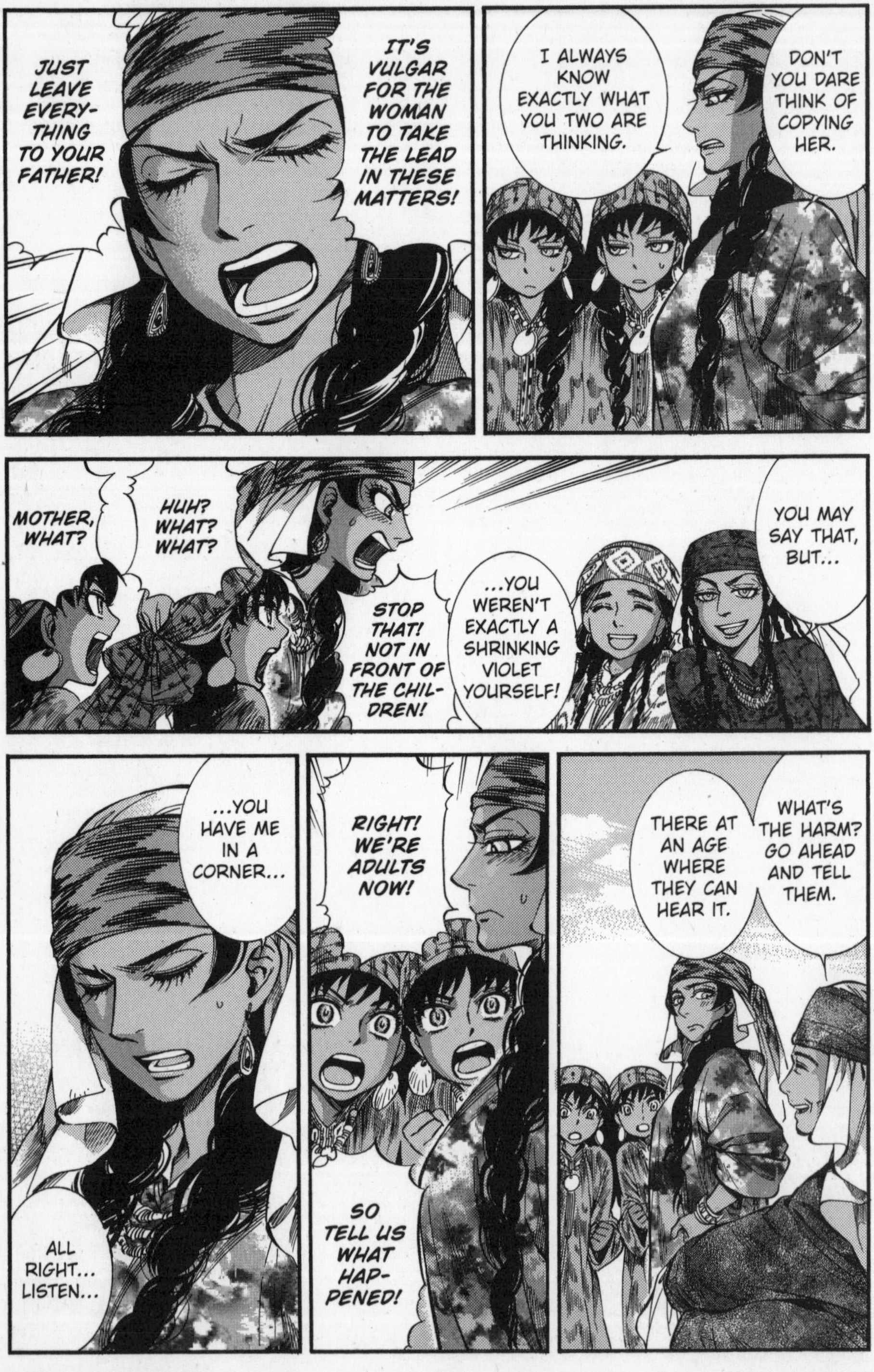

DON'T YOU DARE THINK OF COPYING HER.
I ALWAYS KNOW EXACTLY WHAT YOU TWO ARE THINKING.
IT'S VULGAR FOR THE WOMAN TO TAKE THE LEAD IN THESE MATTERS!
JUST LEAVE EVERYTHING TO YOUR FATHER!
YOU MAY SAY THAT, BUT...
...YOU WEREN'T EXACTLY A SHRINKING VIOLET YOURSELF!
STOP THAT! NOT IN FRONT OF THE CHILDREN!
HUH? WHAT? WHAT?
MOTHER, WHAT?
WHAT'S THE HARM? GO AHEAD AND TELL THEM.
THERE AT AN AGE WHERE THEY CAN HEAR IT.
RIGHT! WE'RE ADULTS NOW!
SO TELL US WHAT HAPPENED!
...YOU HAVE ME IN A CORNER...
ALL RIGHT... LISTEN...

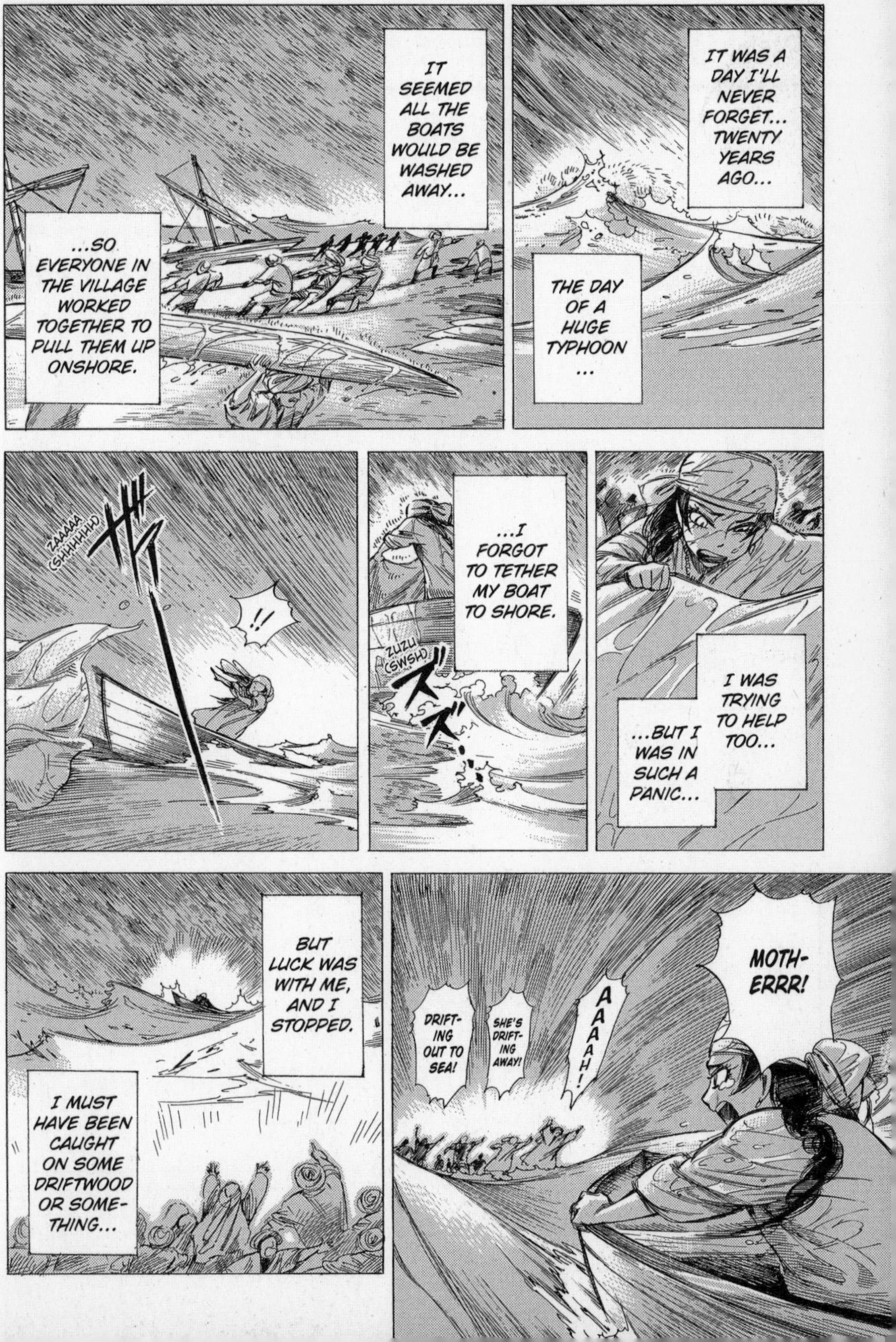
IT WAS A DAY I'LL NEVER FORGET... TWENTY YEARS AGO...
THE DAY OF A HUGE TYPHOON...
IT SEEMED ALL THE BOATS WOULD BE WASHED AWAY...
...SO EVERYONE IN THE VILLAGE WORKED TOGETHER TO PULL THEM UP ONSHORE.
I WAS TRYING TO HELP TOO...
...BUT I WAS IN SUCH A PANIC...
...I FORGOT TO TETHER MY BOAT TO SHORE.
ZUZU (SWSH)
ZAAAAA (SHHHHH)
!!
MOTH-ERRR!
AAAAAH!
SHE'S DRIFT-ING AWAY!
DRIFT-ING OUT TO SEA!
BUT LUCK WAS WITH ME, AND I STOPPED.
I MUST HAVE BEEN CAUGHT ON SOME DRIFTWOOD OR SOME-THING...

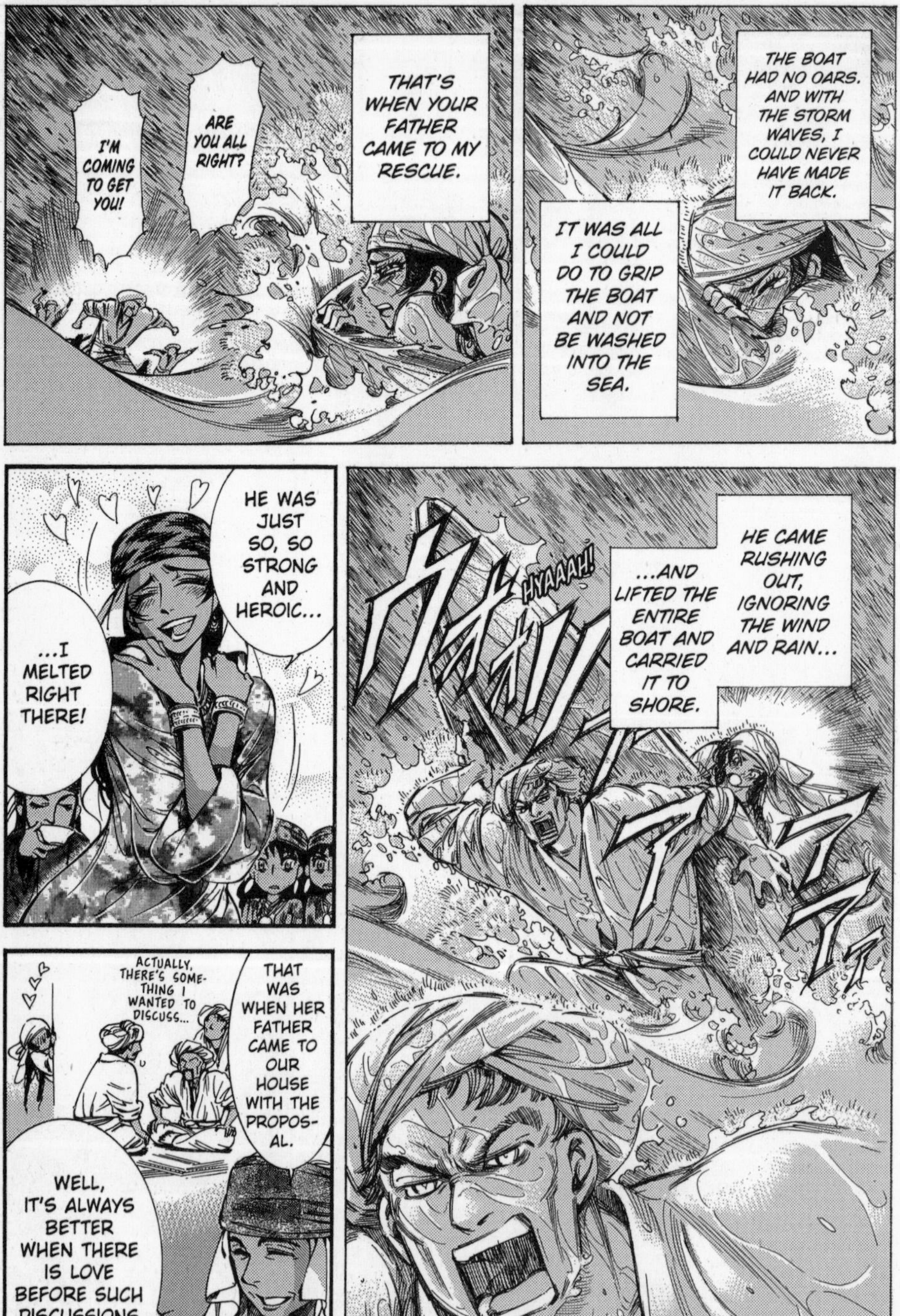
THE BOAT HAD NO OARS. AND WITH THE STORM WAVES, I COULD NEVER HAVE MADE IT BACK.
IT WAS ALL I COULD DO TO GRIP THE BOAT AND NOT BE WASHED INTO THE SEA.
THAT'S WHEN YOUR FATHER CAME TO MY RESCUE.
ARE YOU ALL RIGHT?
I'M COMING TO GET YOU!
HE CAME RUSHING OUT, IGNORING THE WIND AND RAIN...
...AND LIFTED THE ENTIRE BOAT AND CARRIED IT TO SHORE.
HYAAAH!
HE WAS JUST SO, SO STRONG AND HEROIC...
...I MELTED RIGHT THERE!
THAT WAS WHEN HER FATHER CAME TO OUR HOUSE WITH THE PROPOSAL.
ACTUALLY, THERE'S SOMETHING I WANTED TO DISCUSS...
WELL, IT'S ALWAYS BETTER WHEN THERE IS LOVE BEFORE SUCH DISCUSSIONS BEGIN.

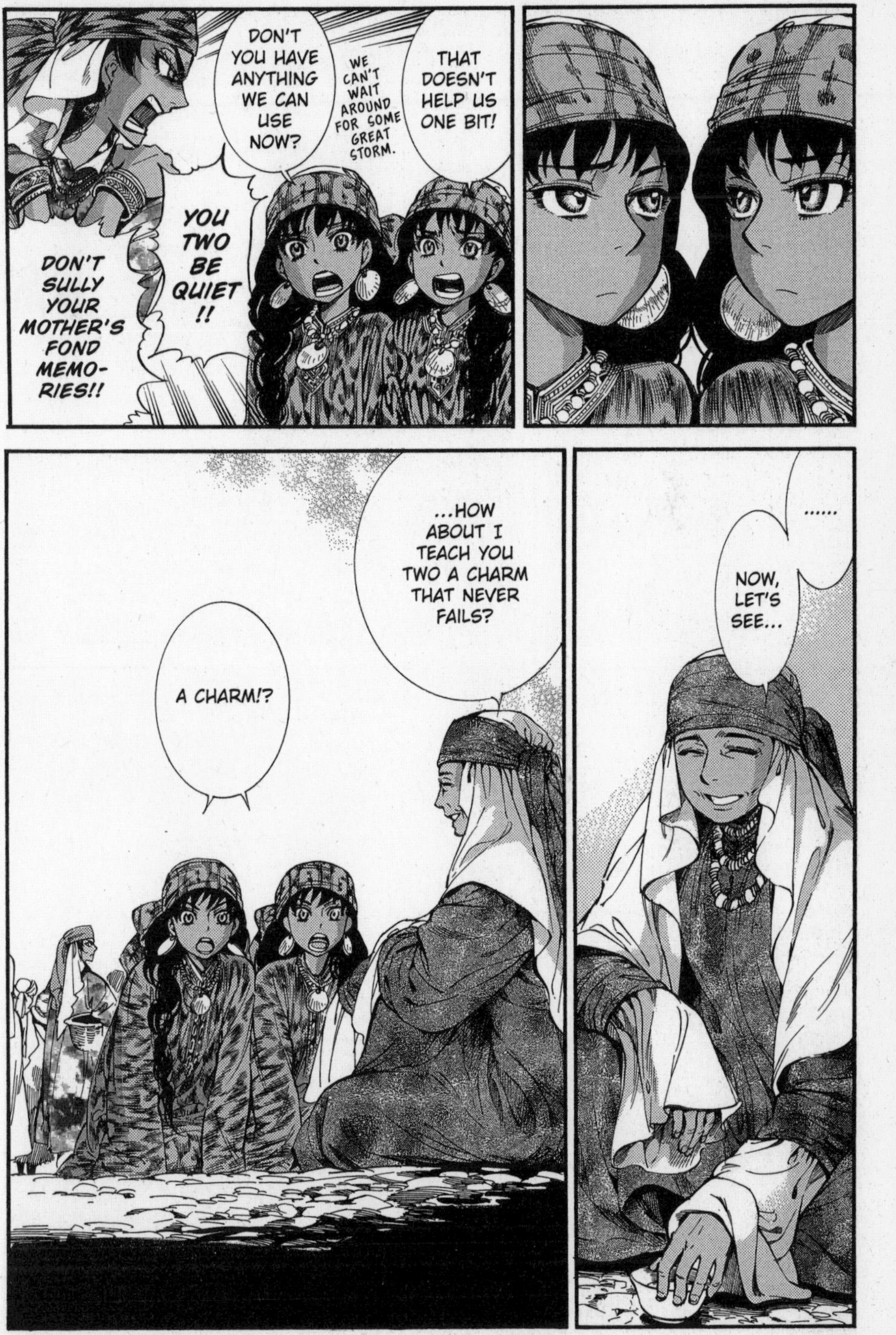

THAT DOESN'T HELP US ONE BIT!
WE CAN'T WAIT AROUND FOR SOME GREAT STORM.
DON'T YOU HAVE ANYTHING WE CAN USE NOW?
YOU TWO BE QUIET!!
DON'T SULLY YOUR MOTHER'S FOND MEMORIES!!
......
NOW, LET'S SEE...
...HOW ABOUT I TEACH YOU TWO A CHARM THAT NEVER FAILS?
A CHARM!?

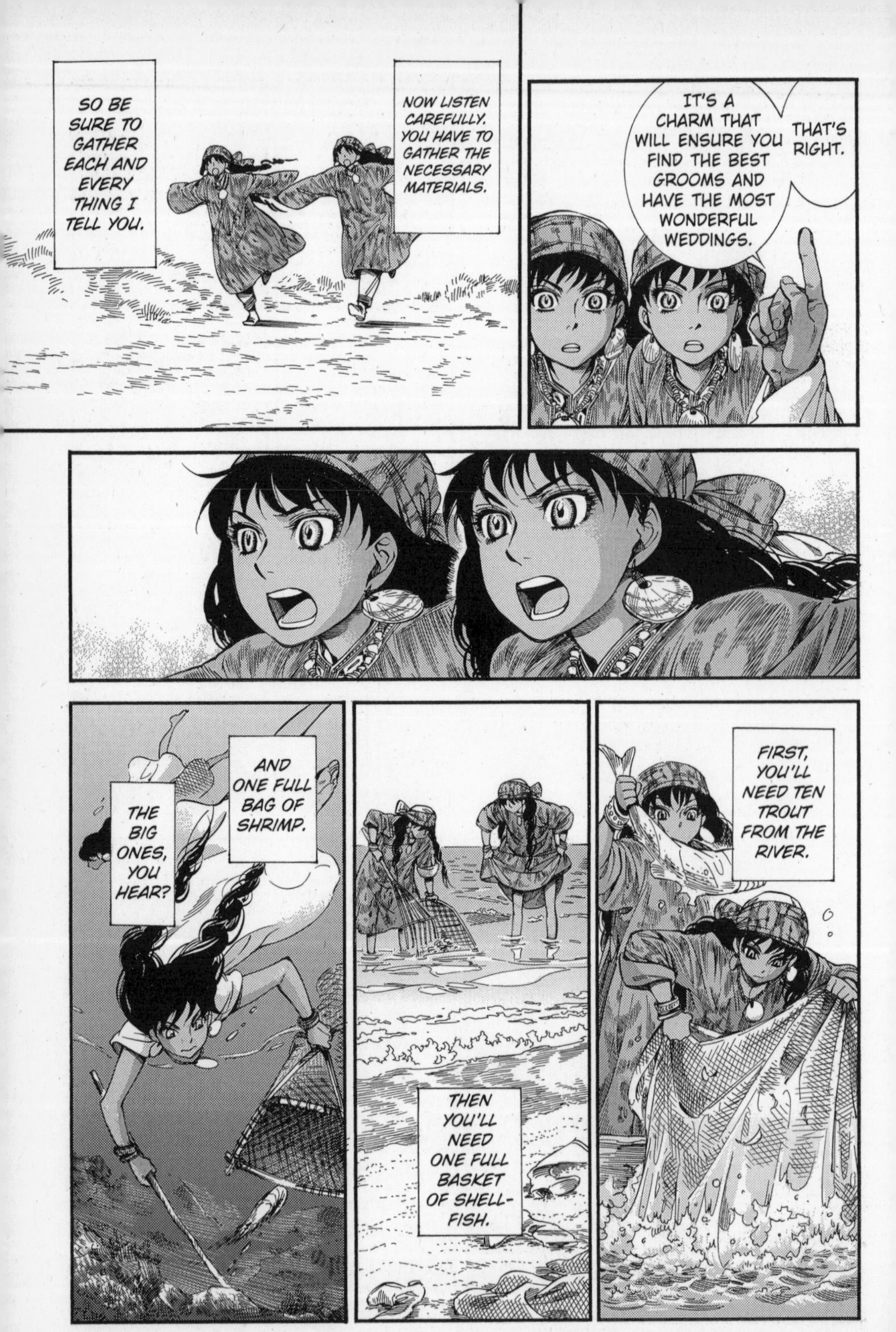
THAT'S RIGHT.
IT'S A CHARM THAT WILL ENSURE YOU FIND THE BEST GROOMS AND HAVE THE MOST WONDERFUL WEDDINGS.
NOW LISTEN CAREFULLY. YOU HAVE TO GATHER THE NECESSARY MATERIALS.
SO BE SURE TO GATHER EACH AND EVERY THING I TELL YOU.
FIRST, YOU'LL NEED TEN TROUT FROM THE RIVER.
THEN YOU'LL NEED ONE FULL BASKET OF SHELL-FISH.
AND ONE FULL BAG OF SHRIMP.
THE BIG ONES, YOU HEAR?

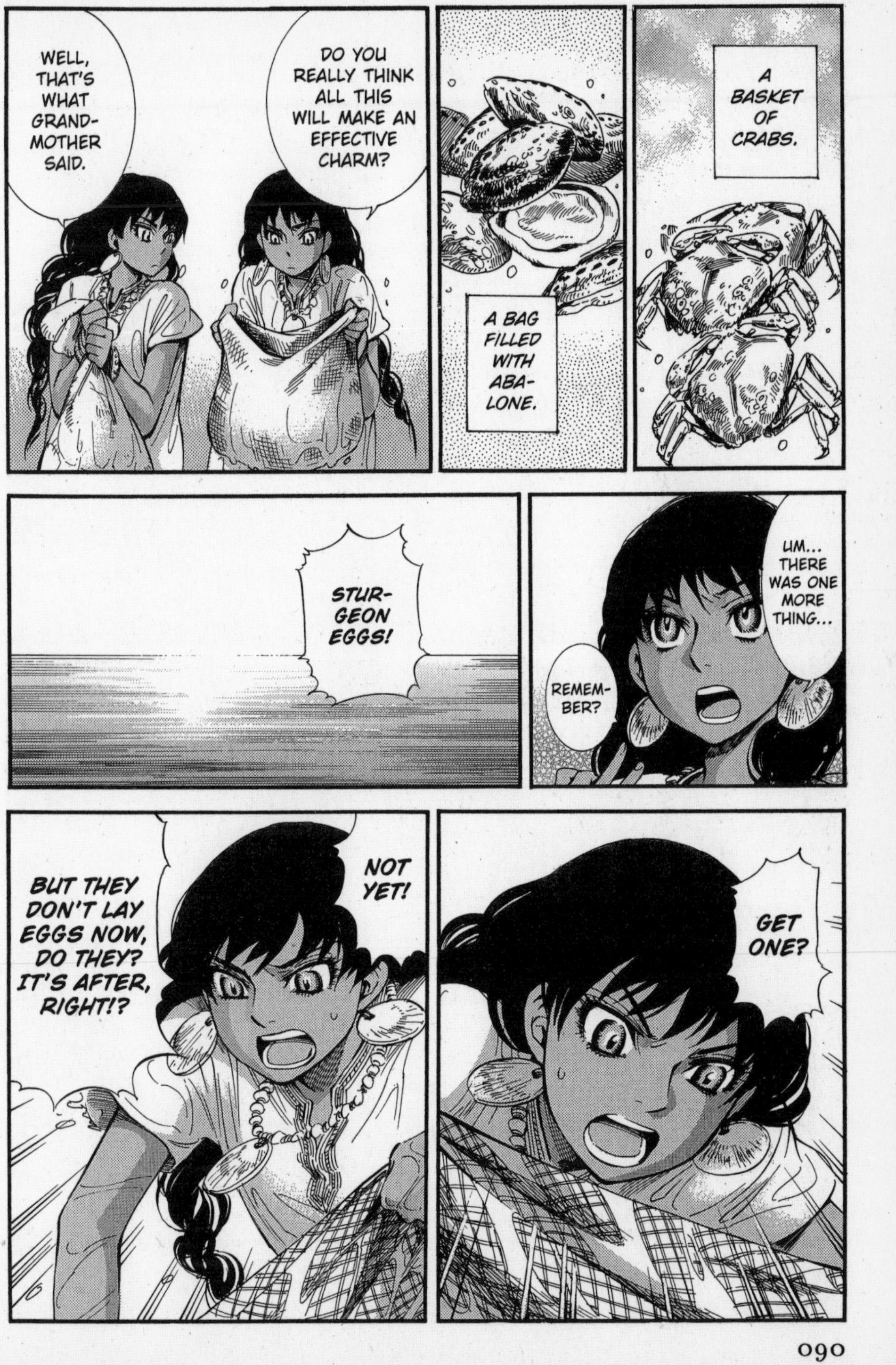
A BASKET OF CRABS.
A BAG FILLED WITH ABA-LONE.
DO YOU REALLY THINK ALL THIS WILL MAKE AN EFFECTIVE CHARM?
WELL, THAT'S WHAT GRAND-MOTHER SAID.
UM... THERE WAS ONE MORE THING...
REMEM-BER?
STUR-GEON EGGS!
GET ONE?
NOT YET!
BUT THEY DON'T LAY EGGS NOW, DO THEY? IT'S AFTER, RIGHT!?

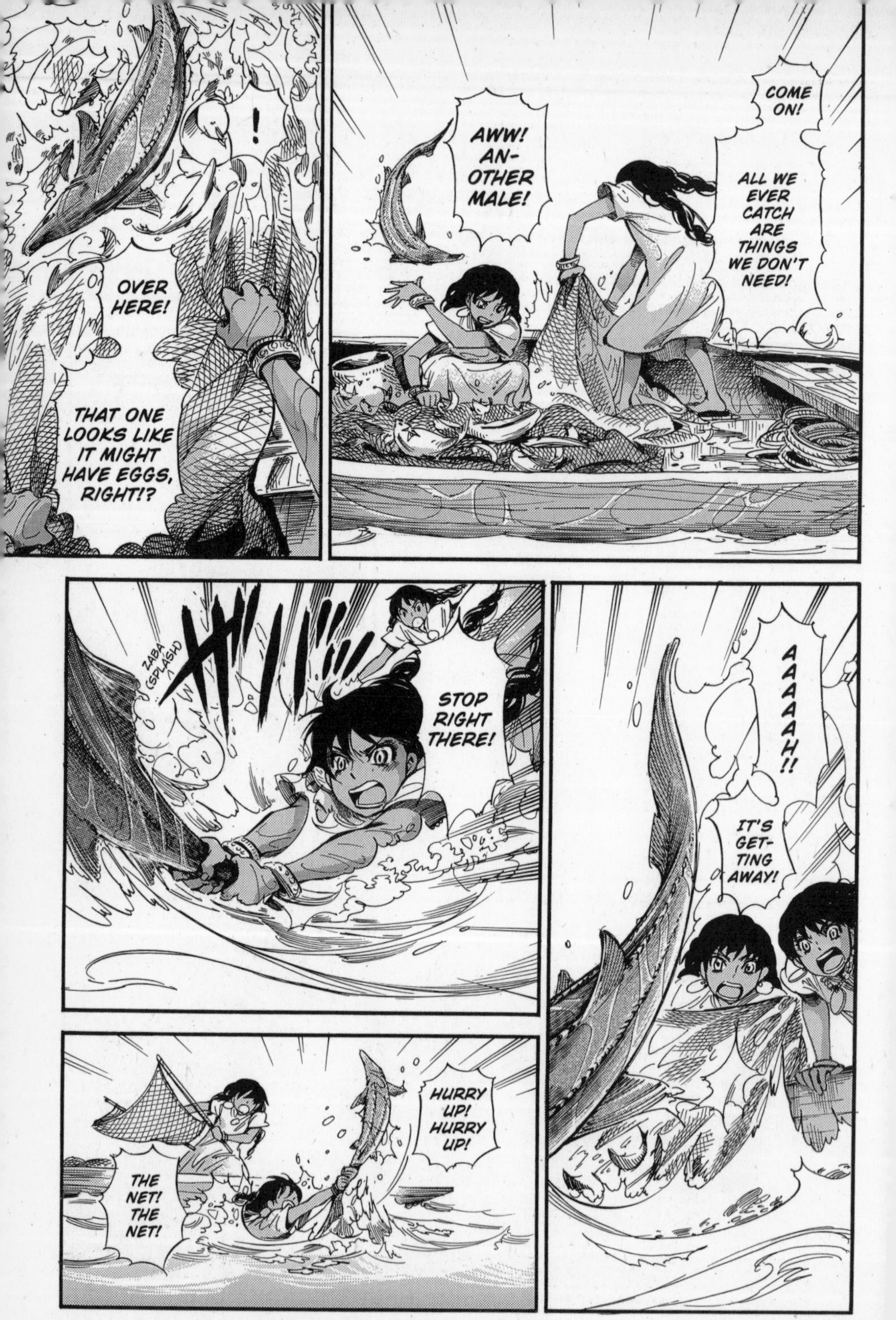

COME ON!
ALL WE EVER CATCH ARE THINGS WE DON'T NEED!
AWW! AN-OTHER MALE!
!
OVER HERE!
THAT ONE LOOKS LIKE IT MIGHT HAVE EGGS, RIGHT!?
AAAAAH!!
IT'S GET-TING AWAY!
STOP RIGHT THERE!
ZABA (SPLASH)
HURRY UP! HURRY UP!
THE NET! THE NET!

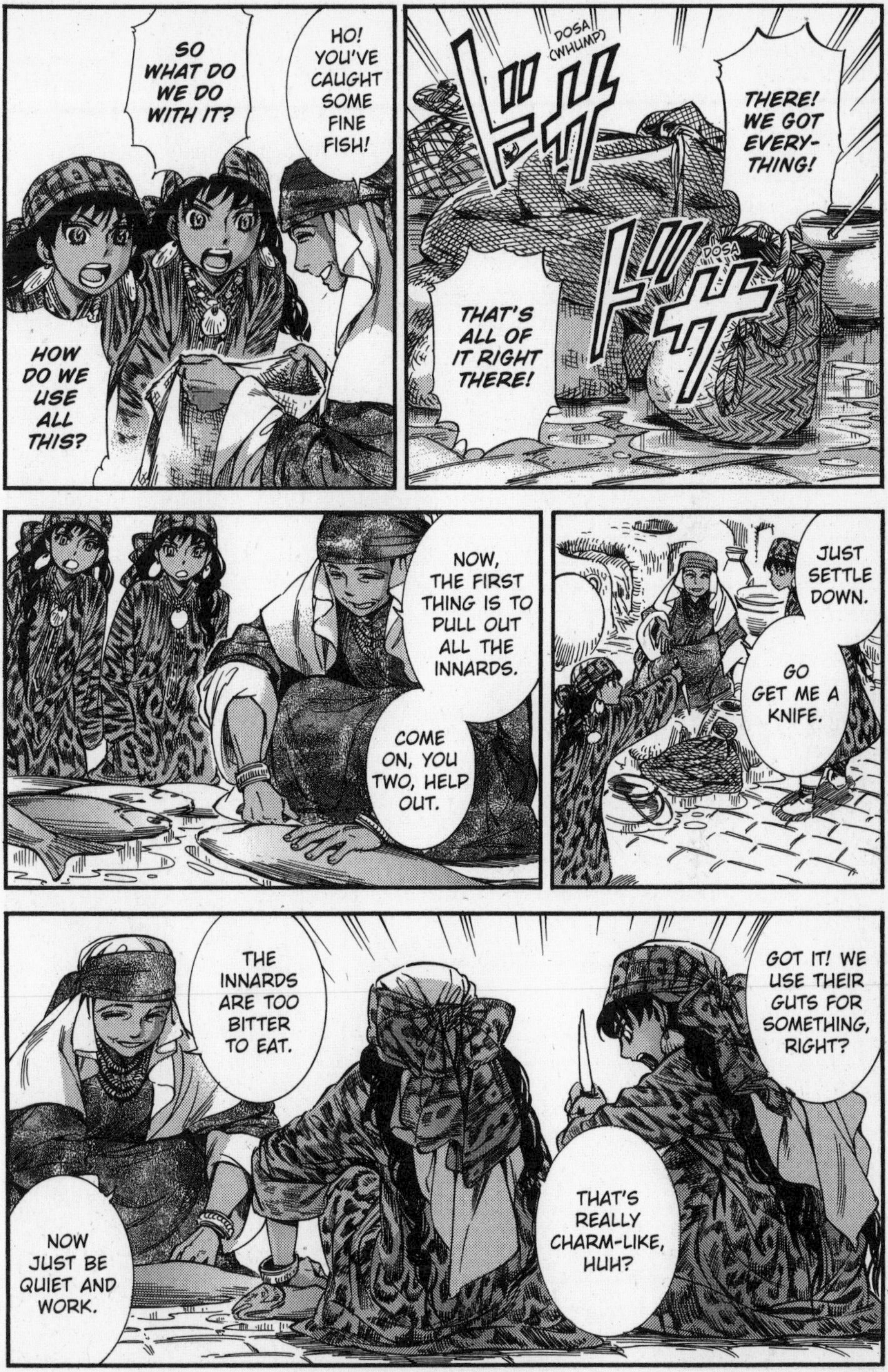
THERE! WE GOT EVERY-THING!
DOSA (WHUMP)
DOSA
THAT'S ALL OF IT RIGHT THERE!
HO! YOU'VE CAUGHT SOME FINE FISH!
SO WHAT DO WE DO WITH IT?
HOW DO WE USE ALL THIS?
JUST SETTLE DOWN.
GO GET ME A KNIFE.
NOW, THE FIRST THING IS TO PULL OUT ALL THE INNARDS.
COME ON, YOU TWO, HELP OUT.
GOT IT! WE USE THEIR GUTS FOR SOMETHING, RIGHT?
THE INNARDS ARE TOO BITTER TO EAT.
THAT'S REALLY CHARM-LIKE, HUH?
NOW JUST BE QUIET AND WORK.

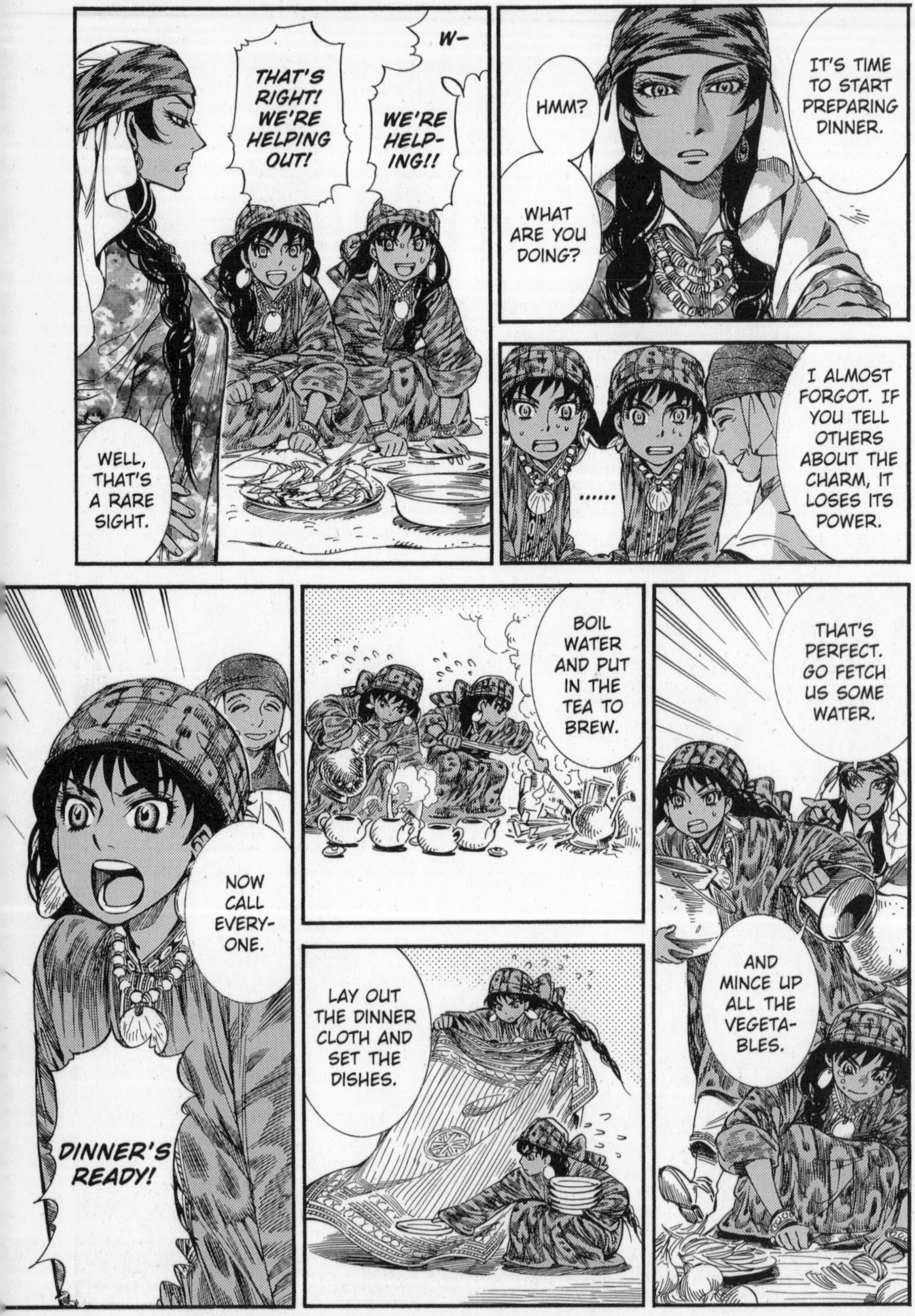
IT'S TIME TO START PREPARING DINNER.
HMM?
WHAT ARE YOU DOING?
I ALMOST FORGOT. IF YOU TELL OTHERS ABOUT THE CHARM, IT LOSES ITS POWER.
......
W-
WE'RE HELP-ING!!
THAT'S RIGHT! WE'RE HELPING OUT!
WELL, THAT'S A RARE SIGHT.
THAT'S PERFECT. GO FETCH US SOME WATER.
AND MINCE UP ALL THE VEGETA-BLES.
BOIL WATER AND PUT IN THE TEA TO BREW.
LAY OUT THE DINNER CLOTH AND SET THE DISHES.
NOW CALL EVERY-ONE.
DINNER'S READY!

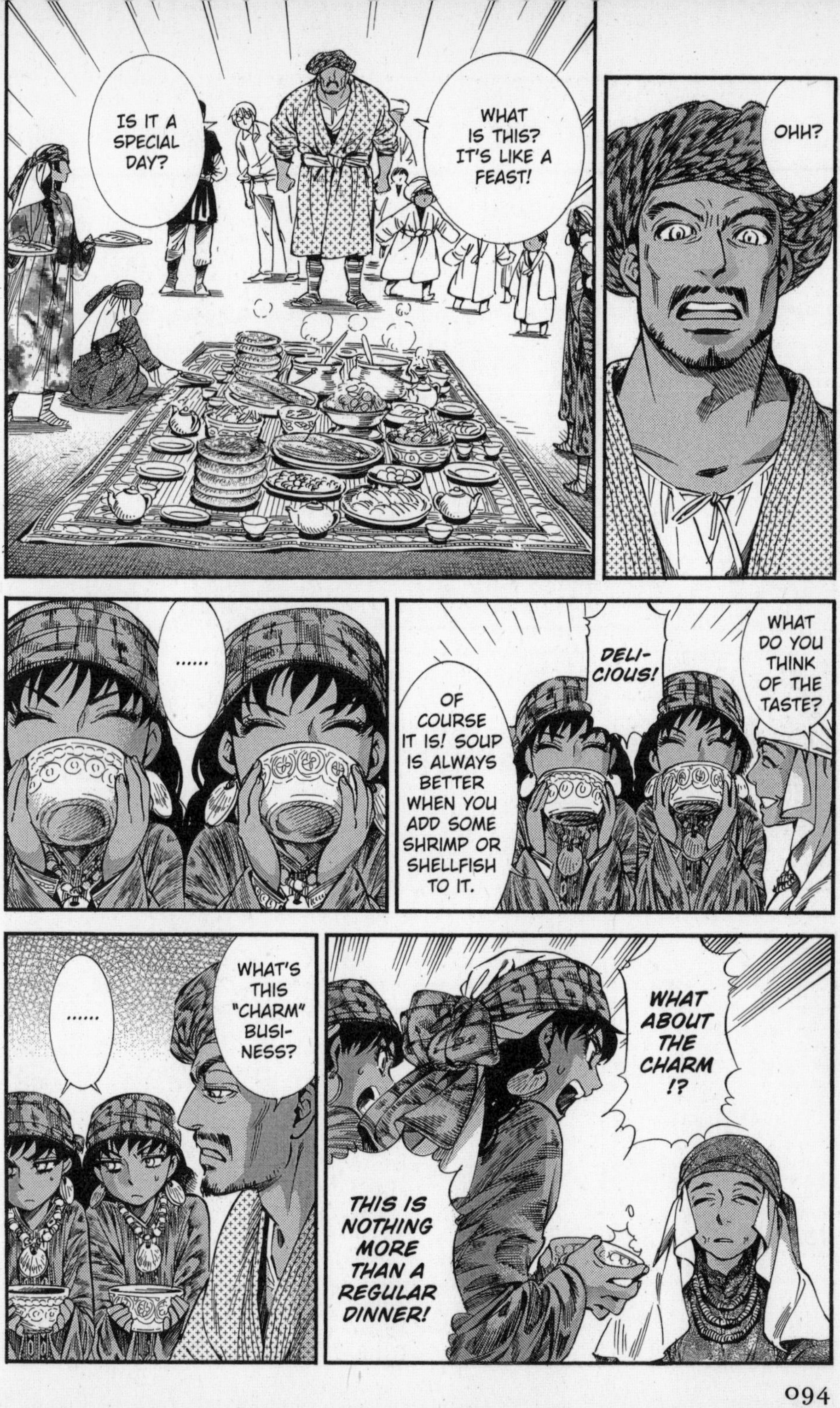
OHH?
WHAT IS THIS? IT'S LIKE A FEAST!
IS IT A SPECIAL DAY?
WHAT DO YOU THINK OF THE TASTE?
DELI-CIOUS!
OF COURSE IT IS! SOUP IS ALWAYS BETTER WHEN YOU ADD SOME SHRIMP OR SHELLFISH TO IT.
......
WHAT ABOUT THE CHARM !?
THIS IS NOTHING MORE THAN A REGULAR DINNER!
WHAT'S THIS "CHARM" BUSI-NESS?
......

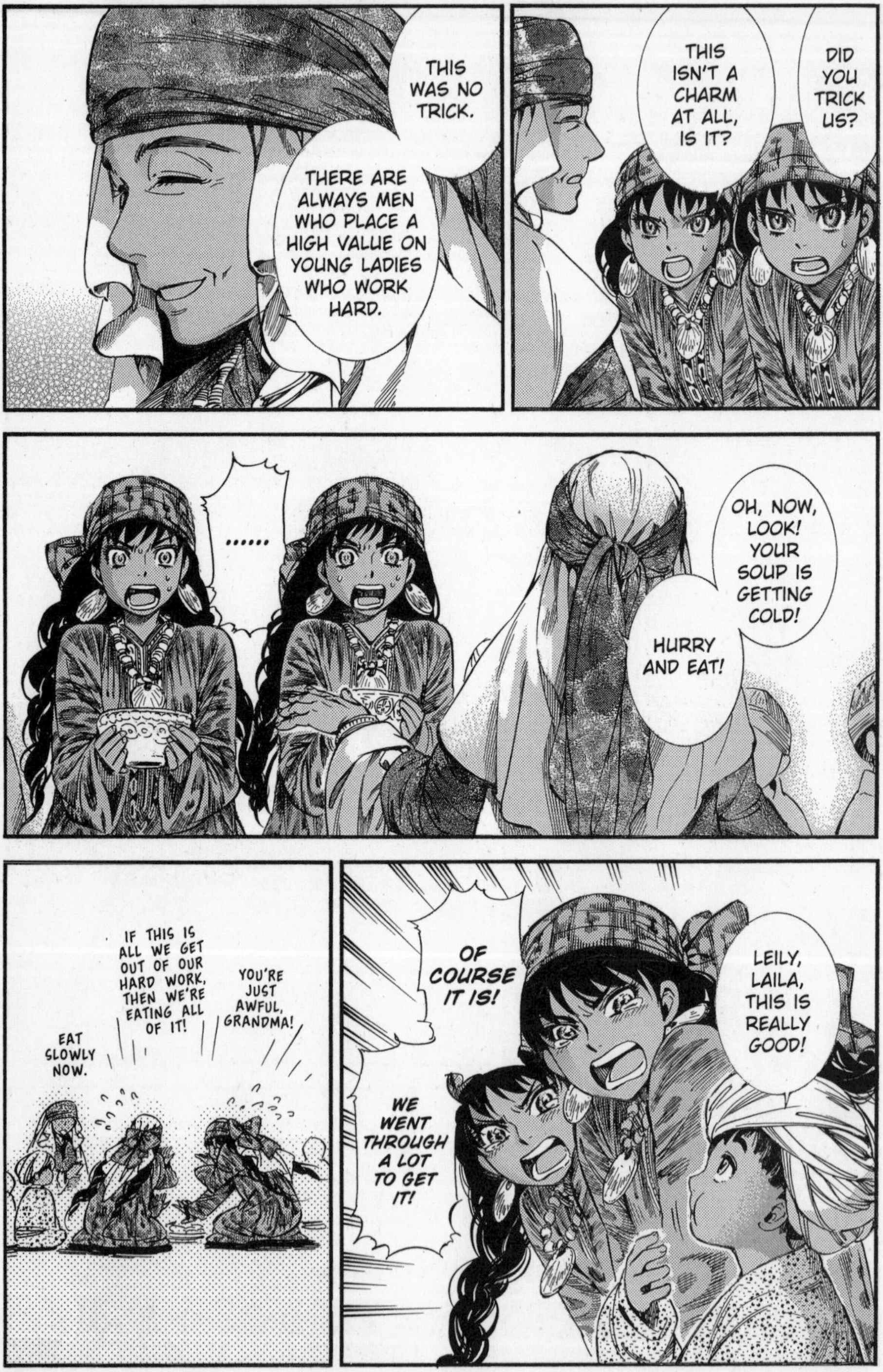
DID YOU TRICK US?
THIS ISN'T A CHARM AT ALL, IS IT?
THIS WAS NO TRICK.
THERE ARE ALWAYS MEN WHO PLACE A HIGH VALUE ON YOUNG LADIES WHO WORK HARD.
OH, NOW, LOOK! YOUR SOUP IS GETTING COLD!
HURRY AND EAT!
......
LEILY, LAILA, THIS IS REALLY GOOD!
OF COURSE IT IS!
WE WENT THROUGH A LOT TO GET IT!
YOU'RE JUST AWFUL, GRANDMA!
IF THIS IS ALL WE GET OUT OF OUR HARD WORK, THEN WE'RE EATING ALL OF IT!
EAT SLOWLY NOW.

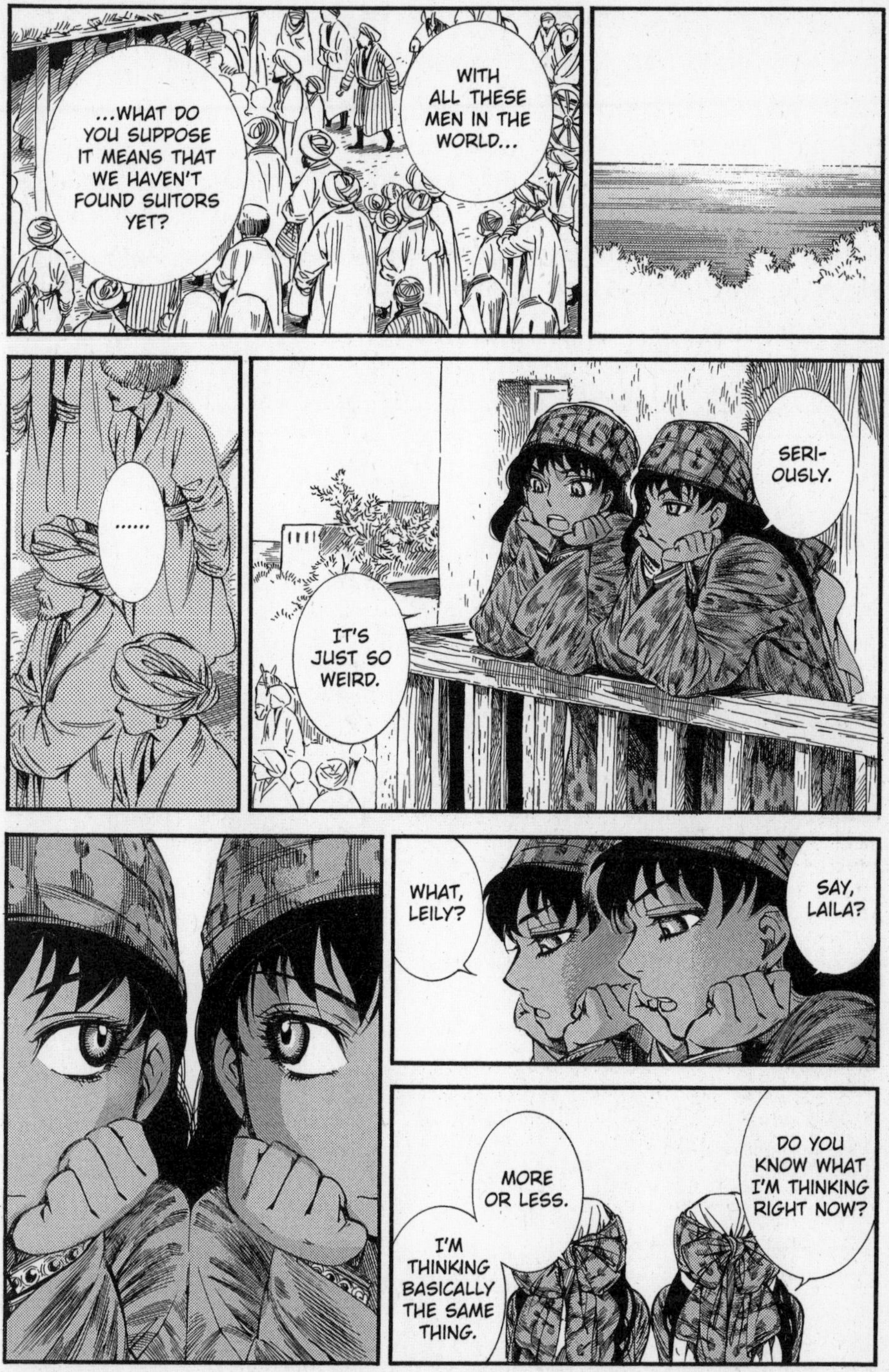
WITH ALL THESE MEN IN THE WORLD...
...WHAT DO YOU SUPPOSE IT MEANS THAT WE HAVEN'T FOUND SUITORS YET?
SERI-OUSLY.
IT'S JUST SO WEIRD.
......
SAY, LAILA?
WHAT, LEILY?
DO YOU KNOW WHAT I'M THINKING RIGHT NOW?
MORE OR LESS.
I'M THINKING BASICALLY THE SAME THING.

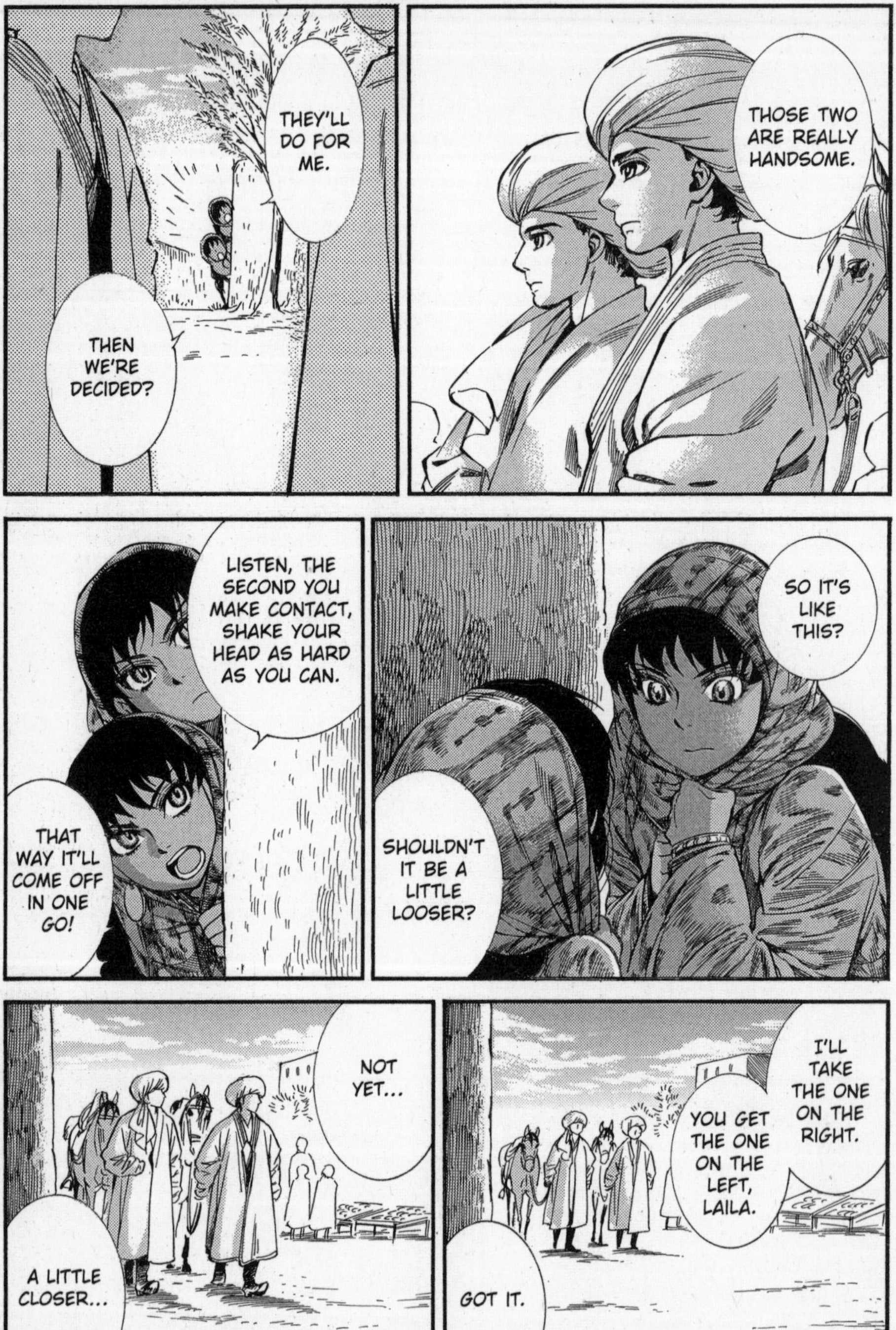
THOSE TWO ARE REALLY HANDSOME.
THEY'LL DO FOR ME.
THEN WE'RE DECIDED?
SO IT'S LIKE THIS?
SHOULDN'T IT BE A LITTLE LOOSER?
LISTEN, THE SECOND YOU MAKE CONTACT, SHAKE YOUR HEAD AS HARD AS YOU CAN.
THAT WAY IT'LL COME OFF IN ONE GO!
I'LL TAKE THE ONE ON THE RIGHT.
YOU GET THE ONE ON THE LEFT, LAILA.
GOT IT.
NOT YET...
A LITTLE CLOSER...

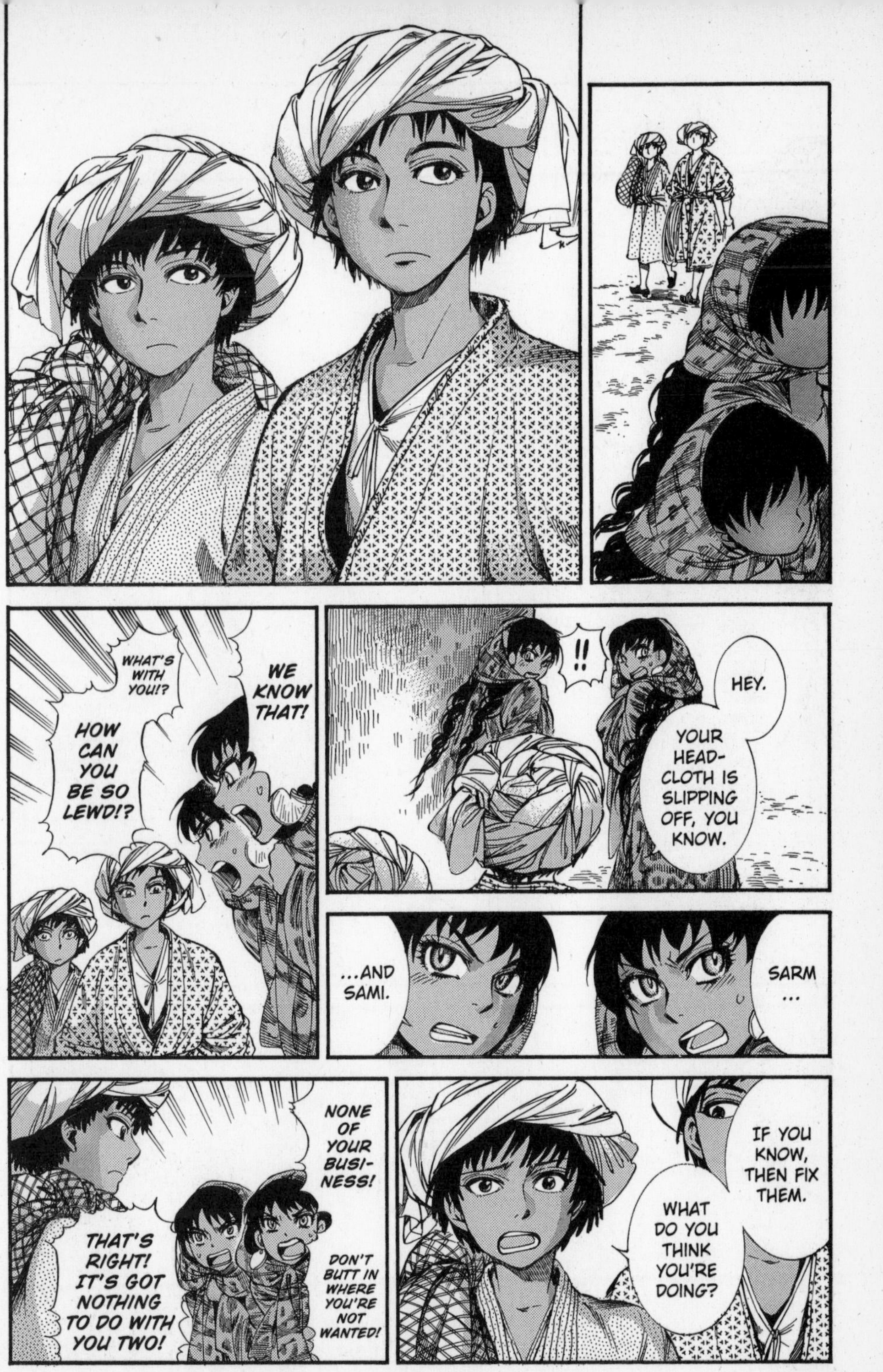

!!
HEY.
YOUR HEAD-CLOTH IS SLIPPING OFF, YOU KNOW.
SARM ...
...AND SAMI.
WE KNOW THAT!
WHAT'S WITH YOU!?
HOW CAN YOU BE SO LEWD!?
IF YOU KNOW, THEN FIX THEM.
WHAT DO YOU THINK YOU'RE DOING?
NONE OF YOUR BUSI-NESS!
DON'T BUTT IN WHERE YOU'RE NOT WANTED!
THAT'S RIGHT! IT'S GOT NOTHING TO DO WITH YOU TWO!

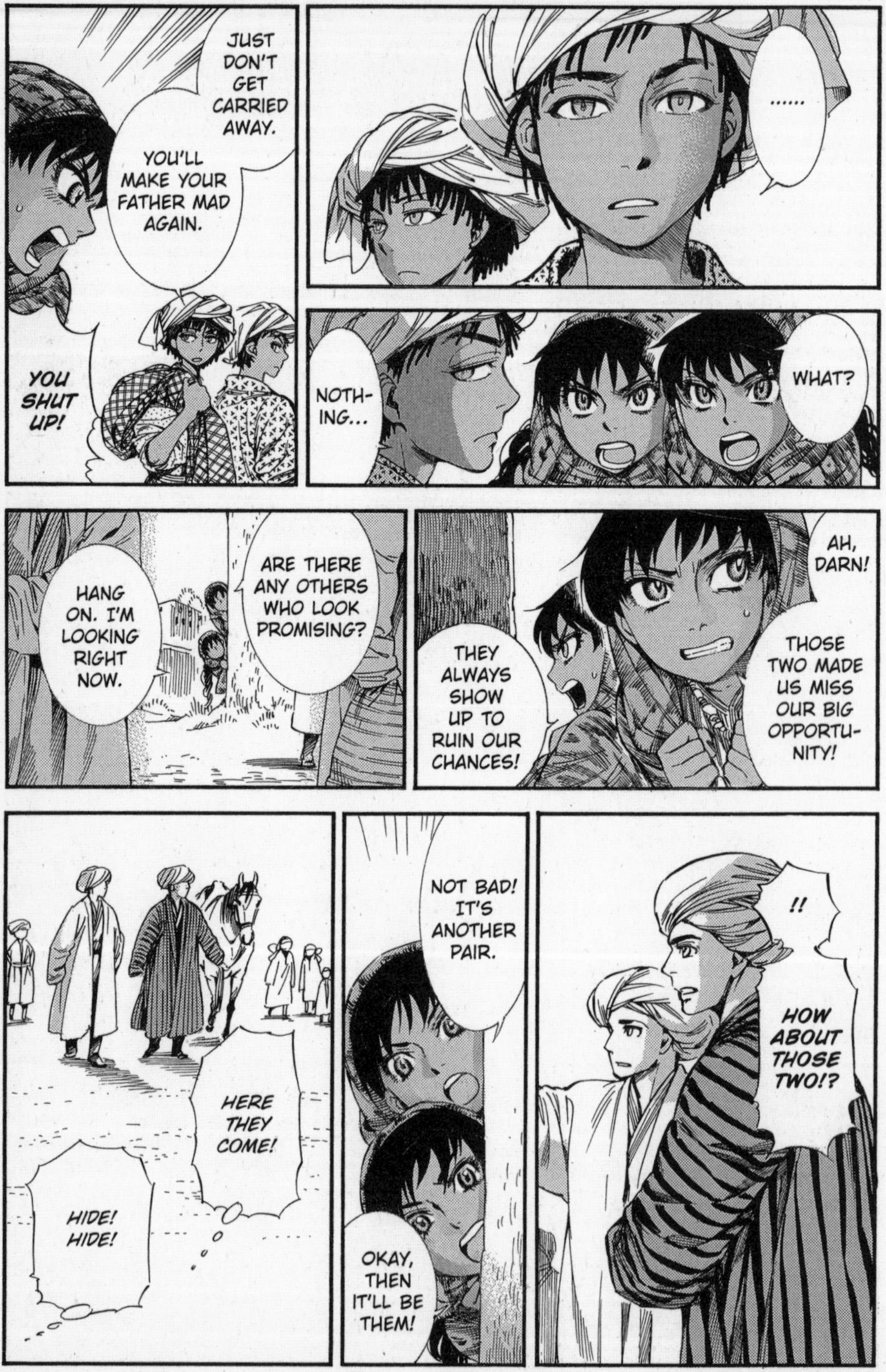
......
WHAT?
NOTHING...
JUST DON'T GET CARRIED AWAY.
YOU'LL MAKE YOUR FATHER MAD AGAIN.
YOU SHUT UP!
AH, DARN!
THOSE TWO MADE US MISS OUR BIG OPPORTUNITY!
THEY ALWAYS SHOW UP TO RUIN OUR CHANCES!
ARE THERE ANY OTHERS WHO LOOK PROMISING?
HANG ON. I'M LOOKING RIGHT NOW.
!!
HOW ABOUT THOSE TWO!?
NOT BAD! IT'S ANOTHER PAIR.
OKAY, THEN IT'LL BE THEM!
HERE THEY COME!
HIDE! HIDE!

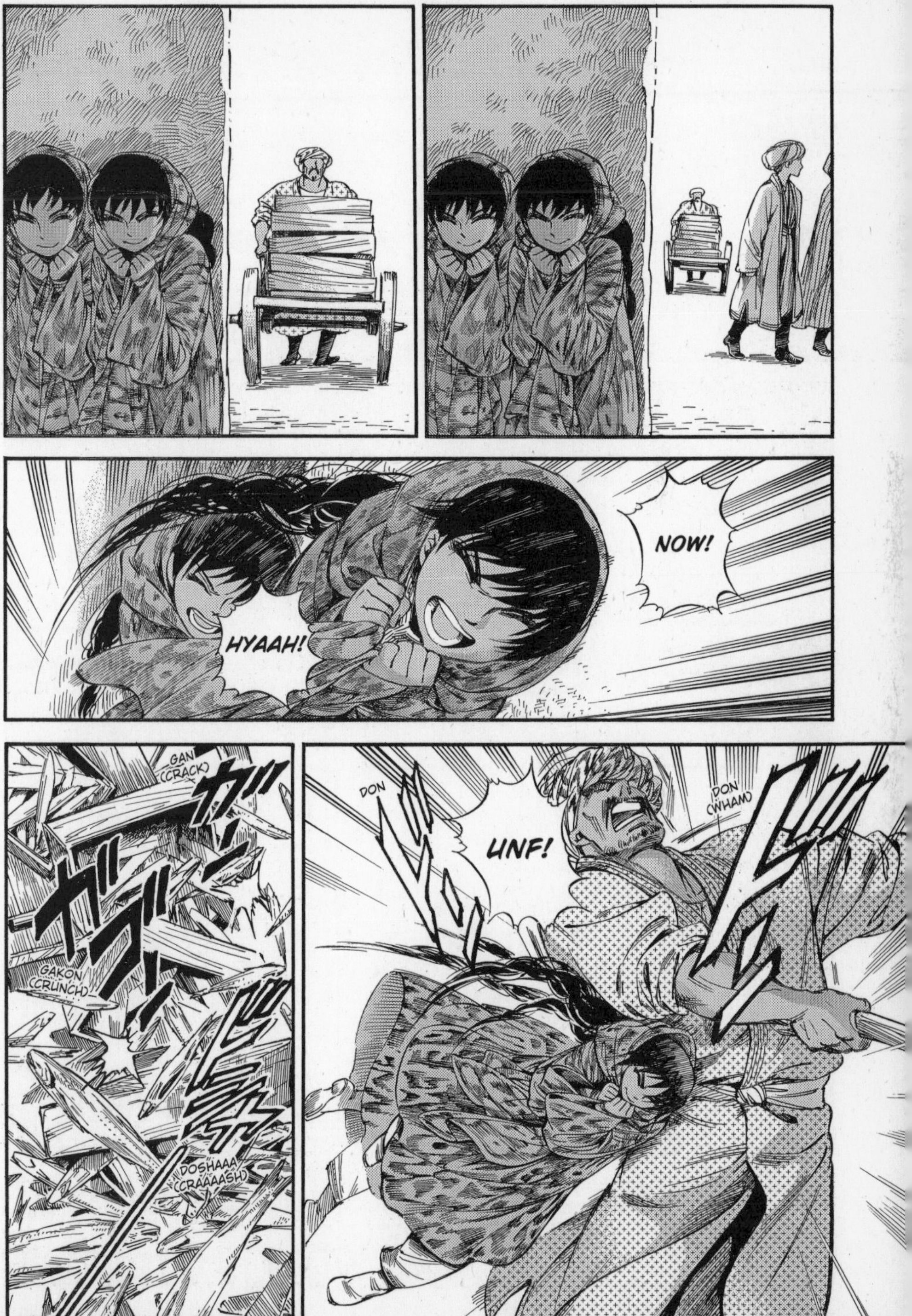
NOW!
HYAAH!
DON (WHAM)
DON
UNF!
GAN (CRACK)
GAKON (CRUNCH)
DOSHAAA (CRAAAASH)

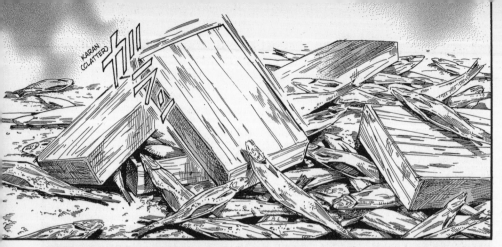

KARAN
(CLATTER)

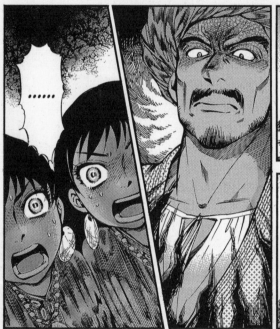

......

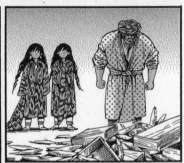

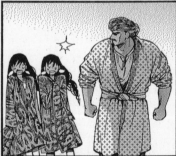

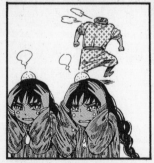

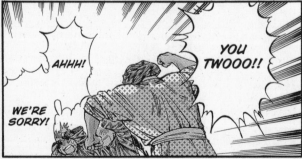

AHHH!

WE'RE
SORRY!

YOU
TWOOO!!

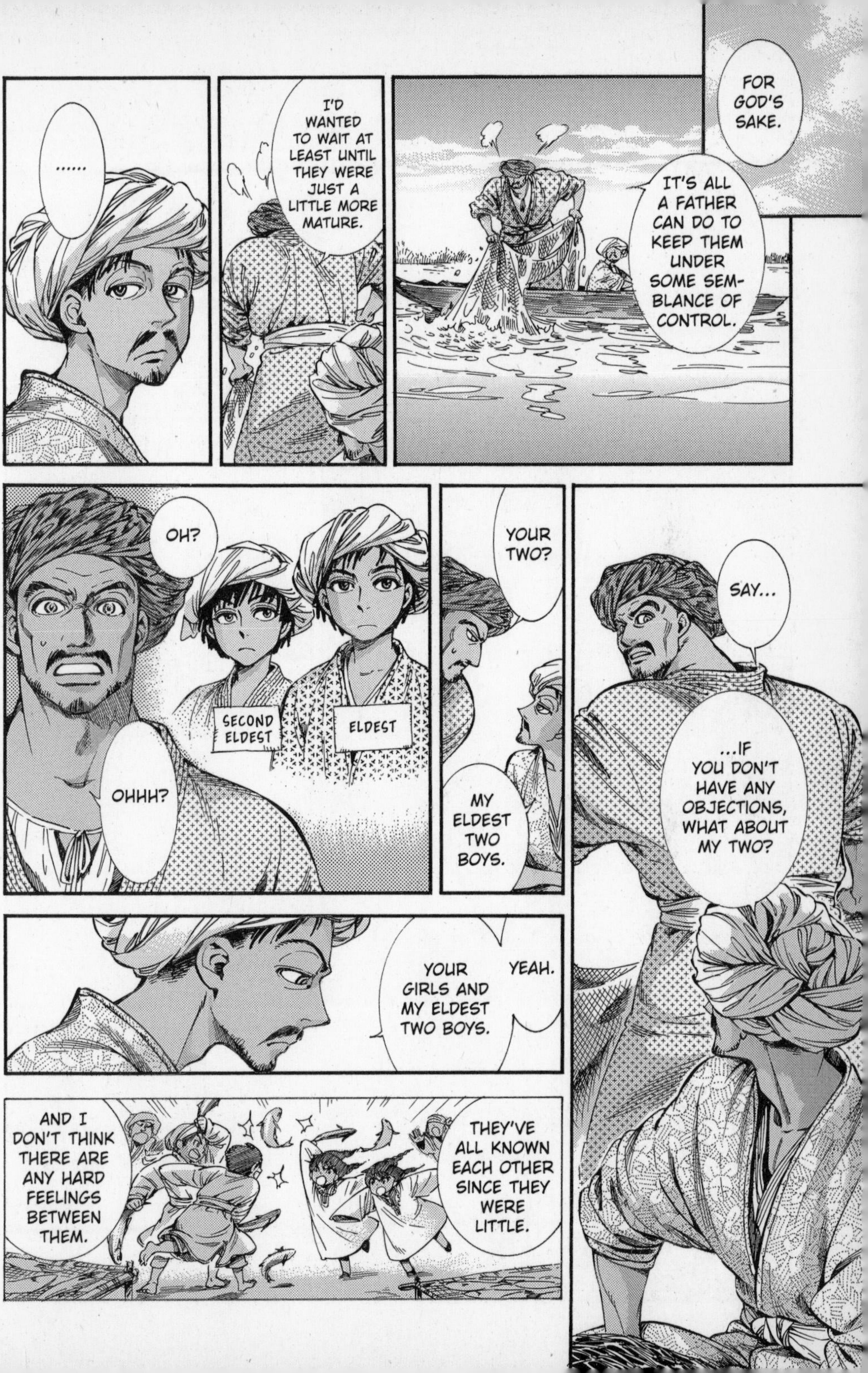
FOR GOD'S SAKE.
IT'S ALL A FATHER CAN DO TO KEEP THEM UNDER SOME SEM-BLANCE OF CONTROL.
I'D WANTED TO WAIT AT LEAST UNTIL THEY WERE JUST A LITTLE MORE MATURE.
......
SAY...
...IF YOU DON'T HAVE ANY OBJECTIONS, WHAT ABOUT MY TWO?
YOUR TWO?
MY ELDEST TWO BOYS.
OH?
ELDEST
SECOND ELDEST
OHHH?
YEAH.
YOUR GIRLS AND MY ELDEST TWO BOYS.
THEY'VE ALL KNOWN EACH OTHER SINCE THEY WERE LITTLE.
AND I DON'T THINK THERE ARE ANY HARD FEELINGS BETWEEN THEM.

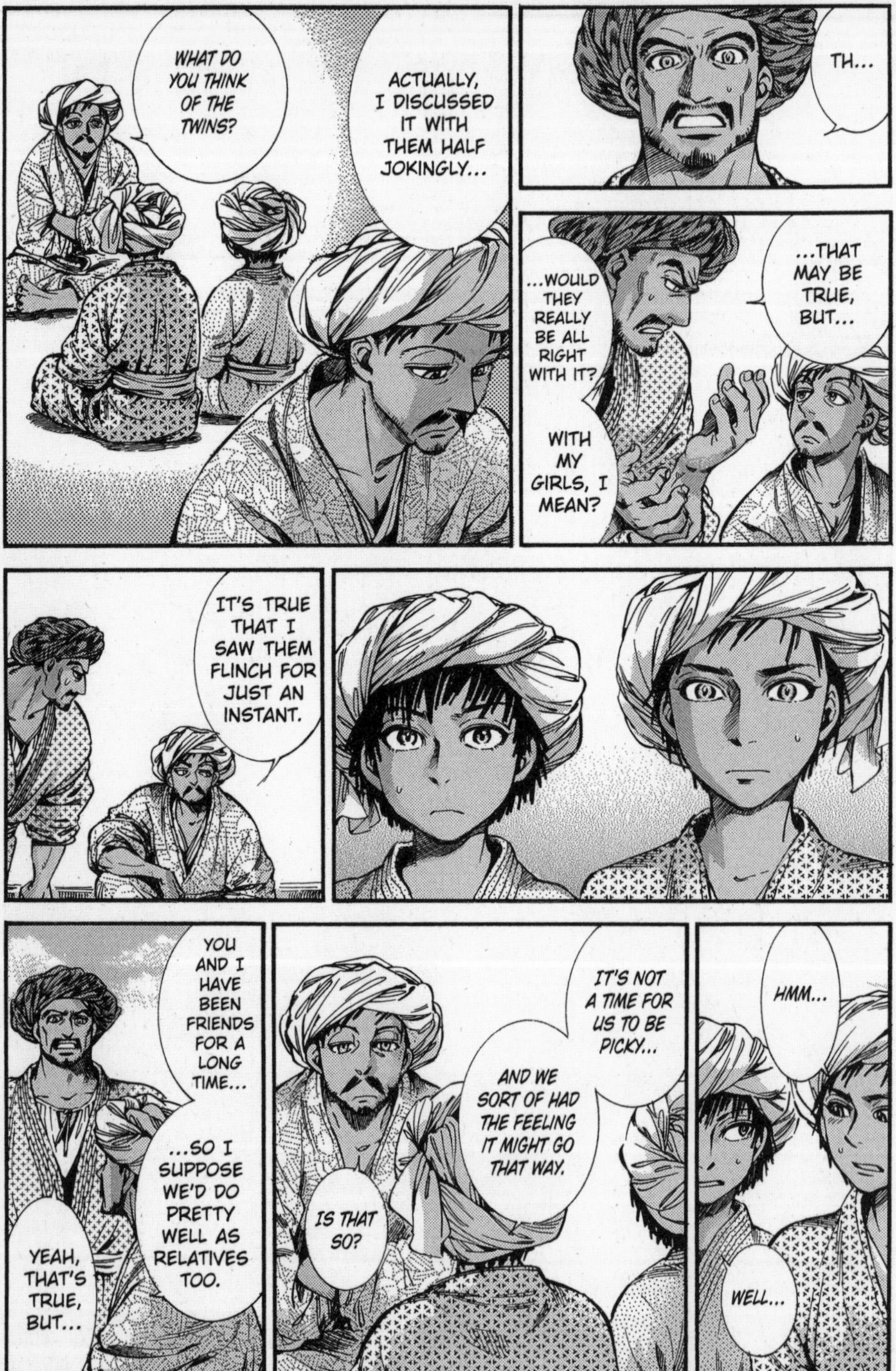
TH...
...THAT MAY BE TRUE, BUT...
...WOULD THEY REALLY BE ALL RIGHT WITH IT?
WITH MY GIRLS, I MEAN?
ACTUALLY, I DISCUSSED IT WITH THEM HALF JOKINGLY...
WHAT DO YOU THINK OF THE TWINS?
IT'S TRUE THAT I SAW THEM FLINCH FOR JUST AN INSTANT.
HMM...
WELL...
IT'S NOT A TIME FOR US TO BE PICKY...
AND WE SORT OF HAD THE FEELING IT MIGHT GO THAT WAY.
IS THAT SO?
YOU AND I HAVE BEEN FRIENDS FOR A LONG TIME...
...SO I SUPPOSE WE'D DO PRETTY WELL AS RELATIVES TOO.
YEAH, THAT'S TRUE, BUT...

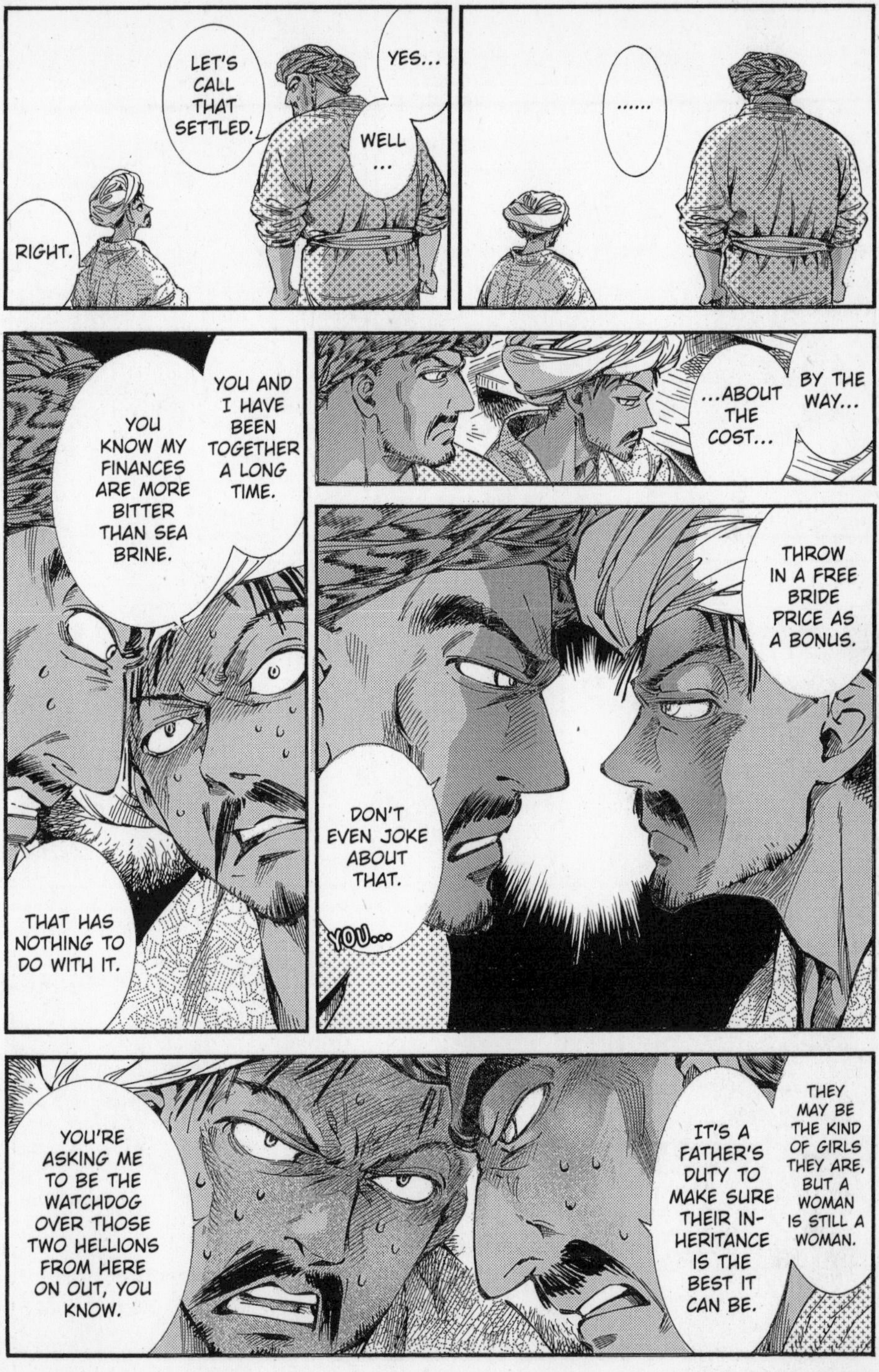
......
YES...
WELL ...
LET'S CALL THAT SETTLED.
RIGHT.
BY THE WAY...
...ABOUT THE COST...
THROW IN A FREE BRIDE PRICE AS A BONUS.
DON'T EVEN JOKE ABOUT THAT.
YOU...
YOU AND I HAVE BEEN TOGETHER A LONG TIME.
YOU KNOW MY FINANCES ARE MORE BITTER THAN SEA BRINE.
THAT HAS NOTHING TO DO WITH IT.
THEY MAY BE THE KIND OF GIRLS THEY ARE, BUT A WOMAN IS STILL A WOMAN.
IT'S A FATHER'S DUTY TO MAKE SURE THEIR IN-HERITANCE IS THE BEST IT CAN BE.
YOU'RE ASKING ME TO BE THE WATCHDOG OVER THOSE TWO HELLIONS FROM HERE ON OUT, YOU KNOW.

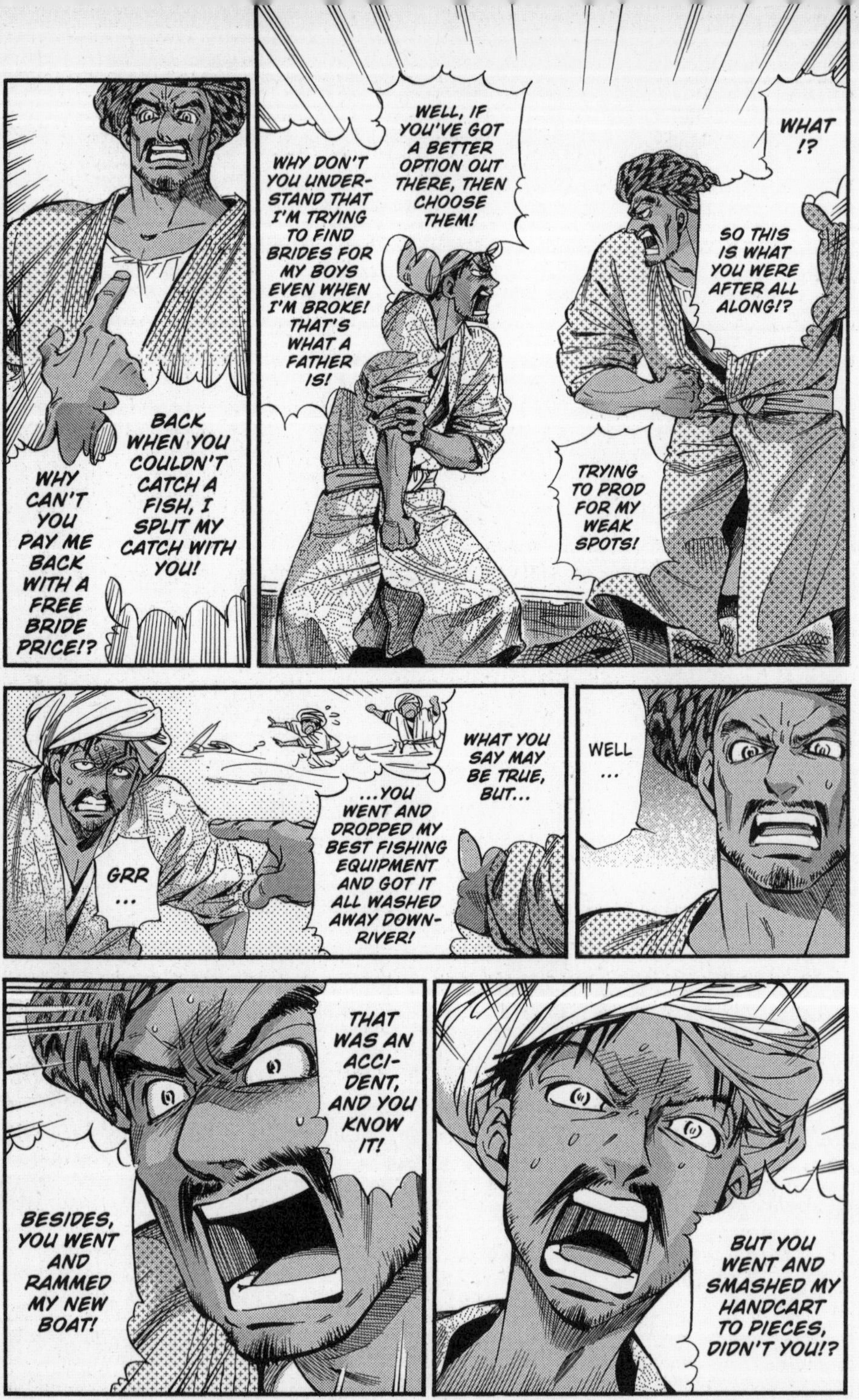
WHAT !?
SO THIS IS WHAT YOU WERE AFTER ALL ALONG!?
TRYING TO PROD FOR MY WEAK SPOTS!
WELL, IF YOU'VE GOT A BETTER OPTION OUT THERE, THEN CHOOSE THEM!
WHY DON'T YOU UNDERSTAND THAT I'M TRYING TO FIND BRIDES FOR MY BOYS EVEN WHEN I'M BROKE! THAT'S WHAT A FATHER IS!
BACK WHEN YOU COULDN'T CATCH A FISH, I SPLIT MY CATCH WITH YOU!
WHY CAN'T YOU PAY ME BACK WITH A FREE BRIDE PRICE!?
WELL ...
WHAT YOU SAY MAY BE TRUE, BUT...
...YOU WENT AND DROPPED MY BEST FISHING EQUIPMENT AND GOT IT ALL WASHED AWAY DOWN-RIVER!
GRR ...
BUT YOU WENT AND SMASHED MY HANDCART TO PIECES, DIDN'T YOU!?
THAT WAS AN ACCI-DENT, AND YOU KNOW IT!
BESIDES, YOU WENT AND RAMMED MY NEW BOAT!

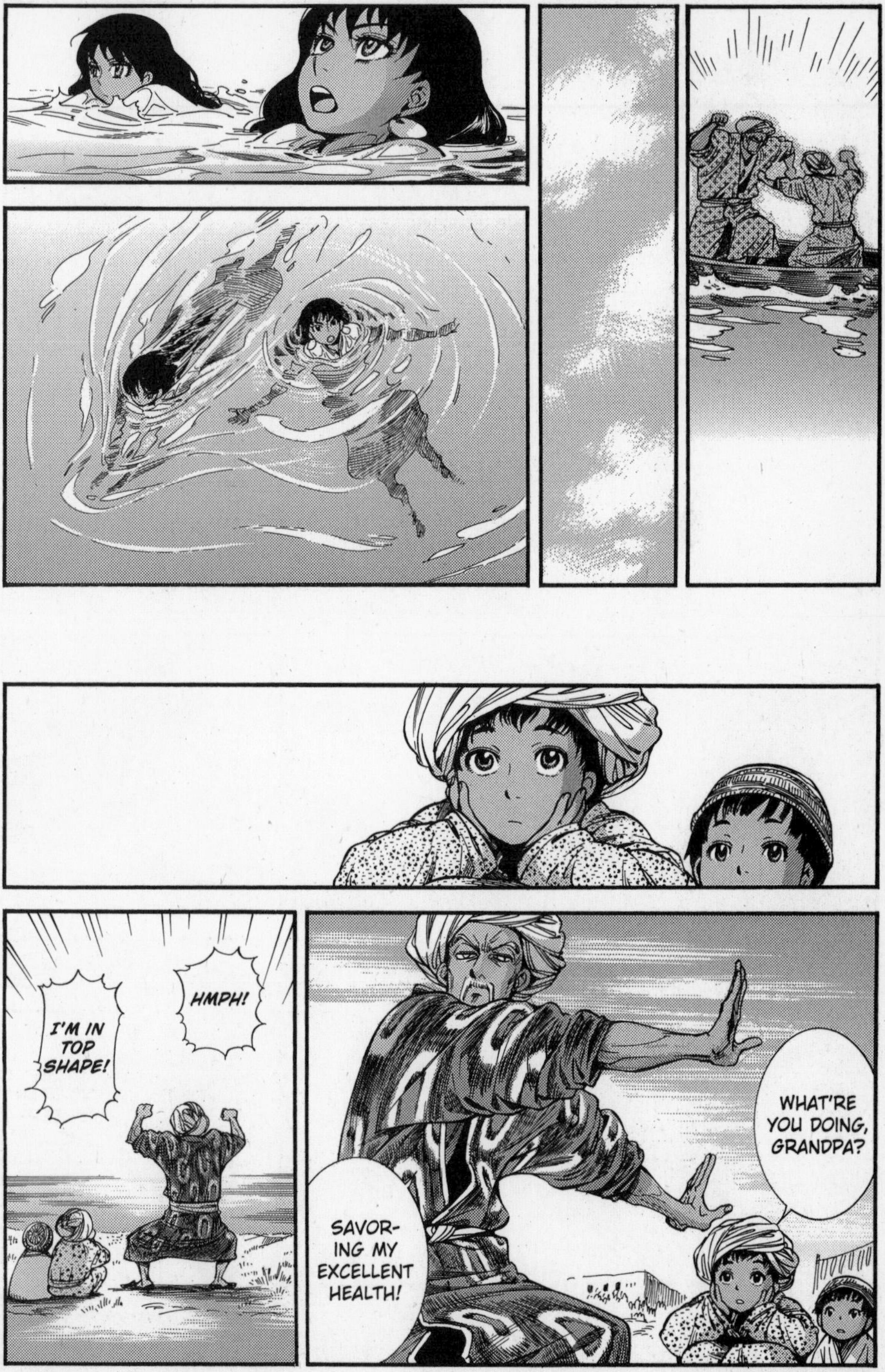
WHAT'RE YOU DOING, GRANDPA?
SAVOR-ING MY EXCELLENT HEALTH!
HMPH!
I'M IN TOP SHAPE!

✦ CHAPTER 20: END ✦

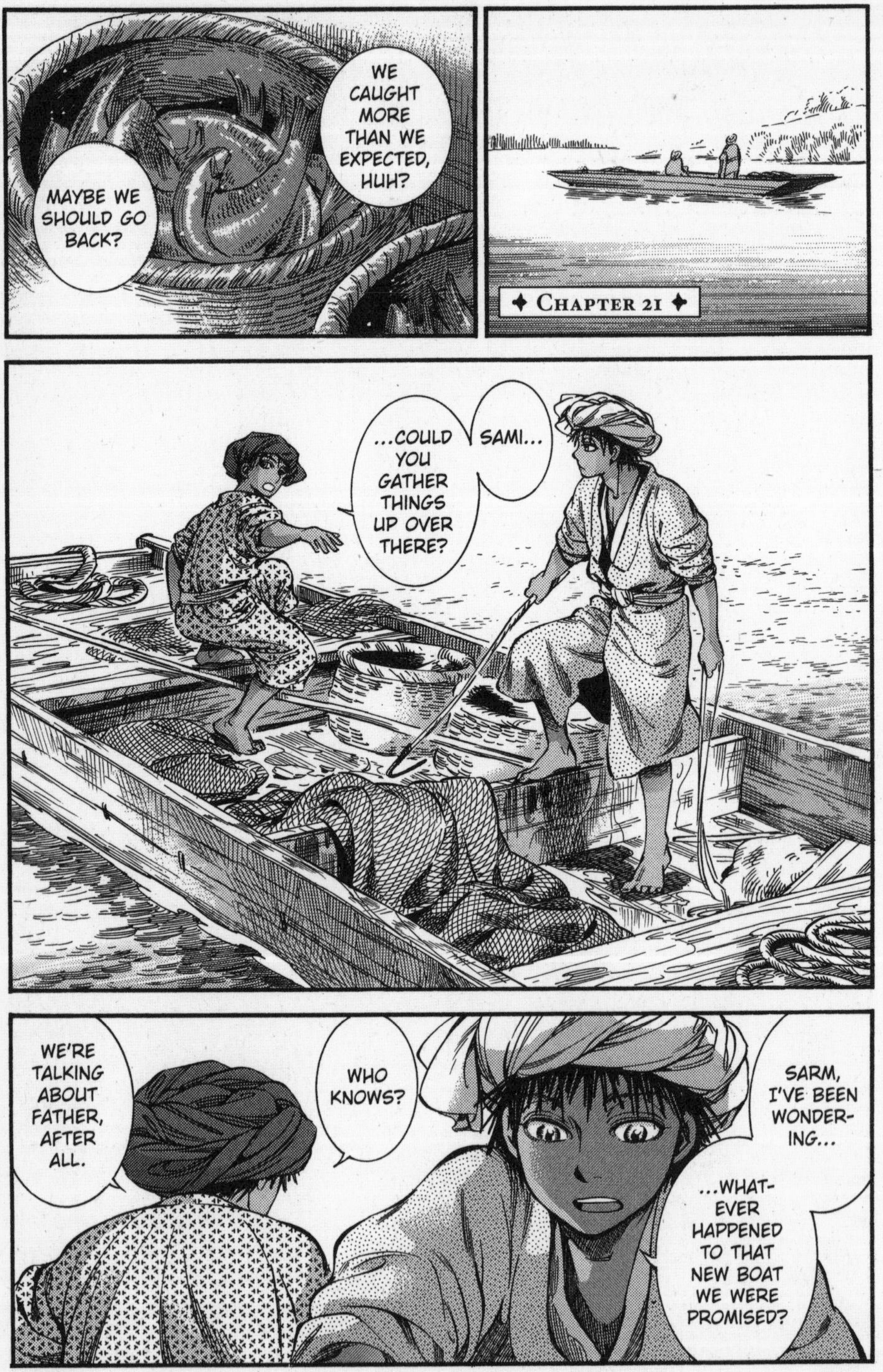
✦ CHAPTER 21 ✦
WE CAUGHT MORE THAN WE EXPECTED, HUH?
MAYBE WE SHOULD GO BACK?
SAMI...
...COULD YOU GATHER THINGS UP OVER THERE?
SARM, I'VE BEEN WONDER-ING...
...WHAT-EVER HAPPENED TO THAT NEW BOAT WE WERE PROMISED?
WHO KNOWS?
WE'RE TALKING ABOUT FATHER, AFTER ALL.

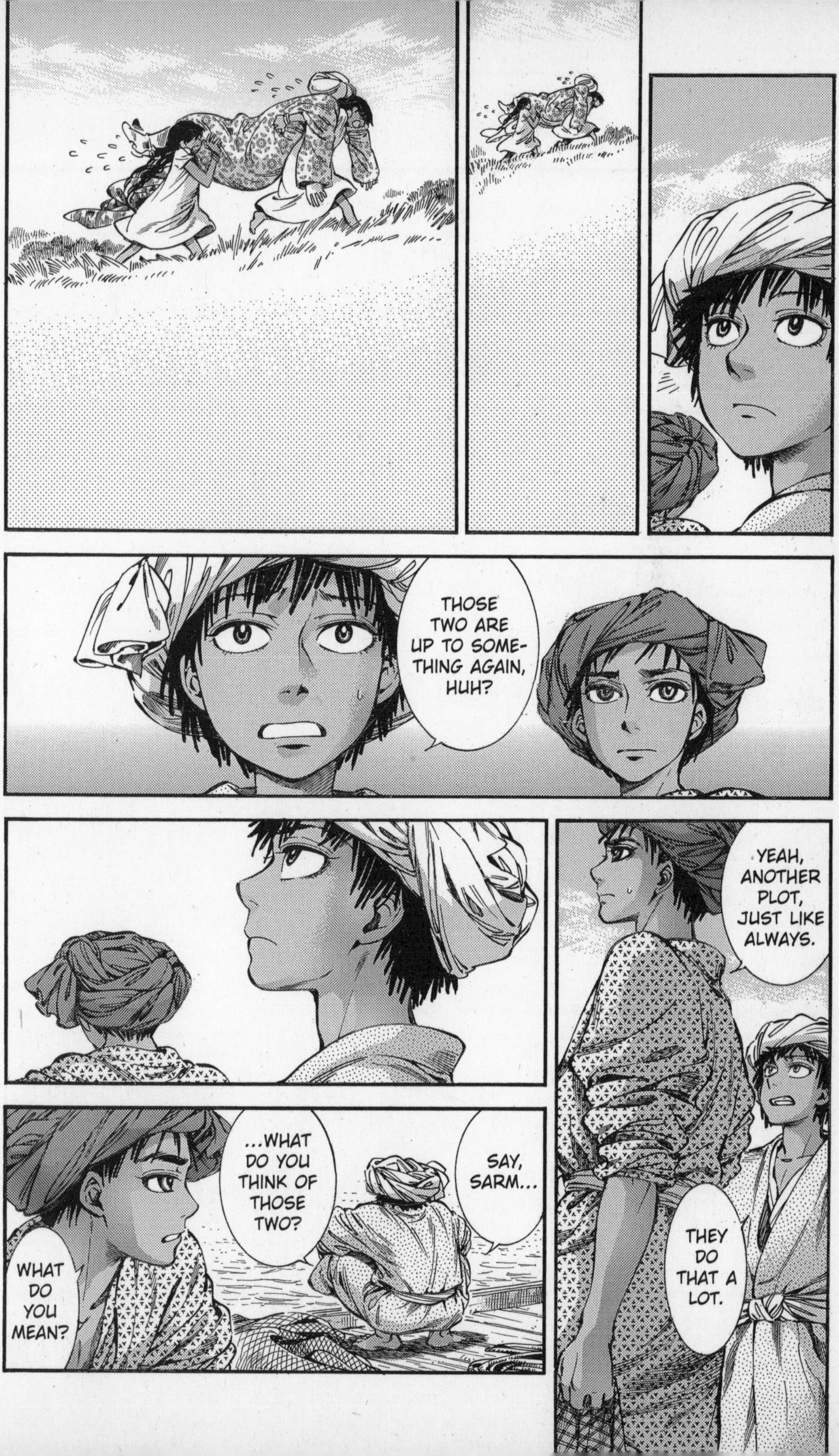
THOSE TWO ARE UP TO SOMETHING AGAIN, HUH?
YEAH, ANOTHER PLOT, JUST LIKE ALWAYS.
THEY DO THAT A LOT.
SAY, SARM...
...WHAT DO YOU THINK OF THOSE TWO?
WHAT DO YOU MEAN?

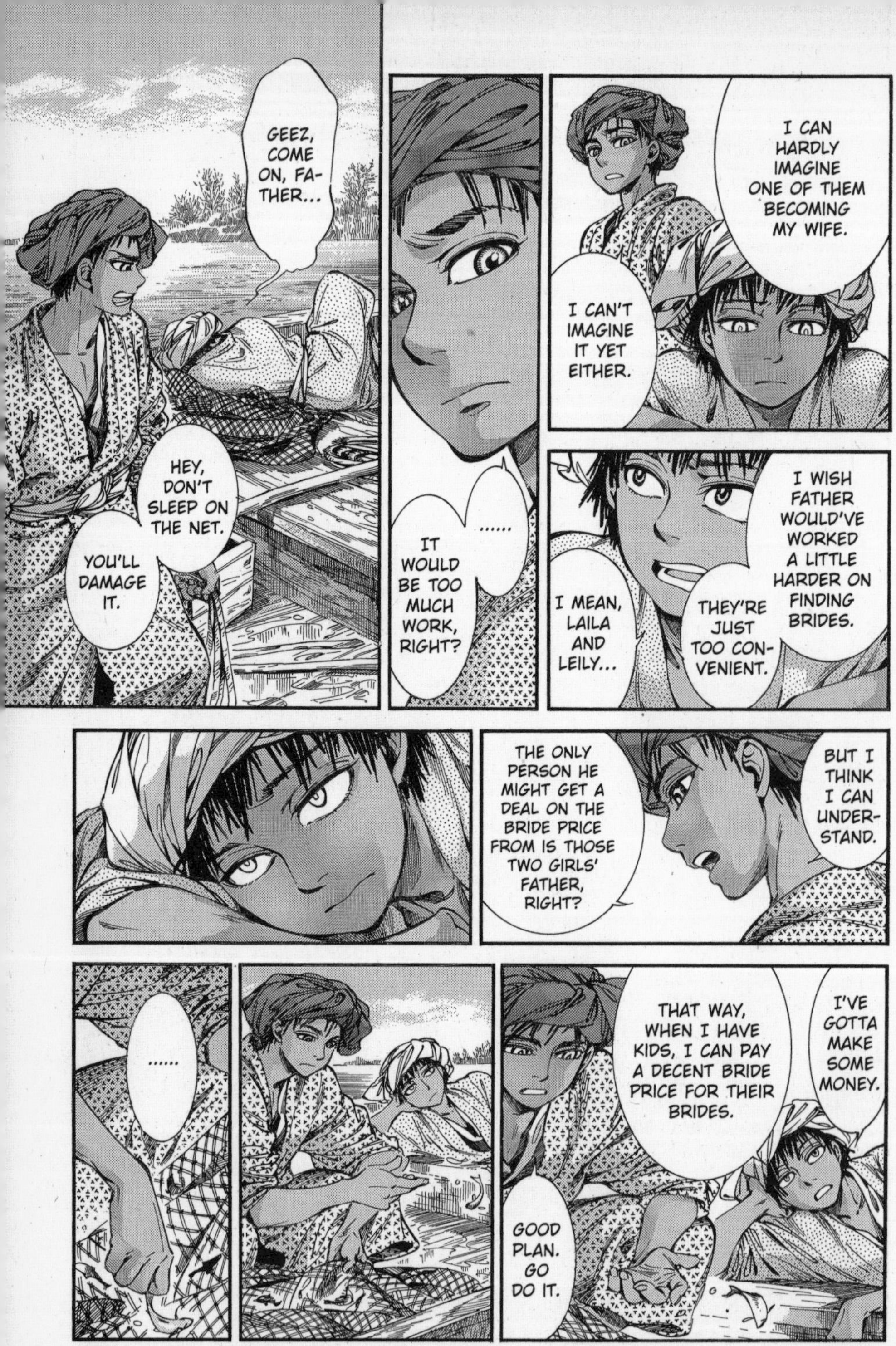
I CAN HARDLY IMAGINE ONE OF THEM BECOMING MY WIFE.
I CAN'T IMAGINE IT YET EITHER.
I WISH FATHER WOULD'VE WORKED A LITTLE HARDER ON FINDING BRIDES.
THEY'RE JUST TOO CON-VENIENT.
I MEAN, LAILA AND LEILY...
......
IT WOULD BE TOO MUCH WORK, RIGHT?
GEEZ, COME ON, FA-THER...
HEY, DON'T SLEEP ON THE NET.
YOU'LL DAMAGE IT.
BUT I THINK I CAN UNDER-STAND.
THE ONLY PERSON HE MIGHT GET A DEAL ON THE BRIDE PRICE FROM IS THOSE TWO GIRLS' FATHER, RIGHT?
I'VE GOTTA MAKE SOME MONEY.
THAT WAY, WHEN I HAVE KIDS, I CAN PAY A DECENT BRIDE PRICE FOR THEIR BRIDES.
GOOD PLAN. GO DO IT.
......

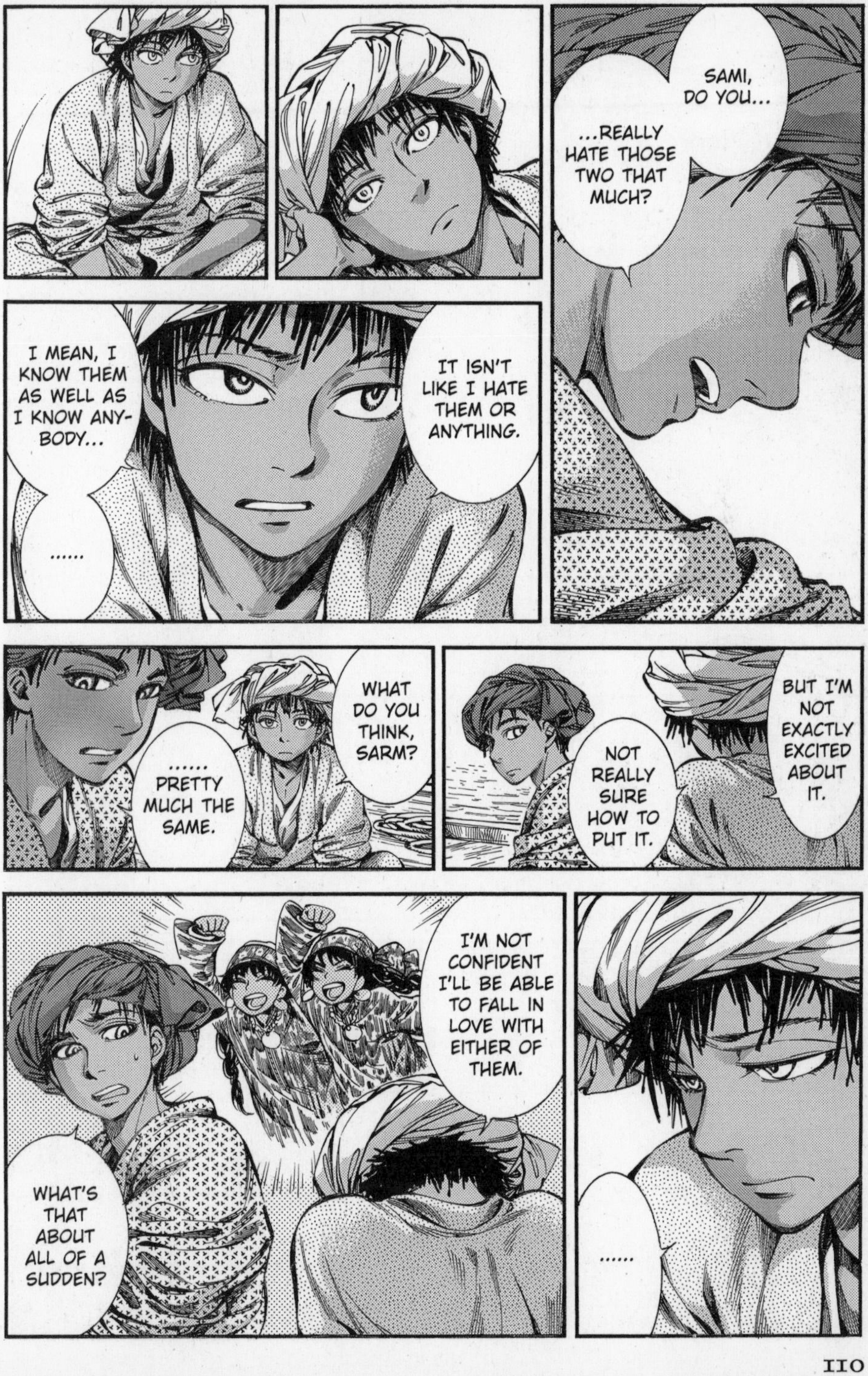
SAMI, DO YOU...
...REALLY HATE THOSE TWO THAT MUCH?
IT ISN'T LIKE I HATE THEM OR ANYTHING.
I MEAN, I KNOW THEM AS WELL AS I KNOW ANY-BODY...
......
BUT I'M NOT EXACTLY EXCITED ABOUT IT.
NOT REALLY SURE HOW TO PUT IT.
WHAT DO YOU THINK, SARM?
...... PRETTY MUCH THE SAME.
......
I'M NOT CONFIDENT I'LL BE ABLE TO FALL IN LOVE WITH EITHER OF THEM.
WHAT'S THAT ABOUT ALL OF A SUDDEN?

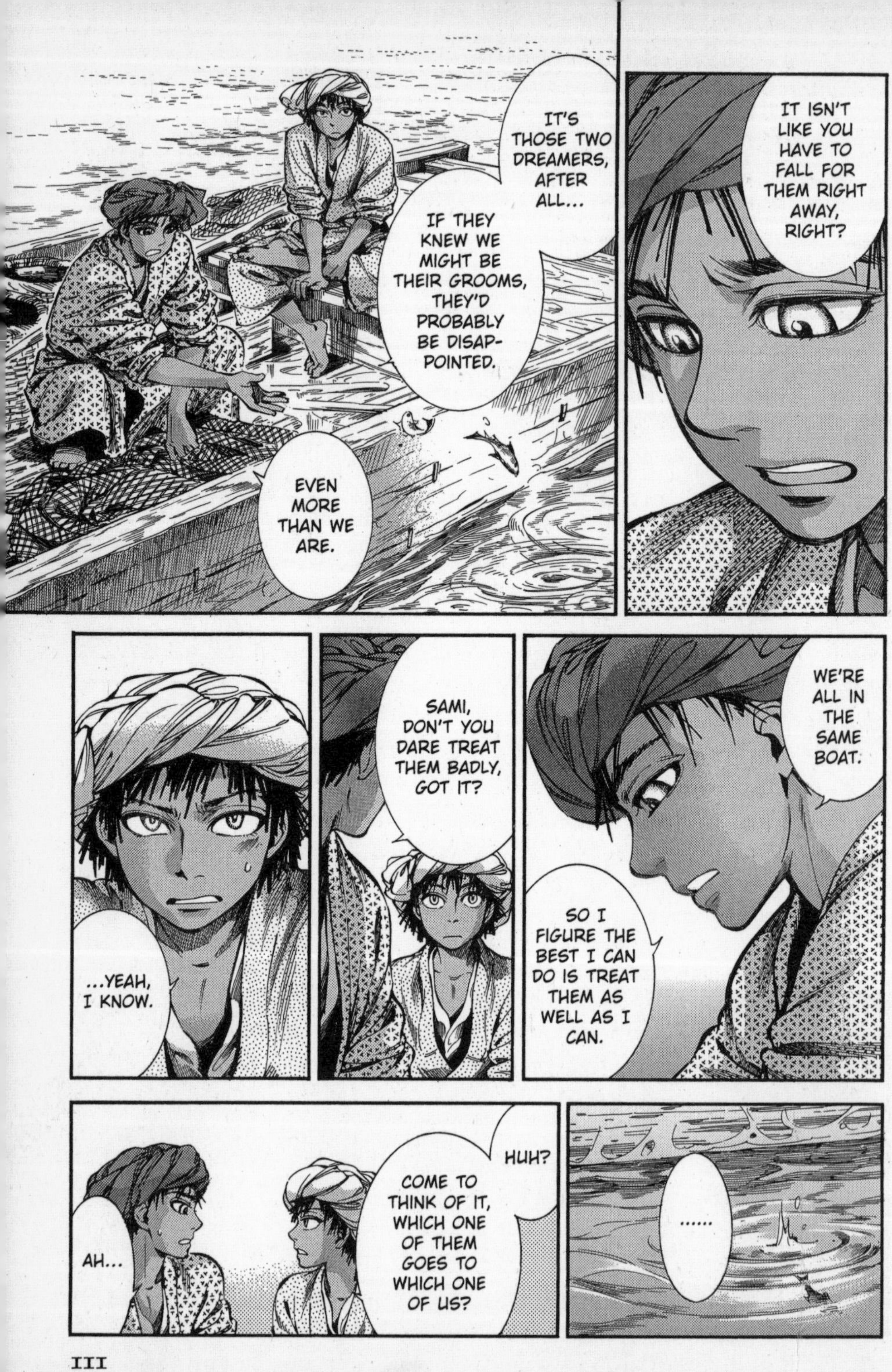
IT ISN'T LIKE YOU HAVE TO FALL FOR THEM RIGHT AWAY, RIGHT?
IT'S THOSE TWO DREAMERS, AFTER ALL...
IF THEY KNEW WE MIGHT BE THEIR GROOMS, THEY'D PROBABLY BE DISAP-POINTED.
EVEN MORE THAN WE ARE.
WE'RE ALL IN THE SAME BOAT.
SO I FIGURE THE BEST I CAN DO IS TREAT THEM AS WELL AS I CAN.
SAMI, DON'T YOU DARE TREAT THEM BADLY, GOT IT?
...YEAH, I KNOW.
......
HUH?
COME TO THINK OF IT, WHICH ONE OF THEM GOES TO WHICH ONE OF US?
AH...

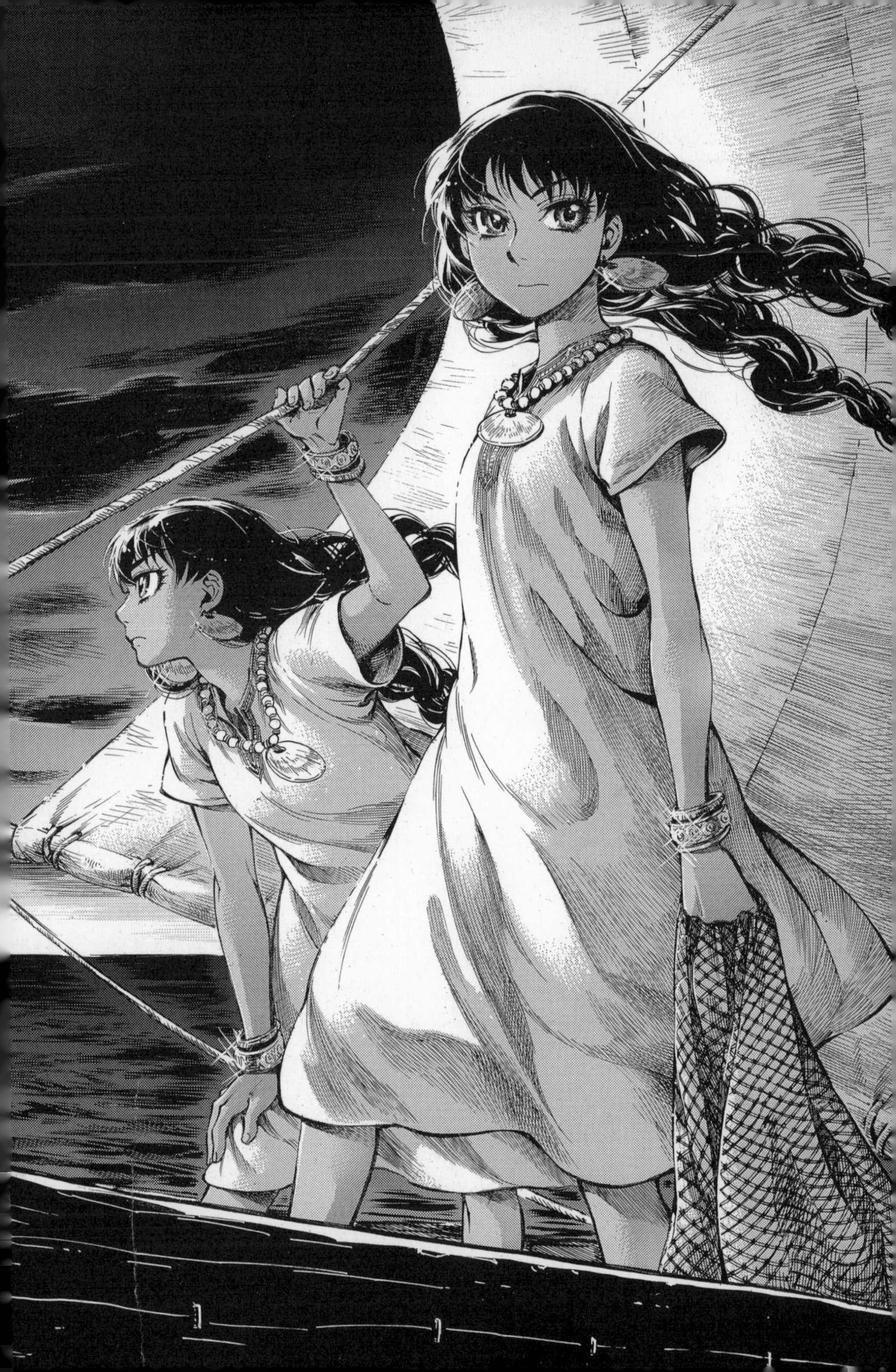

Chapter Twenty-One
Possibilities for the Twins

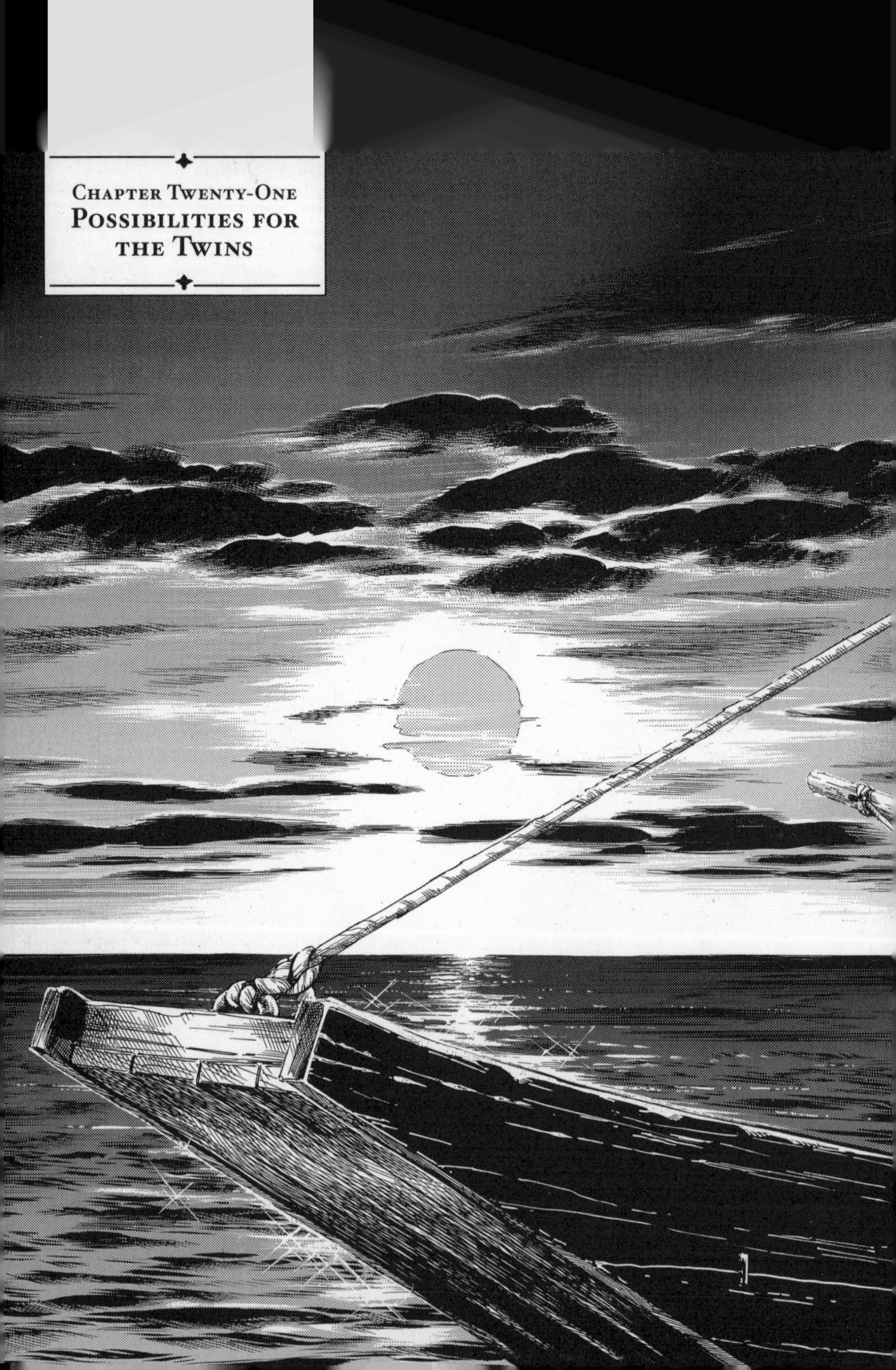

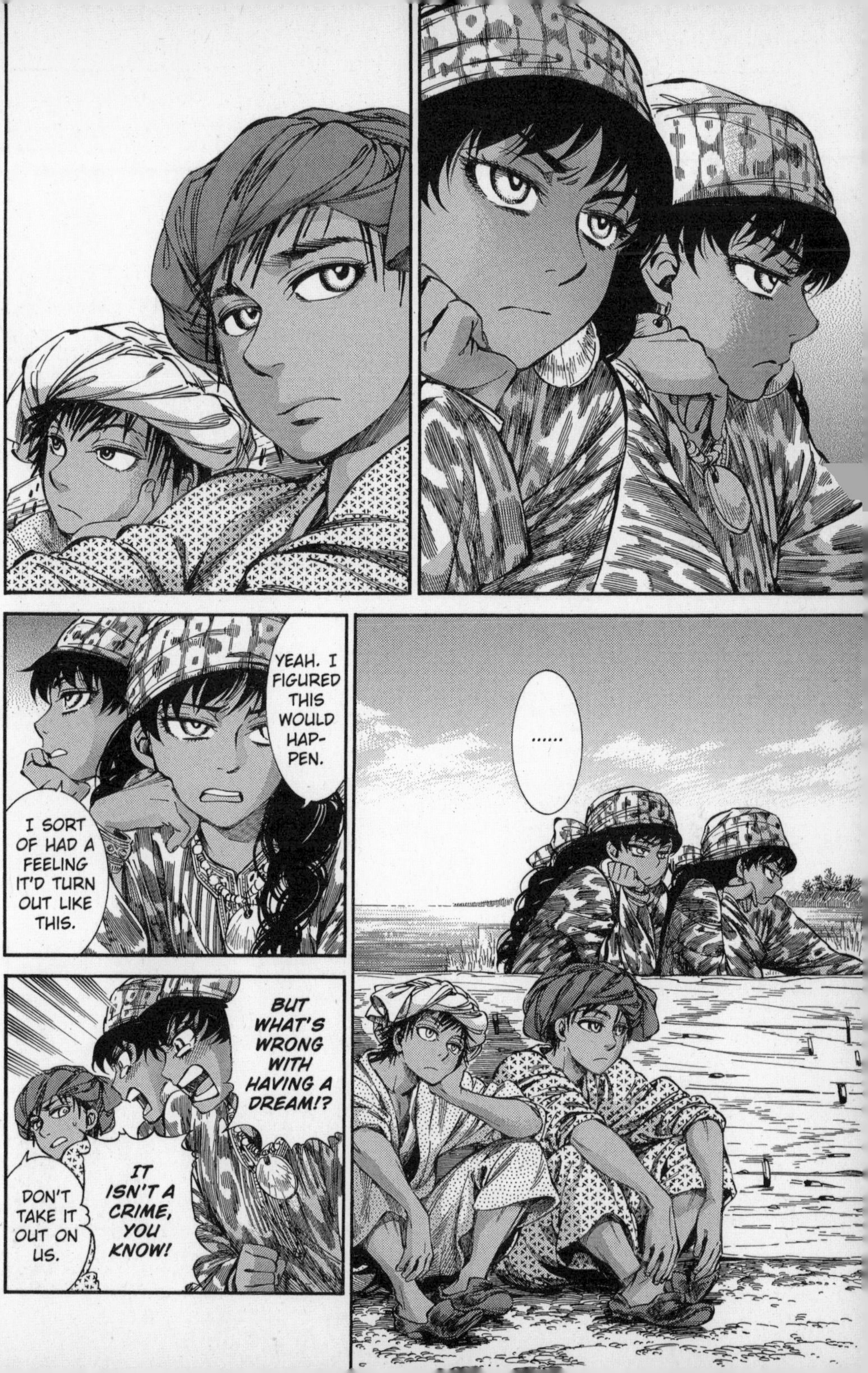
......
YEAH. I FIGURED THIS WOULD HAP-PEN.
I SORT OF HAD A FEELING IT'D TURN OUT LIKE THIS.
BUT WHAT'S WRONG WITH HAVING A DREAM!?
IT ISN'T A CRIME, YOU KNOW!
DON'T TAKE IT OUT ON US.

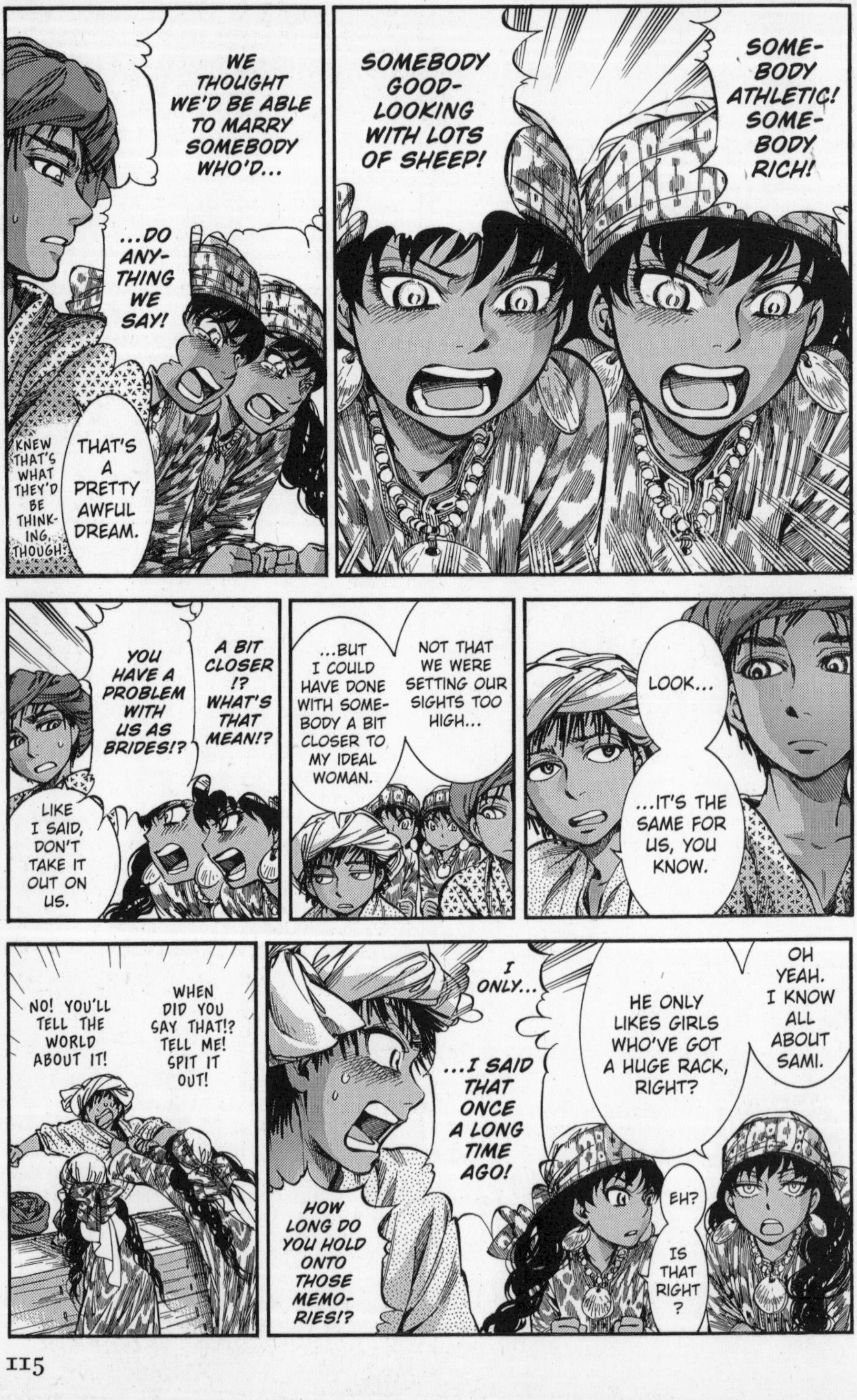
SOMEBODY ATHLETIC! SOMEBODY RICH!
SOMEBODY GOOD-LOOKING WITH LOTS OF SHEEP!
WE THOUGHT WE'D BE ABLE TO MARRY SOMEBODY WHO'D...
...DO ANYTHING WE SAY!
THAT'S A PRETTY AWFUL DREAM.
KNEW THAT'S WHAT THEY'D BE THINKING, THOUGH.
LOOK...
...IT'S THE SAME FOR US, YOU KNOW.
NOT THAT WE WERE SETTING OUR SIGHTS TOO HIGH...
...BUT I COULD HAVE DONE WITH SOMEBODY A BIT CLOSER TO MY IDEAL WOMAN.
A BIT CLOSER!? WHAT'S THAT MEAN!?
YOU HAVE A PROBLEM WITH US AS BRIDES!?
LIKE I SAID, DON'T TAKE IT OUT ON US.
OH YEAH. I KNOW ALL ABOUT SAMI.
HE ONLY LIKES GIRLS WHO'VE GOT A HUGE RACK, RIGHT?
I ONLY...
...I SAID THAT ONCE A LONG TIME AGO!
EH?
IS THAT RIGHT?
HOW LONG DO YOU HOLD ONTO THOSE MEMORIES!?
WHEN DID YOU SAY THAT!? TELL ME! SPIT IT OUT!
NO! YOU'LL TELL THE WORLD ABOUT IT!

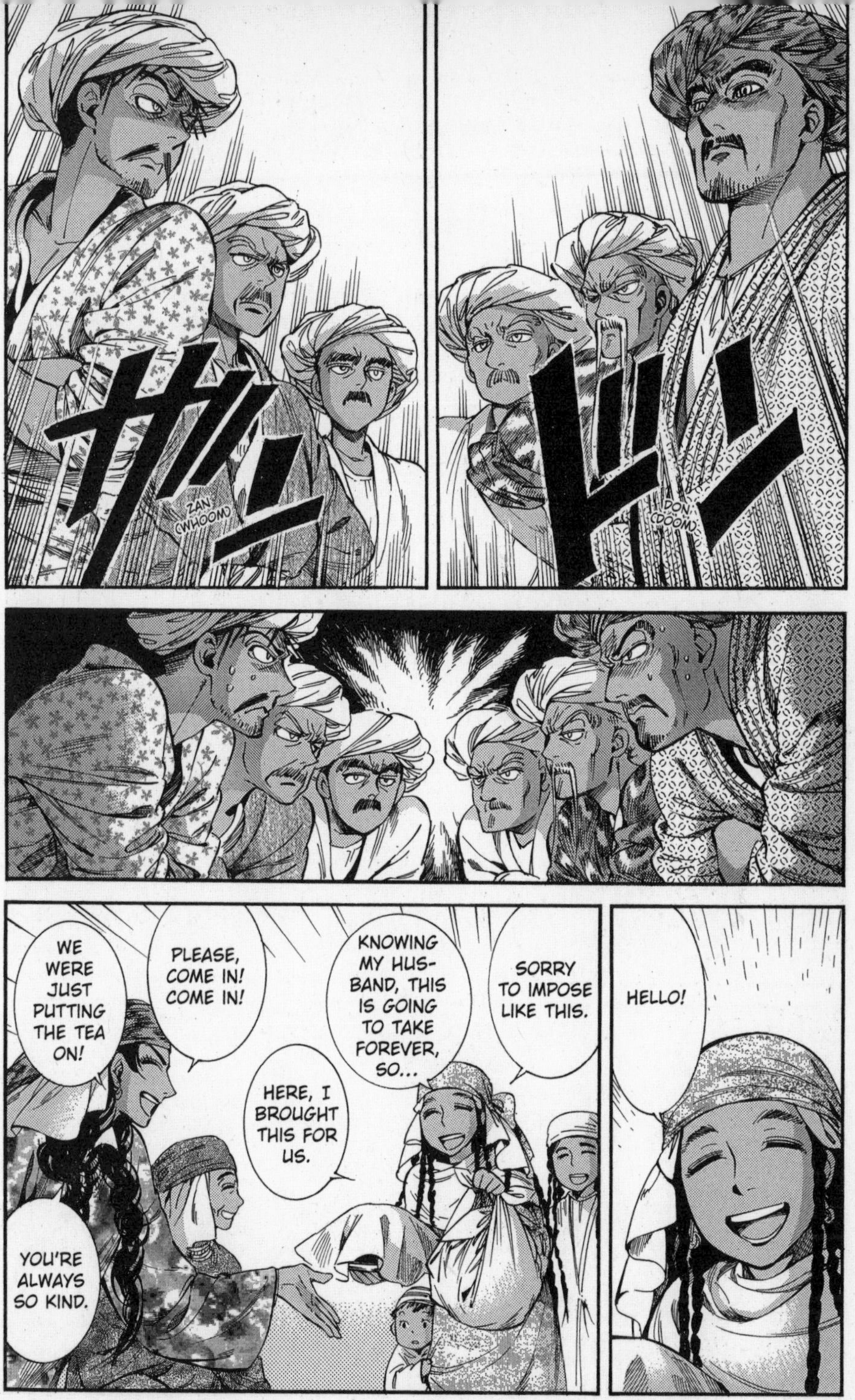
ドン
DON (DOOM)
ザン
ZAN (WHOOM)
HELLO!
SORRY TO IMPOSE LIKE THIS.
KNOWING MY HUS-BAND, THIS IS GOING TO TAKE FOREVER, SO...
HERE, I BROUGHT THIS FOR US.
PLEASE, COME IN! COME IN!
WE WERE JUST PUTTING THE TEA ON!
YOU'RE ALWAYS SO KIND.

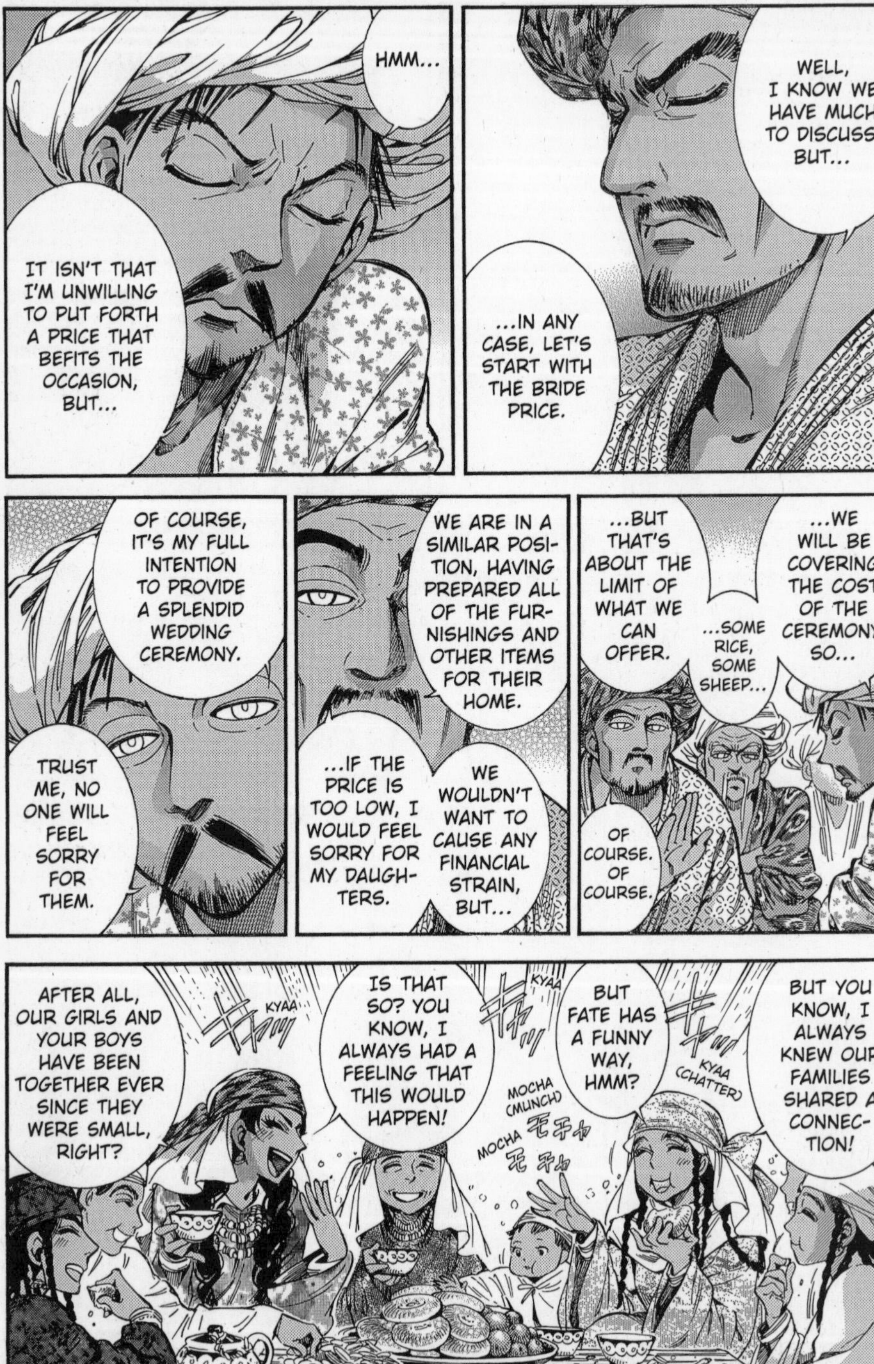
WELL, I KNOW WE HAVE MUCH TO DISCUSS, BUT...
...IN ANY CASE, LET'S START WITH THE BRIDE PRICE.
HMM...
IT ISN'T THAT I'M UNWILLING TO PUT FORTH A PRICE THAT BEFITS THE OCCASION, BUT...
...WE WILL BE COVERING THE COST OF THE CEREMONY, SO...
...SOME RICE, SOME SHEEP...
...BUT THAT'S ABOUT THE LIMIT OF WHAT WE CAN OFFER.
OF COURSE. OF COURSE.
WE ARE IN A SIMILAR POSITION, HAVING PREPARED ALL OF THE FURNISHINGS AND OTHER ITEMS FOR THEIR HOME.
WE WOULDN'T WANT TO CAUSE ANY FINANCIAL STRAIN, BUT...
...IF THE PRICE IS TOO LOW, I WOULD FEEL SORRY FOR MY DAUGHTERS.
OF COURSE, IT'S MY FULL INTENTION TO PROVIDE A SPLENDID WEDDING CEREMONY.
TRUST ME, NO ONE WILL FEEL SORRY FOR THEM.
BUT YOU KNOW, I ALWAYS KNEW OUR FAMILIES SHARED A CONNECTION!
KYAA (CHATTER)
BUT FATE HAS A FUNNY WAY, HMM?
KYAA
MOCHA (MUNCH)
MOCHA
IS THAT SO? YOU KNOW, I ALWAYS HAD A FEELING THAT THIS WOULD HAPPEN!
KYAA
AFTER ALL, OUR GIRLS AND YOUR BOYS HAVE BEEN TOGETHER EVER SINCE THEY WERE SMALL, RIGHT?

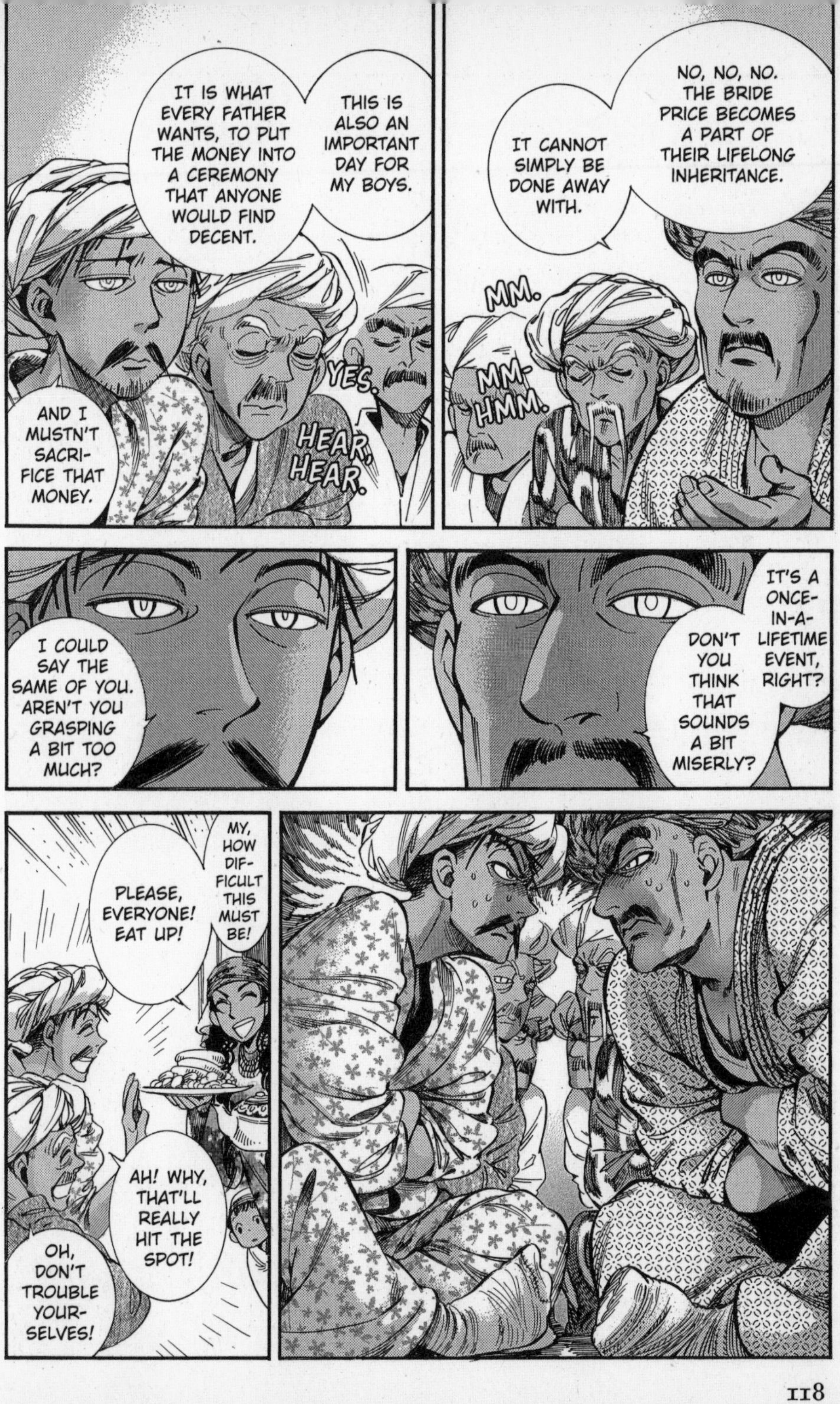
NO, NO, NO. THE BRIDE PRICE BECOMES A PART OF THEIR LIFELONG INHERITANCE.
IT CANNOT SIMPLY BE DONE AWAY WITH.
MM.
MM-HMM.
THIS IS ALSO AN IMPORTANT DAY FOR MY BOYS.
IT IS WHAT EVERY FATHER WANTS, TO PUT THE MONEY INTO A CEREMONY THAT ANYONE WOULD FIND DECENT.
YES.
HEAR, HEAR.
AND I MUSTN'T SACRI-FICE THAT MONEY.
IT'S A ONCE-IN-A-LIFETIME EVENT, RIGHT?
DON'T YOU THINK THAT SOUNDS A BIT MISERLY?
I COULD SAY THE SAME OF YOU. AREN'T YOU GRASPING A BIT TOO MUCH?
MY, HOW DIF-FICULT THIS MUST BE!
PLEASE, EVERYONE! EAT UP!
AH! WHY, THAT'LL REALLY HIT THE SPOT!
OH, DON'T TROUBLE YOUR-SELVES!

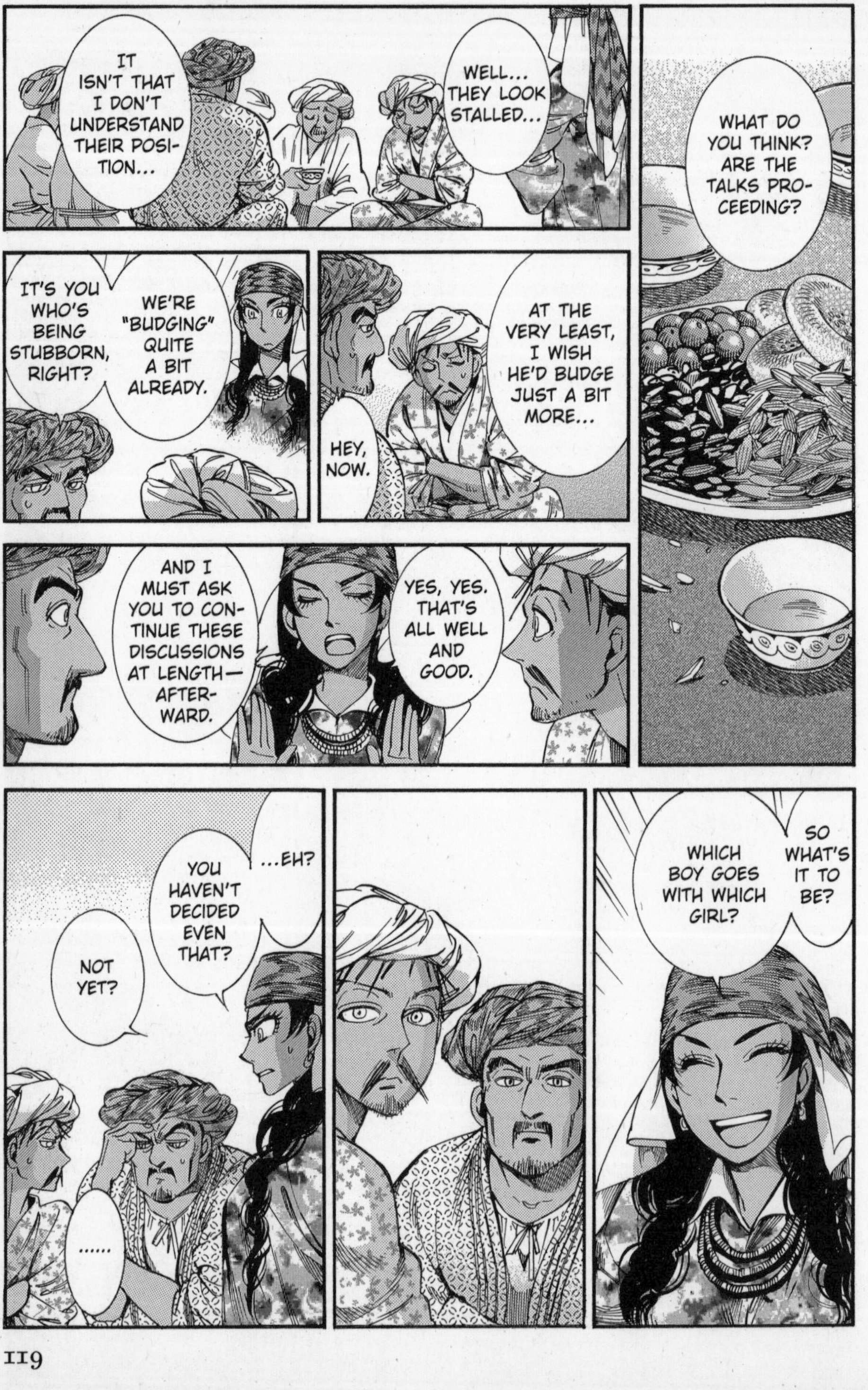
WHAT DO YOU THINK? ARE THE TALKS PROCEEDING?
WELL... THEY LOOK STALLED...
IT ISN'T THAT I DON'T UNDERSTAND THEIR POSITION...
AT THE VERY LEAST, I WISH HE'D BUDGE JUST A BIT MORE...
HEY, NOW.
WE'RE "BUDGING" QUITE A BIT ALREADY.
IT'S YOU WHO'S BEING STUBBORN, RIGHT?
YES, YES. THAT'S ALL WELL AND GOOD.
AND I MUST ASK YOU TO CONTINUE THESE DISCUSSIONS AT LENGTH—AFTERWARD.
SO WHAT'S IT TO BE?
WHICH BOY GOES WITH WHICH GIRL?
...EH?
YOU HAVEN'T DECIDED EVEN THAT?
NOT YET?
......

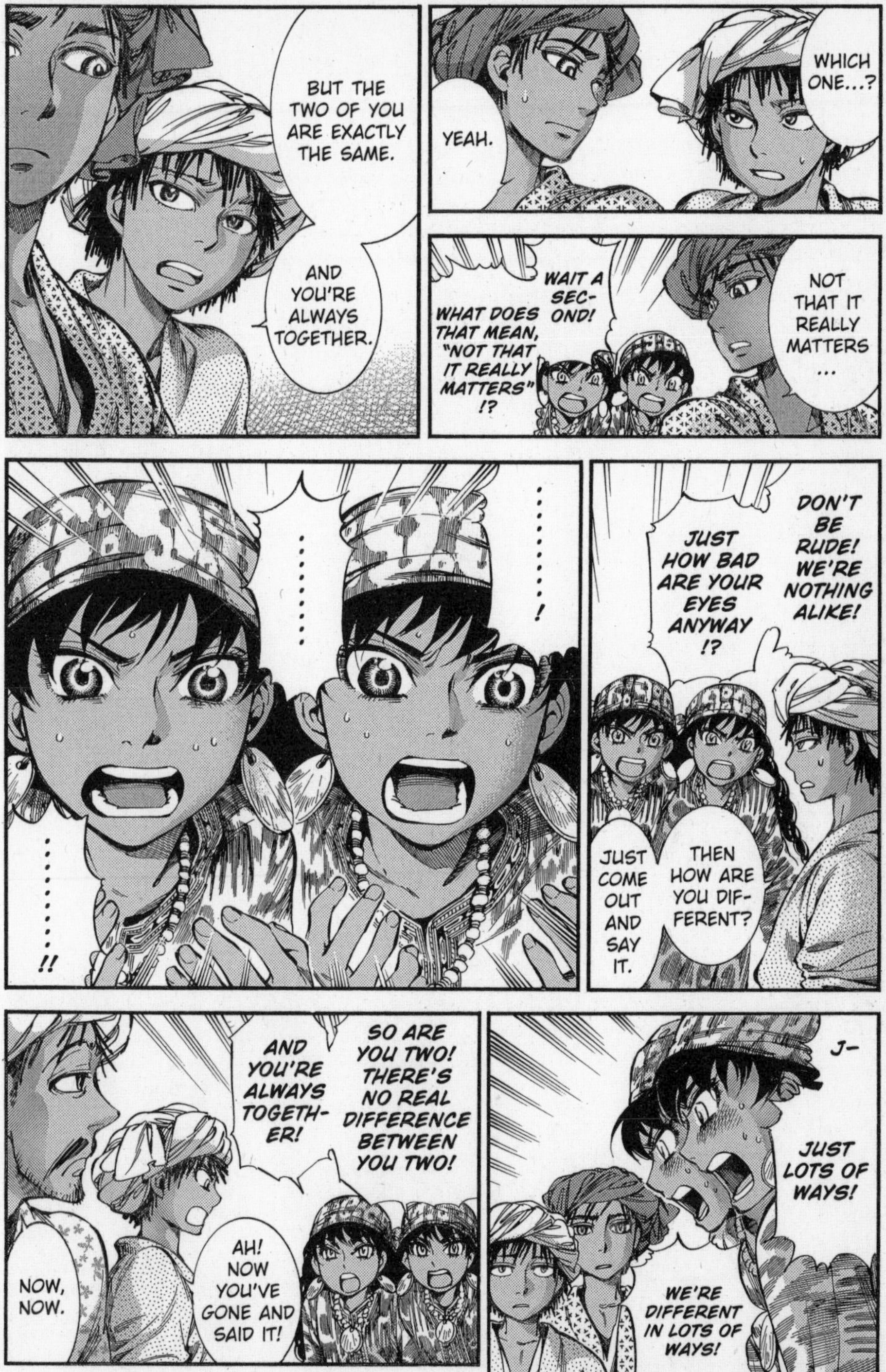
WHICH ONE...?
YEAH.
NOT THAT IT REALLY MATTERS ...
WAIT A SEC-OND!
WHAT DOES THAT MEAN, "NOT THAT IT REALLY MATTERS" !?
BUT THE TWO OF YOU ARE EXACTLY THE SAME.
AND YOU'RE ALWAYS TOGETHER.
DON'T BE RUDE! WE'RE NOTHING ALIKE!
JUST HOW BAD ARE YOUR EYES ANYWAY !?
THEN HOW ARE YOU DIF-FERENT?
JUST COME OUT AND SAY IT.
......!
......
......!!
J-
JUST LOTS OF WAYS!
WE'RE DIFFERENT IN LOTS OF WAYS!
SO ARE YOU TWO! THERE'S NO REAL DIFFERENCE BETWEEN YOU TWO!
AND YOU'RE ALWAYS TOGETH-ER!
AH! NOW YOU'VE GONE AND SAID IT!
NOW, NOW.

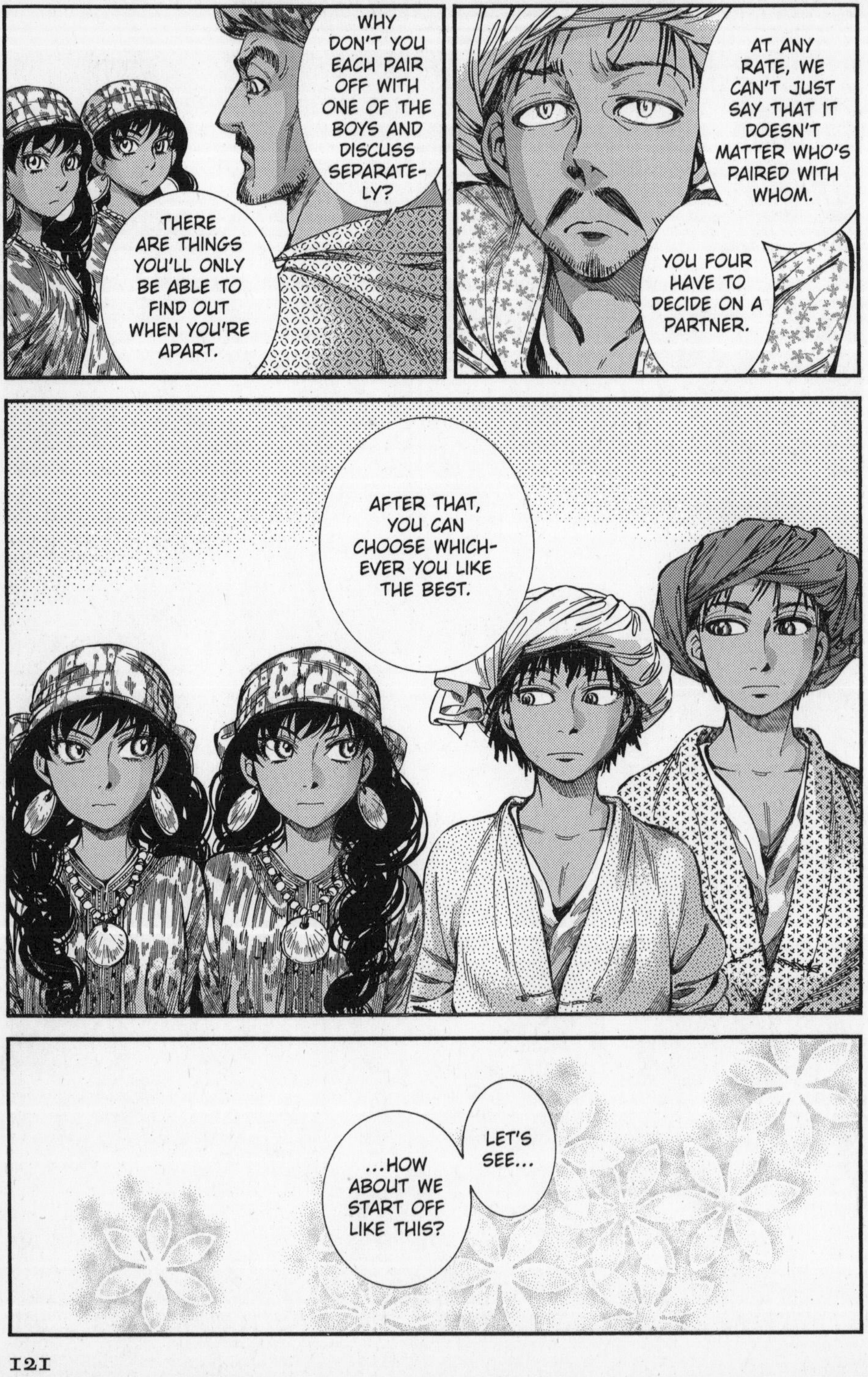
AT ANY RATE, WE CAN'T JUST SAY THAT IT DOESN'T MATTER WHO'S PAIRED WITH WHOM.
YOU FOUR HAVE TO DECIDE ON A PARTNER.
WHY DON'T YOU EACH PAIR OFF WITH ONE OF THE BOYS AND DISCUSS SEPARATE-LY?
THERE ARE THINGS YOU'LL ONLY BE ABLE TO FIND OUT WHEN YOU'RE APART.
AFTER THAT, YOU CAN CHOOSE WHICH-EVER YOU LIKE THE BEST.
LET'S SEE...
...HOW ABOUT WE START OFF LIKE THIS?

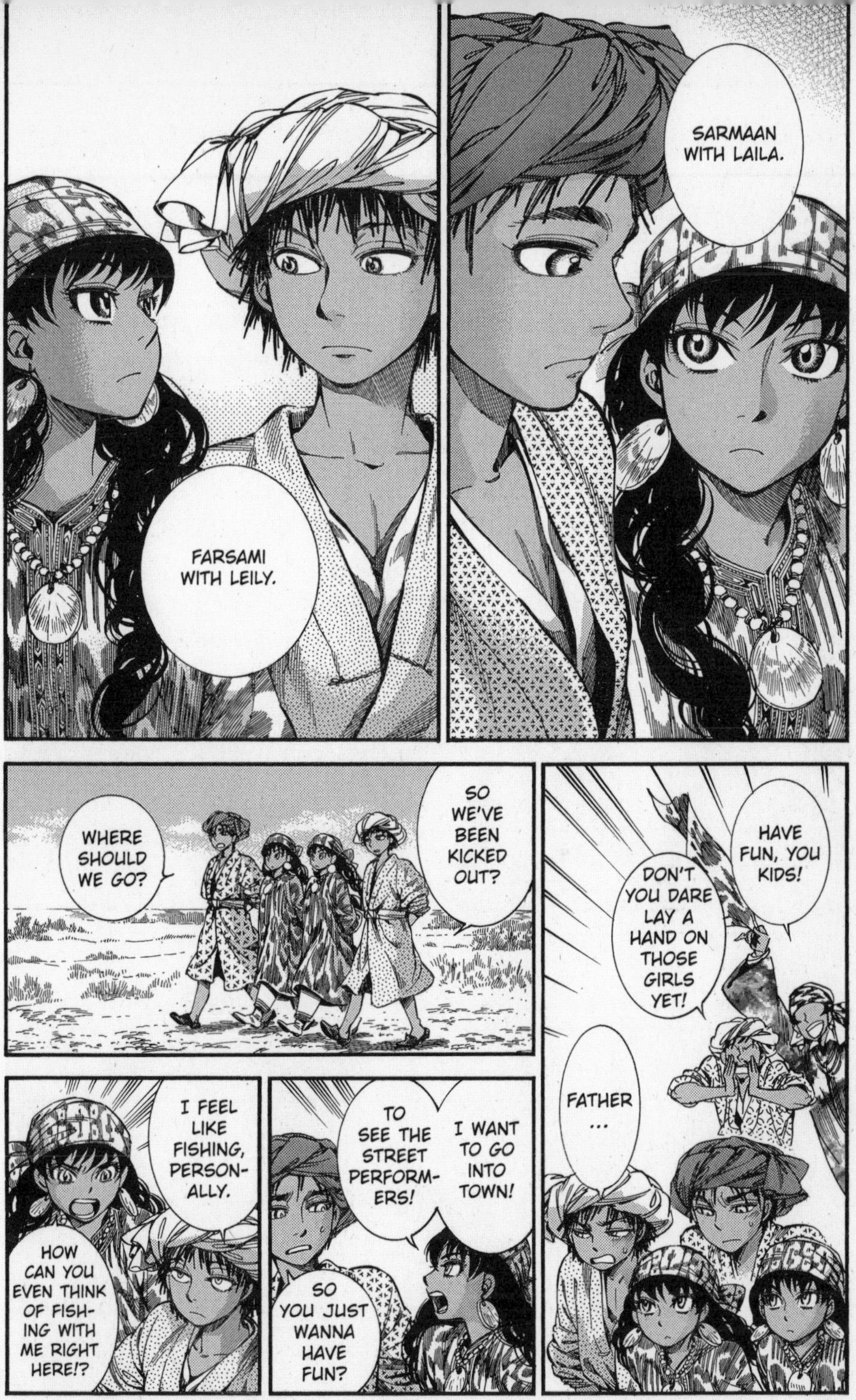
SARMAAN WITH LAILA.
FARSAMI WITH LEILY.
HAVE FUN, YOU KIDS!
DON'T YOU DARE LAY A HAND ON THOSE GIRLS YET!
FATHER...
SO WE'VE BEEN KICKED OUT?
WHERE SHOULD WE GO?
I WANT TO GO INTO TOWN!
TO SEE THE STREET PERFORM-ERS!
SO YOU JUST WANNA HAVE FUN?
I FEEL LIKE FISHING, PERSON-ALLY.
HOW CAN YOU EVEN THINK OF FISH-ING WITH ME RIGHT HERE!?

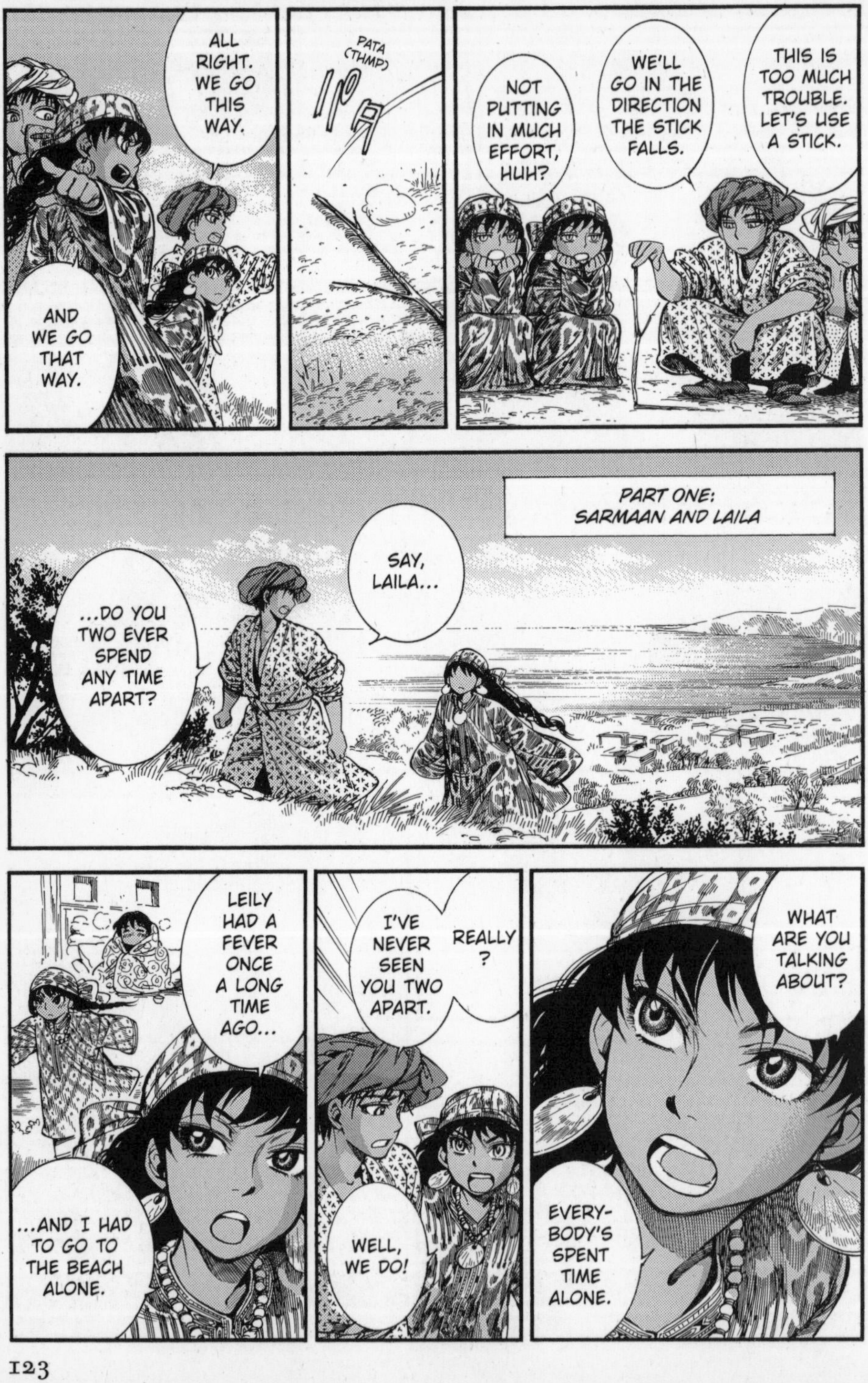
THIS IS TOO MUCH TROUBLE. LET'S USE A STICK.
WE'LL GO IN THE DIRECTION THE STICK FALLS.
NOT PUTTING IN MUCH EFFORT, HUH?
PATA (THMP)
ALL RIGHT. WE GO THIS WAY.
AND WE GO THAT WAY.
PART ONE: SARMAAN AND LAILA
SAY, LAILA...
...DO YOU TWO EVER SPEND ANY TIME APART?
WHAT ARE YOU TALKING ABOUT?
EVERY-BODY'S SPENT TIME ALONE.
REALLY?
I'VE NEVER SEEN YOU TWO APART.
WELL, WE DO!
LEILY HAD A FEVER ONCE A LONG TIME AGO...
...AND I HAD TO GO TO THE BEACH ALONE.

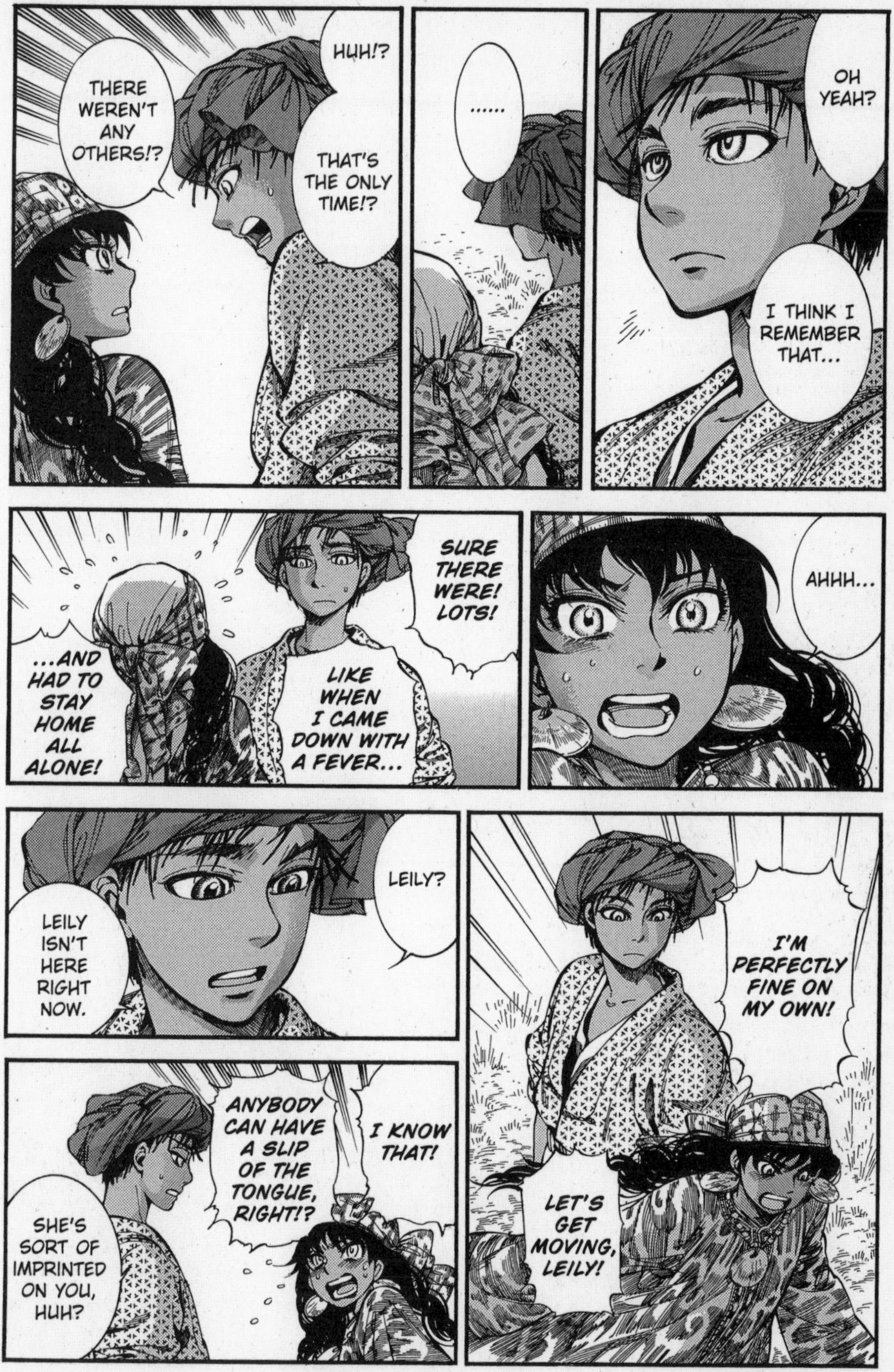
OH YEAH?
I THINK I REMEMBER THAT...
......
HUH!?
THAT'S THE ONLY TIME!?
THERE WEREN'T ANY OTHERS!?
AHHH...
SURE THERE WERE! LOTS!
LIKE WHEN I CAME DOWN WITH A FEVER...
...AND HAD TO STAY HOME ALL ALONE!
I'M PERFECTLY FINE ON MY OWN!
LET'S GET MOVING, LEILY!
LEILY?
LEILY ISN'T HERE RIGHT NOW.
I KNOW THAT!
ANYBODY CAN HAVE A SLIP OF THE TONGUE, RIGHT!?
SHE'S SORT OF IMPRINTED ON YOU, HUH?

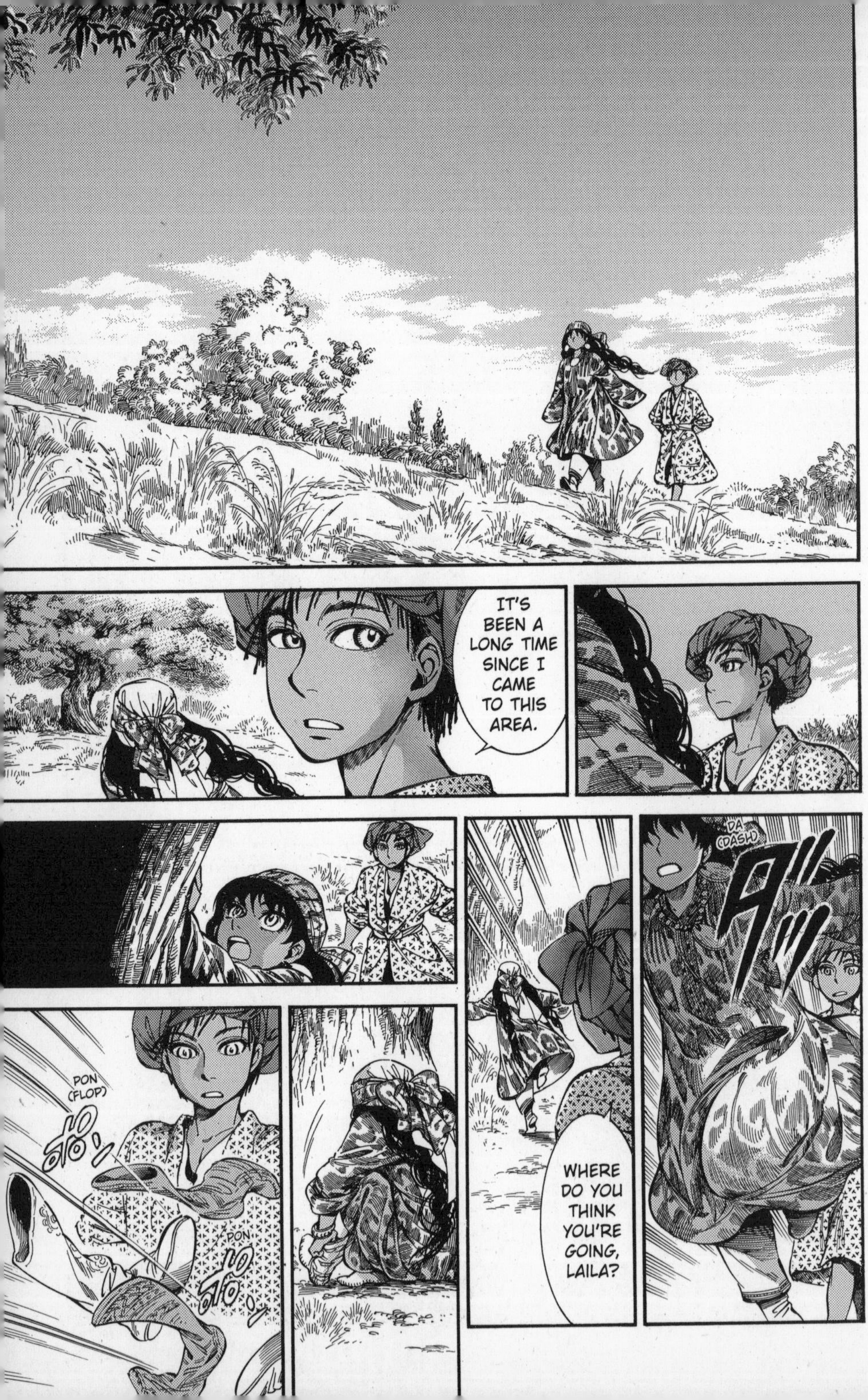
IT'S BEEN A LONG TIME SINCE I CAME TO THIS AREA.
DA (DASH)
WHERE DO YOU THINK YOU'RE GOING, LAILA?
PON (FLOP)
PON

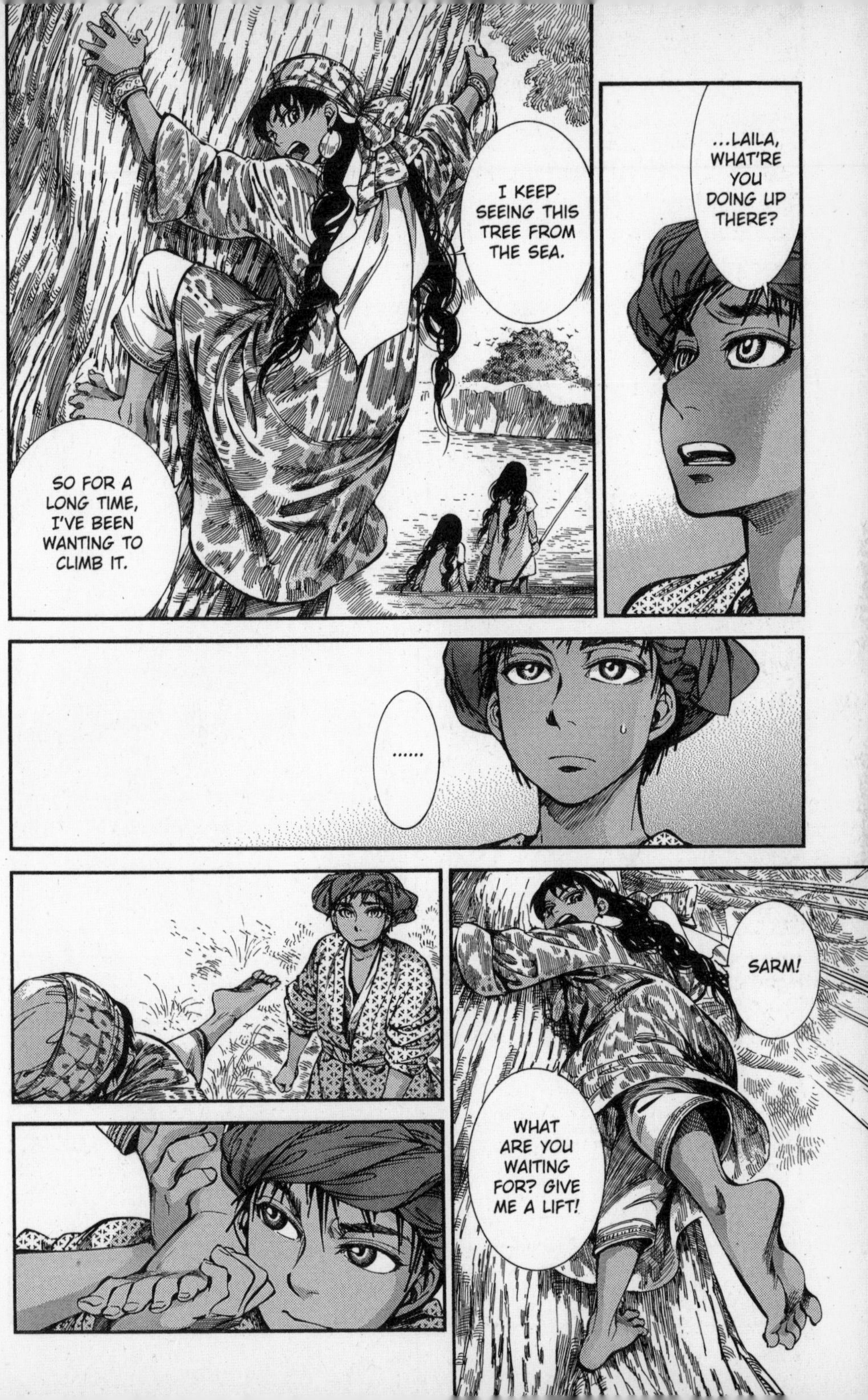
...LAILA, WHAT'RE YOU DOING UP THERE?
I KEEP SEEING THIS TREE FROM THE SEA.
SO FOR A LONG TIME, I'VE BEEN WANTING TO CLIMB IT.
......
SARM!
WHAT ARE YOU WAITING FOR? GIVE ME A LIFT!

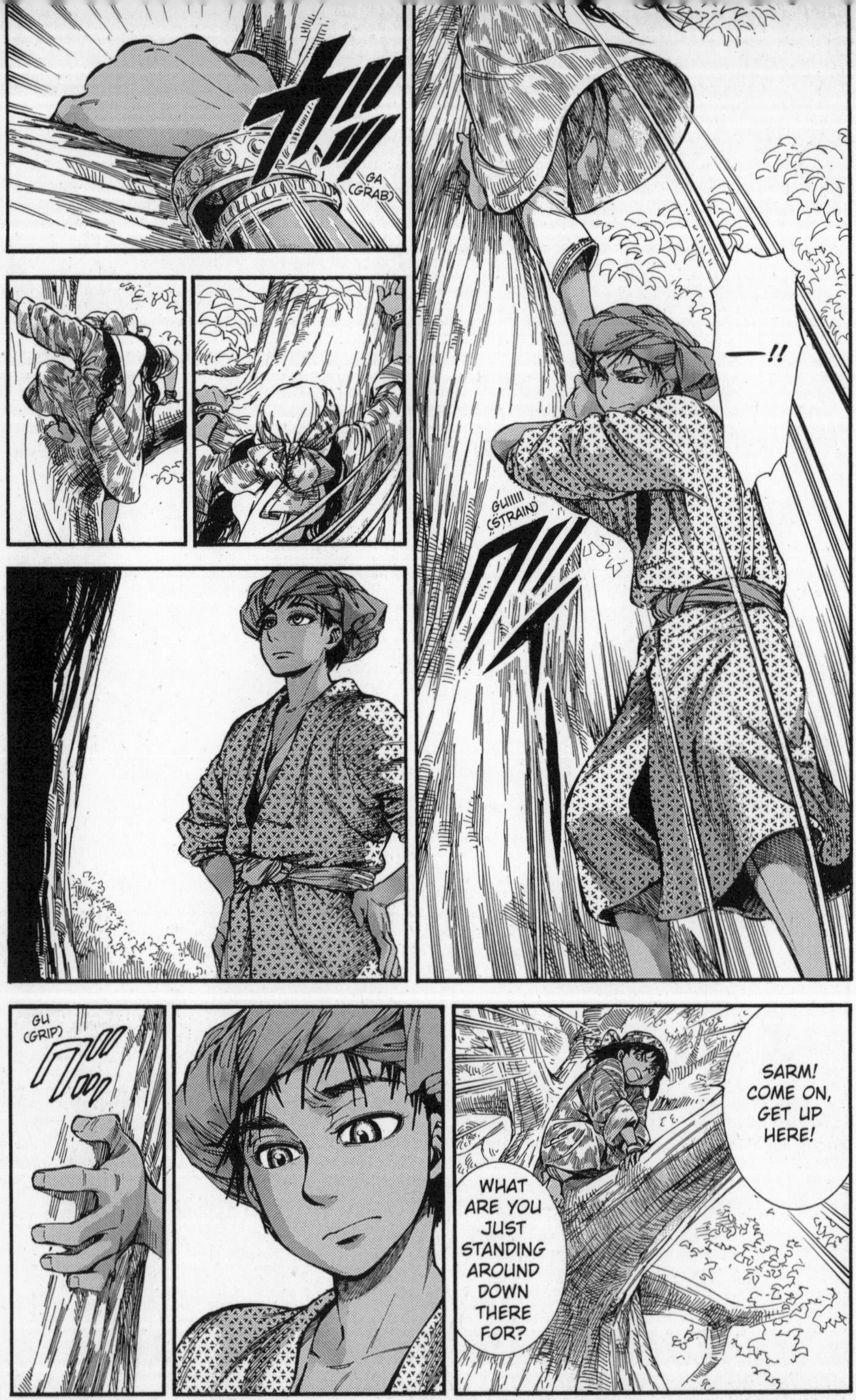
—!!
GUIIIII (STRAIN)
GA (GRAB)
SARM! COME ON, GET UP HERE!
WHAT ARE YOU JUST STANDING AROUND DOWN THERE FOR?
GU (GRIP)

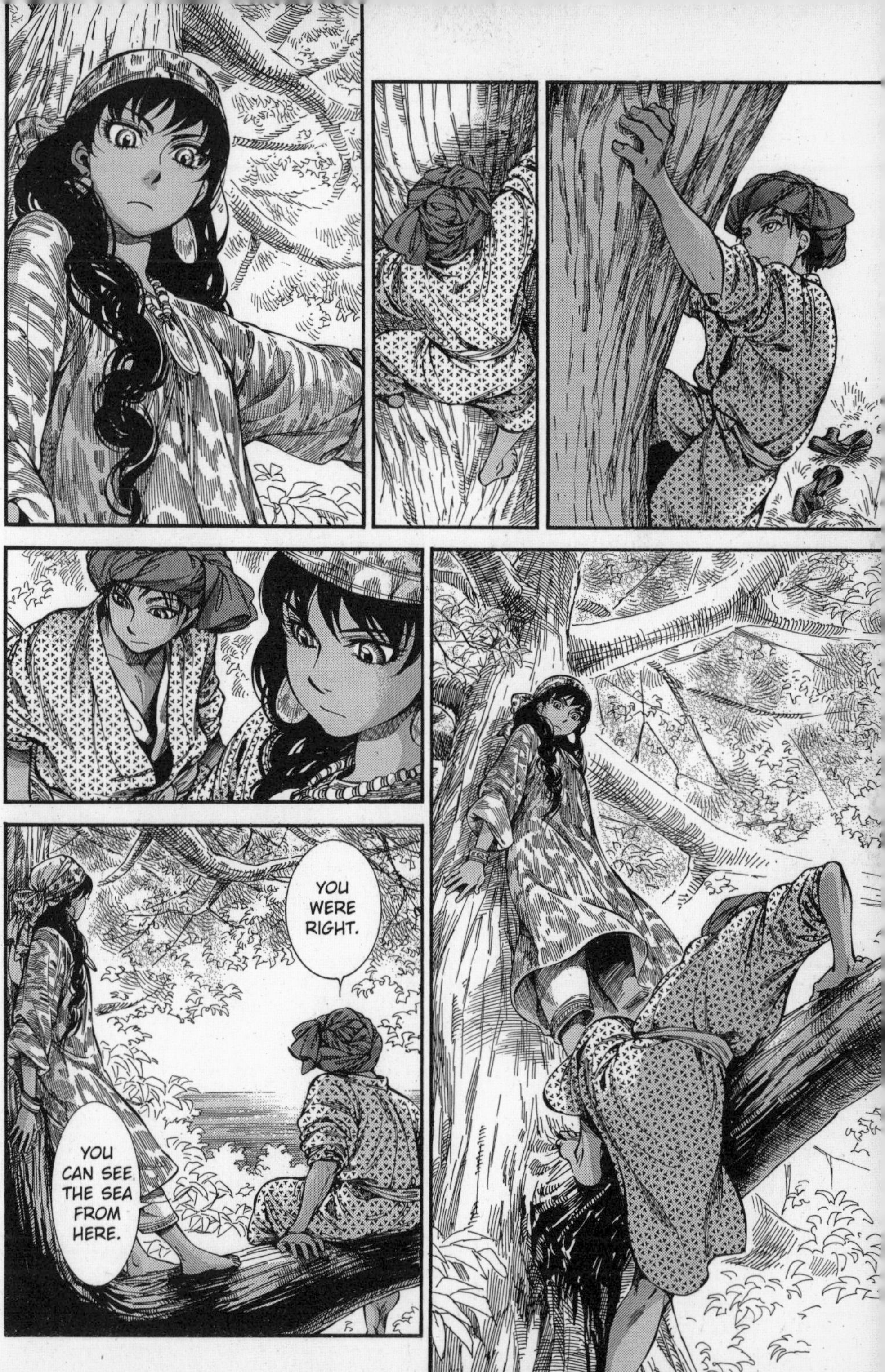
YOU WERE RIGHT.
YOU CAN SEE THE SEA FROM HERE.

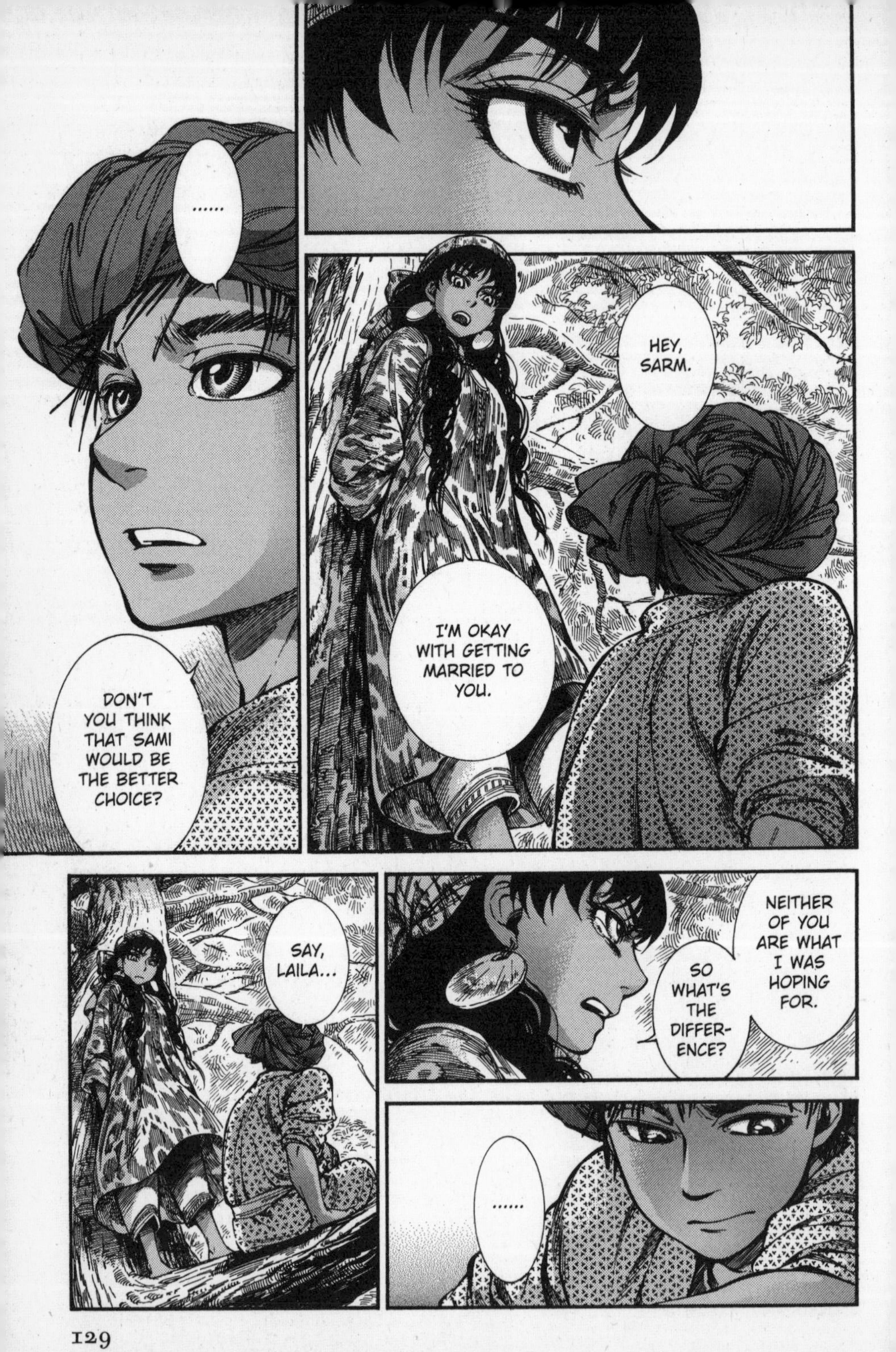
HEY, SARM.
I'M OKAY WITH GETTING MARRIED TO YOU.
......
DON'T YOU THINK THAT SAMI WOULD BE THE BETTER CHOICE?
NEITHER OF YOU ARE WHAT I WAS HOPING FOR.
SO WHAT'S THE DIFFER-ENCE?
......
SAY, LAILA...

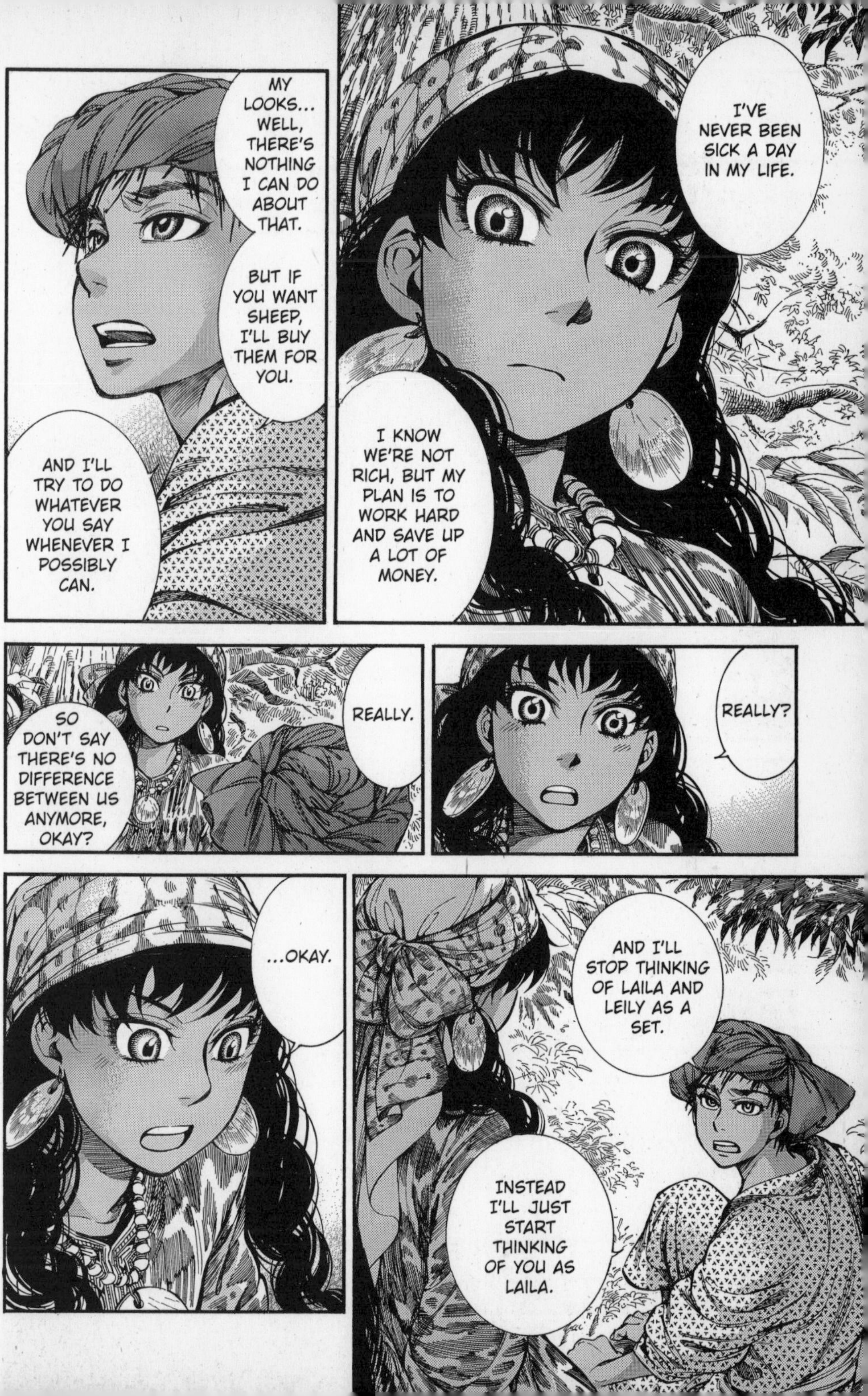
I'VE NEVER BEEN SICK A DAY IN MY LIFE.
I KNOW WE'RE NOT RICH, BUT MY PLAN IS TO WORK HARD AND SAVE UP A LOT OF MONEY.
MY LOOKS... WELL, THERE'S NOTHING I CAN DO ABOUT THAT.
BUT IF YOU WANT SHEEP, I'LL BUY THEM FOR YOU.
AND I'LL TRY TO DO WHATEVER YOU SAY WHENEVER I POSSIBLY CAN.
REALLY?
REALLY.
SO DON'T SAY THERE'S NO DIFFERENCE BETWEEN US ANYMORE, OKAY?
AND I'LL STOP THINKING OF LAILA AND LEILY AS A SET.
INSTEAD I'LL JUST START THINKING OF YOU AS LAILA.
...OKAY.

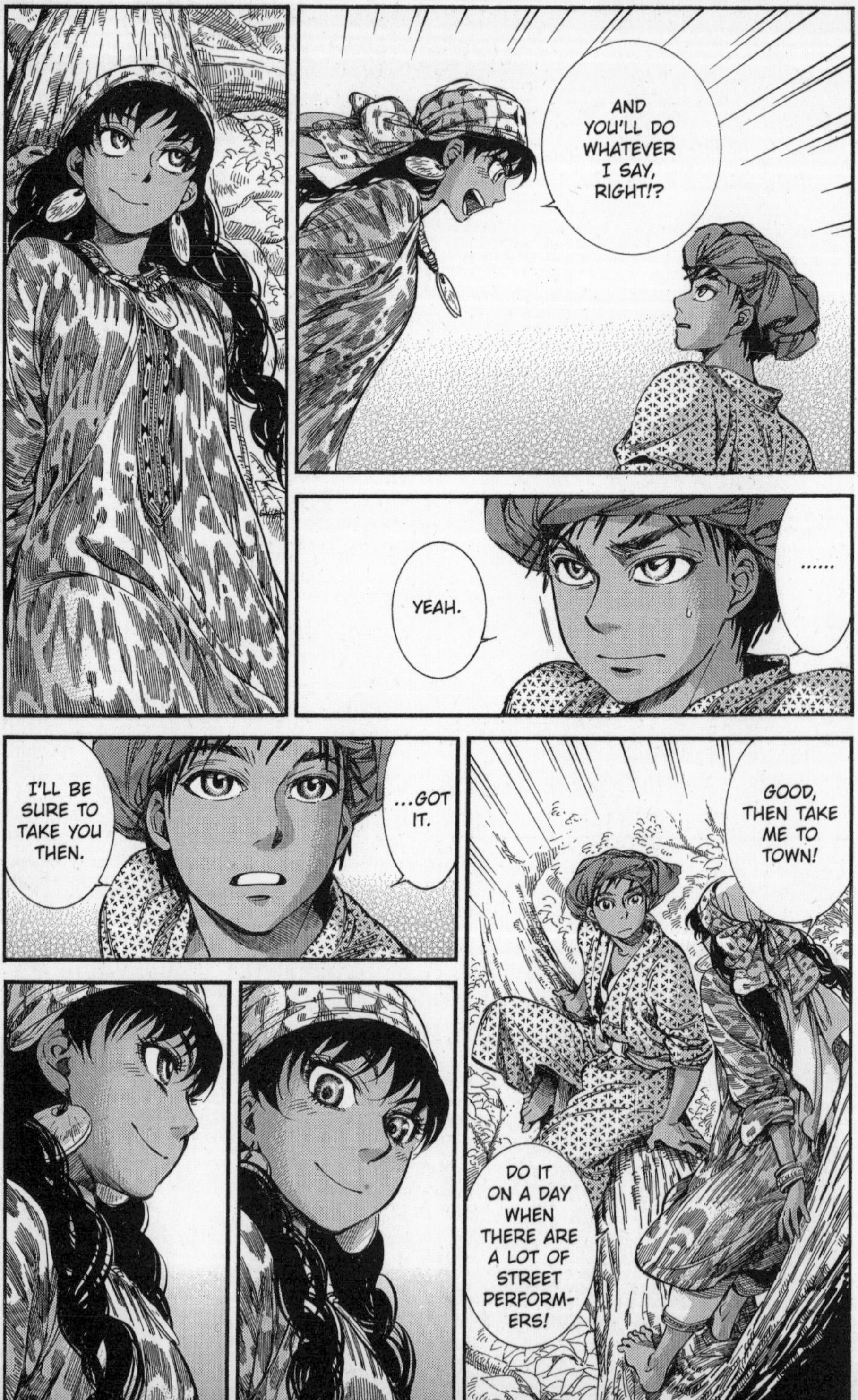
AND YOU'LL DO WHATEVER I SAY, RIGHT!?
......
YEAH.
GOOD, THEN TAKE ME TO TOWN!
DO IT ON A DAY WHEN THERE ARE A LOT OF STREET PERFORM-ERS!
...GOT IT.
I'LL BE SURE TO TAKE YOU THEN.

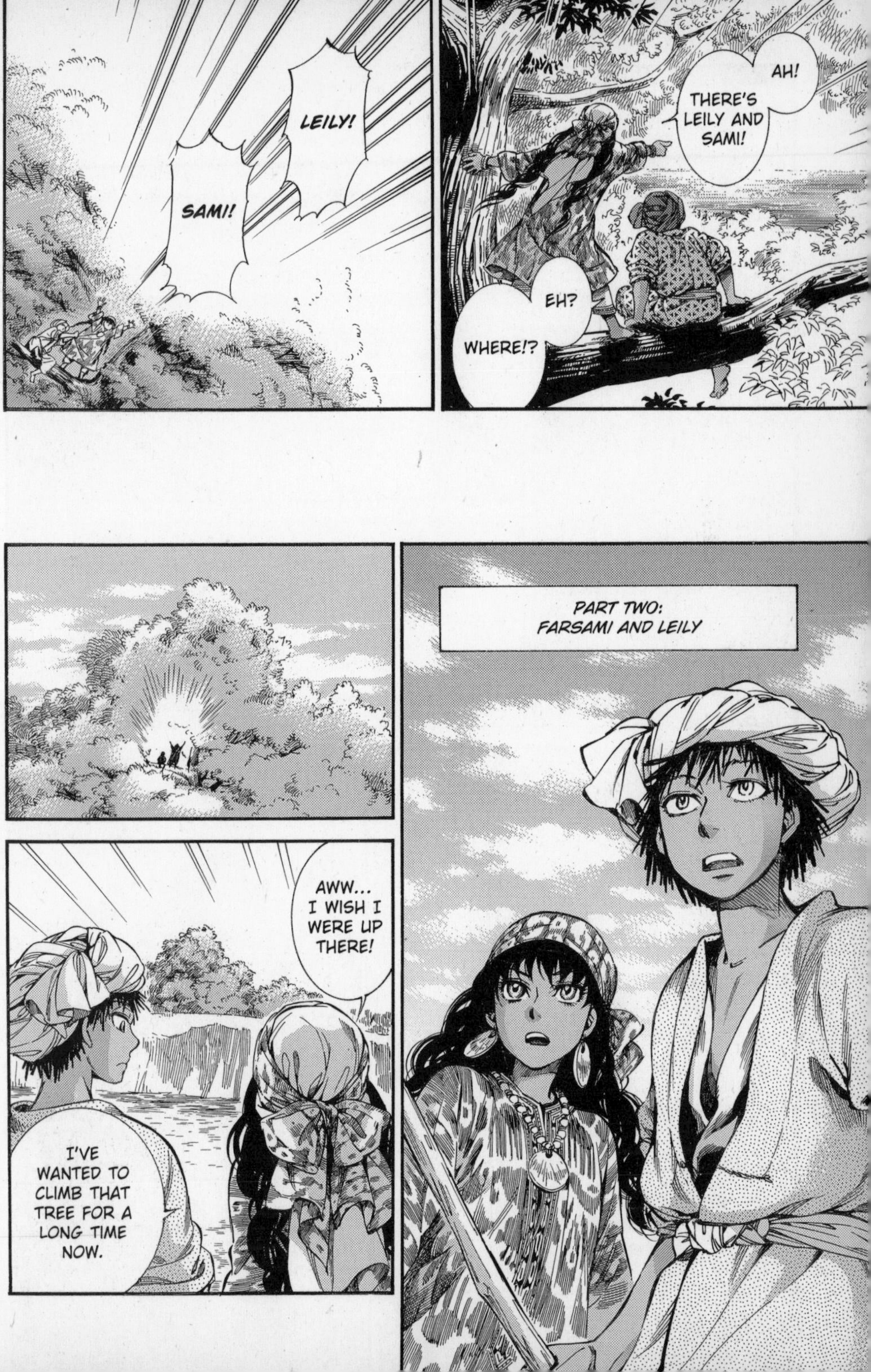
AH!
THERE'S LEILY AND SAMI!
EH?
WHERE!?
LEILY!
SAMI!
PART TWO: FARSAMI AND LEILY
AWW... I WISH I WERE UP THERE!
I'VE WANTED TO CLIMB THAT TREE FOR A LONG TIME NOW.

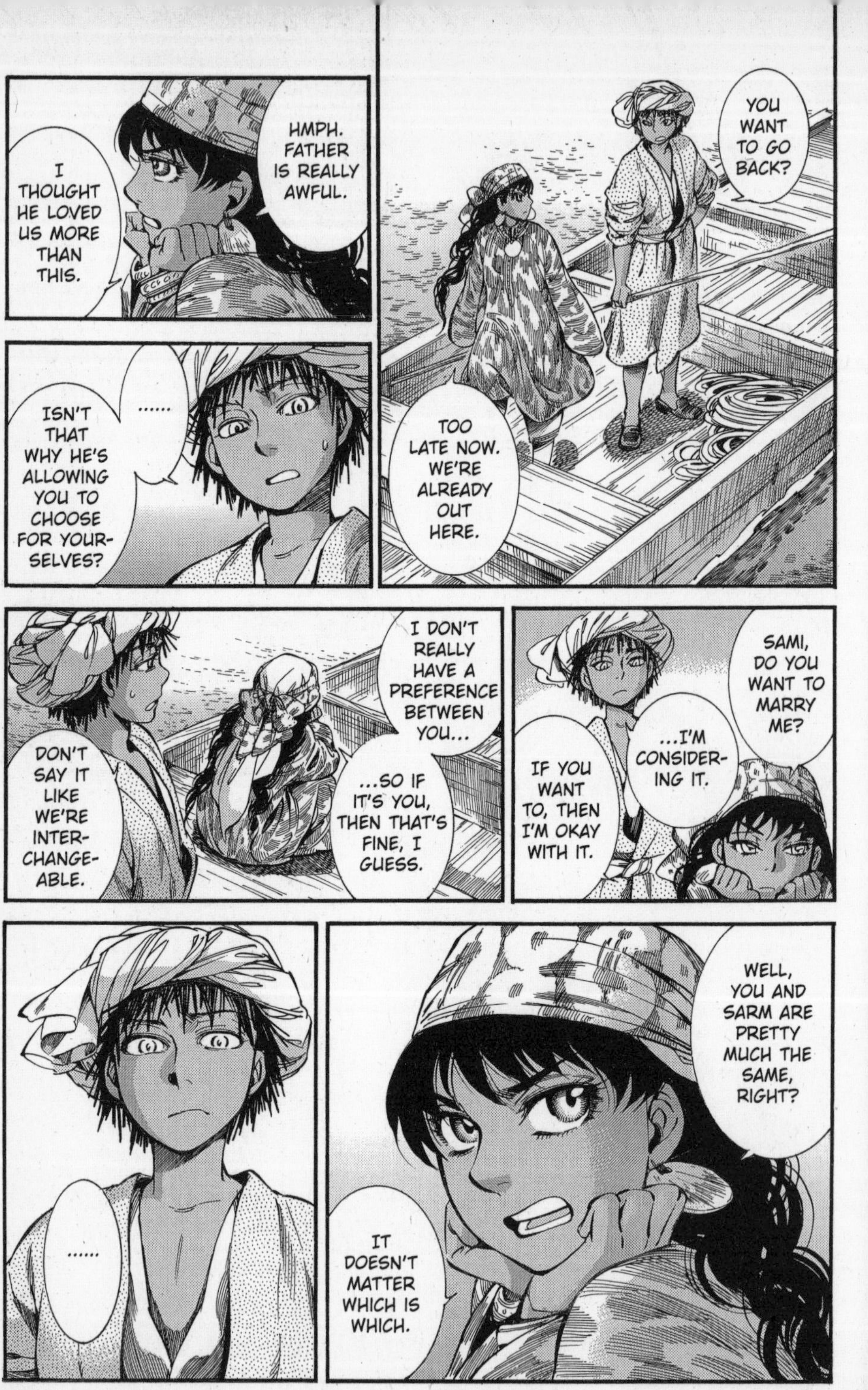
YOU WANT TO GO BACK?
TOO LATE NOW. WE'RE ALREADY OUT HERE.
HMPH. FATHER IS REALLY AWFUL.
I THOUGHT HE LOVED US MORE THAN THIS.
......
ISN'T THAT WHY HE'S ALLOWING YOU TO CHOOSE FOR YOUR-SELVES?
SAMI, DO YOU WANT TO MARRY ME?
...I'M CONSIDER-ING IT.
IF YOU WANT TO, THEN I'M OKAY WITH IT.
I DON'T REALLY HAVE A PREFERENCE BETWEEN YOU...
...SO IF IT'S YOU, THEN THAT'S FINE, I GUESS.
DON'T SAY IT LIKE WE'RE INTER-CHANGE-ABLE.
WELL, YOU AND SARM ARE PRETTY MUCH THE SAME, RIGHT?
IT DOESN'T MATTER WHICH IS WHICH.
......

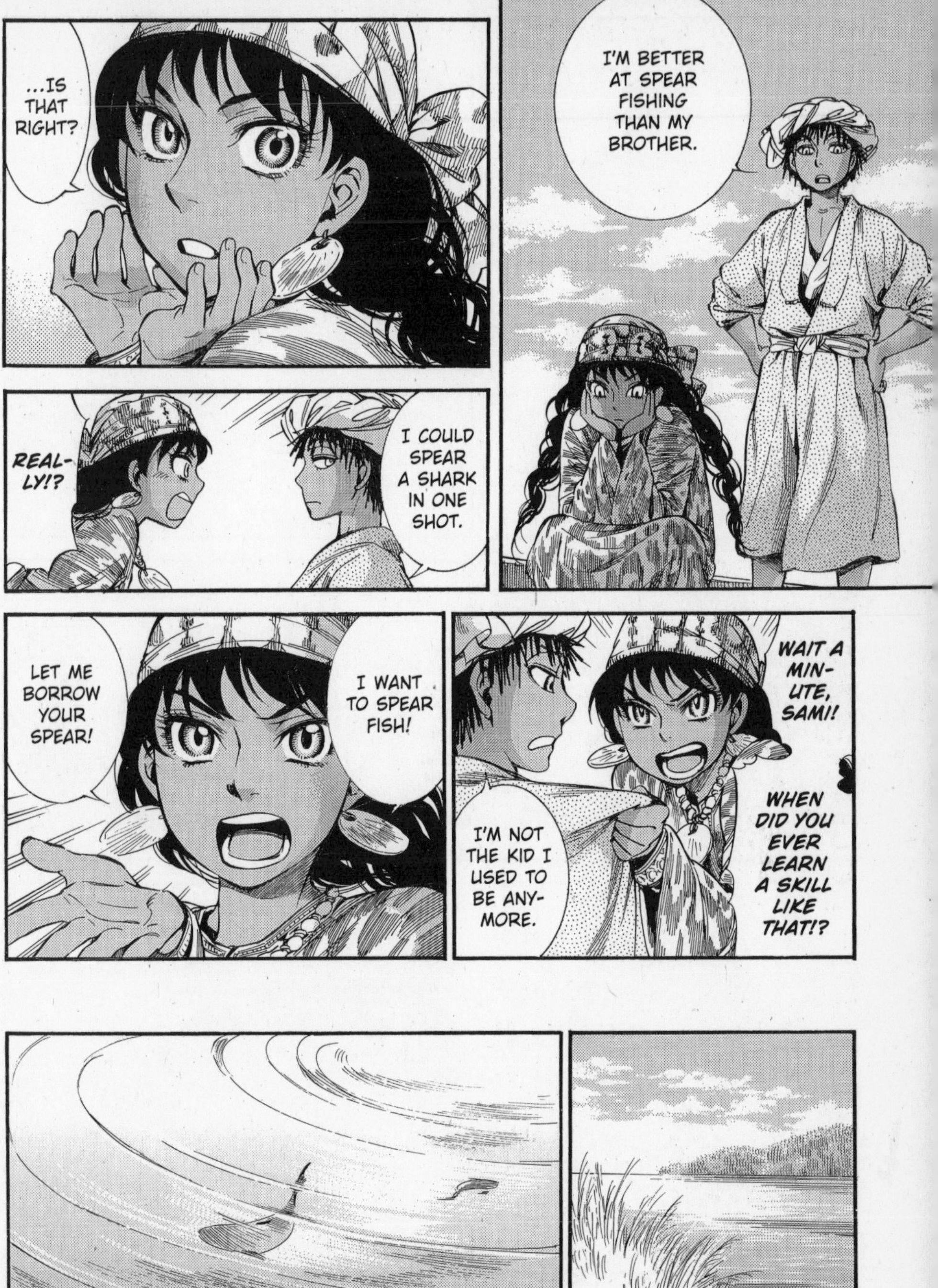
I'M BETTER AT SPEAR FISHING THAN MY BROTHER.
...IS THAT RIGHT?
I COULD SPEAR A SHARK IN ONE SHOT.
REAL-LY!?
WAIT A MIN-UTE, SAMI!
WHEN DID YOU EVER LEARN A SKILL LIKE THAT!?
I'M NOT THE KID I USED TO BE ANY-MORE.
I WANT TO SPEAR FISH!
LET ME BORROW YOUR SPEAR!

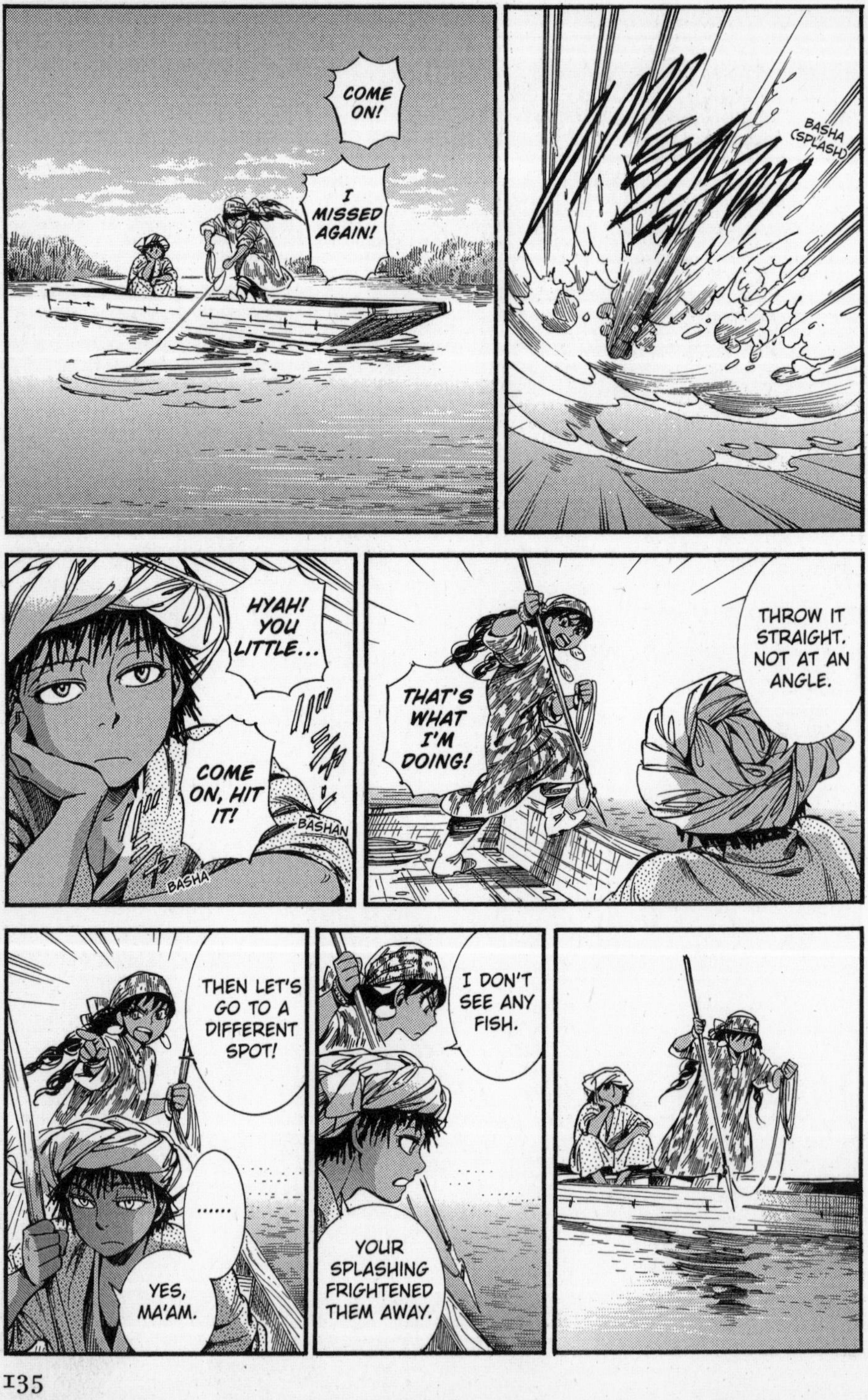

BASHA (SPLASH)
COME ON!
I MISSED AGAIN!
THROW IT STRAIGHT. NOT AT AN ANGLE.
THAT'S WHAT I'M DOING!
HYAH! YOU LITTLE...
COME ON, HIT IT!
BASHAN
BASHA
I DON'T SEE ANY FISH.
YOUR SPLASHING FRIGHTENED THEM AWAY.
THEN LET'S GO TO A DIFFERENT SPOT!
......
YES, MA'AM.

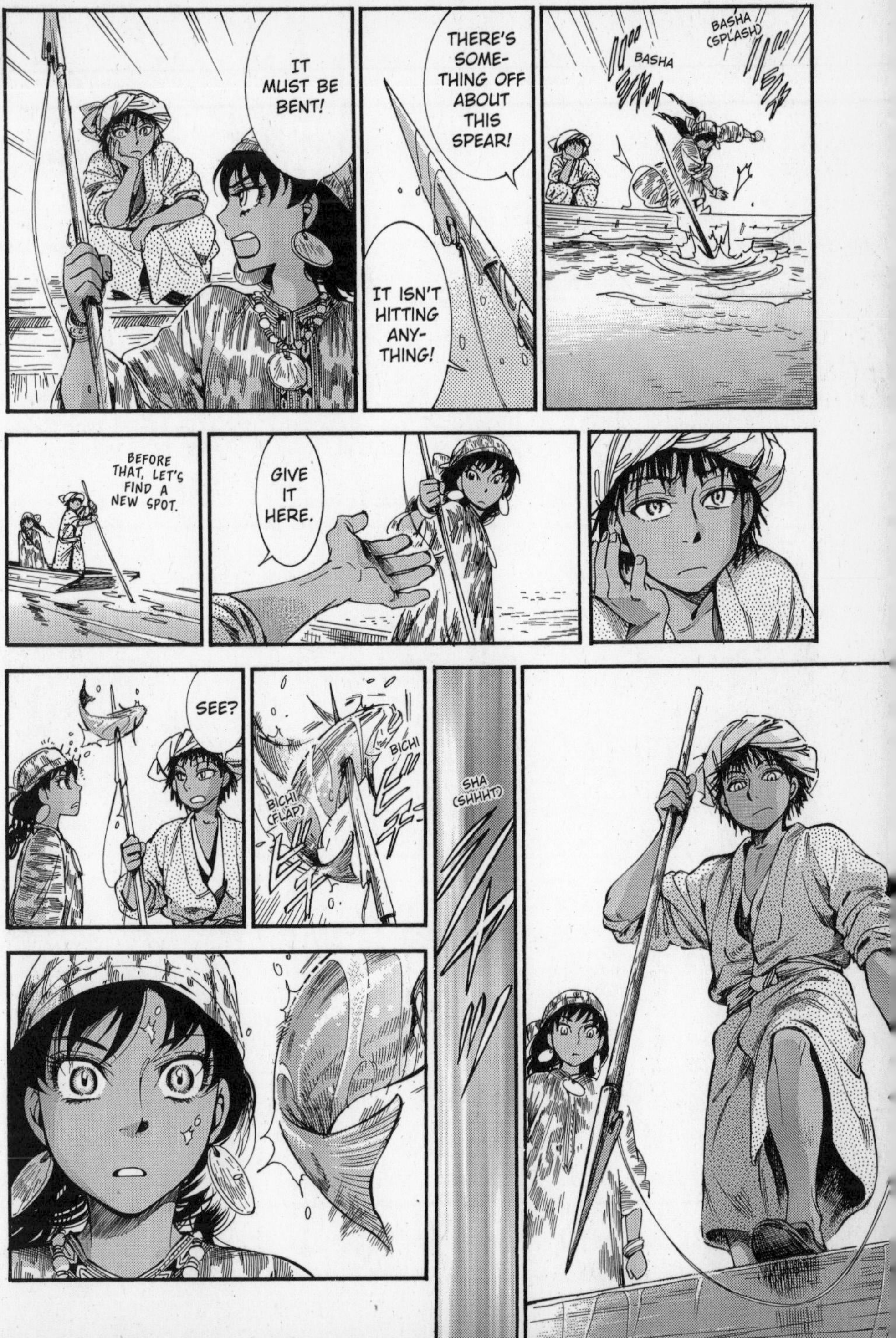
BASHA (SPLASH)
BASHA
THERE'S SOME- THING OFF ABOUT THIS SPEAR!
IT ISN'T HITTING ANY- THING!
IT MUST BE BENT!
GIVE IT HERE.
BEFORE THAT, LET'S FIND A NEW SPOT.
SHA (SHHHT)
BICHI
BICHI (FLAP)
SEE?

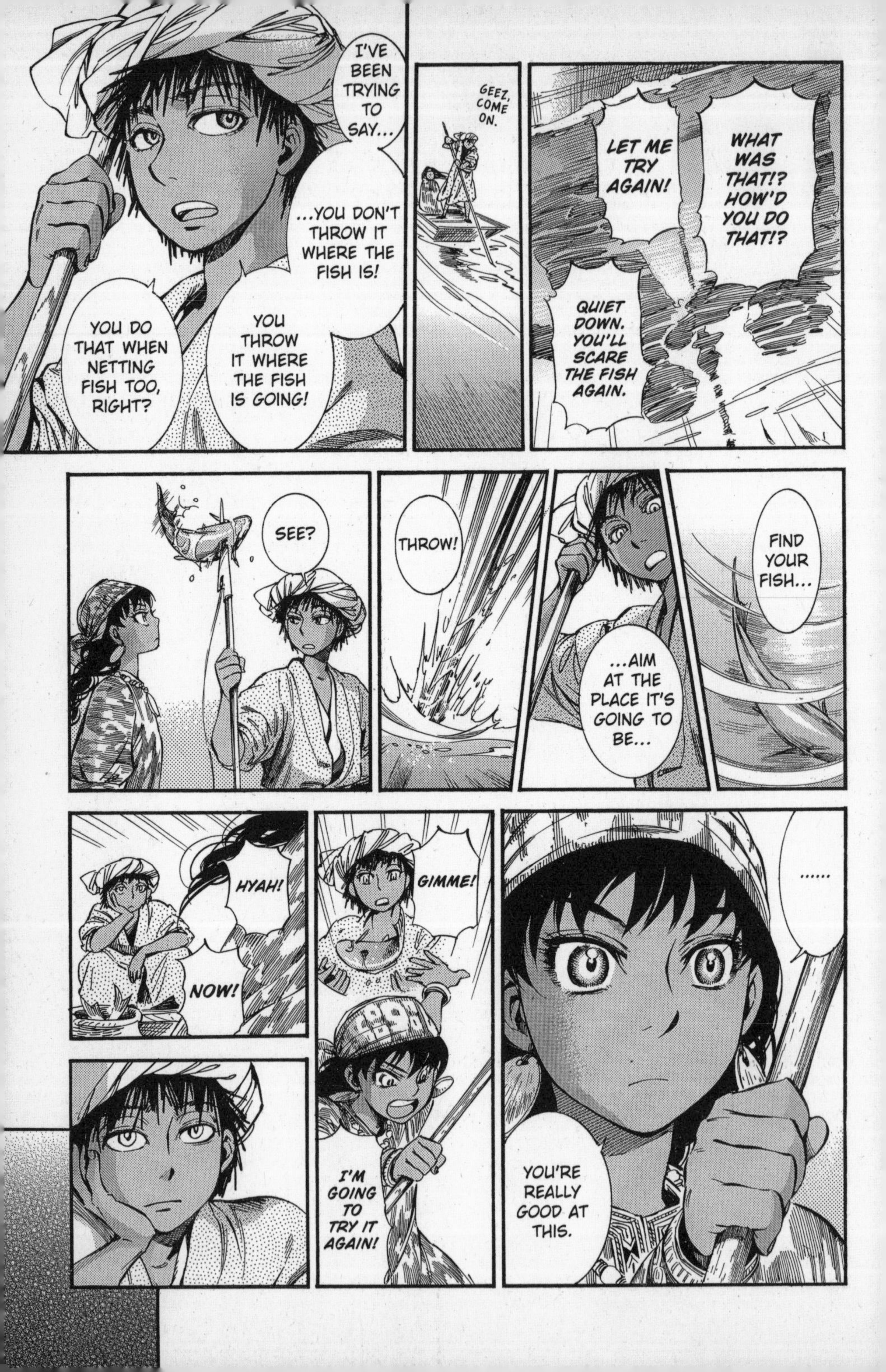
WHAT WAS THAT!? HOW'D YOU DO THAT!?
LET ME TRY AGAIN!
QUIET DOWN. YOU'LL SCARE THE FISH AGAIN.
GEEZ, COME ON.
I'VE BEEN TRYING TO SAY...
...YOU DON'T THROW IT WHERE THE FISH IS!
YOU THROW IT WHERE THE FISH IS GOING!
YOU DO THAT WHEN NETTING FISH TOO, RIGHT?
FIND YOUR FISH...
...AIM AT THE PLACE IT'S GOING TO BE...
THROW!
SEE?
......
YOU'RE REALLY GOOD AT THIS.
GIMME!
I'M GOING TO TRY IT AGAIN!
HYAH!
NOW!

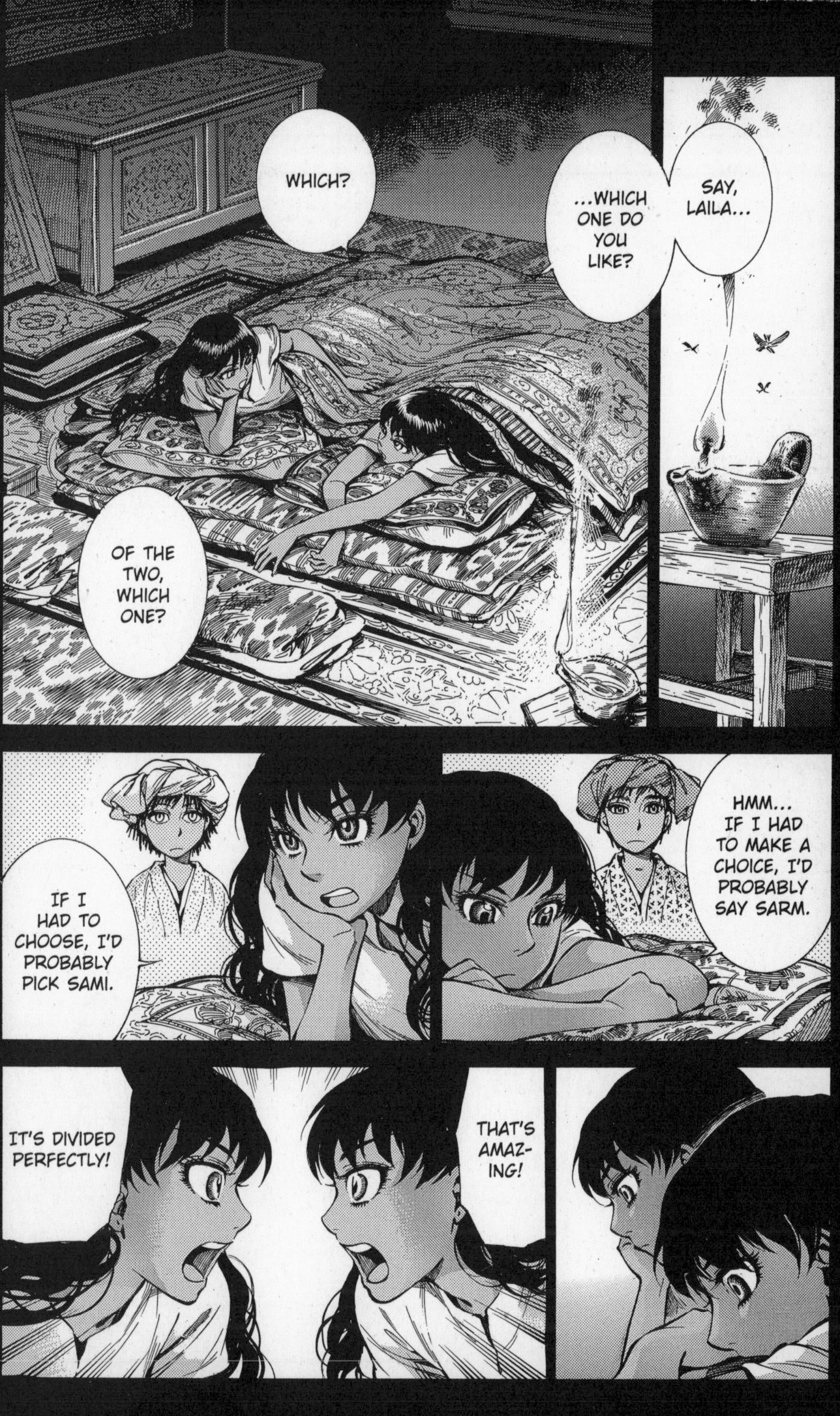
SAY, LAILA...
...WHICH ONE DO YOU LIKE?
WHICH?
OF THE TWO, WHICH ONE?
HMM... IF I HAD TO MAKE A CHOICE, I'D PROBABLY SAY SARM.
IF I HAD TO CHOOSE, I'D PROBABLY PICK SAMI.
THAT'S AMAZ-ING!
IT'S DIVIDED PERFECTLY!

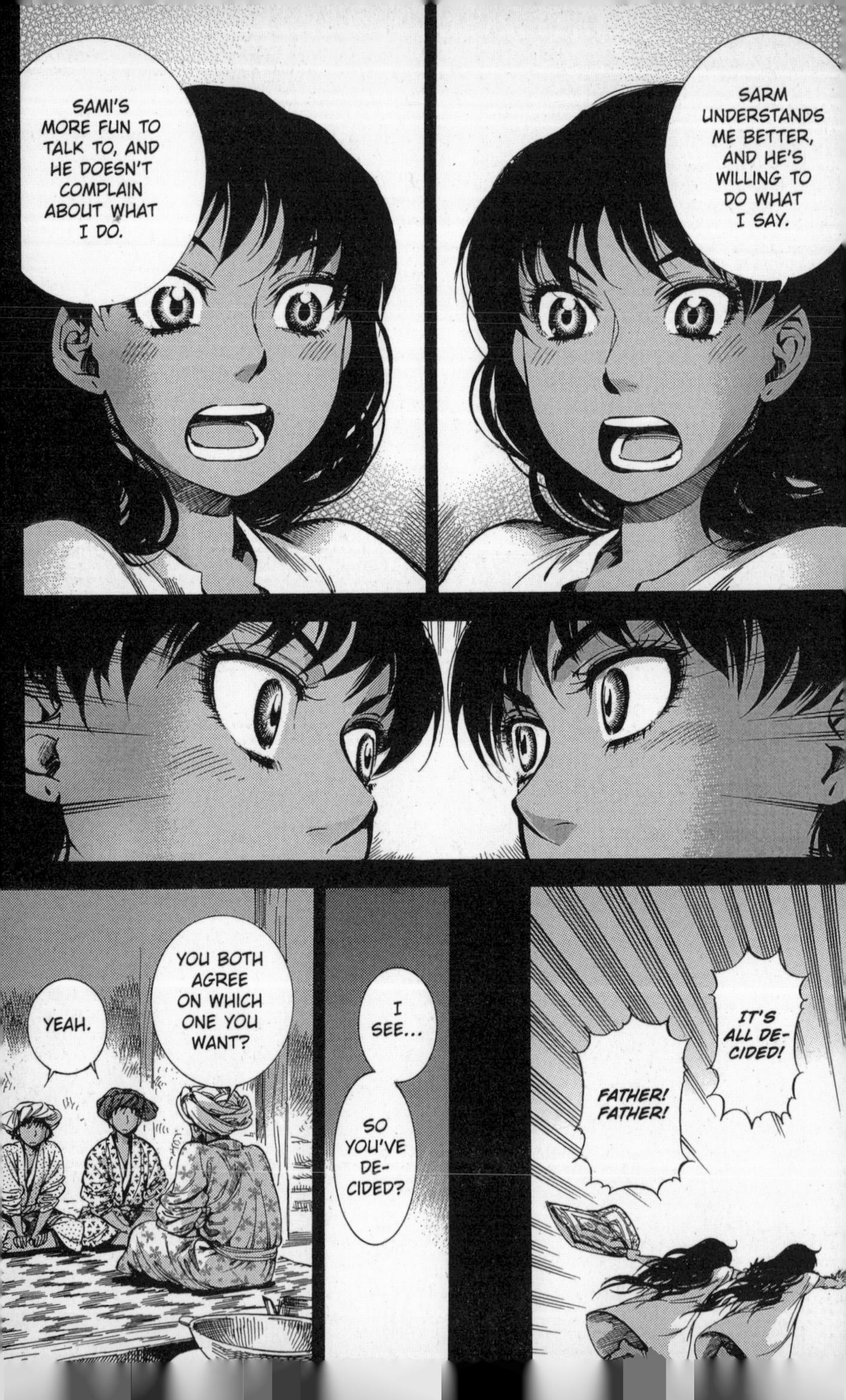
SARM UNDERSTANDS ME BETTER, AND HE'S WILLING TO DO WHAT I SAY.
SAMI'S MORE FUN TO TALK TO, AND HE DOESN'T COMPLAIN ABOUT WHAT I DO.
IT'S ALL DE-CIDED!
FATHER! FATHER!
I SEE...
SO YOU'VE DE-CIDED?
YOU BOTH AGREE ON WHICH ONE YOU WANT?
YEAH.

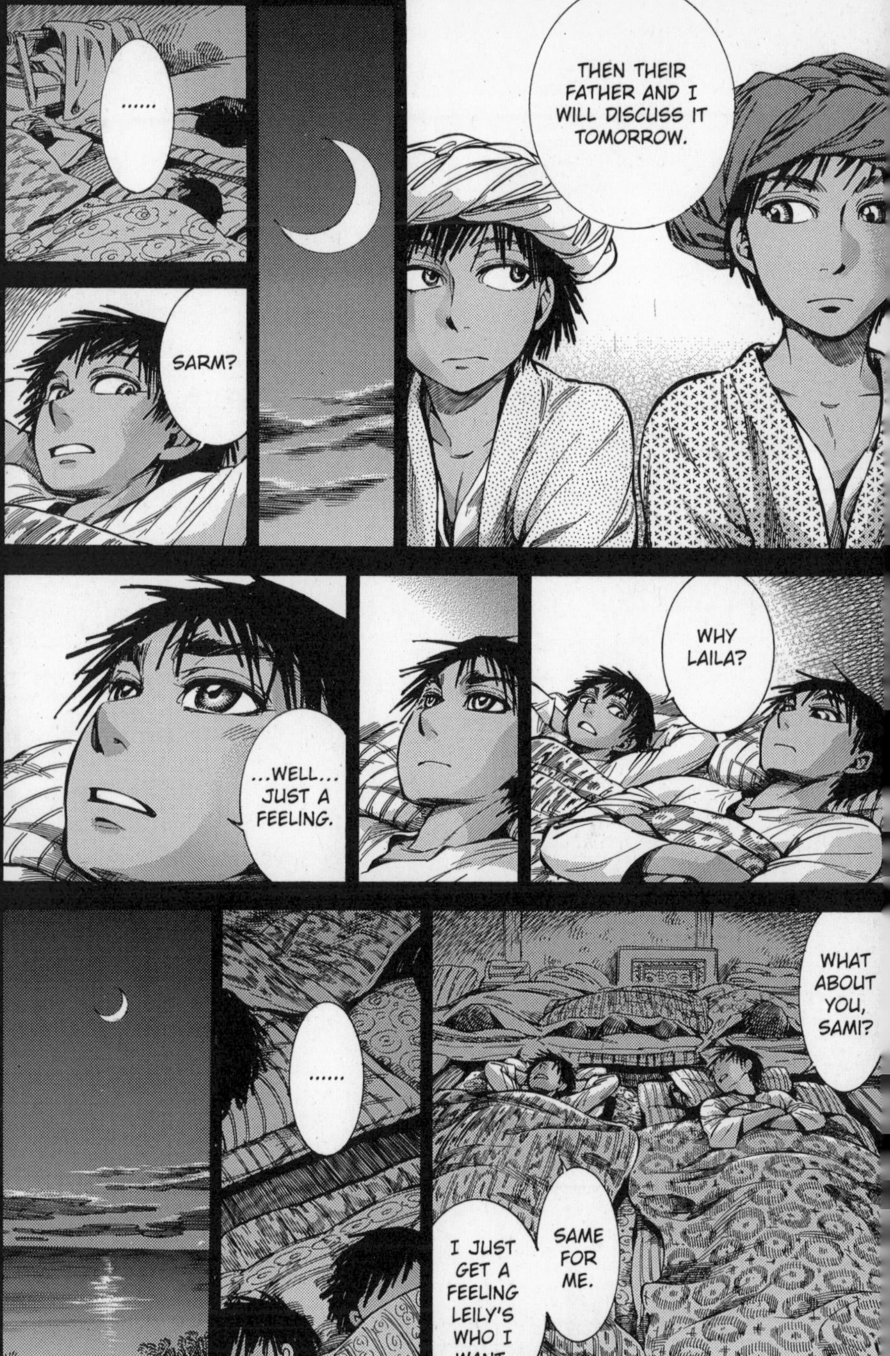
THEN THEIR FATHER AND I WILL DISCUSS IT TOMORROW.
......
SARM?
WHY LAILA?
...WELL... JUST A FEELING.
WHAT ABOUT YOU, SAMI?
SAME FOR ME.
I JUST GET A FEELING LEILY'S WHO I WANT.
......

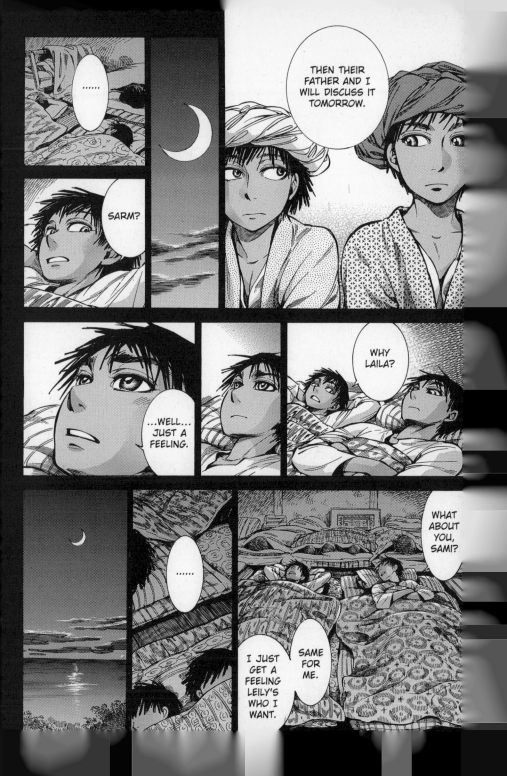

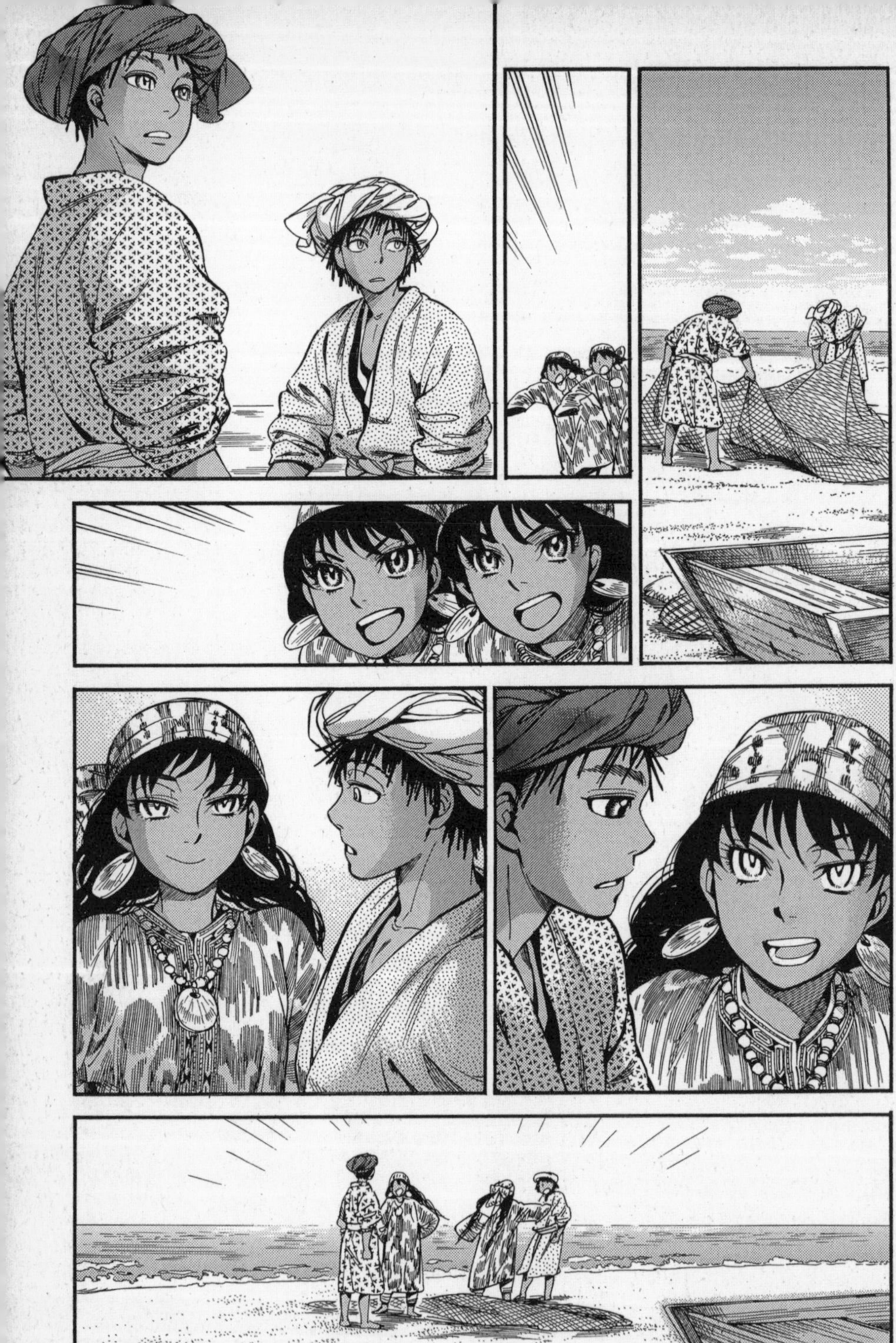

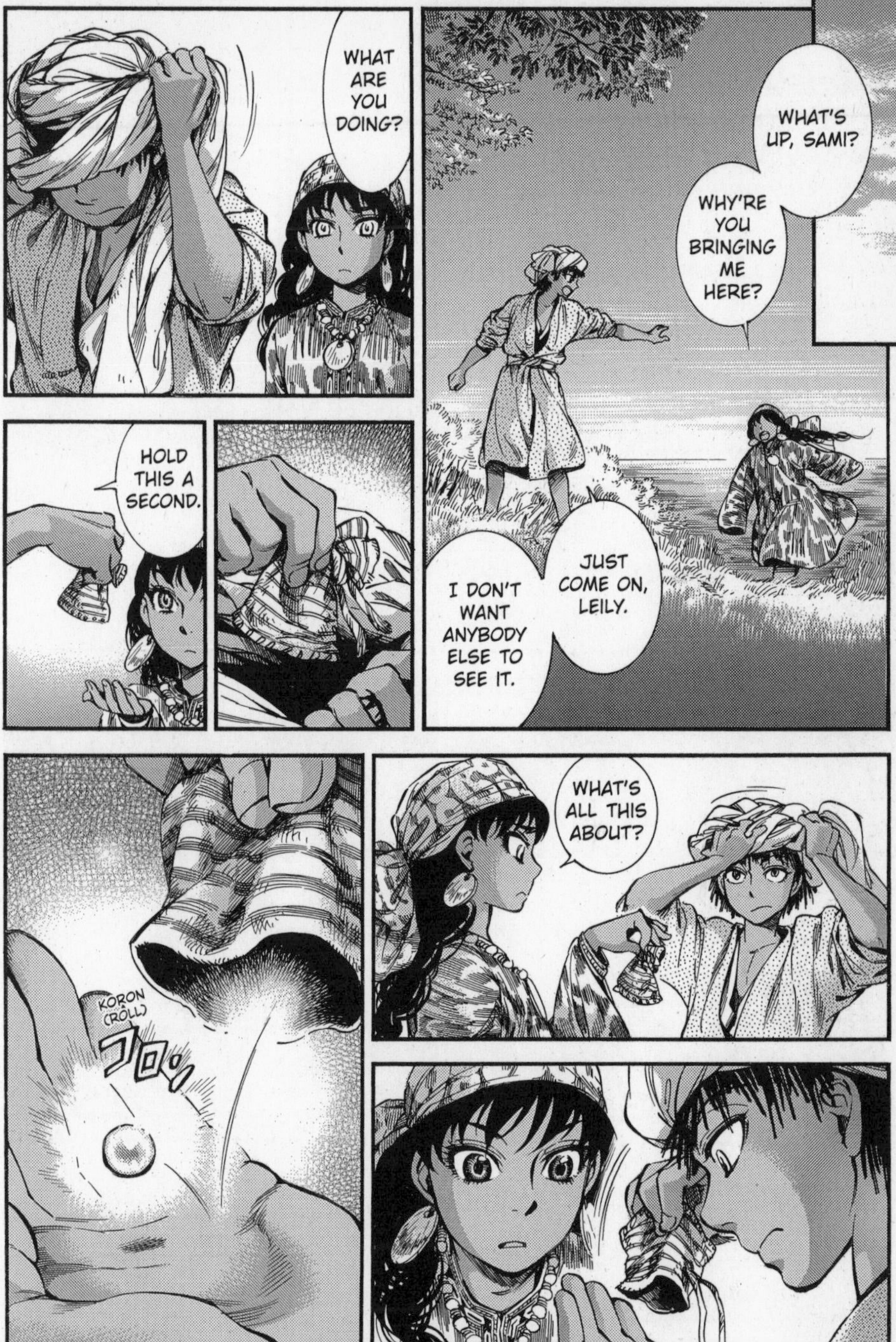
WHAT'S UP, SAMI?
WHY'RE YOU BRINGING ME HERE?
JUST COME ON, LEILY.
I DON'T WANT ANYBODY ELSE TO SEE IT.
WHAT ARE YOU DOING?
HOLD THIS A SECOND.
WHAT'S ALL THIS ABOUT?
KORON (ROLL)

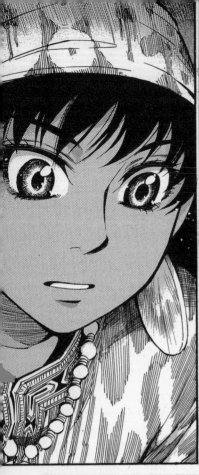
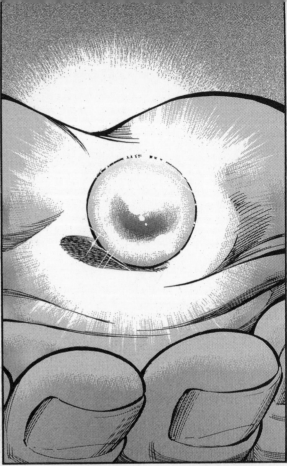

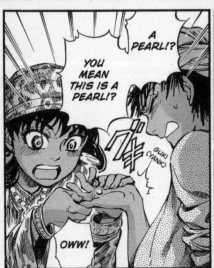
A PEARL!?

YOU MEAN THIS IS A PEARL!?

GLIKI CYANKO

OWW!

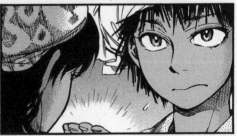

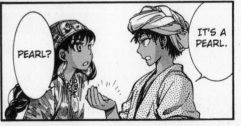
PEARL?

IT'S A PEARL.

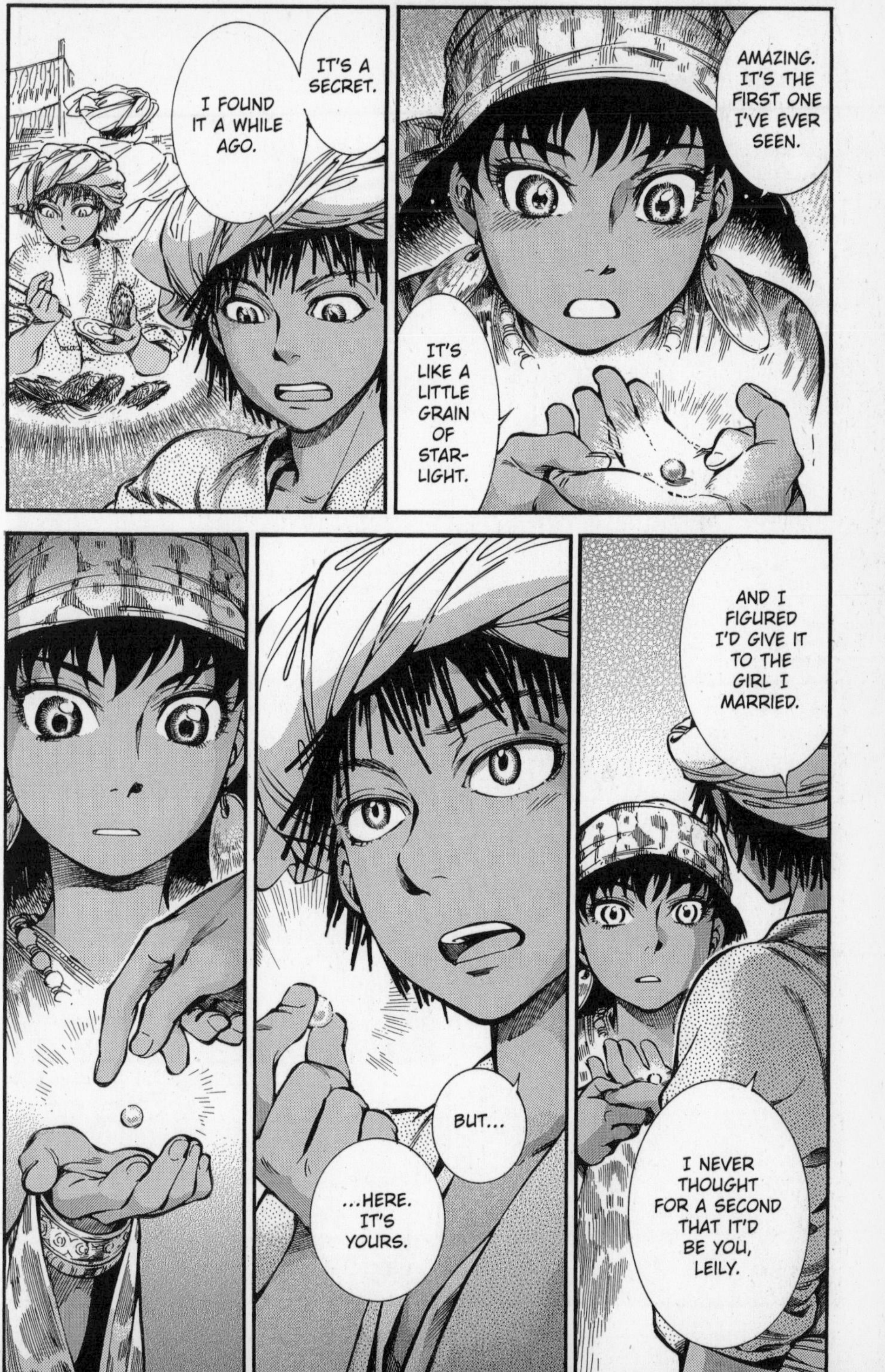
AMAZING. IT'S THE FIRST ONE I'VE EVER SEEN.
IT'S LIKE A LITTLE GRAIN OF STAR-LIGHT.
IT'S A SECRET.
I FOUND IT A WHILE AGO.
AND I FIGURED I'D GIVE IT TO THE GIRL I MARRIED.
I NEVER THOUGHT FOR A SECOND THAT IT'D BE YOU, LEILY.
BUT...
...HERE. IT'S YOURS.

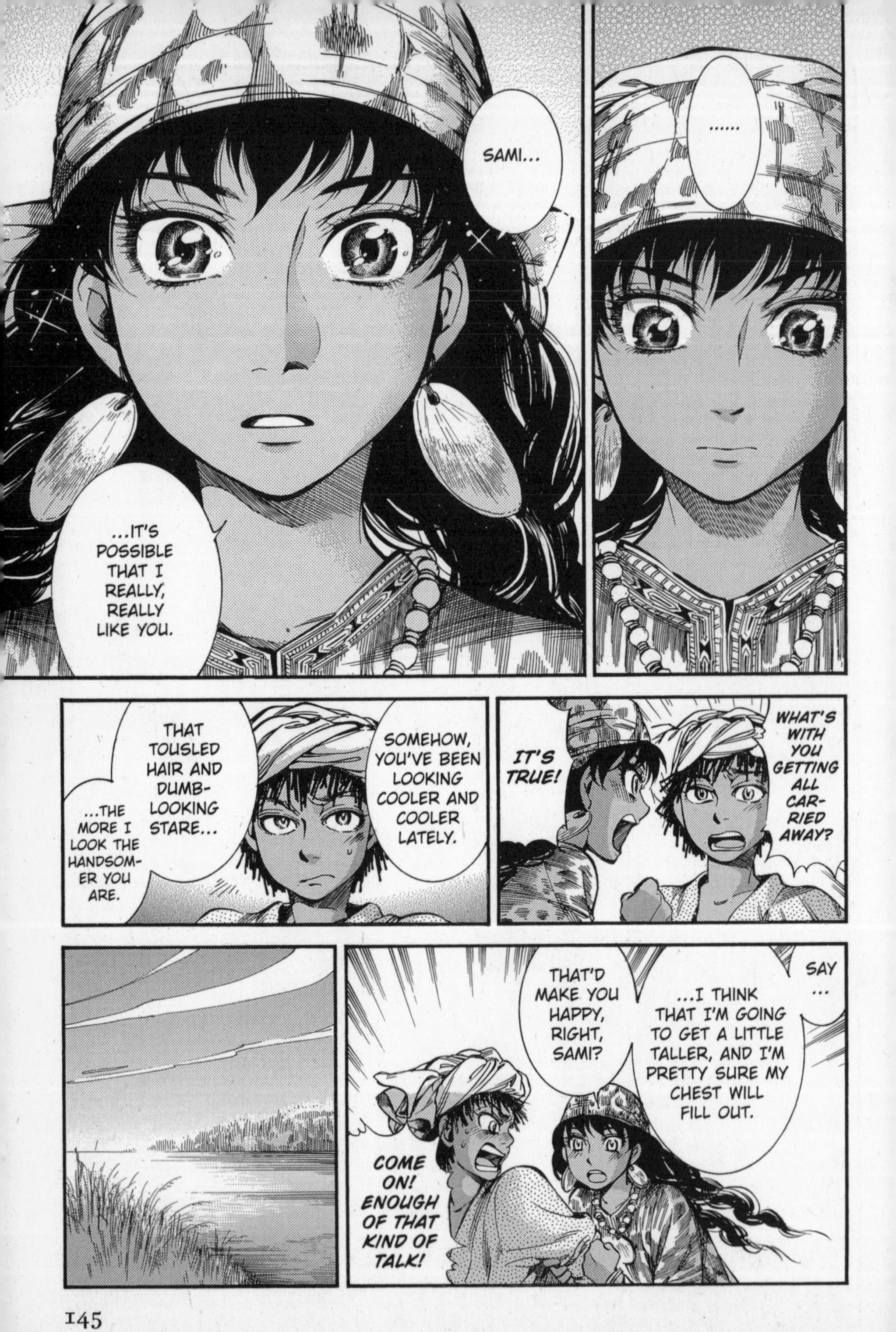
......
SAMI...
...IT'S POSSIBLE THAT I REALLY, REALLY LIKE YOU.
WHAT'S WITH YOU GETTING ALL CARRIED AWAY?
IT'S TRUE!
SOMEHOW, YOU'VE BEEN LOOKING COOLER AND COOLER LATELY.
THAT TOUSLED HAIR AND DUMB-LOOKING STARE...
...THE MORE I LOOK THE HANDSOMER YOU ARE.
SAY ...
...I THINK THAT I'M GOING TO GET A LITTLE TALLER, AND I'M PRETTY SURE MY CHEST WILL FILL OUT.
THAT'D MAKE YOU HAPPY, RIGHT, SAMI?
COME ON! ENOUGH OF THAT KIND OF TALK!

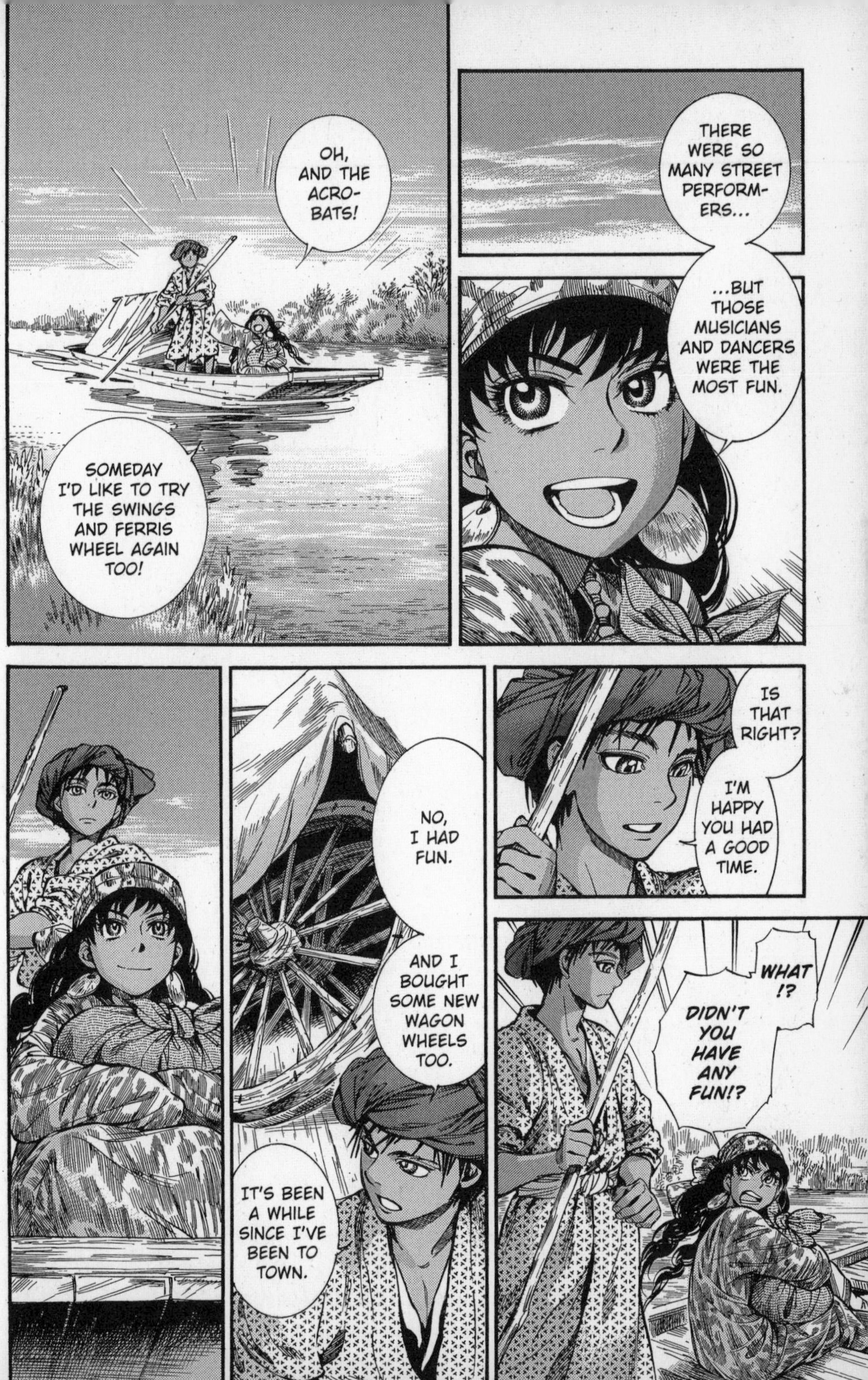

THERE WERE SO MANY STREET PERFORMERS...
...BUT THOSE MUSICIANS AND DANCERS WERE THE MOST FUN.
OH, AND THE ACROBATS!
SOMEDAY I'D LIKE TO TRY THE SWINGS AND FERRIS WHEEL AGAIN TOO!
IS THAT RIGHT?
I'M HAPPY YOU HAD A GOOD TIME.
WHAT!?
DIDN'T YOU HAVE ANY FUN!?
NO, I HAD FUN.
AND I BOUGHT SOME NEW WAGON WHEELS TOO.
IT'S BEEN A WHILE SINCE I'VE BEEN TO TOWN.

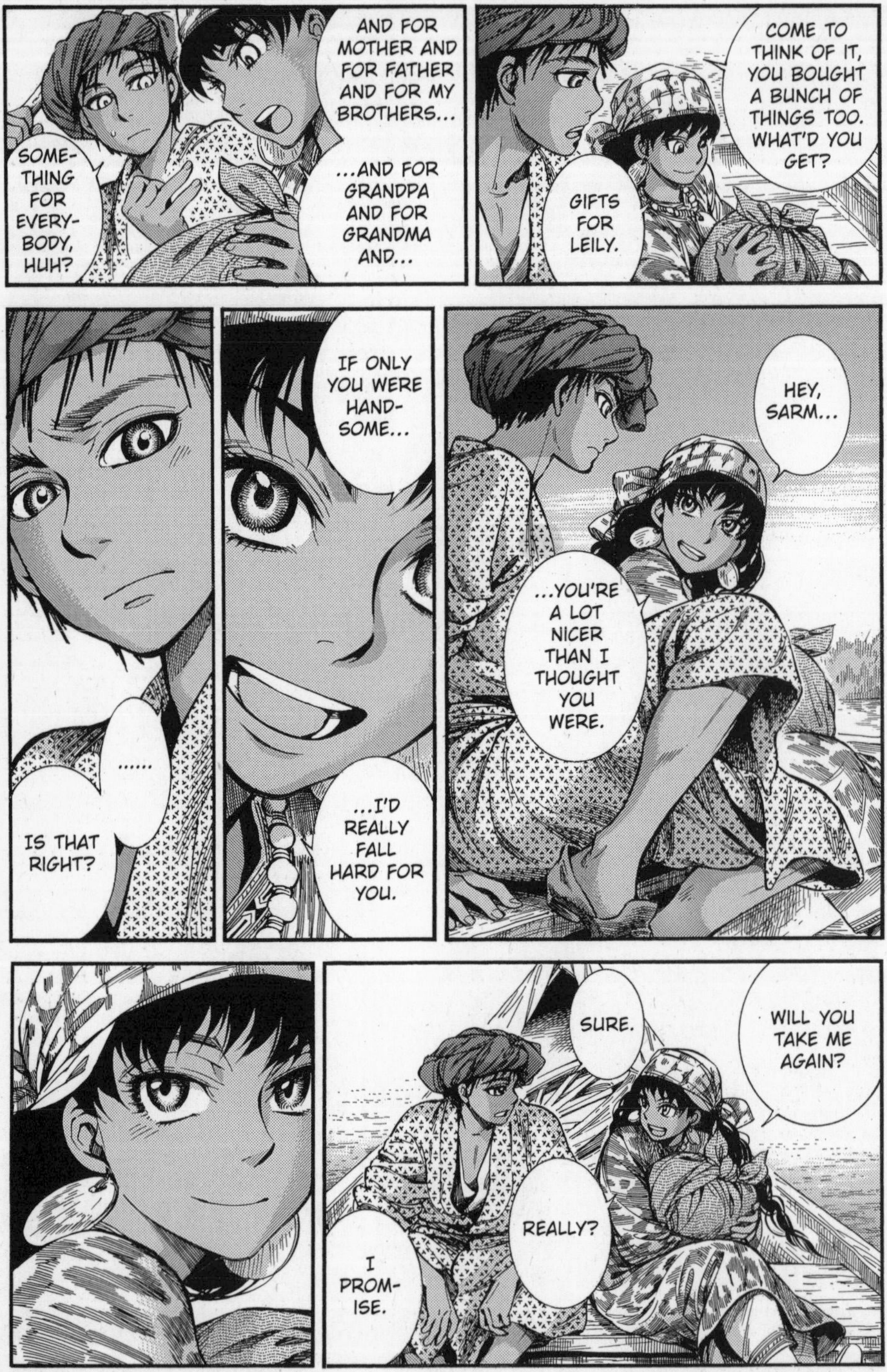
COME TO THINK OF IT, YOU BOUGHT A BUNCH OF THINGS TOO. WHAT'D YOU GET?
GIFTS FOR LEILY.
AND FOR MOTHER AND FOR FATHER AND FOR MY BROTHERS...
...AND FOR GRANDPA AND FOR GRANDMA AND...
SOME-THING FOR EVERY-BODY, HUH?
HEY, SARM...
...YOU'RE A LOT NICER THAN I THOUGHT YOU WERE.
IF ONLY YOU WERE HAND-SOME...
...I'D REALLY FALL HARD FOR YOU.
......
IS THAT RIGHT?
WILL YOU TAKE ME AGAIN?
SURE.
REALLY?
I PROM-ISE.

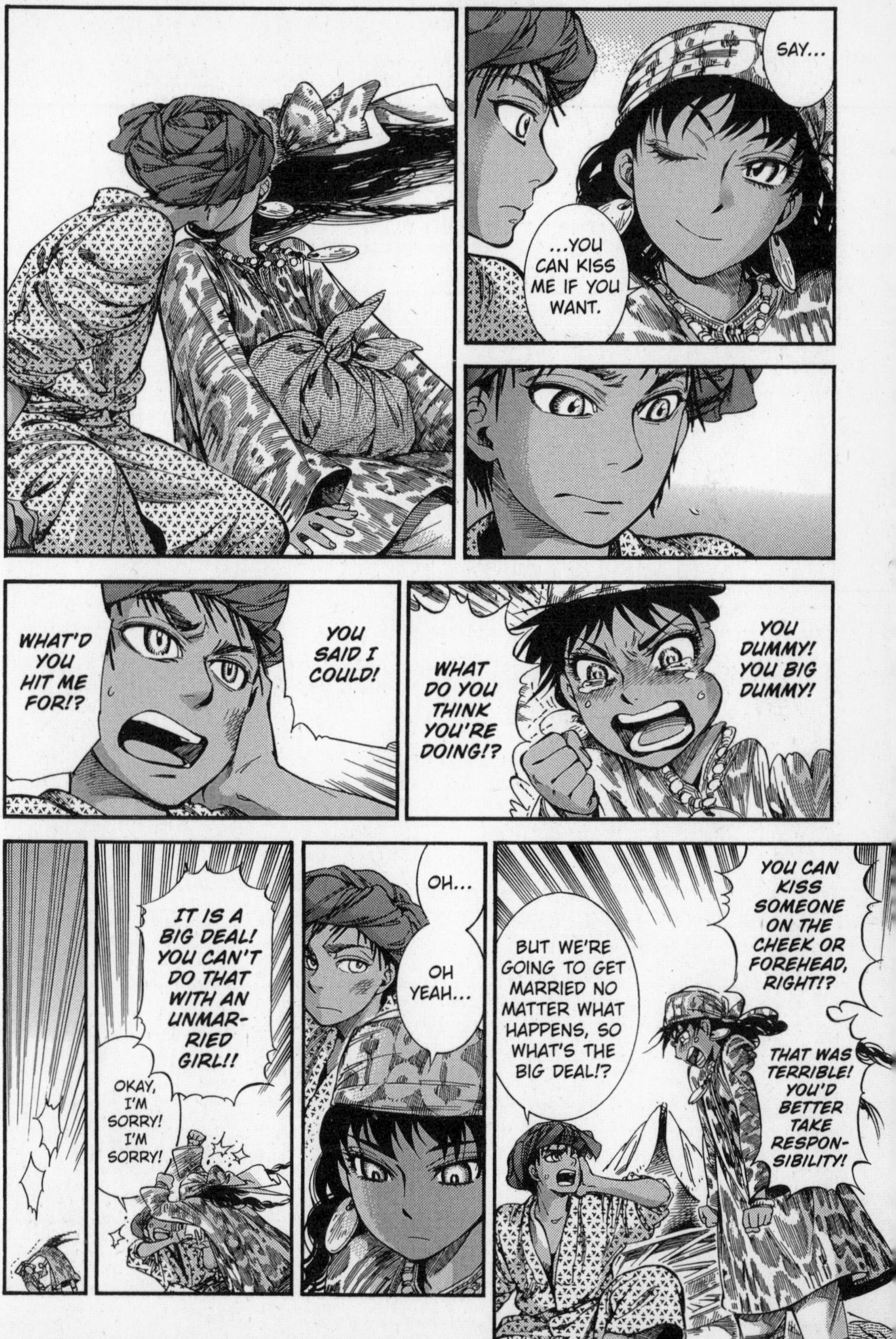
SAY...
...YOU CAN KISS ME IF YOU WANT.
YOU DUMMY! YOU BIG DUMMY!
WHAT DO YOU THINK YOU'RE DOING!?
YOU SAID I COULD!
WHAT'D YOU HIT ME FOR!?
YOU CAN KISS SOMEONE ON THE CHEEK OR FOREHEAD, RIGHT!?
THAT WAS TERRIBLE! YOU'D BETTER TAKE RESPON-SIBILITY!
BUT WE'RE GOING TO GET MARRIED NO MATTER WHAT HAPPENS, SO WHAT'S THE BIG DEAL!?
OH...
OH YEAH...
IT IS A BIG DEAL! YOU CAN'T DO THAT WITH AN UNMAR-RIED GIRL!!
OKAY, I'M SORRY! I'M SORRY!

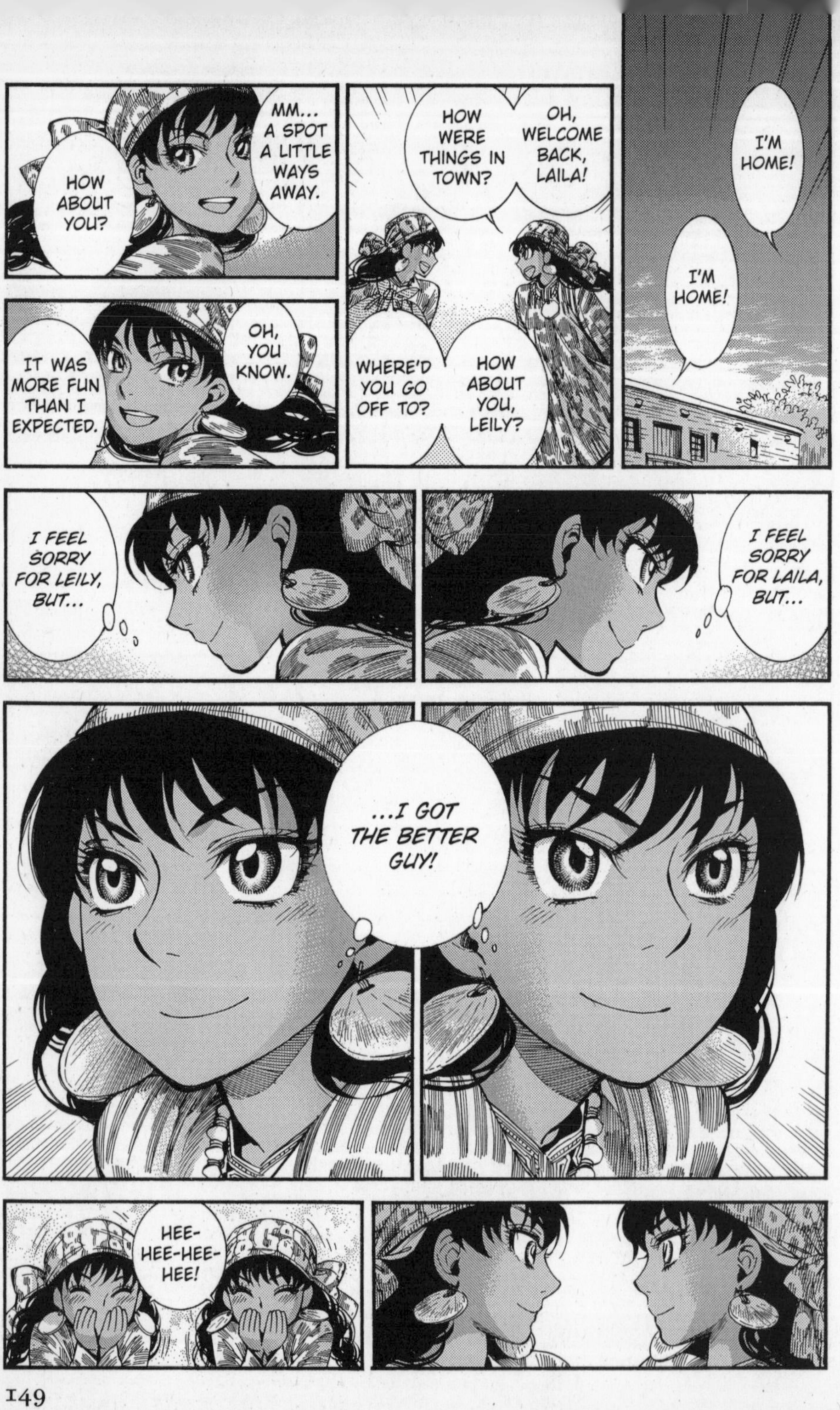
I'M HOME!
I'M HOME!
OH, WELCOME BACK, LAILA!
HOW WERE THINGS IN TOWN?
HOW ABOUT YOU, LEILY?
WHERE'D YOU GO OFF TO?
MM... A SPOT A LITTLE WAYS AWAY.
HOW ABOUT YOU?
OH, YOU KNOW.
IT WAS MORE FUN THAN I EXPECTED.
I FEEL SORRY FOR LAILA, BUT...
I FEEL SORRY FOR LEILY, BUT...
...I GOT THE BETTER GUY!
HEE-HEE-HEE-HEE!

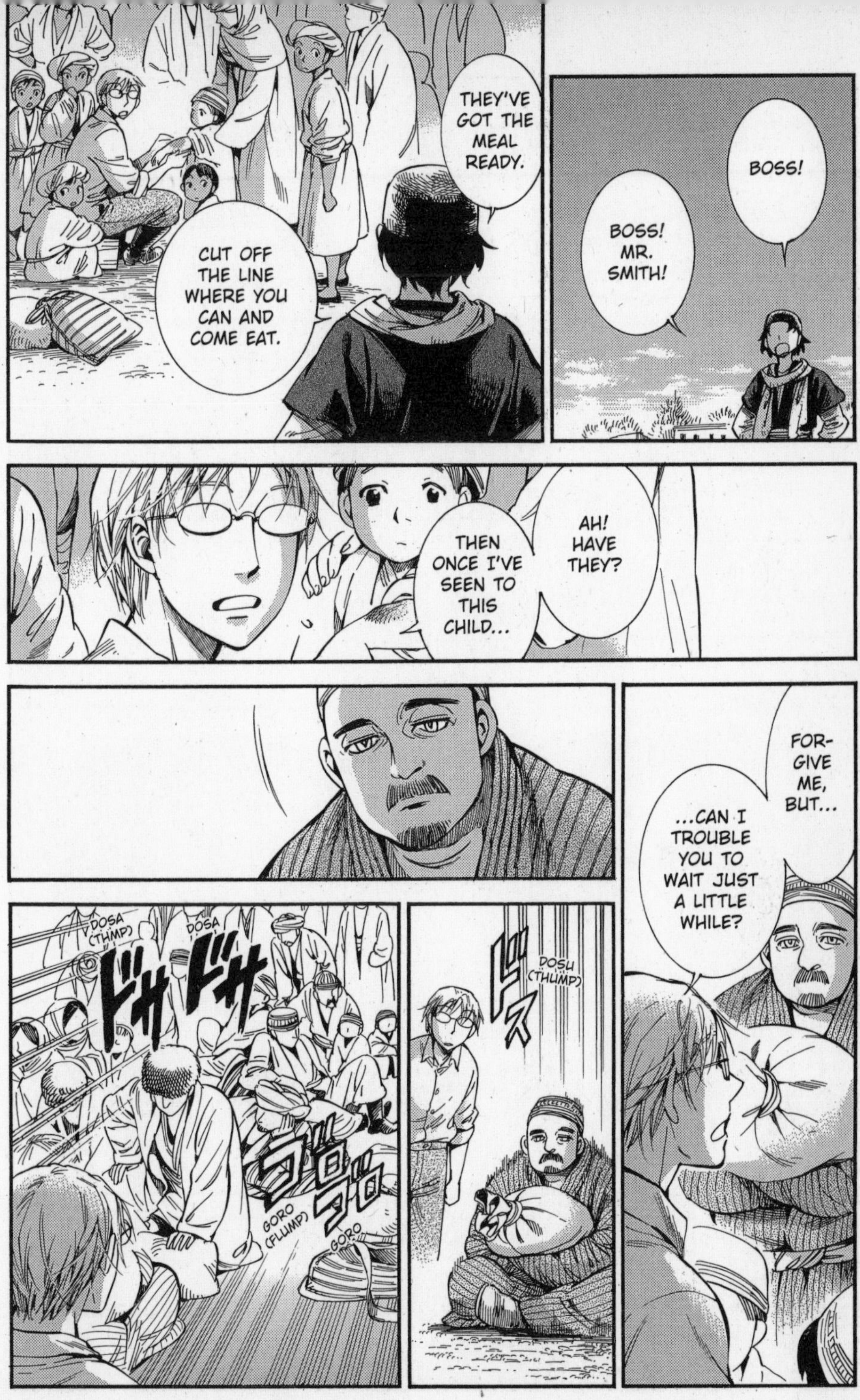
BOSS!
BOSS! MR. SMITH!
THEY'VE GOT THE MEAL READY.
CUT OFF THE LINE WHERE YOU CAN AND COME EAT.
AH! HAVE THEY?
THEN ONCE I'VE SEEN TO THIS CHILD...
FOR-GIVE ME, BUT...
...CAN I TROUBLE YOU TO WAIT JUST A LITTLE WHILE?
ドス
DOSU (THUMP)
ドサドサ
DOSA (THUMP)
DOSA
ゴロゴロ
GORO (FLUMP)
GORO

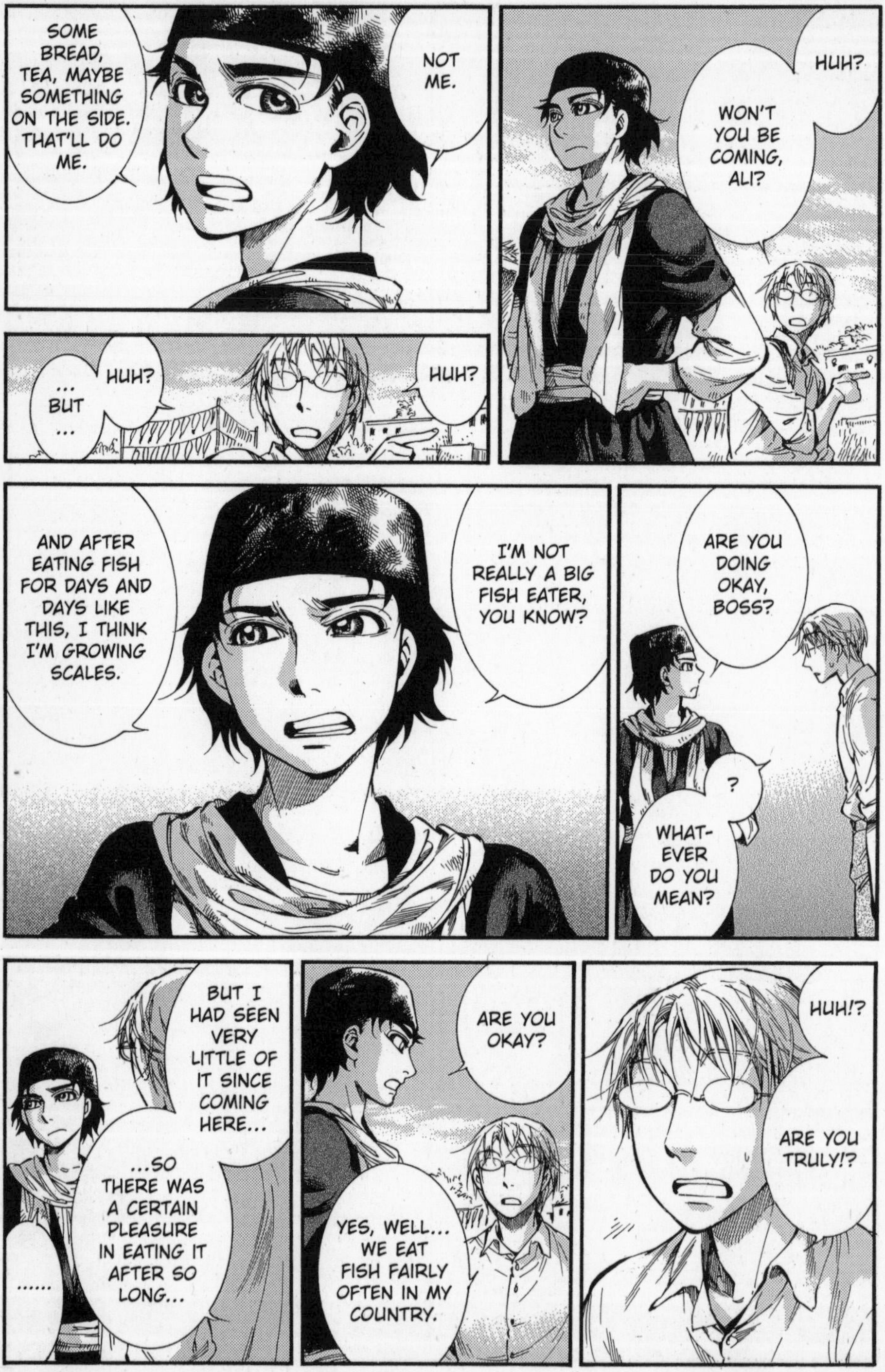
HUH?
WON'T YOU BE COMING, ALI?
NOT ME.
SOME BREAD, TEA, MAYBE SOMETHING ON THE SIDE. THAT'LL DO ME.
HUH?
HUH?
... BUT ...
ARE YOU DOING OKAY, BOSS?
?
WHAT-EVER DO YOU MEAN?
I'M NOT REALLY A BIG FISH EATER, YOU KNOW?
AND AFTER EATING FISH FOR DAYS AND DAYS LIKE THIS, I THINK I'M GROWING SCALES.
HUH!?
ARE YOU TRULY!?
ARE YOU OKAY?
YES, WELL... WE EAT FISH FAIRLY OFTEN IN MY COUNTRY.
BUT I HAD SEEN VERY LITTLE OF IT SINCE COMING HERE...
...SO THERE WAS A CERTAIN PLEASURE IN EATING IT AFTER SO LONG...
......

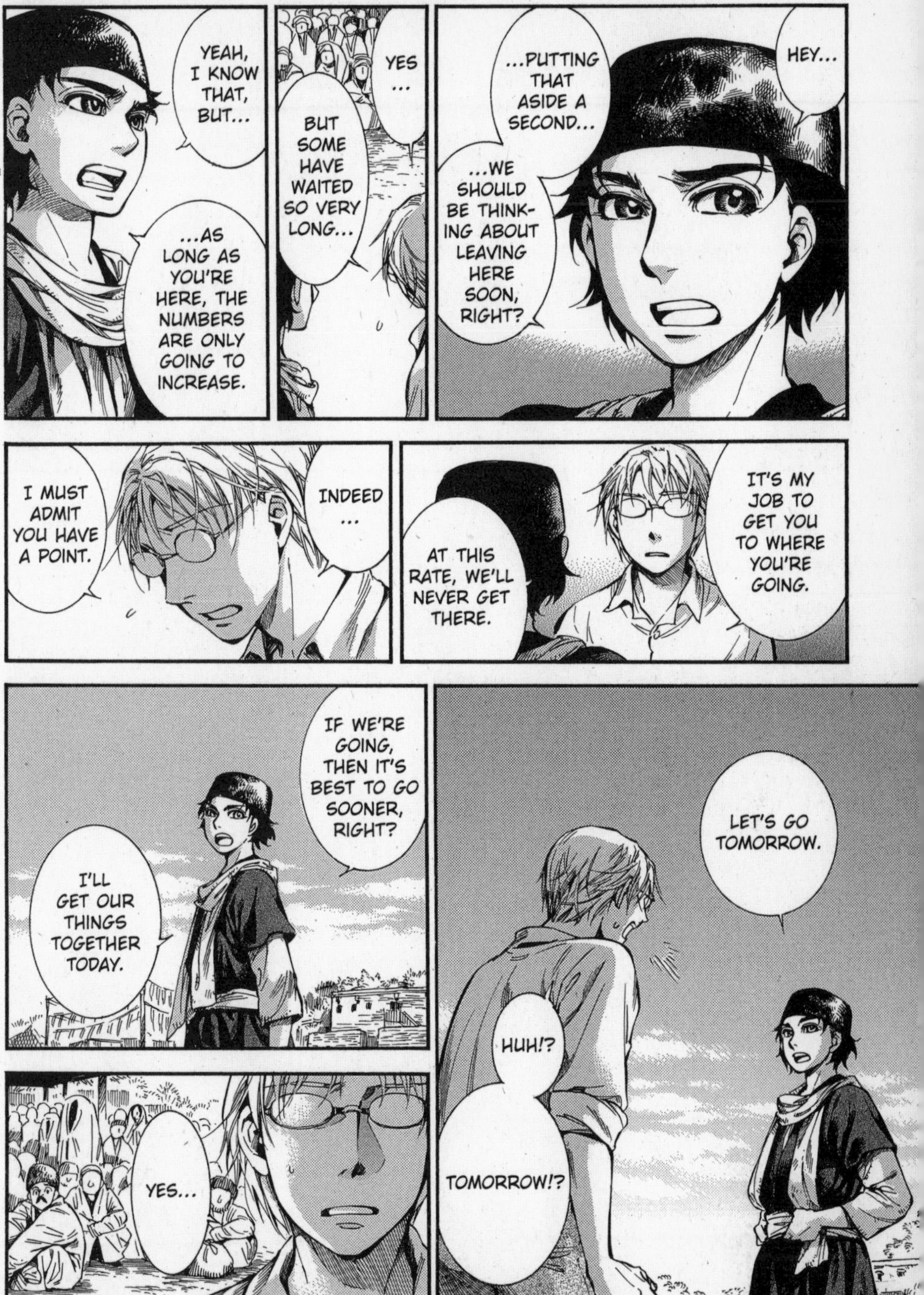
HEY...
...PUTTING THAT ASIDE A SECOND...
...WE SHOULD BE THINKING ABOUT LEAVING HERE SOON, RIGHT?
YES...
BUT SOME HAVE WAITED SO VERY LONG...
YEAH, I KNOW THAT, BUT...
...AS LONG AS YOU'RE HERE, THE NUMBERS ARE ONLY GOING TO INCREASE.
IT'S MY JOB TO GET YOU TO WHERE YOU'RE GOING.
AT THIS RATE, WE'LL NEVER GET THERE.
INDEED...
I MUST ADMIT YOU HAVE A POINT.
LET'S GO TOMORROW.
HUH!?
TOMORROW!?
IF WE'RE GOING, THEN IT'S BEST TO GO SOONER, RIGHT?
I'LL GET OUR THINGS TOGETHER TODAY.
YES...

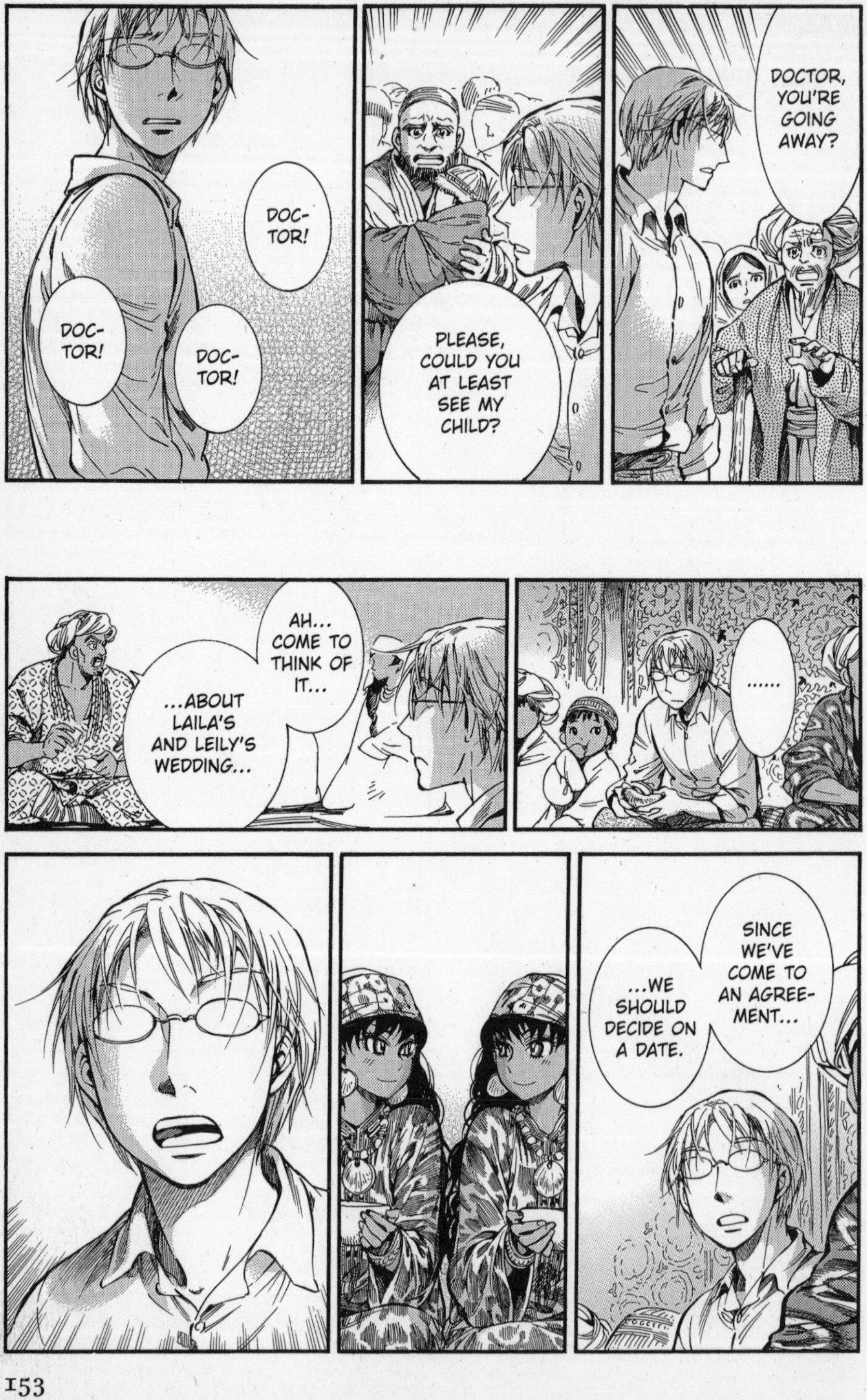
DOCTOR, YOU'RE GOING AWAY?
PLEASE, COULD YOU AT LEAST SEE MY CHILD?
DOC-TOR!
DOC-TOR!
DOC-TOR!
......
AH... COME TO THINK OF IT...
...ABOUT LAILA'S AND LEILY'S WEDDING...
SINCE WE'VE COME TO AN AGREE-MENT...
...WE SHOULD DECIDE ON A DATE.

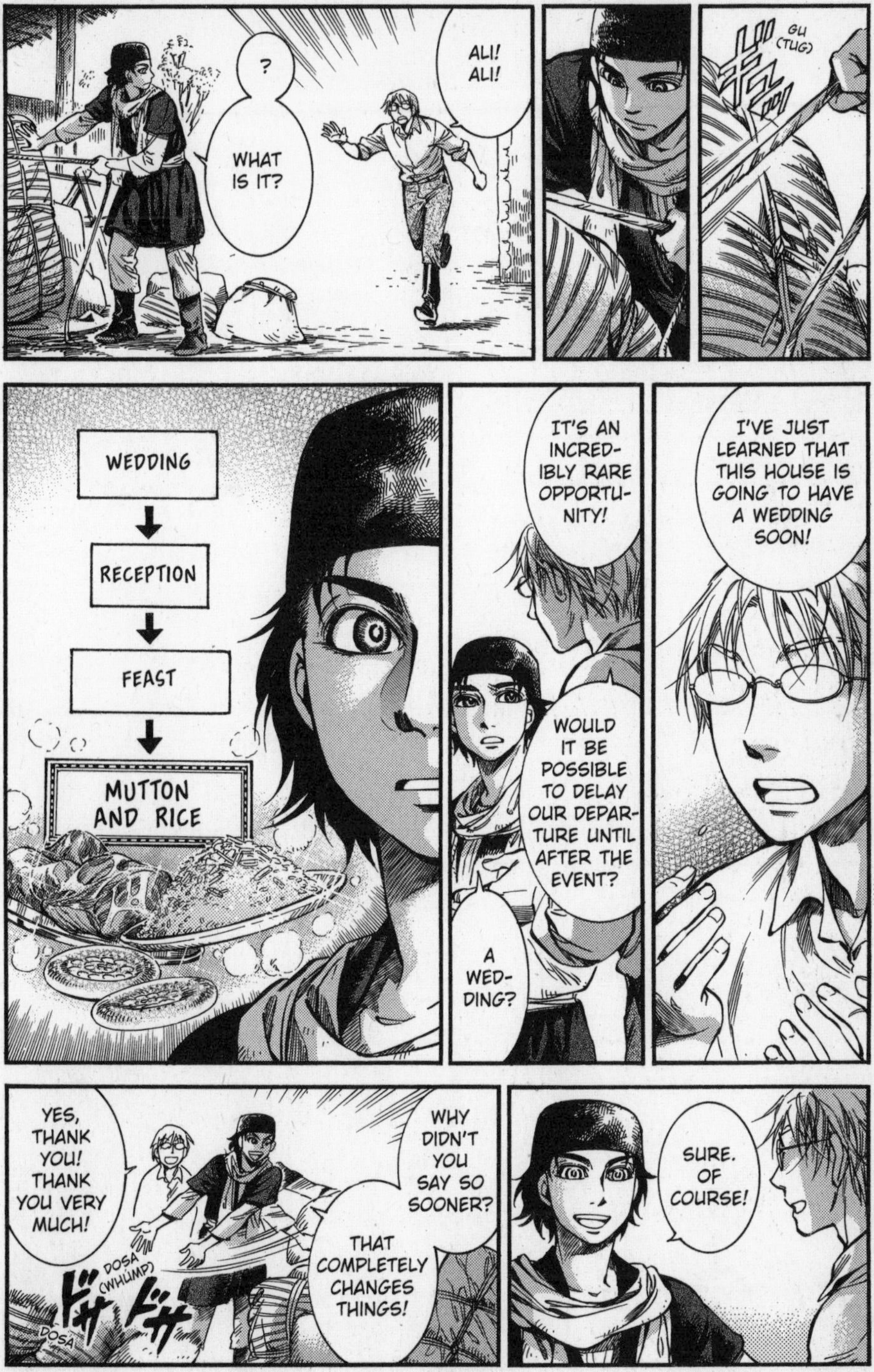
GU (TUG)
ALI! ALI!
?
WHAT IS IT?
I'VE JUST LEARNED THAT THIS HOUSE IS GOING TO HAVE A WEDDING SOON!
IT'S AN INCREDIBLY RARE OPPORTUNITY!
WOULD IT BE POSSIBLE TO DELAY OUR DEPARTURE UNTIL AFTER THE EVENT?
A WEDDING?
WEDDING
RECEPTION
FEAST
MUTTON AND RICE
SURE. OF COURSE!
WHY DIDN'T YOU SAY SO SOONER?
THAT COMPLETELY CHANGES THINGS!
YES, THANK YOU! THANK YOU VERY MUCH!
DOSA (WHUMP)
DOSA

✦ **Chapter 21: End** ✦

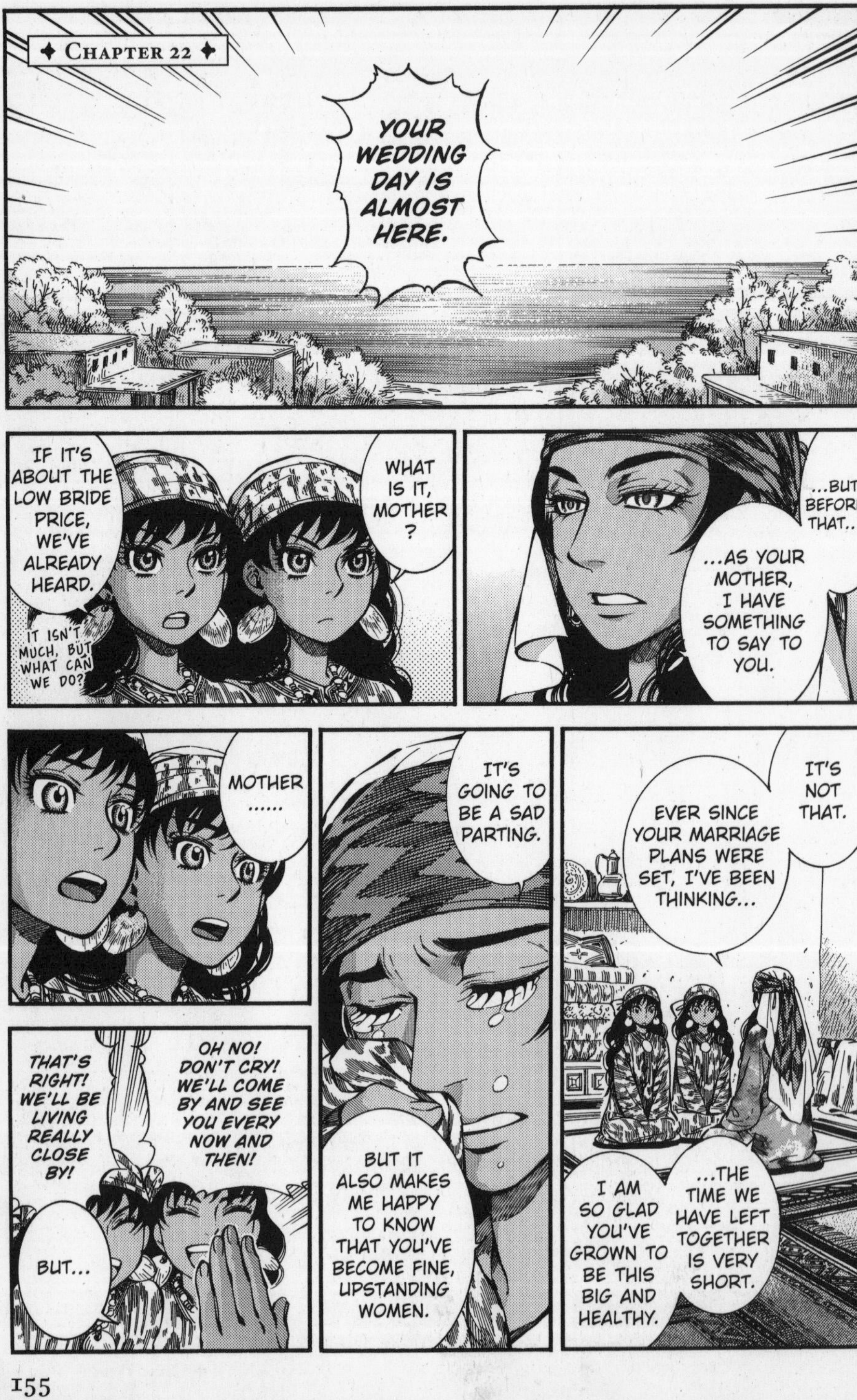

Chapter 22
YOUR WEDDING DAY IS ALMOST HERE.
...BUT BEFORE THAT...
...AS YOUR MOTHER, I HAVE SOMETHING TO SAY TO YOU.
WHAT IS IT, MOTHER?
IF IT'S ABOUT THE LOW BRIDE PRICE, WE'VE ALREADY HEARD.
IT ISN'T MUCH, BUT WHAT CAN WE DO?
IT'S NOT THAT.
EVER SINCE YOUR MARRIAGE PLANS WERE SET, I'VE BEEN THINKING...
...THE TIME WE HAVE LEFT TOGETHER IS VERY SHORT.
I AM SO GLAD YOU'VE GROWN TO BE THIS BIG AND HEALTHY.
IT'S GOING TO BE A SAD PARTING.
BUT IT ALSO MAKES ME HAPPY TO KNOW THAT YOU'VE BECOME FINE, UPSTANDING WOMEN.
MOTHER ......
OH NO! DON'T CRY! WE'LL COME BY AND SEE YOU EVERY NOW AND THEN!
THAT'S RIGHT! WE'LL BE LIVING REALLY CLOSE BY!
BUT...

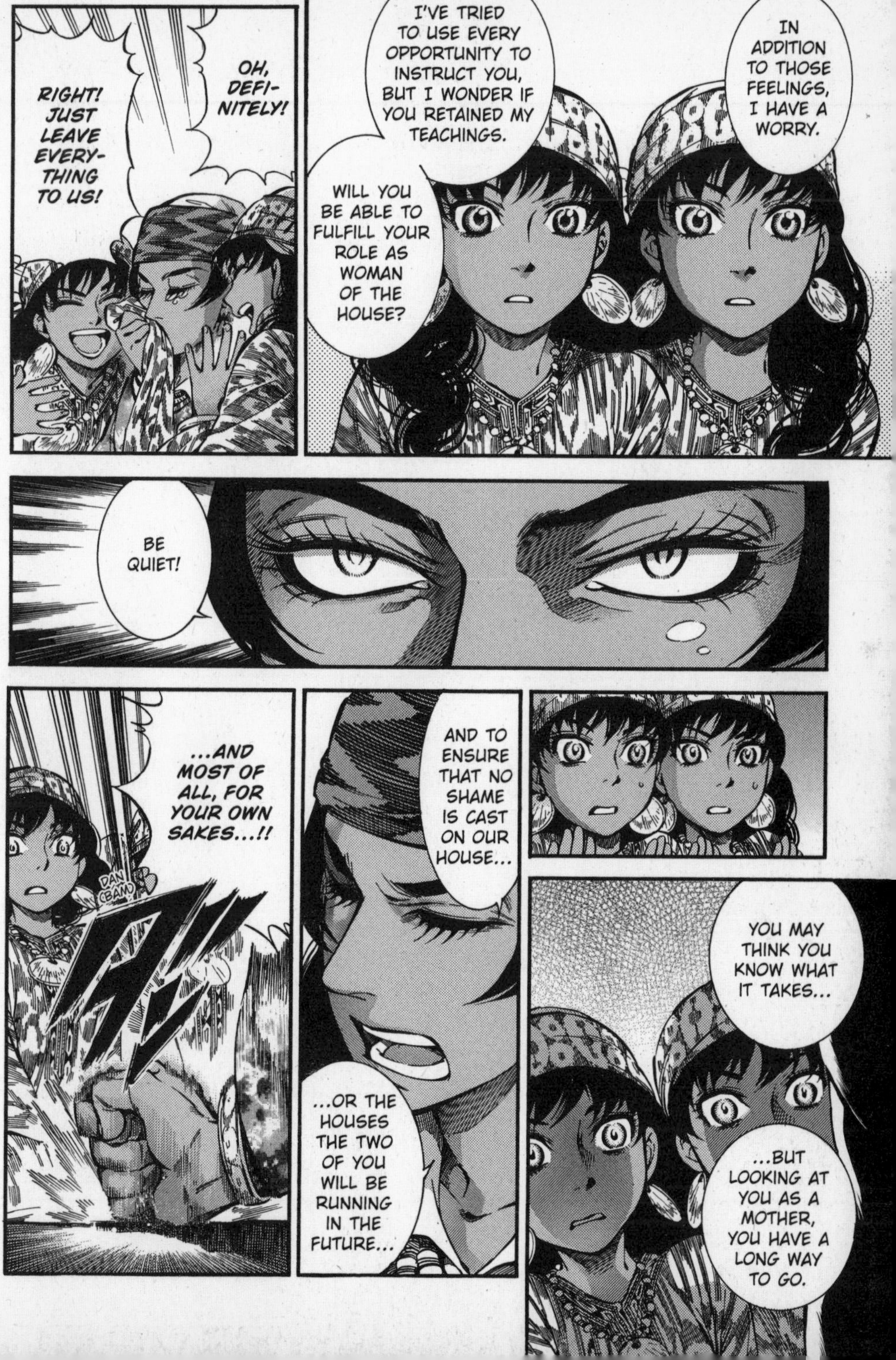
IN ADDITION TO THOSE FEELINGS, I HAVE A WORRY.
I'VE TRIED TO USE EVERY OPPORTUNITY TO INSTRUCT YOU, BUT I WONDER IF YOU RETAINED MY TEACHINGS.
WILL YOU BE ABLE TO FULFILL YOUR ROLE AS WOMAN OF THE HOUSE?
OH, DEFI-NITELY!
RIGHT! JUST LEAVE EVERY-THING TO US!
BE QUIET!
YOU MAY THINK YOU KNOW WHAT IT TAKES...
...BUT LOOKING AT YOU AS A MOTHER, YOU HAVE A LONG WAY TO GO.
AND TO ENSURE THAT NO SHAME IS CAST ON OUR HOUSE...
...OR THE HOUSES THE TWO OF YOU WILL BE RUNNING IN THE FUTURE...
...AND MOST OF ALL, FOR YOUR OWN SAKES...!!
DAN (BAM)

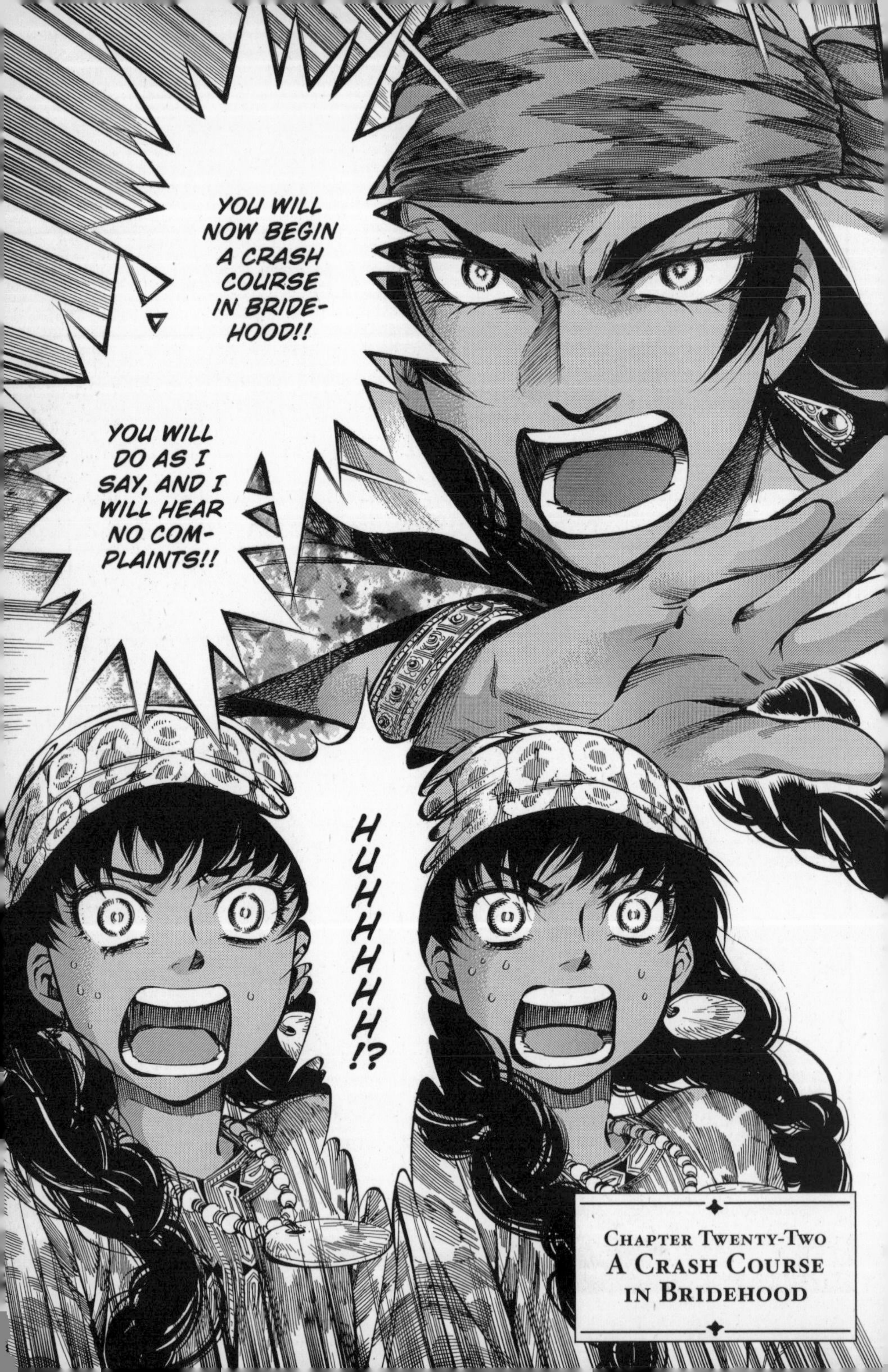
YOU WILL NOW BEGIN A CRASH COURSE IN BRIDE-HOOD!!
YOU WILL DO AS I SAY, AND I WILL HEAR NO COM-PLAINTS!!
HUHHHHHH!?

Chapter Twenty-Two
A Crash Course in Bridehood

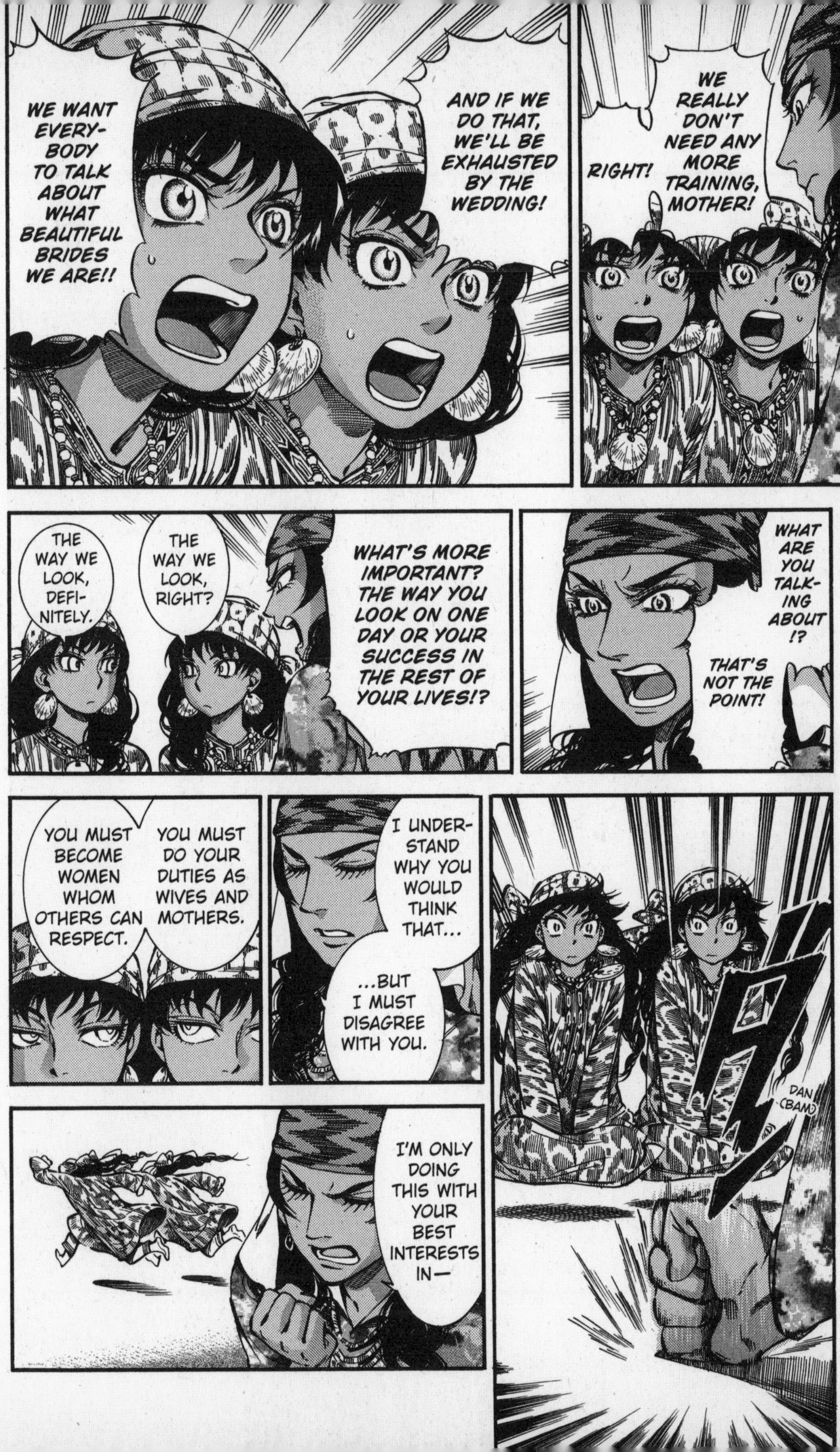
WE REALLY DON'T NEED ANY MORE TRAINING, MOTHER!
RIGHT!
AND IF WE DO THAT, WE'LL BE EXHAUSTED BY THE WEDDING!
WE WANT EVERY-BODY TO TALK ABOUT WHAT BEAUTIFUL BRIDES WE ARE!!
WHAT ARE YOU TALK-ING ABOUT !?
THAT'S NOT THE POINT!
WHAT'S MORE IMPORTANT? THE WAY YOU LOOK ON ONE DAY OR YOUR SUCCESS IN THE REST OF YOUR LIVES!?
THE WAY WE LOOK, RIGHT?
THE WAY WE LOOK, DEFI-NITELY.
DAN (BAM)
I UNDER-STAND WHY YOU WOULD THINK THAT...
...BUT I MUST DISAGREE WITH YOU.
YOU MUST DO YOUR DUTIES AS WIVES AND MOTHERS.
YOU MUST BECOME WOMEN WHOM OTHERS CAN RESPECT.
I'M ONLY DOING THIS WITH YOUR BEST INTERESTS IN—

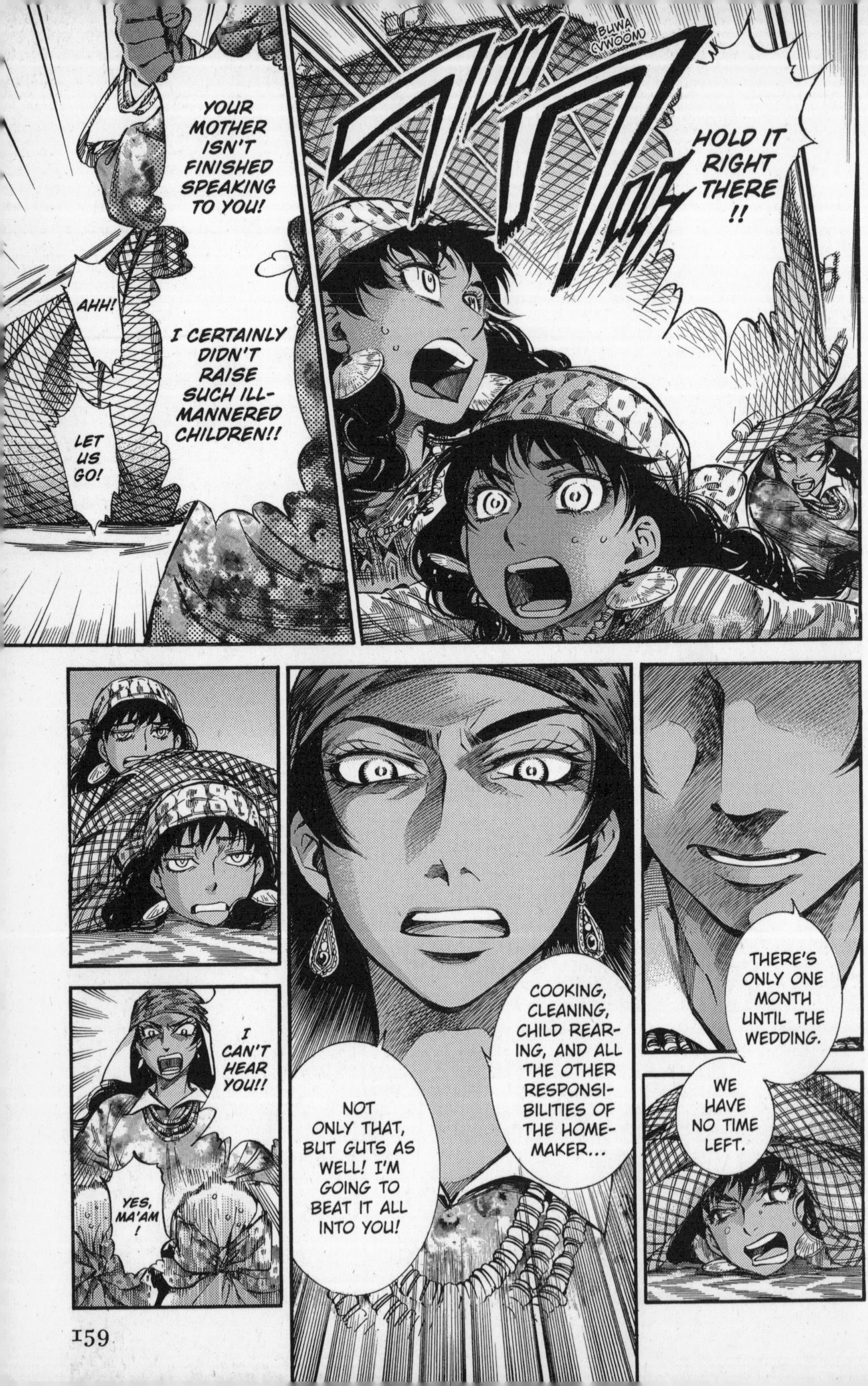
BUWA (VWOOM)
HOLD IT RIGHT THERE!!
YOUR MOTHER ISN'T FINISHED SPEAKING TO YOU!
I CERTAINLY DIDN'T RAISE SUCH ILL-MANNERED CHILDREN!!
AHH!
LET US GO!
THERE'S ONLY ONE MONTH UNTIL THE WEDDING.
WE HAVE NO TIME LEFT.
COOKING, CLEANING, CHILD REARING, AND ALL THE OTHER RESPONSIBILITIES OF THE HOMEMAKER...
NOT ONLY THAT, BUT GUTS AS WELL! I'M GOING TO BEAT IT ALL INTO YOU!
I CAN'T HEAR YOU!!
YES, MA'AM!

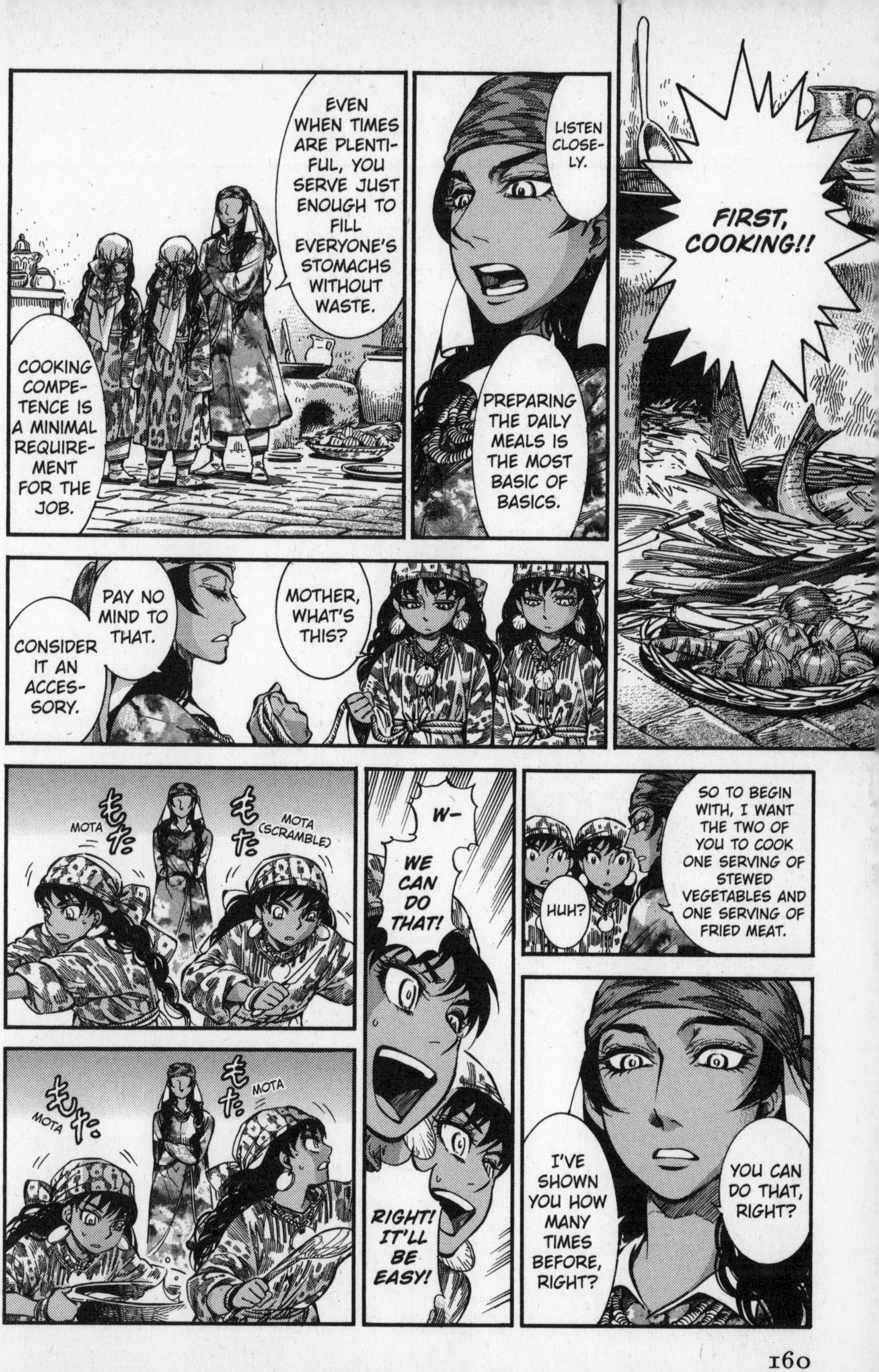
FIRST, COOKING!!
LISTEN CLOSE-LY.
PREPARING THE DAILY MEALS IS THE MOST BASIC OF BASICS.
EVEN WHEN TIMES ARE PLENTI-FUL, YOU SERVE JUST ENOUGH TO FILL EVERYONE'S STOMACHS WITHOUT WASTE.
COOKING COMPE-TENCE IS A MINIMAL REQUIRE-MENT FOR THE JOB.
MOTHER, WHAT'S THIS?
PAY NO MIND TO THAT.
CONSIDER IT AN ACCES-SORY.
SO TO BEGIN WITH, I WANT THE TWO OF YOU TO COOK ONE SERVING OF STEWED VEGETABLES AND ONE SERVING OF FRIED MEAT.
HUH?
YOU CAN DO THAT, RIGHT?
I'VE SHOWN YOU HOW MANY TIMES BEFORE, RIGHT?
W-
WE CAN DO THAT!
RIGHT! IT'LL BE EASY!
もた
MOTA (SCRAMBLE)
もた
MOTA
もた
MOTA
もた。
MOTA

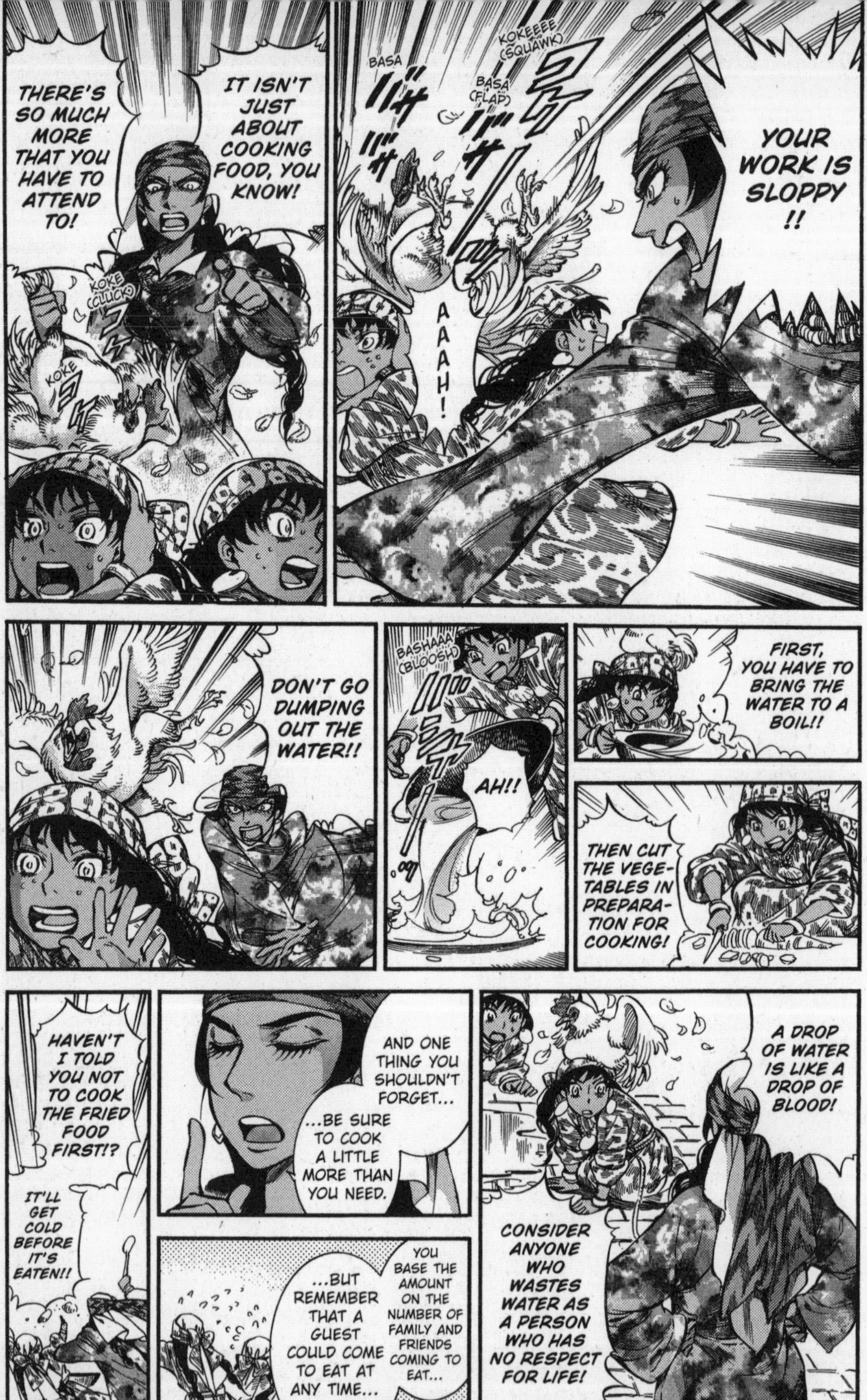
KOKEEEE (SQUAWK)
BASA (FLAP)
BASA
YOUR WORK IS SLOPPY!!
AAAAH!
IT ISN'T JUST ABOUT COOKING FOOD, YOU KNOW!
THERE'S SO MUCH MORE THAT YOU HAVE TO ATTEND TO!
KOKE (CLUCK)
KOKE
FIRST, YOU HAVE TO BRING THE WATER TO A BOIL!!
THEN CUT THE VEGETABLES IN PREPARATION FOR COOKING!
BASHAAA (BLOOSH)
AH!!
DON'T GO DUMPING OUT THE WATER!!
A DROP OF WATER IS LIKE A DROP OF BLOOD!
CONSIDER ANYONE WHO WASTES WATER AS A PERSON WHO HAS NO RESPECT FOR LIFE!
AND ONE THING YOU SHOULDN'T FORGET...
...BE SURE TO COOK A LITTLE MORE THAN YOU NEED.
YOU BASE THE AMOUNT ON THE NUMBER OF FAMILY AND FRIENDS COMING TO EAT...
...BUT REMEMBER THAT A GUEST COULD COME TO EAT AT ANY TIME...
HAVEN'T I TOLD YOU NOT TO COOK THE FRIED FOOD FIRST!?
IT'LL GET COLD BEFORE IT'S EATEN!!

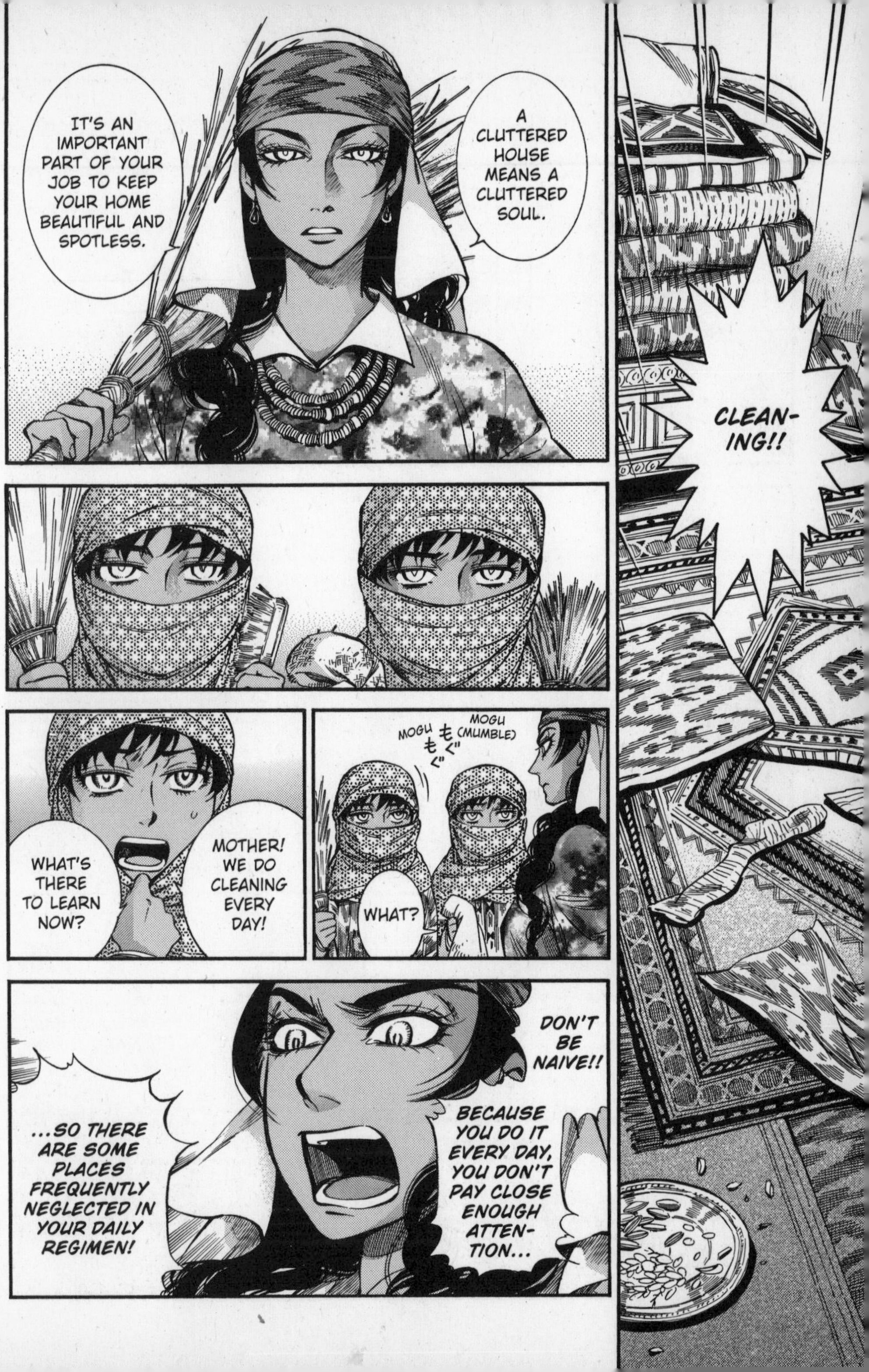
CLEAN-ING!!
A CLUTTERED HOUSE MEANS A CLUTTERED SOUL.
IT'S AN IMPORTANT PART OF YOUR JOB TO KEEP YOUR HOME BEAUTIFUL AND SPOTLESS.
MOGU もぐ
MOGU (MUMBLE) もぐ
WHAT?
MOTHER! WE DO CLEANING EVERY DAY!
WHAT'S THERE TO LEARN NOW?
DON'T BE NAIVE!!
BECAUSE YOU DO IT EVERY DAY, YOU DON'T PAY CLOSE ENOUGH ATTEN-TION...
...SO THERE ARE SOME PLACES FREQUENTLY NEGLECTED IN YOUR DAILY REGIMEN!

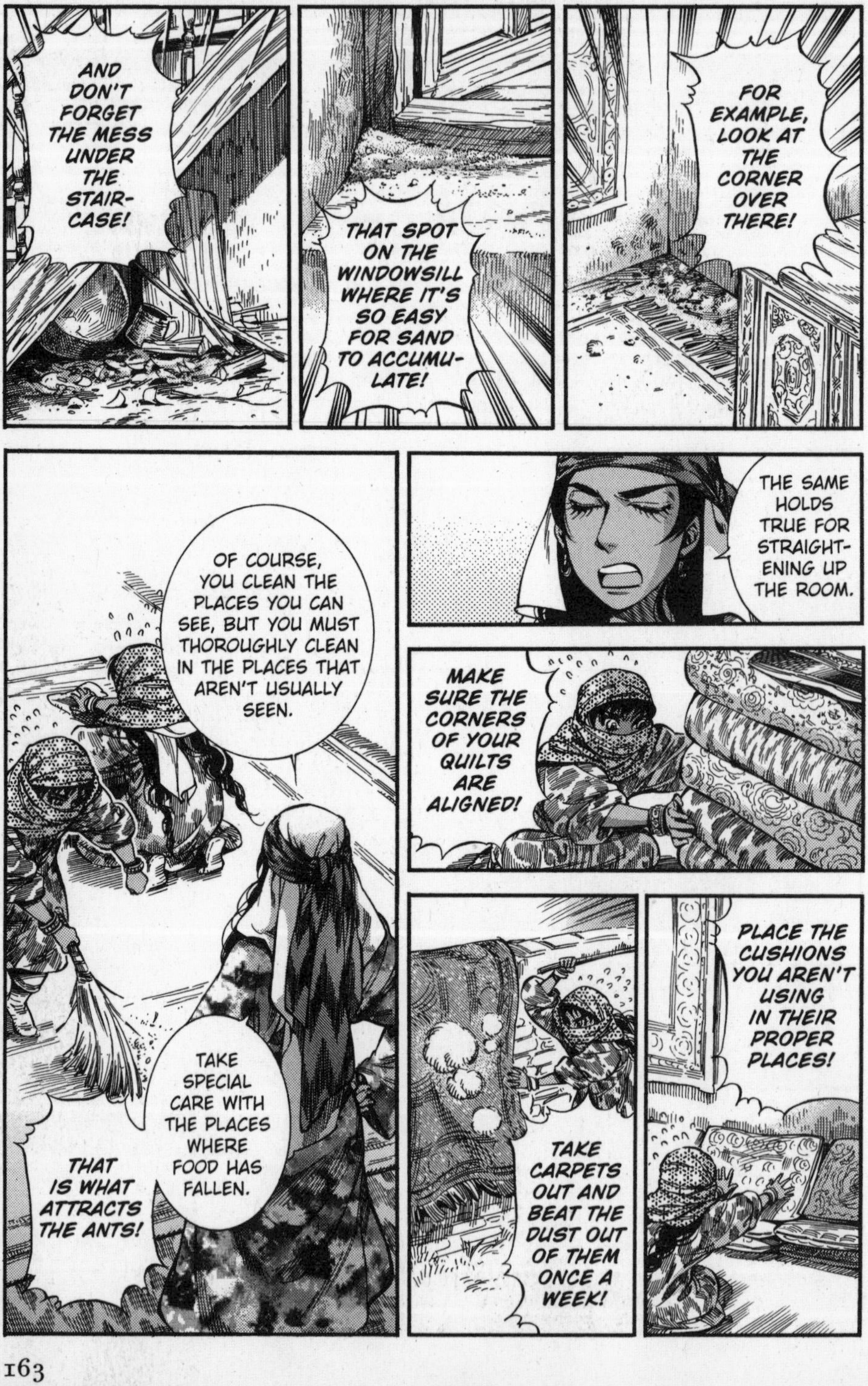
FOR EXAMPLE, LOOK AT THE CORNER OVER THERE!
THAT SPOT ON THE WINDOWSILL WHERE IT'S SO EASY FOR SAND TO ACCUMULATE!
AND DON'T FORGET THE MESS UNDER THE STAIRCASE!
THE SAME HOLDS TRUE FOR STRAIGHTENING UP THE ROOM.
MAKE SURE THE CORNERS OF YOUR QUILTS ARE ALIGNED!
PLACE THE CUSHIONS YOU AREN'T USING IN THEIR PROPER PLACES!
TAKE CARPETS OUT AND BEAT THE DUST OUT OF THEM ONCE A WEEK!
OF COURSE, YOU CLEAN THE PLACES YOU CAN SEE, BUT YOU MUST THOROUGHLY CLEAN IN THE PLACES THAT AREN'T USUALLY SEEN.
TAKE SPECIAL CARE WITH THE PLACES WHERE FOOD HAS FALLEN.
THAT IS WHAT ATTRACTS THE ANTS!

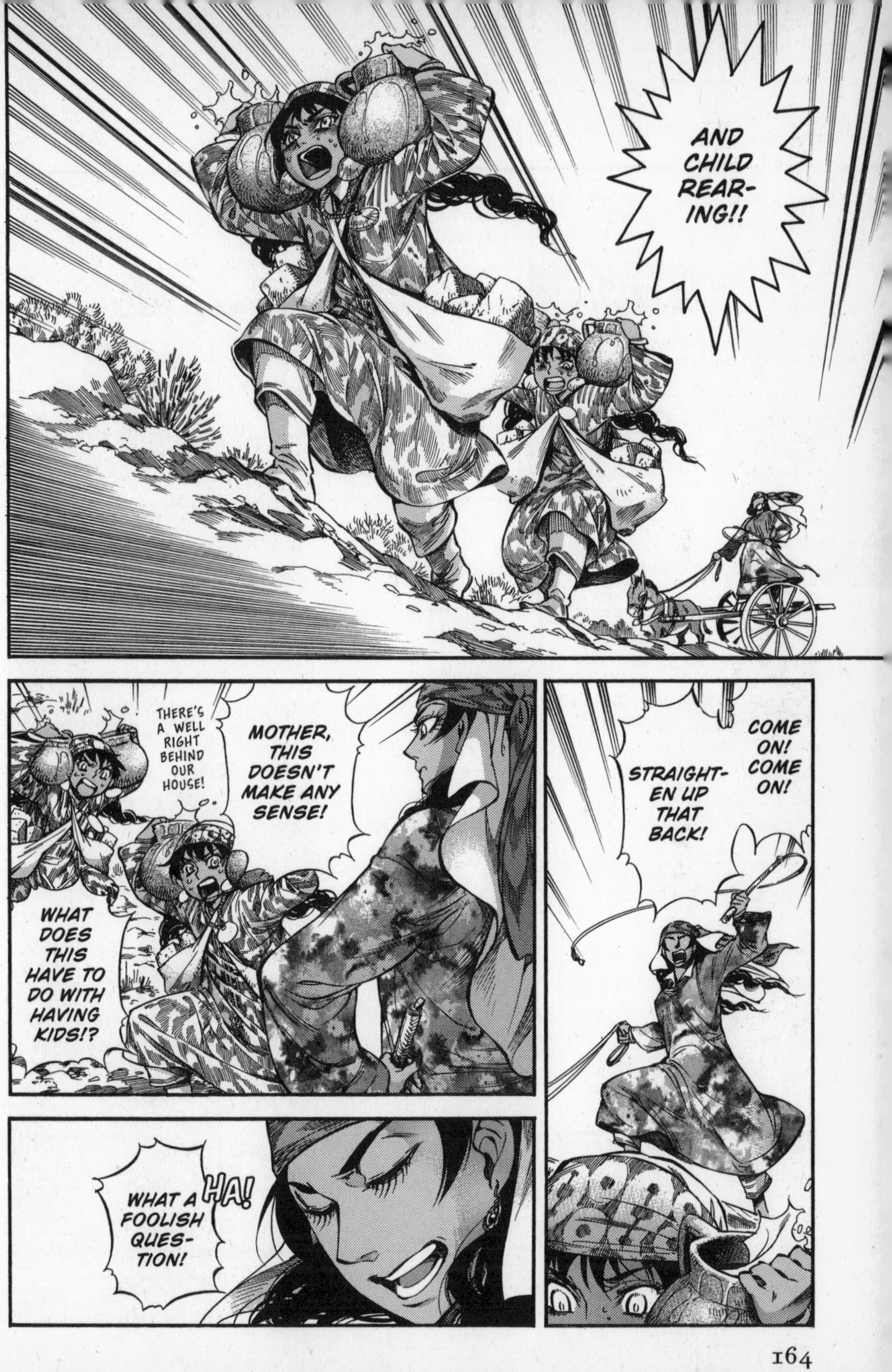
AND CHILD REARING!!
COME ON! COME ON!
STRAIGHTEN UP THAT BACK!
MOTHER, THIS DOESN'T MAKE ANY SENSE!
THERE'S A WELL RIGHT BEHIND OUR HOUSE!
WHAT DOES THIS HAVE TO DO WITH HAVING KIDS!?
HA!
WHAT A FOOLISH QUESTION!

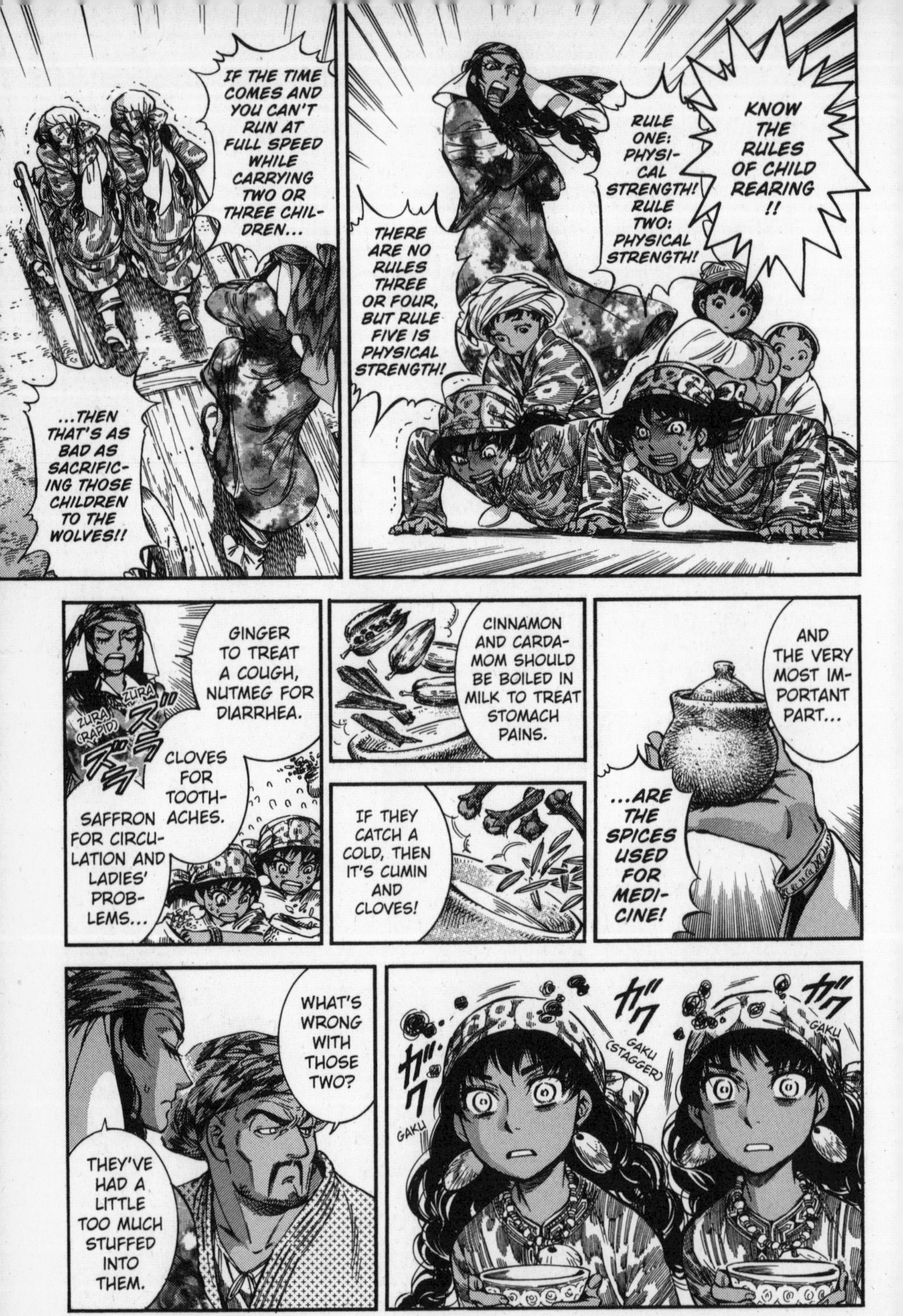
KNOW THE RULES OF CHILD REARING !!
RULE ONE: PHYSICAL STRENGTH! RULE TWO: PHYSICAL STRENGTH!
THERE ARE NO RULES THREE OR FOUR, BUT RULE FIVE IS PHYSICAL STRENGTH!
IF THE TIME COMES AND YOU CAN'T RUN AT FULL SPEED WHILE CARRYING TWO OR THREE CHILDREN...
...THEN THAT'S AS BAD AS SACRIFICING THOSE CHILDREN TO THE WOLVES!!
AND THE VERY MOST IMPORTANT PART...
...ARE THE SPICES USED FOR MEDICINE!
CINNAMON AND CARDAMOM SHOULD BE BOILED IN MILK TO TREAT STOMACH PAINS.
IF THEY CATCH A COLD, THEN IT'S CUMIN AND CLOVES!
GINGER TO TREAT A COUGH, NUTMEG FOR DIARRHEA.
ZURA
ZURA (RAPID)
CLOVES FOR TOOTHACHES.
SAFFRON FOR CIRCULATION AND LADIES' PROBLEMS...
GAKU
GAKU (STAGGER)
GAKU
WHAT'S WRONG WITH THOSE TWO?
THEY'VE HAD A LITTLE TOO MUCH STUFFED INTO THEM.

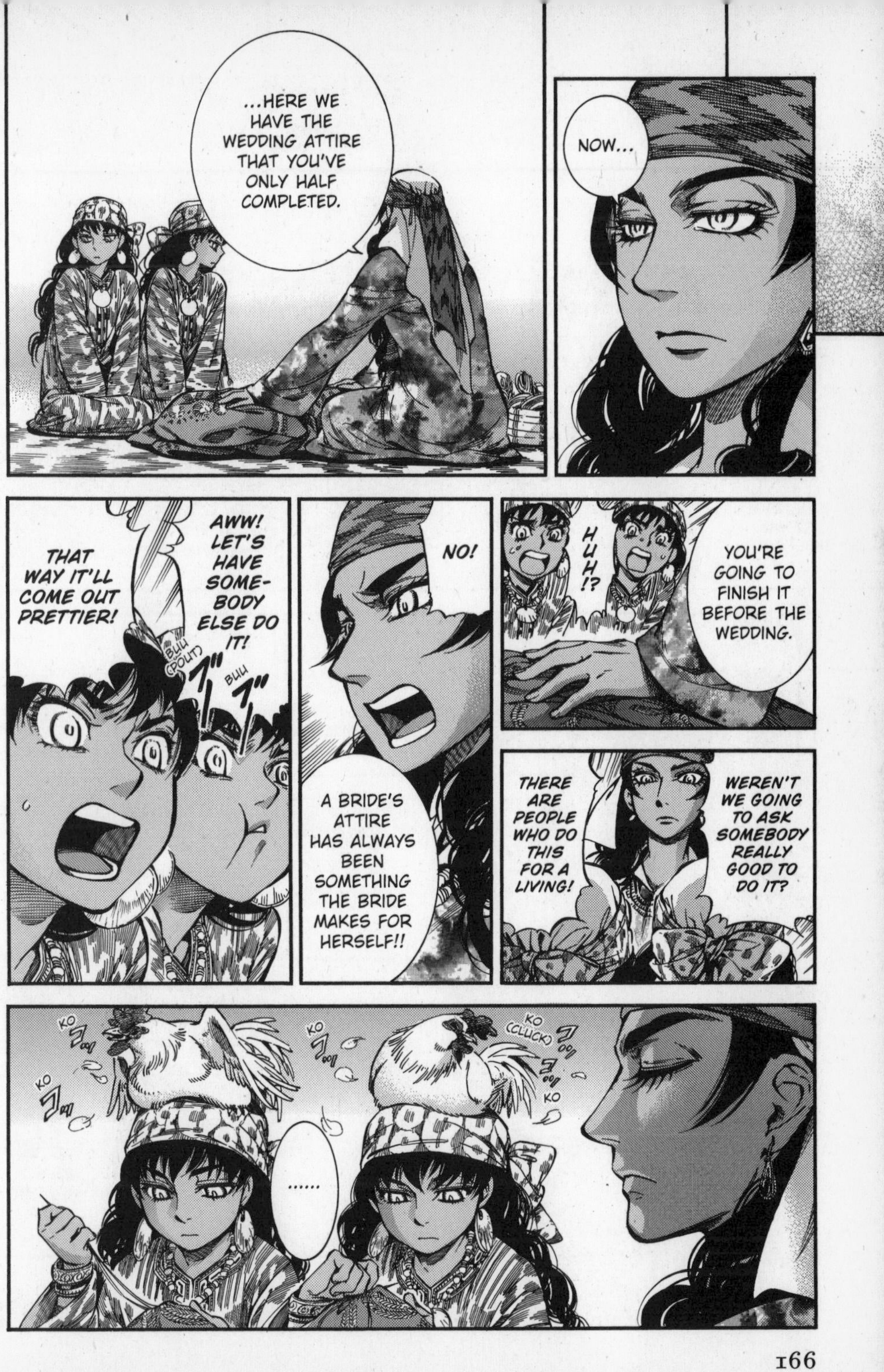
NOW...
...HERE WE HAVE THE WEDDING ATTIRE THAT YOU'VE ONLY HALF COMPLETED.
YOU'RE GOING TO FINISH IT BEFORE THE WEDDING.
HUH!?
WEREN'T WE GOING TO ASK SOMEBODY REALLY GOOD TO DO IT?
THERE ARE PEOPLE WHO DO THIS FOR A LIVING!
NO!
A BRIDE'S ATTIRE HAS ALWAYS BEEN SOMETHING THE BRIDE MAKES FOR HERSELF!!
AWW! LET'S HAVE SOMEBODY ELSE DO IT!
THAT WAY IT'LL COME OUT PRETTIER!
BUU (POUT)
BUU
KO (CLUCK)
KO
KO
KO
KO
......

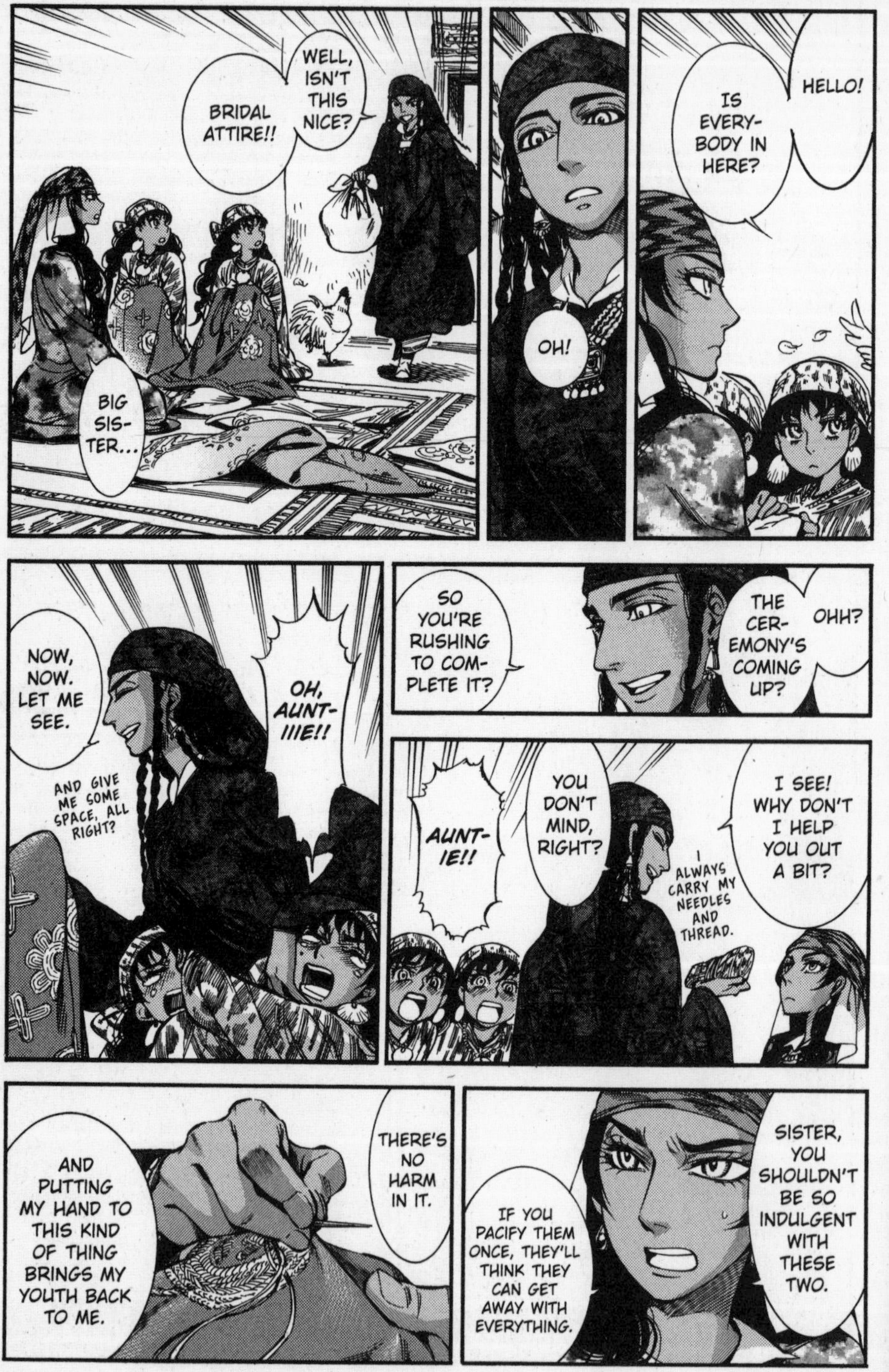
HELLO!
IS EVERYBODY IN HERE?
OH!
WELL, ISN'T THIS NICE?
BRIDAL ATTIRE!!
BIG SISTER...
OHH?
THE CEREMONY'S COMING UP?
SO YOU'RE RUSHING TO COMPLETE IT?
I SEE! WHY DON'T I HELP YOU OUT A BIT?
I ALWAYS CARRY MY NEEDLES AND THREAD.
YOU DON'T MIND, RIGHT?
AUNTIE!!
OH, AUNTIIIE!!
NOW, NOW. LET ME SEE.
AND GIVE ME SOME SPACE, ALL RIGHT?
SISTER, YOU SHOULDN'T BE SO INDULGENT WITH THESE TWO.
IF YOU PACIFY THEM ONCE, THEY'LL THINK THEY CAN GET AWAY WITH EVERYTHING.
THERE'S NO HARM IN IT.
AND PUTTING MY HAND TO THIS KIND OF THING BRINGS MY YOUTH BACK TO ME.

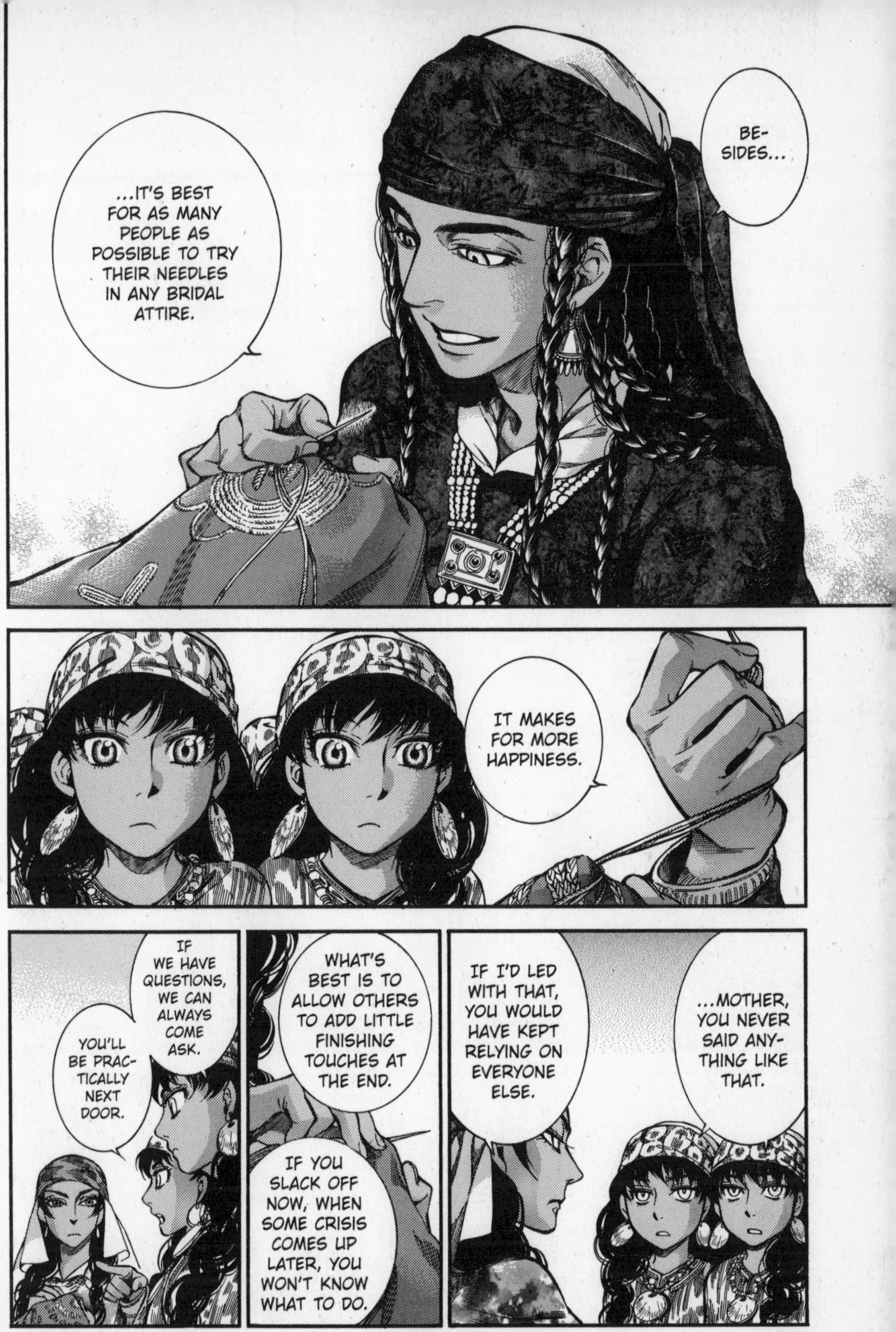
BE-SIDES...
...IT'S BEST FOR AS MANY PEOPLE AS POSSIBLE TO TRY THEIR NEEDLES IN ANY BRIDAL ATTIRE.
IT MAKES FOR MORE HAPPINESS.
...MOTHER, YOU NEVER SAID ANY-THING LIKE THAT.
IF I'D LED WITH THAT, YOU WOULD HAVE KEPT RELYING ON EVERYONE ELSE.
WHAT'S BEST IS TO ALLOW OTHERS TO ADD LITTLE FINISHING TOUCHES AT THE END.
IF YOU SLACK OFF NOW, WHEN SOME CRISIS COMES UP LATER, YOU WON'T KNOW WHAT TO DO.
IF WE HAVE QUESTIONS, WE CAN ALWAYS COME ASK.
YOU'LL BE PRAC-TICALLY NEXT DOOR.

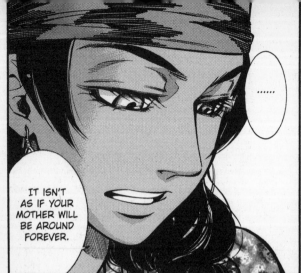

......

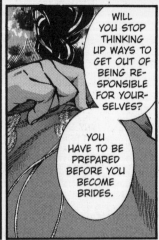

WILL YOU STOP THINKING UP WAYS TO GET OUT OF BEING RE-SPONSIBLE FOR YOUR-SELVES?

YOU HAVE TO BE PREPARED BEFORE YOU BECOME BRIDES.

IT ISN'T AS IF YOUR MOTHER WILL BE AROUND FOREVER.

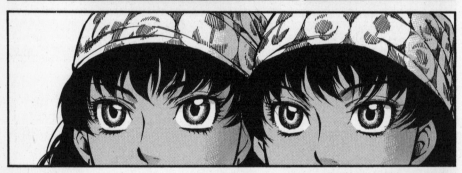

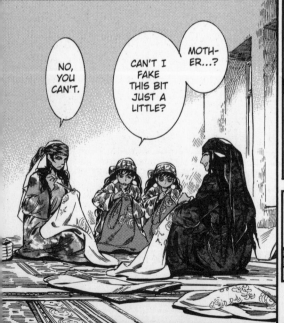

NO, YOU CAN'T.

CAN'T I FAKE THIS BIT JUST A LITTLE?

MOTH-ER...?

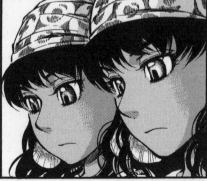

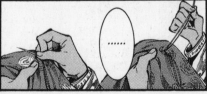

......

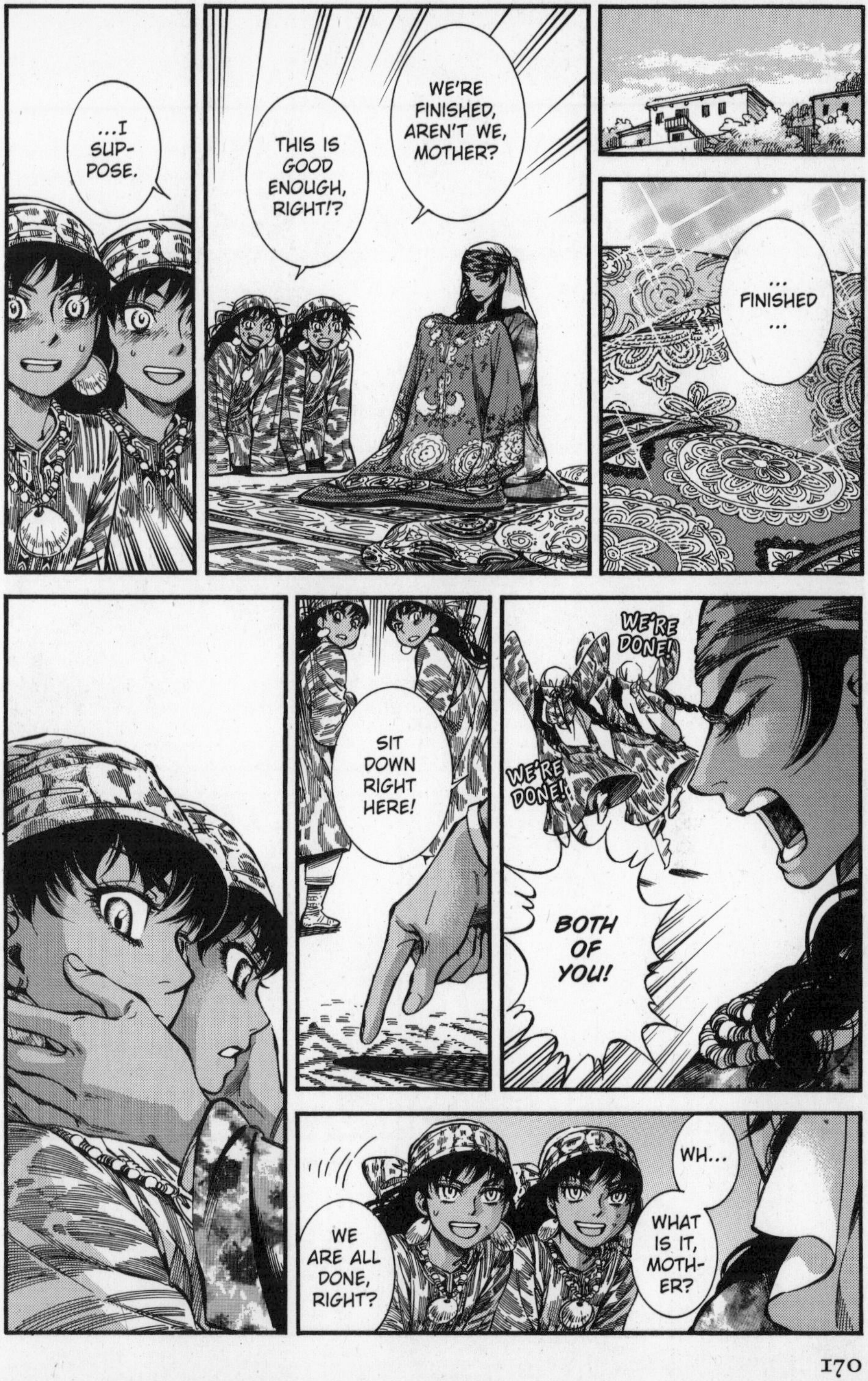
...
FINISHED
...
WE'RE FINISHED, AREN'T WE, MOTHER?
THIS IS GOOD ENOUGH, RIGHT!?
...I SUP-POSE.
WE'RE DONE!
WE'RE DONE!
BOTH OF YOU!
SIT DOWN RIGHT HERE!
WH...
WHAT IS IT, MOTHER?
WE ARE ALL DONE, RIGHT?

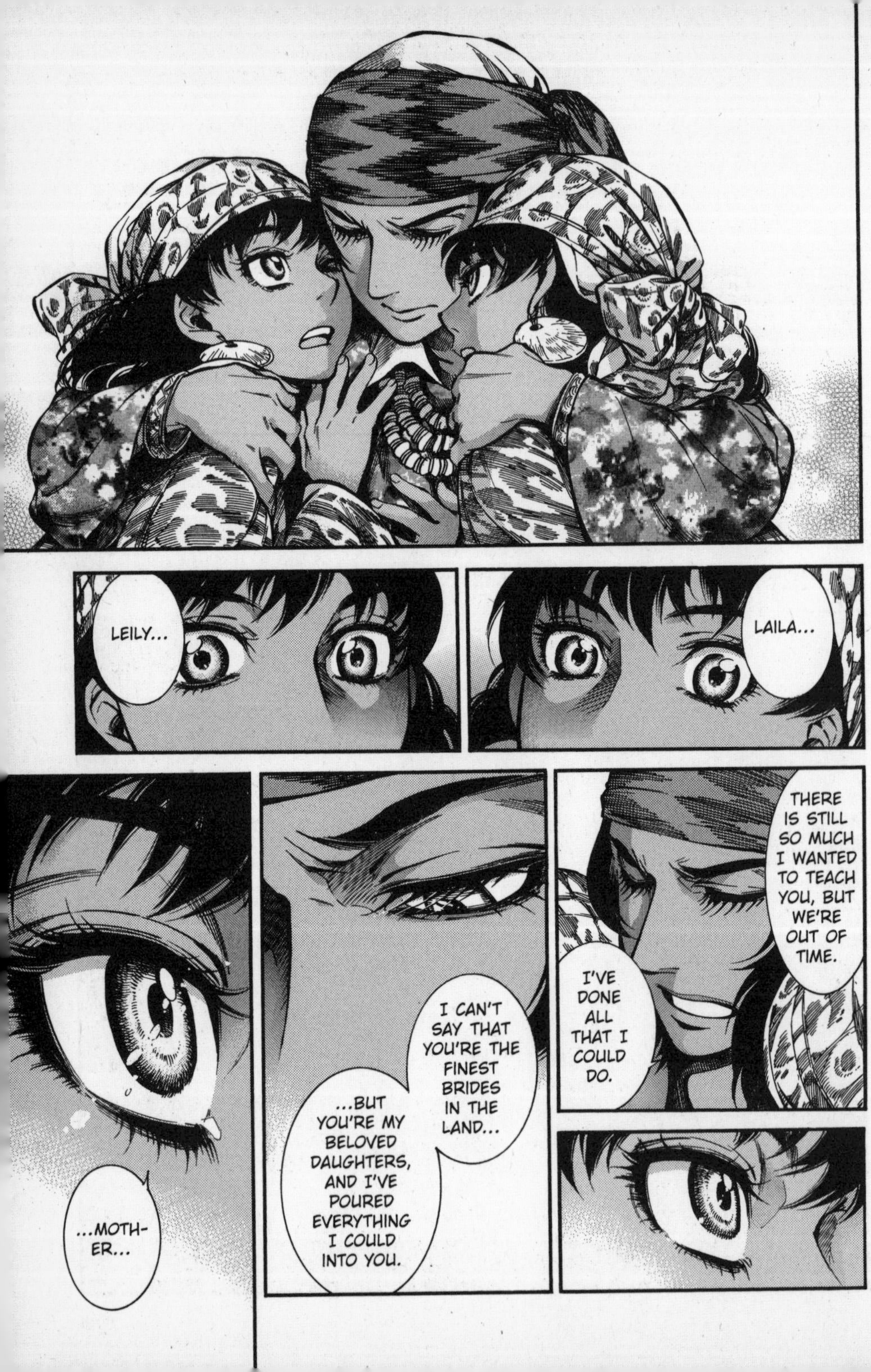
LAILA...
LEILY...
THERE IS STILL SO MUCH I WANTED TO TEACH YOU, BUT WE'RE OUT OF TIME.
I'VE DONE ALL THAT I COULD DO.
I CAN'T SAY THAT YOU'RE THE FINEST BRIDES IN THE LAND...
...BUT YOU'RE MY BELOVED DAUGHTERS, AND I'VE POURED EVERYTHING I COULD INTO YOU.
...MOTH-ER...

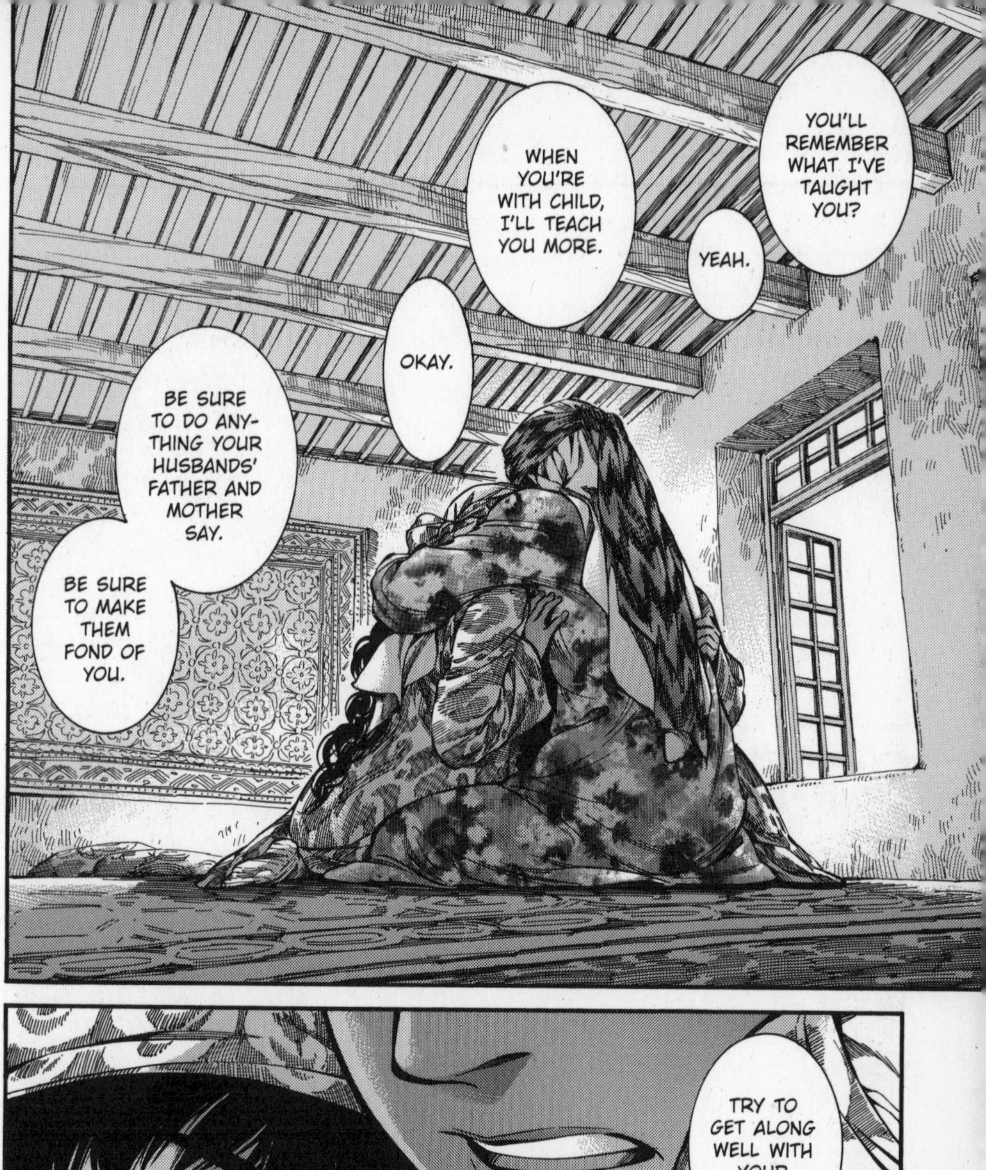
YOU'LL REMEMBER WHAT I'VE TAUGHT YOU?
YEAH.
WHEN YOU'RE WITH CHILD, I'LL TEACH YOU MORE.
OKAY.
BE SURE TO DO ANY-THING YOUR HUSBANDS' FATHER AND MOTHER SAY.
BE SURE TO MAKE THEM FOND OF YOU.

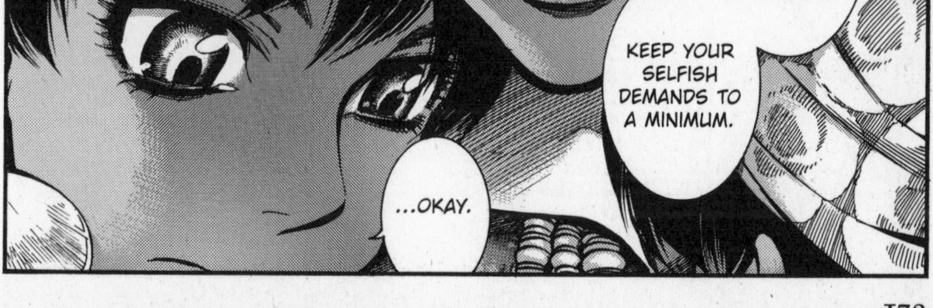
TRY TO GET ALONG WELL WITH YOUR HUSBANDS.
KEEP YOUR SELFISH DEMANDS TO A MINIMUM.
...OKAY.

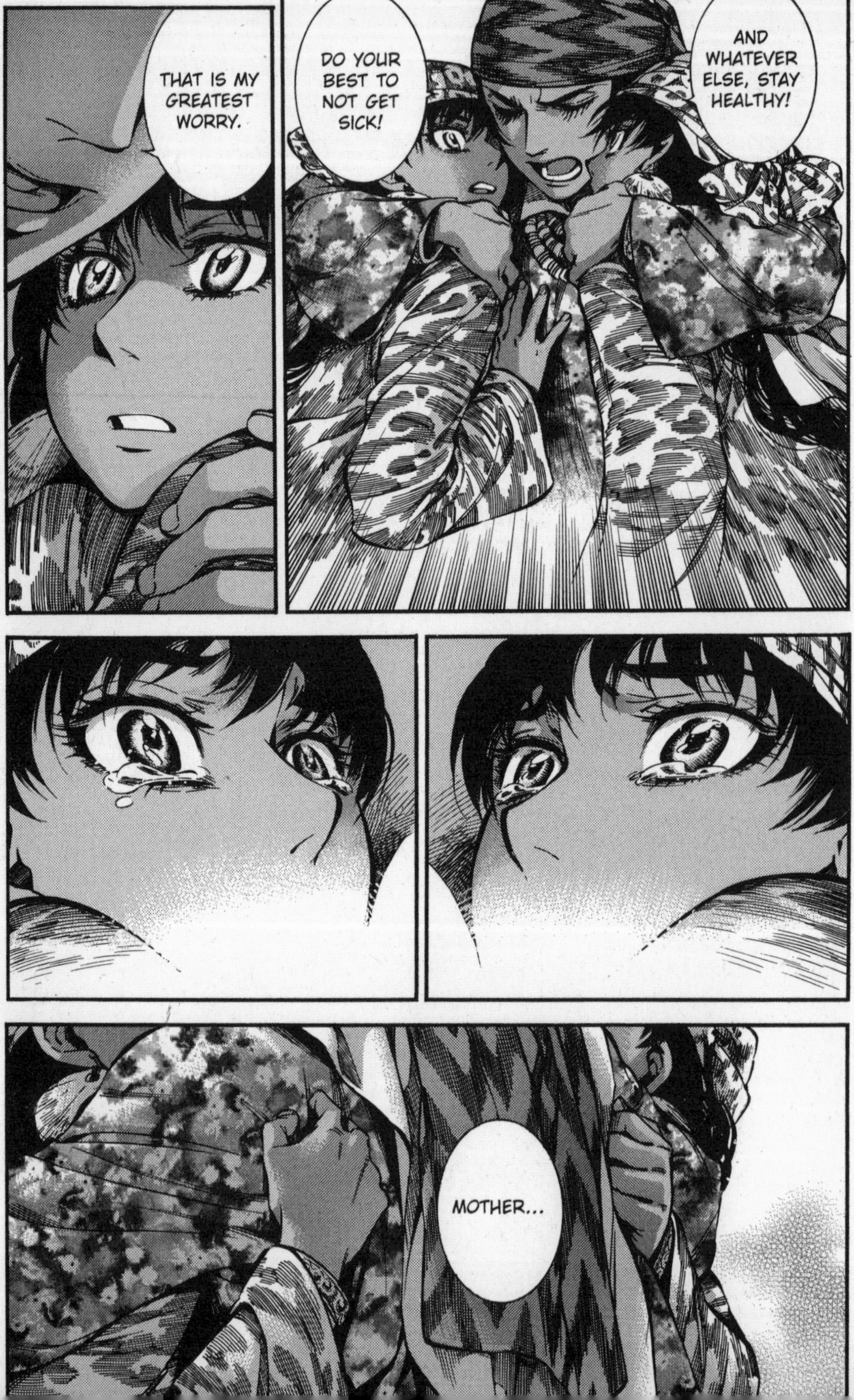
AND WHATEVER ELSE, STAY HEALTHY!
DO YOUR BEST TO NOT GET SICK!
THAT IS MY GREATEST WORRY.
MOTHER...

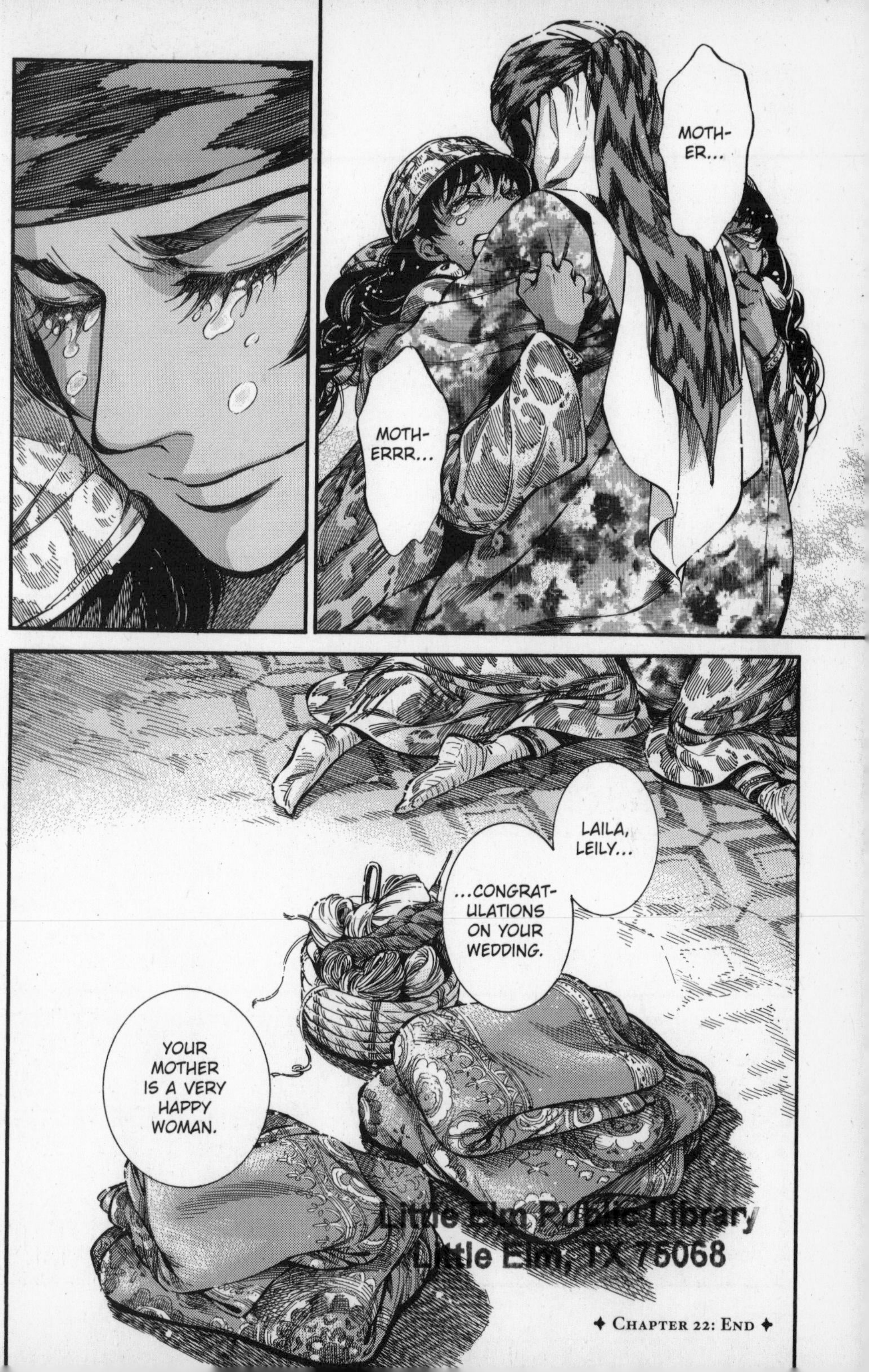
MOTH-ER...
MOTH-ERRR...
LAILA, LEILY...
...CONGRAT-ULATIONS ON YOUR WEDDING.
YOUR MOTHER IS A VERY HAPPY WOMAN.
✦ CHAPTER 22: END ✦

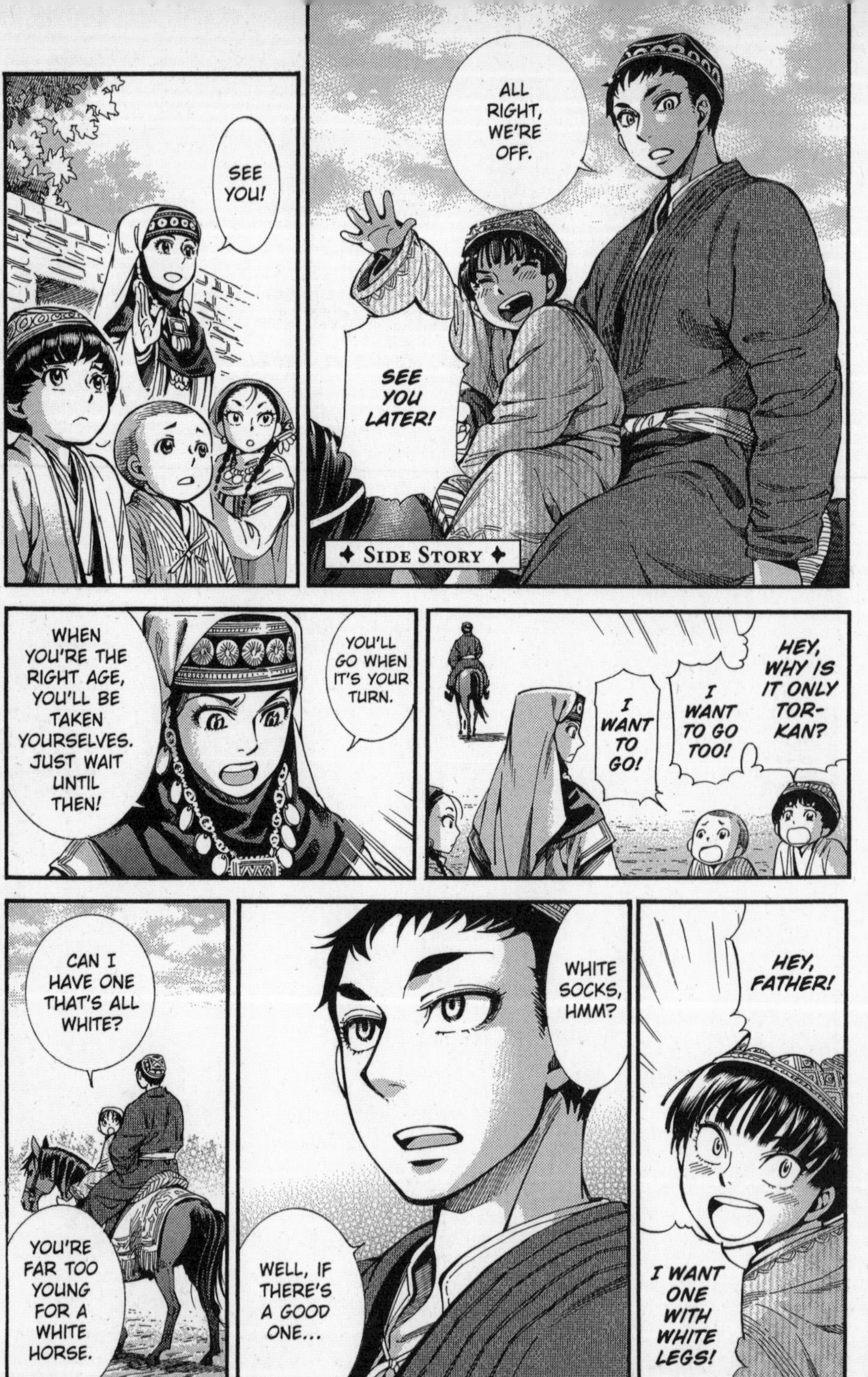
ALL RIGHT, WE'RE OFF.
SEE YOU LATER!
Side Story
SEE YOU!
HEY, WHY IS IT ONLY TOR-KAN?
I WANT TO GO TOO!
I WANT TO GO!
YOU'LL GO WHEN IT'S YOUR TURN.
WHEN YOU'RE THE RIGHT AGE, YOU'LL BE TAKEN YOURSELVES. JUST WAIT UNTIL THEN!
HEY, FATHER!
I WANT ONE WITH WHITE LEGS!
WHITE SOCKS, HMM?
WELL, IF THERE'S A GOOD ONE...
CAN I HAVE ONE THAT'S ALL WHITE?
YOU'RE FAR TOO YOUNG FOR A WHITE HORSE.

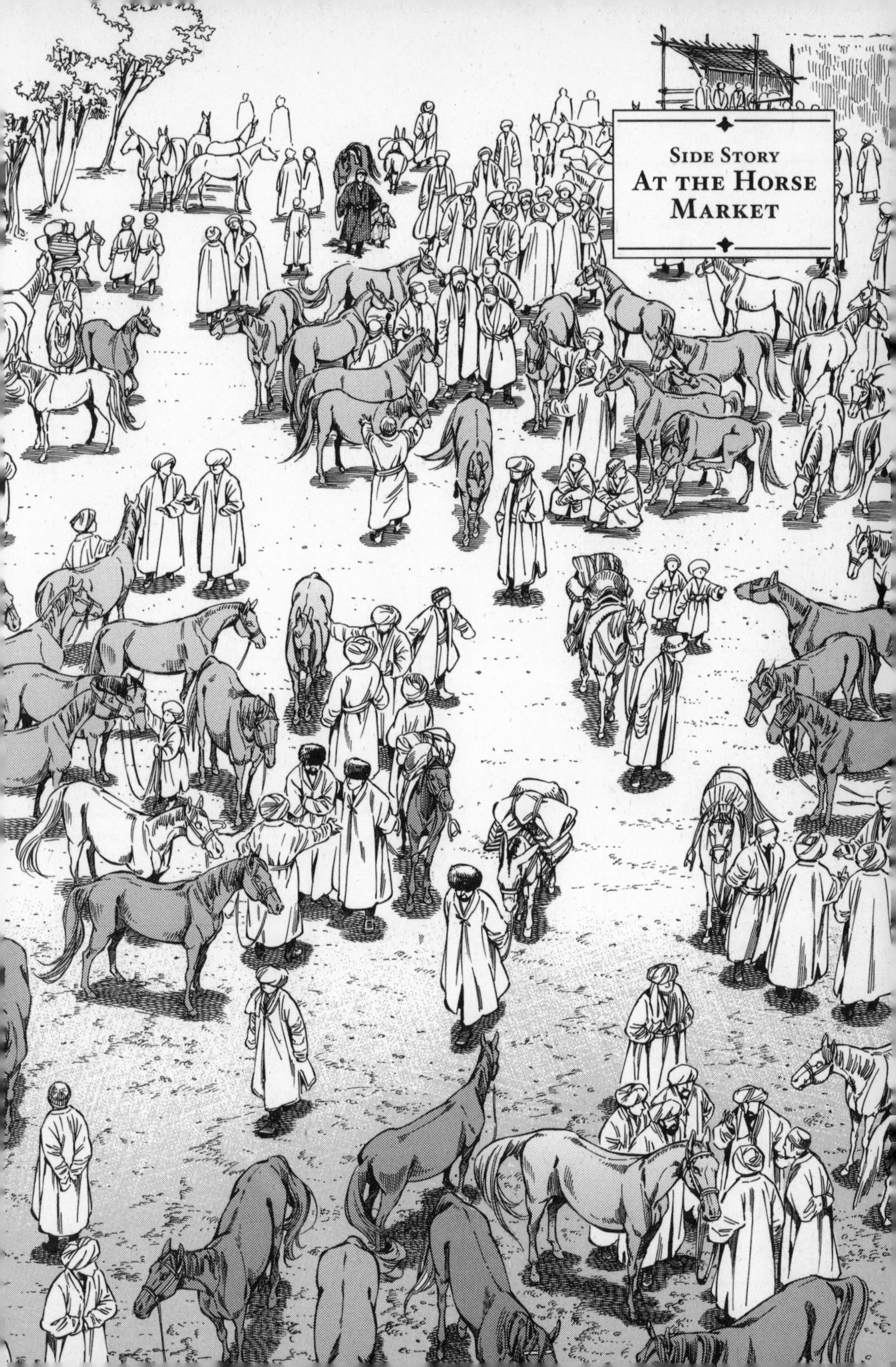
Side Story
At the Horse Market

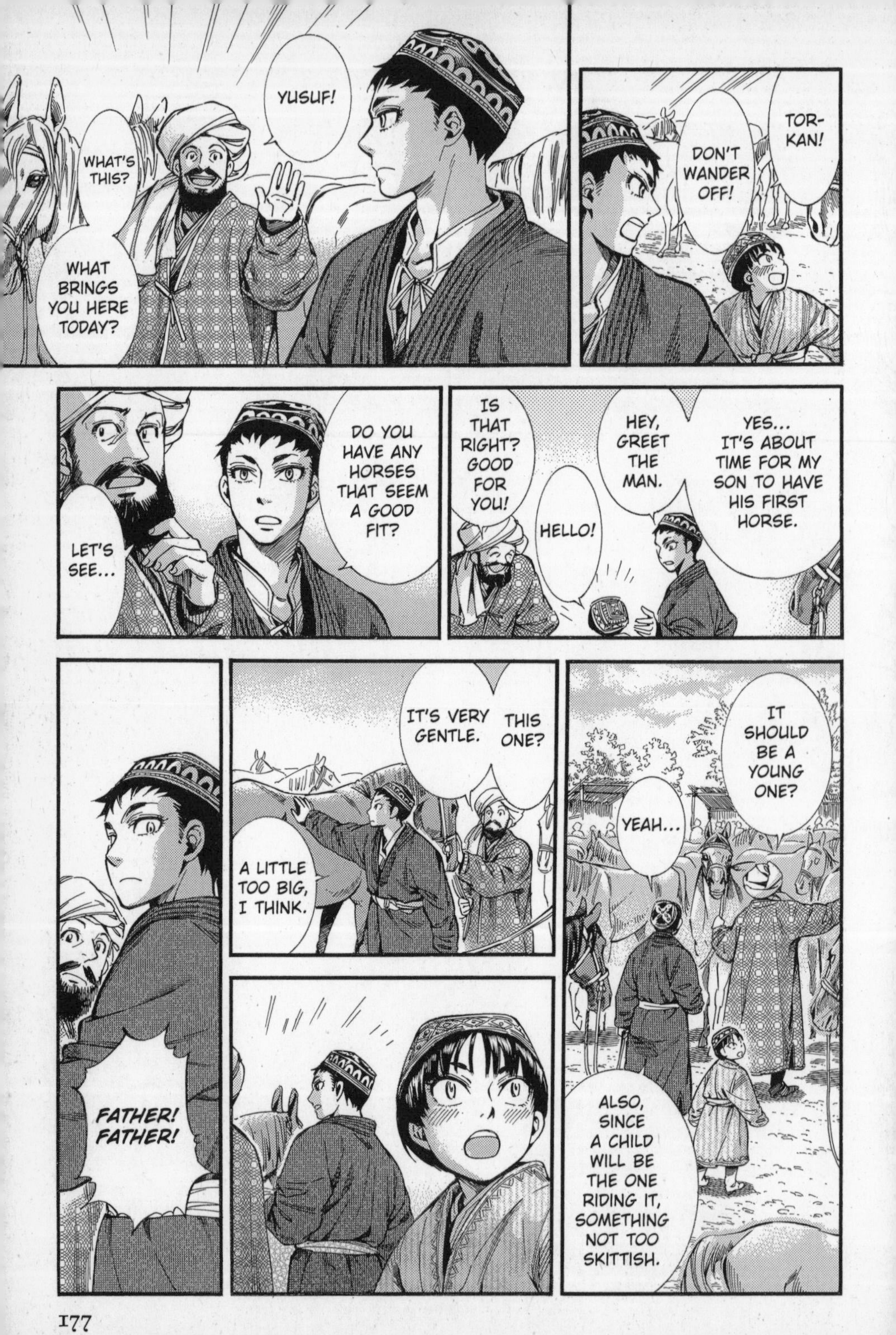
TOR-KAN!
DON'T WANDER OFF!
YUSUF!
WHAT'S THIS?
WHAT BRINGS YOU HERE TODAY?
YES... IT'S ABOUT TIME FOR MY SON TO HAVE HIS FIRST HORSE.
HEY, GREET THE MAN.
IS THAT RIGHT? GOOD FOR YOU!
HELLO!
DO YOU HAVE ANY HORSES THAT SEEM A GOOD FIT?
LET'S SEE...
IT SHOULD BE A YOUNG ONE?
YEAH...
ALSO, SINCE A CHILD WILL BE THE ONE RIDING IT, SOMETHING NOT TOO SKITTISH.
THIS ONE?
IT'S VERY GENTLE.
A LITTLE TOO BIG, I THINK.
FATHER! FATHER!

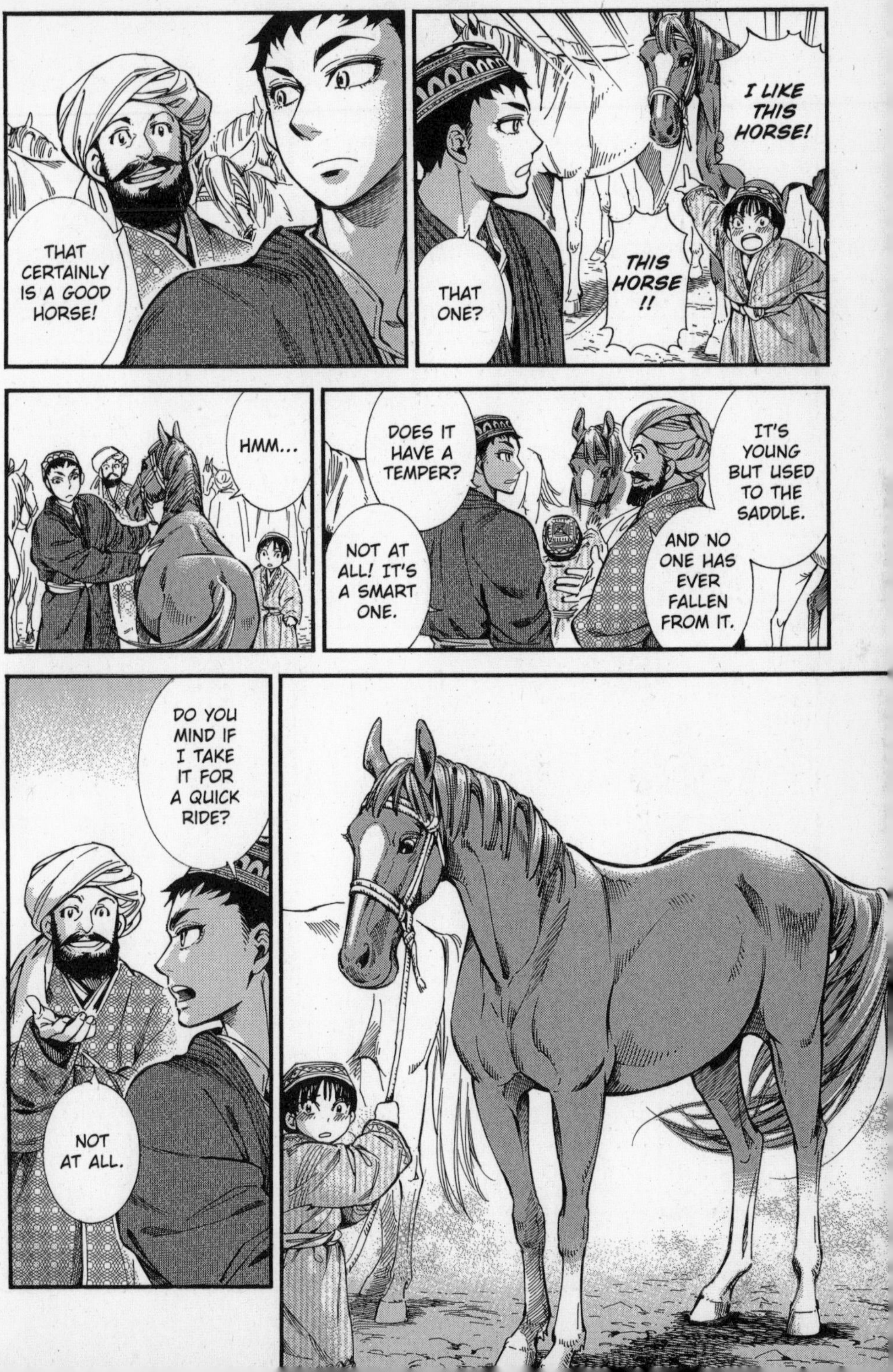
I LIKE THIS HORSE!
THIS HORSE !!
THAT ONE?
THAT CERTAINLY IS A GOOD HORSE!
IT'S YOUNG BUT USED TO THE SADDLE.
AND NO ONE HAS EVER FALLEN FROM IT.
DOES IT HAVE A TEMPER?
NOT AT ALL! IT'S A SMART ONE.
HMM...
DO YOU MIND IF I TAKE IT FOR A QUICK RIDE?
NOT AT ALL.

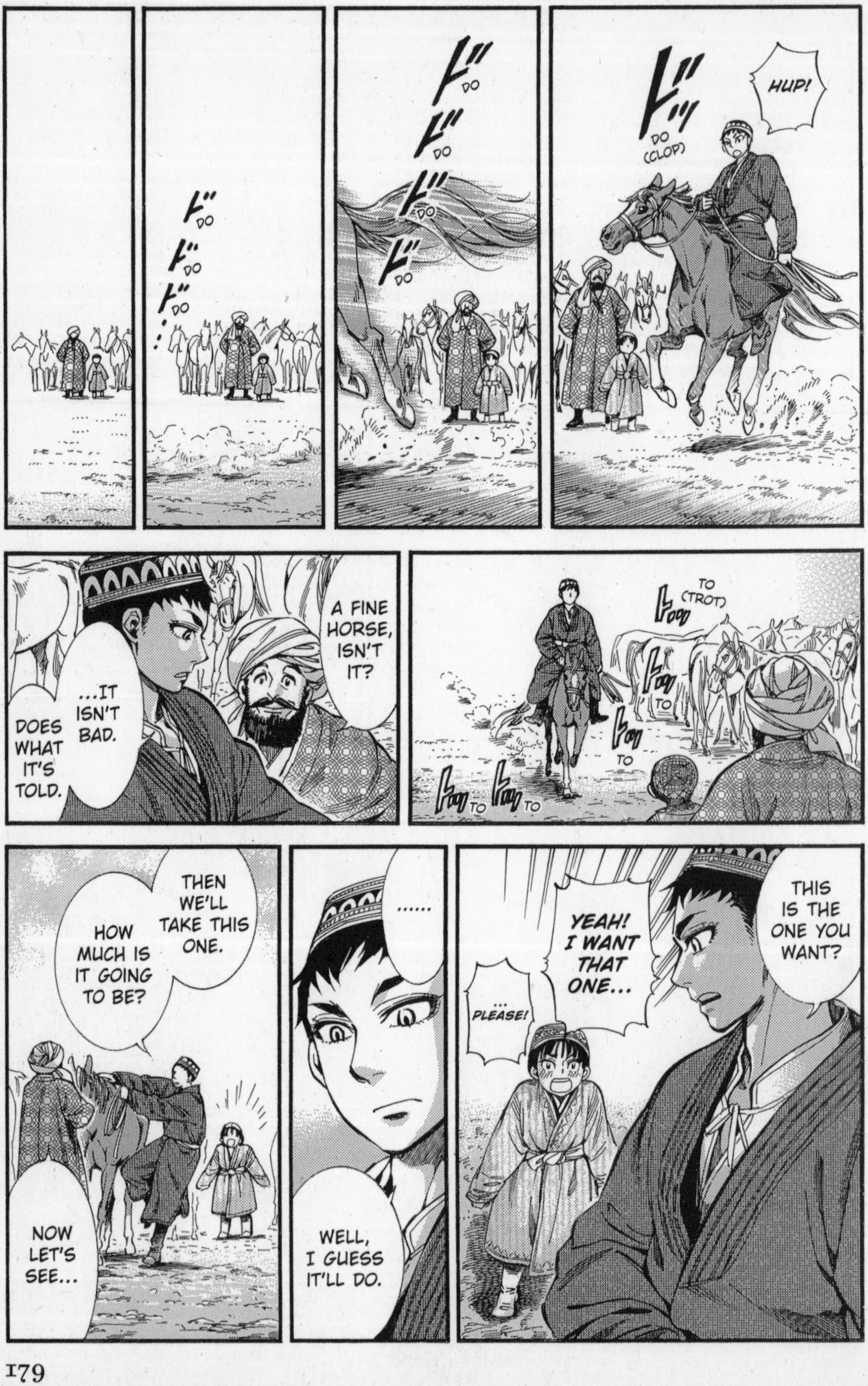

HUP!
ドッ DO (CLOP)
ド DO
ド DO
ド DO
ド DO
ド DO
ド DO
ド DO
ト TO (TROT)
ト TO
ト TO
ト TO
ト TO
A FINE HORSE, ISN'T IT?
...IT ISN'T BAD.
DOES WHAT IT'S TOLD.
THIS IS THE ONE YOU WANT?
YEAH! I WANT THAT ONE...
...PLEASE!
......
WELL, I GUESS IT'LL DO.
THEN WE'LL TAKE THIS ONE.
HOW MUCH IS IT GOING TO BE?
NOW LET'S SEE...

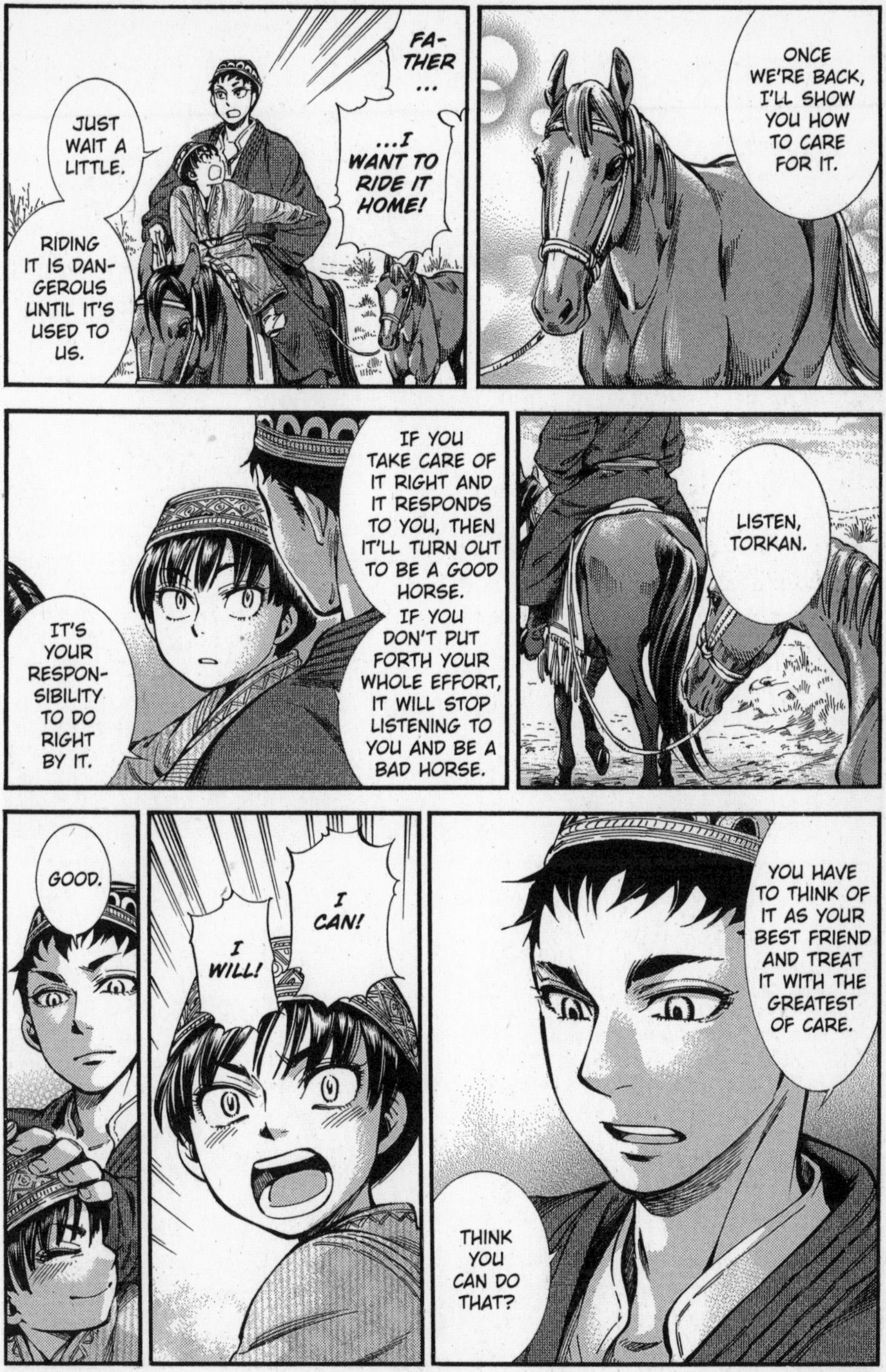
ONCE WE'RE BACK, I'LL SHOW YOU HOW TO CARE FOR IT.
FA-THER ...
...I WANT TO RIDE IT HOME!
JUST WAIT A LITTLE.
RIDING IT IS DAN-GEROUS UNTIL IT'S USED TO US.
LISTEN, TORKAN.
IF YOU TAKE CARE OF IT RIGHT AND IT RESPONDS TO YOU, THEN IT'LL TURN OUT TO BE A GOOD HORSE. IF YOU DON'T PUT FORTH YOUR WHOLE EFFORT, IT WILL STOP LISTENING TO YOU AND BE A BAD HORSE.
IT'S YOUR RESPON-SIBILITY TO DO RIGHT BY IT.
YOU HAVE TO THINK OF IT AS YOUR BEST FRIEND AND TREAT IT WITH THE GREATEST OF CARE.
THINK YOU CAN DO THAT?
I CAN!
I WILL!
GOOD.

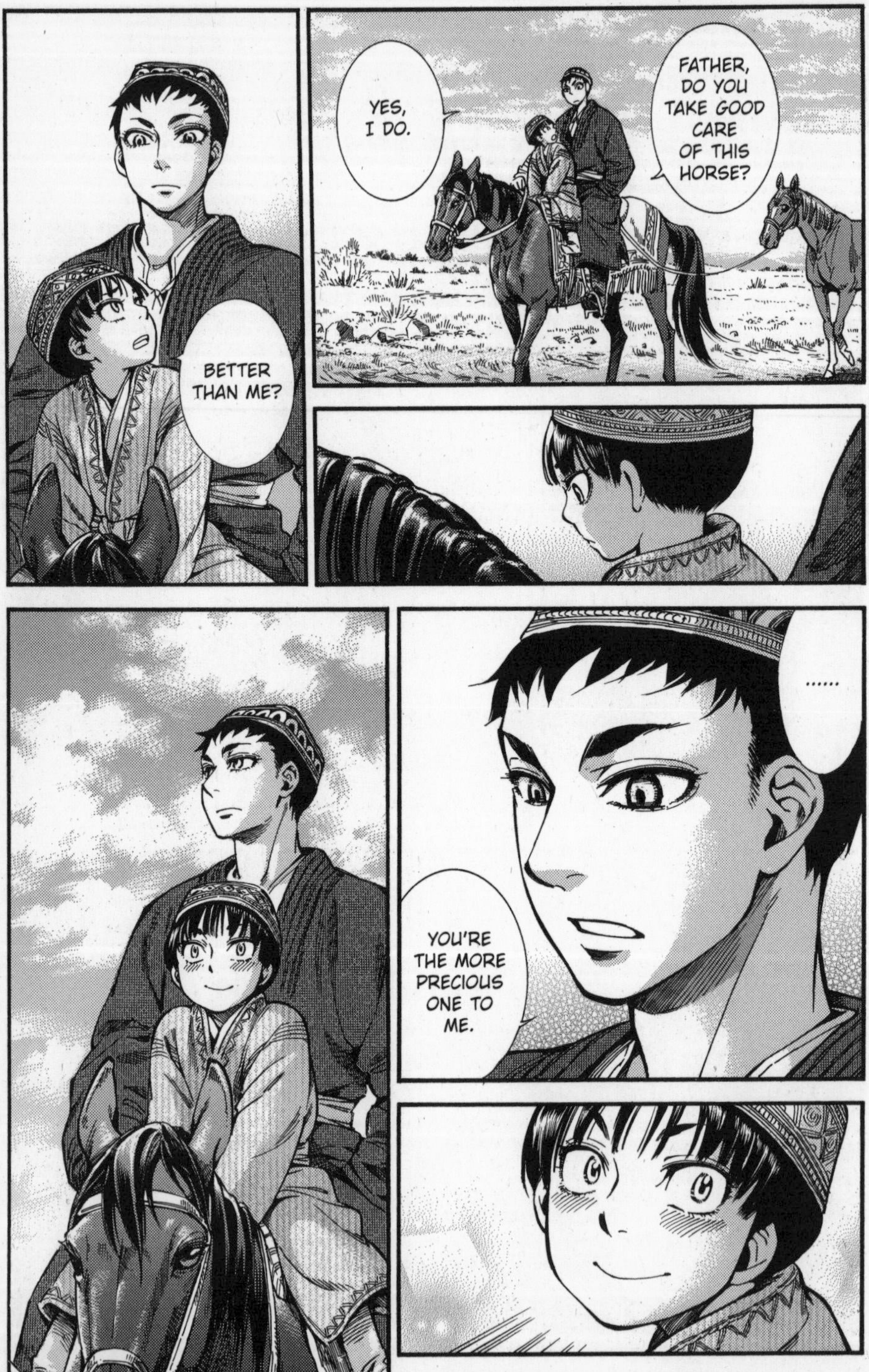
FATHER, DO YOU TAKE GOOD CARE OF THIS HORSE?
YES, I DO.
BETTER THAN ME?
......
YOU'RE THE MORE PRECIOUS ONE TO ME.

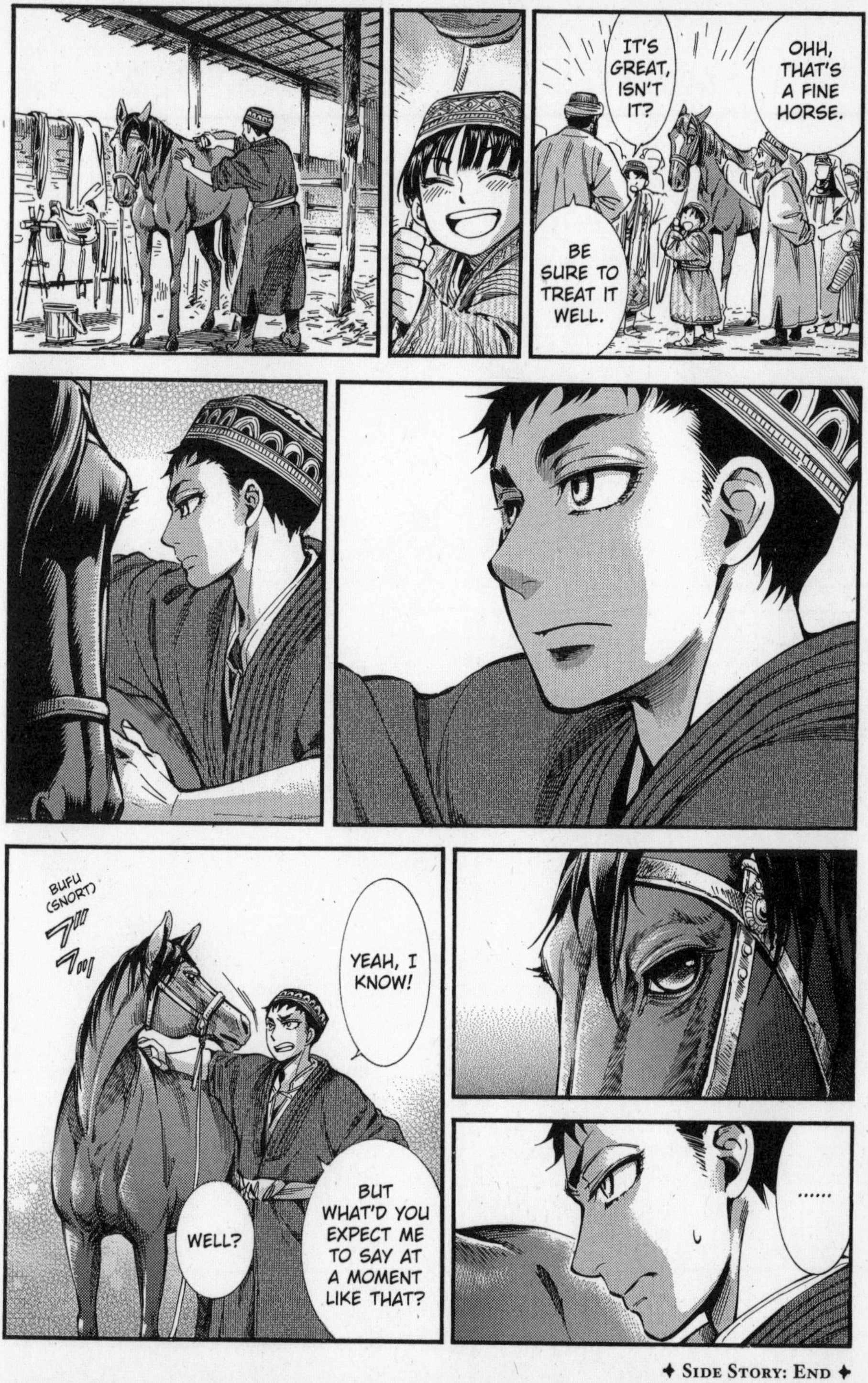
OHH, THAT'S A FINE HORSE.
IT'S GREAT, ISN'T IT?
BE SURE TO TREAT IT WELL.
......
BUFU (SNORT)
YEAH, I KNOW!
BUT WHAT'D YOU EXPECT ME TO SAY AT A MOMENT LIKE THAT?
WELL?

✦ SIDE STORY: END ✦

AFTERWORD

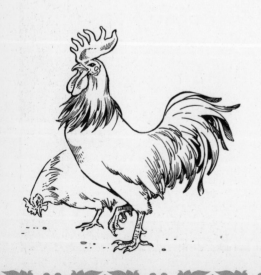

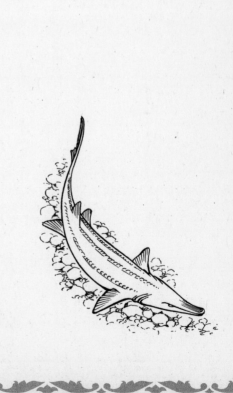

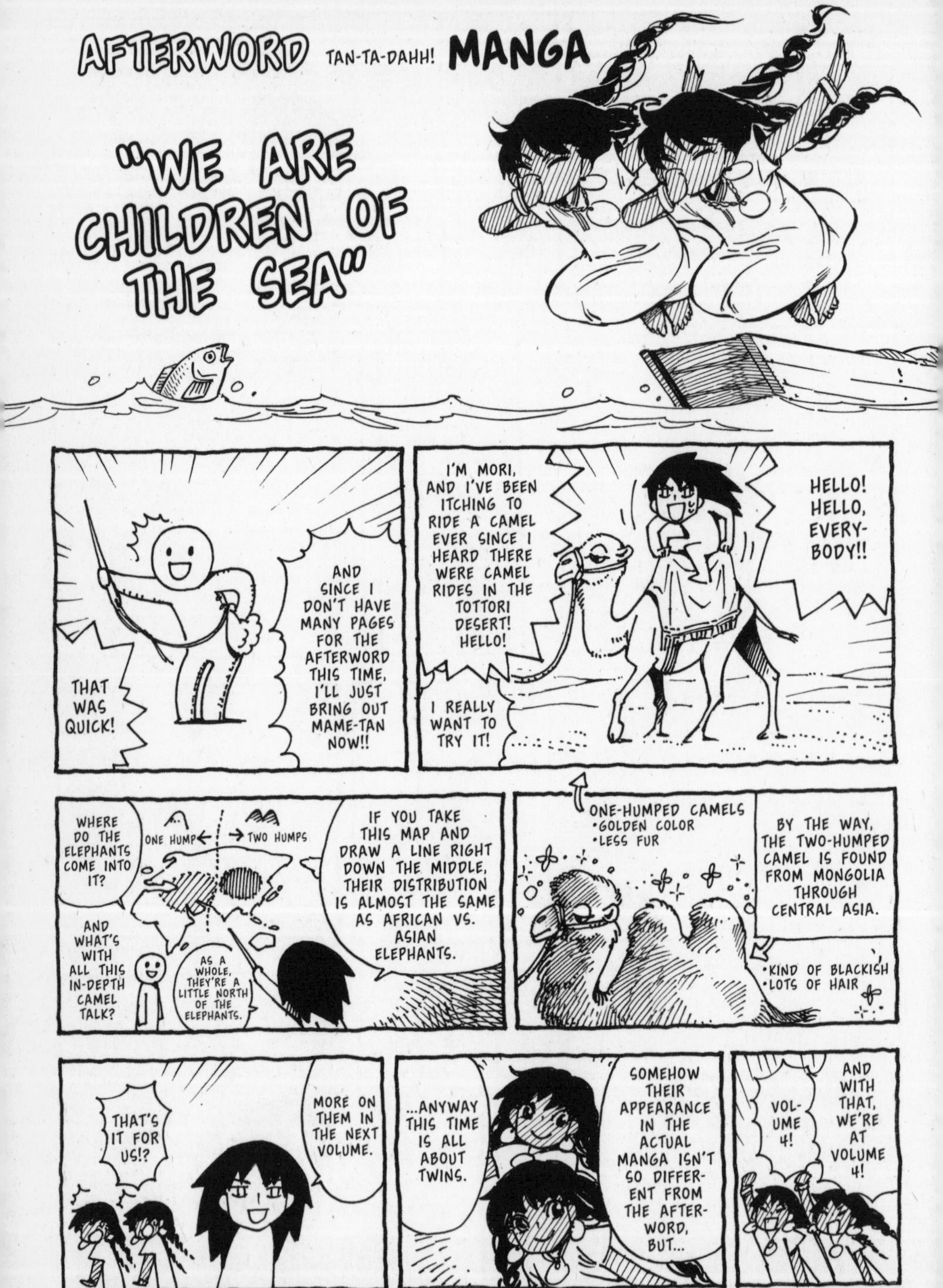
AFTERWORD TAN-TA-DAHH! MANGA
"WE ARE CHILDREN OF THE SEA"*
HELLO! HELLO, EVERYBODY!!
I'M MORI, AND I'VE BEEN ITCHING TO RIDE A CAMEL EVER SINCE I HEARD THERE WERE CAMEL RIDES IN THE TOTTORI DESERT! HELLO!
I REALLY WANT TO TRY IT!
AND SINCE I DON'T HAVE MANY PAGES FOR THE AFTERWORD THIS TIME, I'LL JUST BRING OUT MAME-TAN NOW!!
THAT WAS QUICK!
BY THE WAY, THE TWO-HUMPED CAMEL IS FOUND FROM MONGOLIA THROUGH CENTRAL ASIA.
ONE-HUMPED CAMELS
•GOLDEN COLOR
•LESS FUR
•KIND OF BLACKISH
•LOTS OF HAIR
IF YOU TAKE THIS MAP AND DRAW A LINE RIGHT DOWN THE MIDDLE, THEIR DISTRIBUTION IS ALMOST THE SAME AS AFRICAN VS. ASIAN ELEPHANTS.
AS A WHOLE, THEY'RE A LITTLE NORTH OF THE ELEPHANTS.
ONE HUMP ← → TWO HUMPS
WHERE DO THE ELEPHANTS COME INTO IT?
AND WHAT'S WITH ALL THIS IN-DEPTH CAMEL TALK?
AND WITH THAT, WE'RE AT VOLUME 4!
VOLUME 4!
SOMEHOW THEIR APPEARANCE IN THE ACTUAL MANGA ISN'T SO DIFFERENT FROM THE AFTERWORD, BUT...
...ANYWAY THIS TIME IS ALL ABOUT TWINS.
MORE ON THEM IN THE NEXT VOLUME.
THAT'S IT FOR US!?

*"WARE HA UMI NO KO" (WE ARE CHILDREN OF THE SEA) IS A TRADITIONAL JAPANESE CHILDREN'S SONG THAT RECOUNTS AN IDYLLIC LIFE LIVED ON THE SEASHORE. THE SONG FIRST APPEARED IN PRINT IN 1910 WHEN THE JAPANESE MINISTRY OF EDUCATION PUT OUT A BOOK OF SCHOOL SONGS. AFTER THE WAR, THE AMERICAN OCCUPIERS DECREED THAT THE FINAL SEVENTH VERSE, WHICH REFERENCES PROTECTING THE COUNTRY AND SEAS WITH WARSHIPS, SHOULD BE STRICKEN FROM THE OFFICIAL VERSION OF THE SONG.

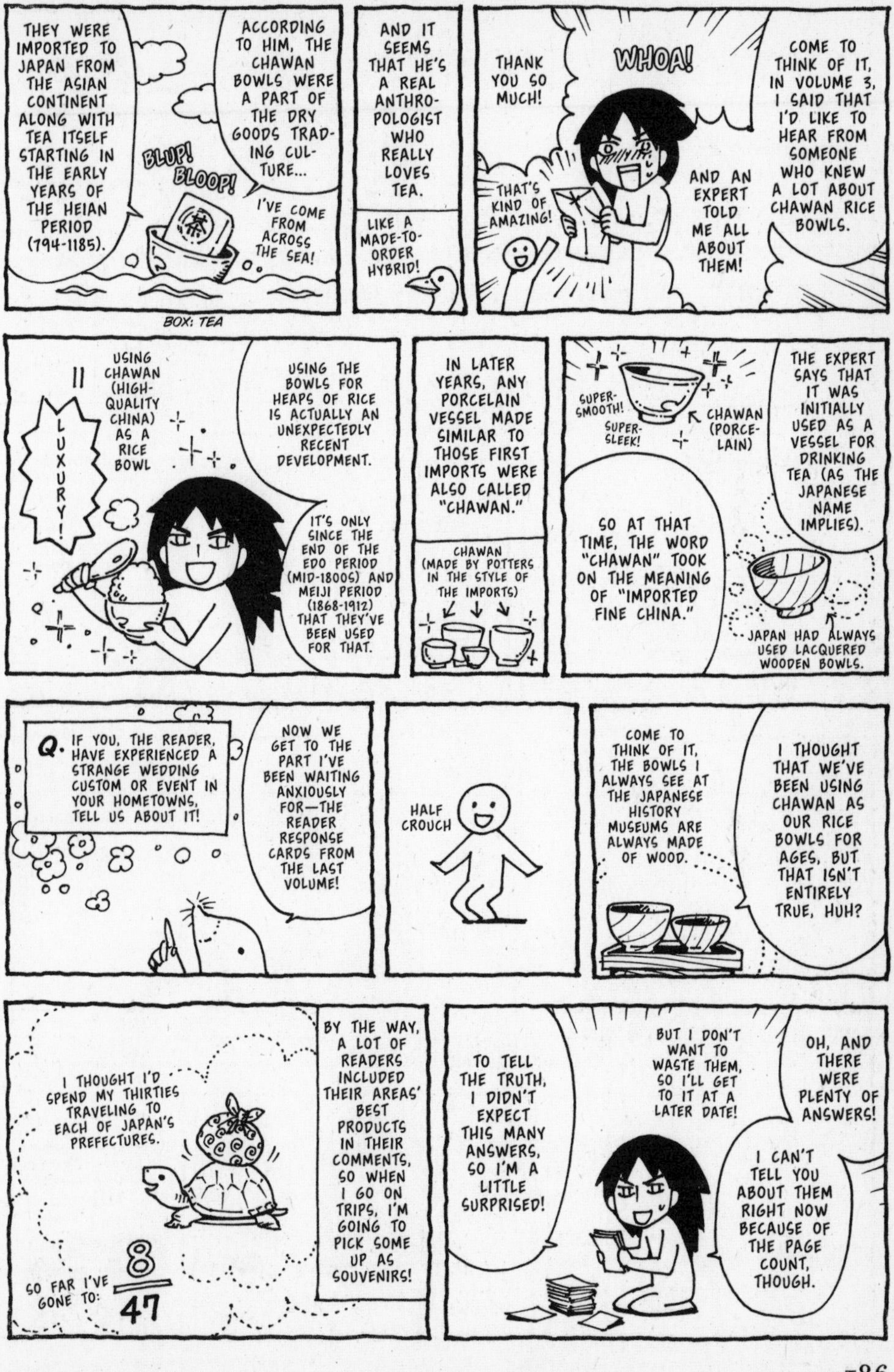
COME TO THINK OF IT, IN VOLUME 3, I SAID THAT I'D LIKE TO HEAR FROM SOMEONE WHO KNEW A LOT ABOUT CHAWAN RICE BOWLS.
AND AN EXPERT TOLD ME ALL ABOUT THEM!
WHOA!
THANK YOU SO MUCH!
THAT'S KIND OF AMAZING!
AND IT SEEMS THAT HE'S A REAL ANTHROPOLOGIST WHO REALLY LOVES TEA.
LIKE A MADE-TO-ORDER HYBRID!
ACCORDING TO HIM, THE CHAWAN BOWLS WERE A PART OF THE DRY GOODS TRADING CULTURE...
THEY WERE IMPORTED TO JAPAN FROM THE ASIAN CONTINENT ALONG WITH TEA ITSELF STARTING IN THE EARLY YEARS OF THE HEIAN PERIOD (794-1185).
I'VE COME FROM ACROSS THE SEA!
BLUP! BLOOP!
BOX: TEA
THE EXPERT SAYS THAT IT WAS INITIALLY USED AS A VESSEL FOR DRINKING TEA (AS THE JAPANESE NAME IMPLIES).
CHAWAN (PORCELAIN)
SUPER-SMOOTH!
SUPER-SLEEK!
SO AT THAT TIME, THE WORD "CHAWAN" TOOK ON THE MEANING OF "IMPORTED FINE CHINA."
JAPAN HAD ALWAYS USED LACQUERED WOODEN BOWLS.
IN LATER YEARS, ANY PORCELAIN VESSEL MADE SIMILAR TO THOSE FIRST IMPORTS WERE ALSO CALLED "CHAWAN."
CHAWAN (MADE BY POTTERS IN THE STYLE OF THE IMPORTS)
USING THE BOWLS FOR HEAPS OF RICE IS ACTUALLY AN UNEXPECTEDLY RECENT DEVELOPMENT.
IT'S ONLY SINCE THE END OF THE EDO PERIOD (MID-1800S) AND MEIJI PERIOD (1868-1912) THAT THEY'VE BEEN USED FOR THAT.
USING CHAWAN (HIGH-QUALITY CHINA) AS A RICE BOWL
= LUXURY!
I THOUGHT THAT WE'VE BEEN USING CHAWAN AS OUR RICE BOWLS FOR AGES, BUT THAT ISN'T ENTIRELY TRUE, HUH?
COME TO THINK OF IT, THE BOWLS I ALWAYS SEE AT THE JAPANESE HISTORY MUSEUMS ARE ALWAYS MADE OF WOOD.
HALF CROUCH
NOW WE GET TO THE PART I'VE BEEN WAITING ANXIOUSLY FOR—THE READER RESPONSE CARDS FROM THE LAST VOLUME!
Q. IF YOU, THE READER, HAVE EXPERIENCED A STRANGE WEDDING CUSTOM OR EVENT IN YOUR HOMETOWNS, TELL US ABOUT IT!
OH, AND THERE WERE PLENTY OF ANSWERS!
I CAN'T TELL YOU ABOUT THEM RIGHT NOW BECAUSE OF THE PAGE COUNT, THOUGH.
BUT I DON'T WANT TO WASTE THEM, SO I'LL GET TO IT AT A LATER DATE!
TO TELL THE TRUTH, I DIDN'T EXPECT THIS MANY ANSWERS, SO I'M A LITTLE SURPRISED!
BY THE WAY, A LOT OF READERS INCLUDED THEIR AREAS' BEST PRODUCTS IN THEIR COMMENTS, SO WHEN I GO ON TRIPS, I'M GOING TO PICK SOME UP AS SOUVENIRS!
I THOUGHT I'D SPEND MY THIRTIES TRAVELING TO EACH OF JAPAN'S PREFECTURES.
SO FAR I'VE GONE TO: 8/47

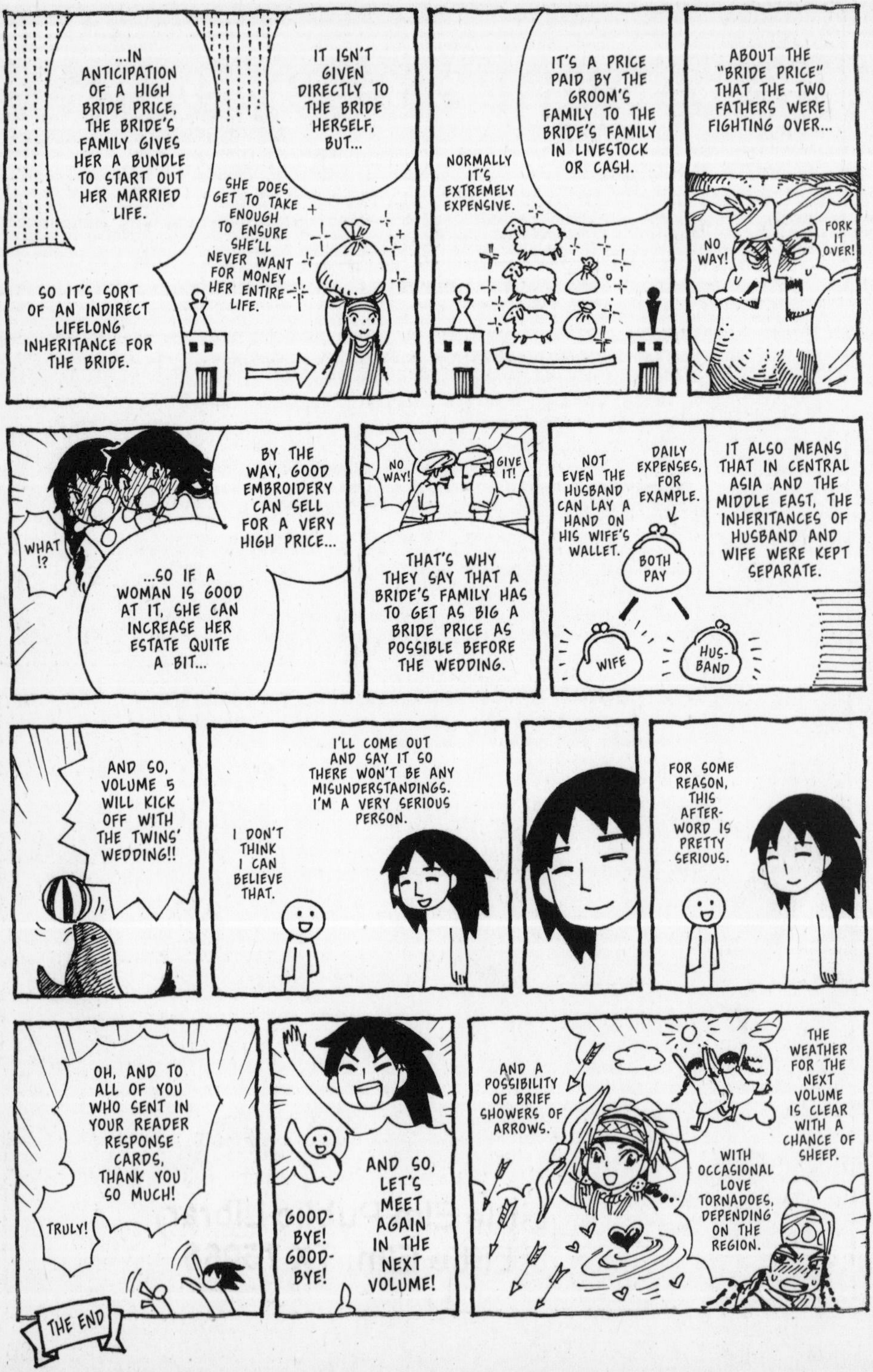
ABOUT THE "BRIDE PRICE" THAT THE TWO FATHERS WERE FIGHTING OVER...
FORK IT OVER!
NO WAY!
IT'S A PRICE PAID BY THE GROOM'S FAMILY TO THE BRIDE'S FAMILY IN LIVESTOCK OR CASH.
NORMALLY IT'S EXTREMELY EXPENSIVE.
IT ISN'T GIVEN DIRECTLY TO THE BRIDE HERSELF, BUT...
...IN ANTICIPATION OF A HIGH BRIDE PRICE, THE BRIDE'S FAMILY GIVES HER A BUNDLE TO START OUT HER MARRIED LIFE.
SHE DOES GET TO TAKE ENOUGH TO ENSURE SHE'LL NEVER WANT FOR MONEY HER ENTIRE LIFE.
SO IT'S SORT OF AN INDIRECT LIFELONG INHERITANCE FOR THE BRIDE.
IT ALSO MEANS THAT IN CENTRAL ASIA AND THE MIDDLE EAST, THE INHERITANCES OF HUSBAND AND WIFE WERE KEPT SEPARATE.
DAILY EXPENSES, FOR EXAMPLE.
NOT EVEN THE HUSBAND CAN LAY A HAND ON HIS WIFE'S WALLET.
BOTH PAY
HUS-BAND
WIFE
GIVE IT!
NO WAY!
THAT'S WHY THEY SAY THAT A BRIDE'S FAMILY HAS TO GET AS BIG A BRIDE PRICE AS POSSIBLE BEFORE THE WEDDING.
BY THE WAY, GOOD EMBROIDERY CAN SELL FOR A VERY HIGH PRICE...
WHAT!?
...SO IF A WOMAN IS GOOD AT IT, SHE CAN INCREASE HER ESTATE QUITE A BIT...
FOR SOME REASON, THIS AFTER-WORD IS PRETTY SERIOUS.
I'LL COME OUT AND SAY IT SO THERE WON'T BE ANY MISUNDERSTANDINGS. I'M A VERY SERIOUS PERSON.
I DON'T THINK I CAN BELIEVE THAT.
AND SO, VOLUME 5 WILL KICK OFF WITH THE TWINS' WEDDING!!
THE WEATHER FOR THE NEXT VOLUME IS CLEAR WITH A CHANCE OF SHEEP.
WITH OCCASIONAL LOVE TORNADOES, DEPENDING ON THE REGION.
AND A POSSIBILITY OF BRIEF SHOWERS OF ARROWS.
AND SO, LET'S MEET AGAIN IN THE NEXT VOLUME!
GOOD-BYE! GOOD-BYE!
OH, AND TO ALL OF YOU WHO SENT IN YOUR READER RESPONSE CARDS, THANK YOU SO MUCH!
TRULY!
THE END

A BRIDE'S STORY ④

KAORU MORI

TRANSLATION: WILLIAM FLANAGAN

LETTERING: ABIGAIL BLACKMAN

A BRIDE'S STORY Volume 4 © 2012 Kaoru Mori All rights reserved. First published in Japan in 2012 by ENTERBRAIN, INC., Tokyo. English translation rights arranged with ENTERBRAIN, INC. through Tuttle-Mori Agency, Inc., Tokyo.

Translation © 2013 by Hachette Book Group

Yen Press
Hachette Book Group
237 Park Avenue, New York, NY 10017

www.HachetteBookGroup.com • www.YenPress.com

Yen Press is an imprint of Hachette Book Group, Inc. The Yen Press name and logo are trademarks of Hachette Book Group, Inc.

First Yen Press Edition: January 2013

ISBN: 978-0-316-23203-6

10 9 8 7 6 5 4 3 2 1

BVG

Printed in the United States of America

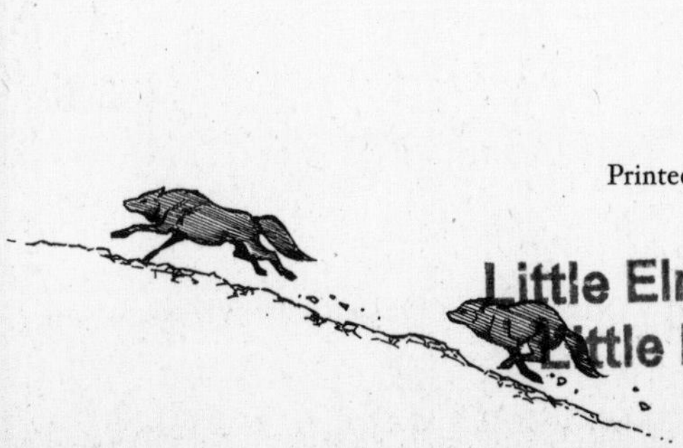

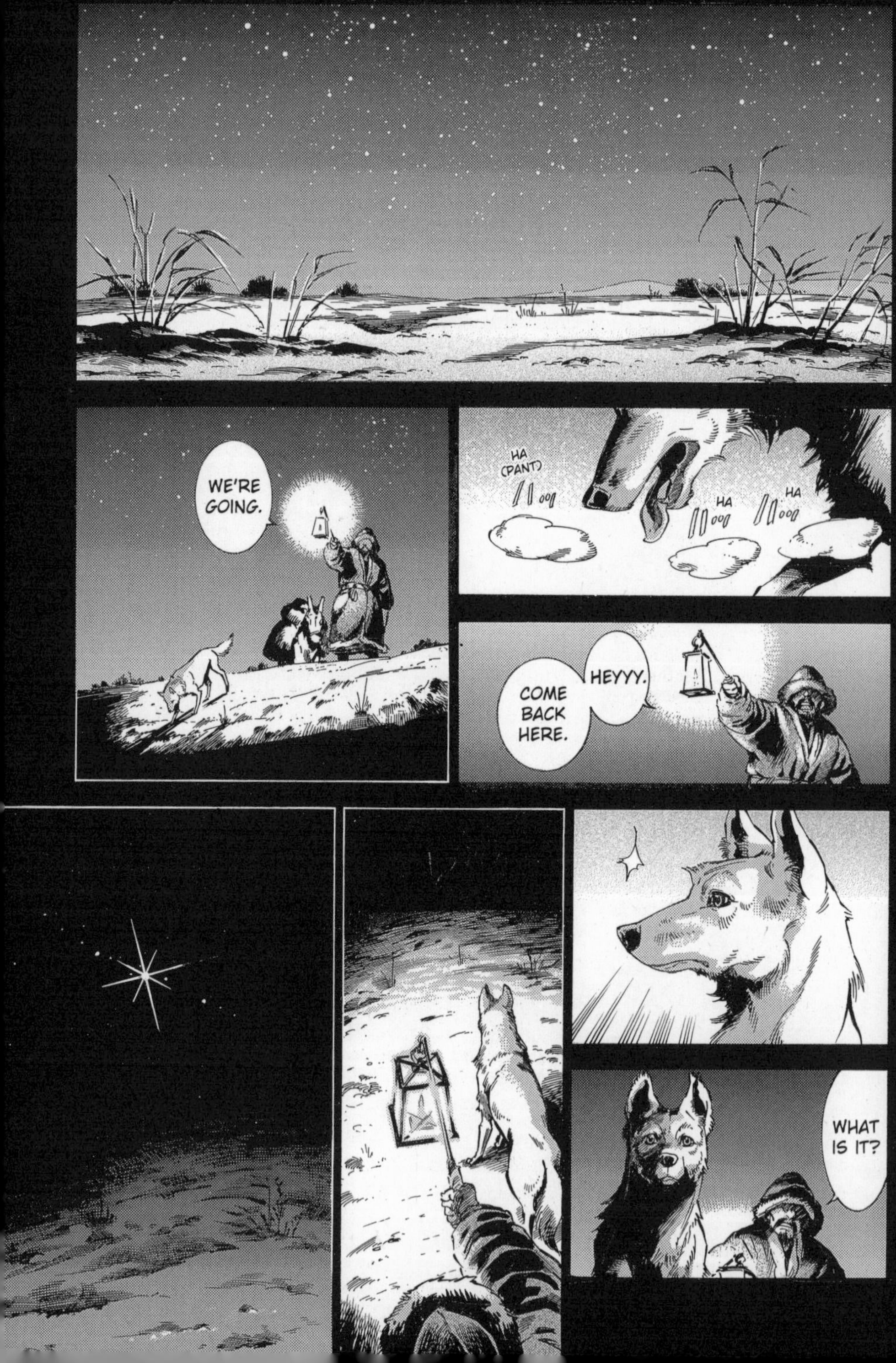
HA
HA
HA (PANT)
HEYYY.
COME BACK HERE.
WE'RE GOING.
WHAT IS IT?

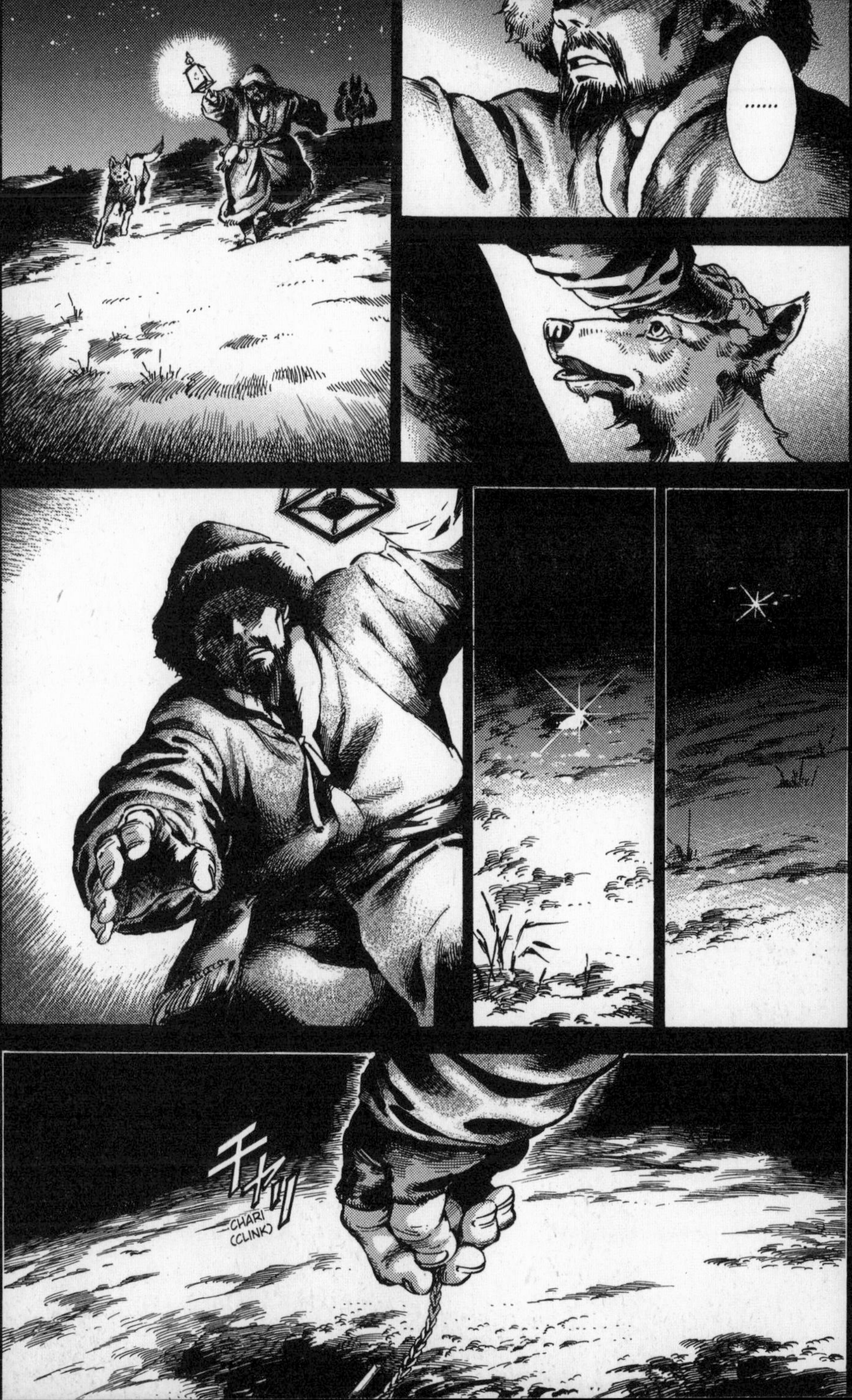
......
CHARI
(CLINK)

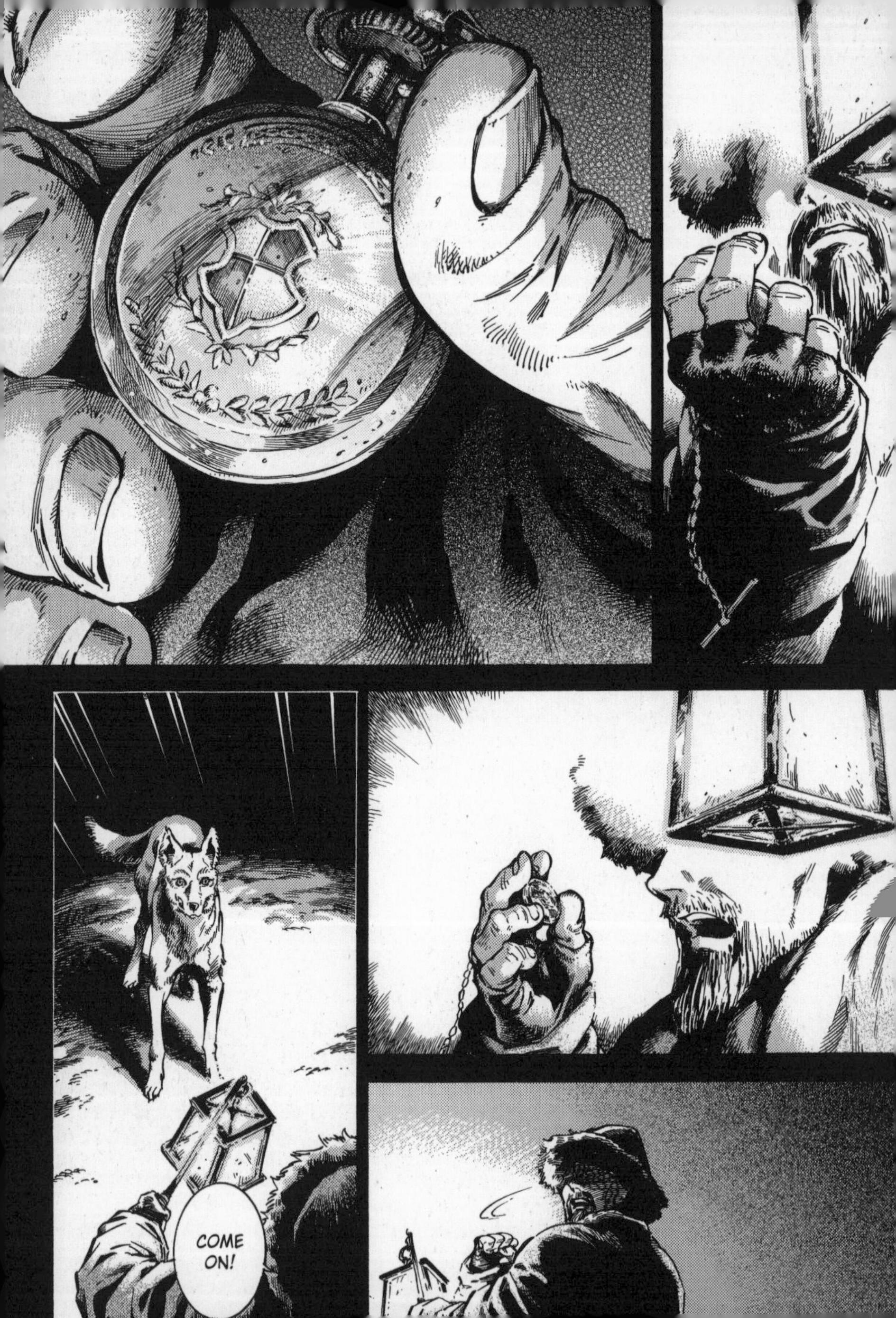
COME ON!

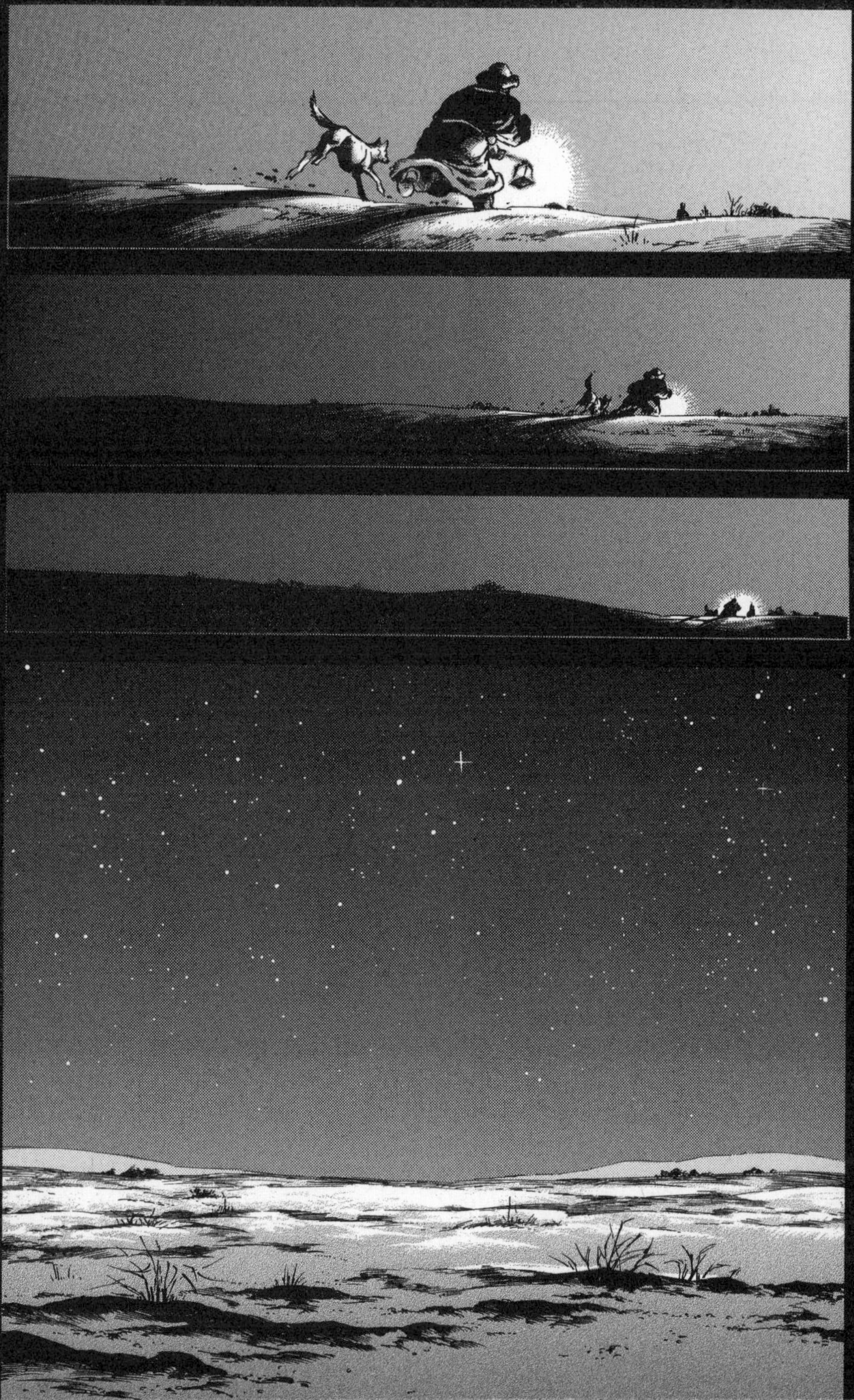